FROM ROCK A SONG

PART 1

The Valley

V.E.Bines

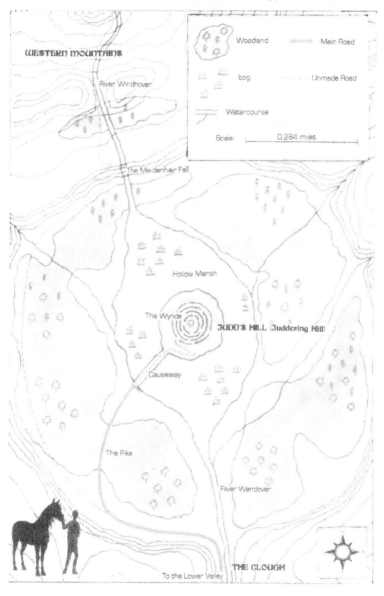

Contents

Dedication

This work is inscribed to all the people who courteously feigned interest when I bored them silly by rabbiting on about my magnum opus as it was in the process of creation, and especially to the ones who undertook the herculean task of reading it from start to finish once I reached the end but was far from completely satisfied with the result. It's a shame that most of them were much too polite to tell me what they really thought because, had they done so, it might have come to you in a greatly improved and quite different form from the one you'll find here.

Foreword

If certain scientific theories are correct, then recognition that other universes exist besides our own may be necessary - in fact there could be an infinite number of parallel universes. If the number of universes is infinite then there are an infinite number of alternatives to our familiar world – everything exists somewhere. There will be other macrocosms containing earth-like planets, a number (an infinite number?) exactly like this one, a number with a few significant differences. You will have multiple doppelgängers distributed across these planets living similar lives to yours, but on some you will be married to a different person or maybe never got married at all, where you have ten children or remain totally childless. Somewhere Americans never fought battles to gain their independence and the Germans won the Second World War; somewhere the Duchy of Luxembourg rules the world. But also, somewhere, Alice is talking to the Caterpillar, following the White Rabbit down the rabbit hole and taking tea with the Mad Hatter while Frodo and Sam are carrying the Ring to Mount Doom.

The following story is set in a universe very like our own: the stars are in their places, the sun shines on a pleasant green and blue globe, the moon rises and sets going through its familiar phases. There are numerous synchronicities that chime with this biosphere: for instance people talk about *Jonahs* (Jonah Benallack, a sailor who survived five ship wrecks while all his fellow crew-members drowned), *Samaritans* (The name of a religious order in ancient Belturbet, famous for succouring the sick and dying), and *Purgatory* (the dark place in which a soul can sometimes become lost between incarnations). But on my planet Terra has two super-continents and a single great ocean, the laws of nature incorporate phenomena to which, in this world, we would assign the term magic and developing life-forms, if not prevented, eventually reach a stage at which they can dispense with their fleshy envelopes and adopt spiritual bodies or, in modern parlance, bodies of pure energy, free to roam throughout the space-time continuum.

Oh - by the way – this is fiction, in our universe at any rate.

Characters in alphabetical order

A PEDDLER – Mrs Humpage's lover. Stays at the Justification whenever he is in the valley.

ASBO – Dando's ginger tom cat.

ATTACK – The Dans' black stallion. King horse of the valley.

BOIKO – age: 16. Duke's younger brother.

CAROLUS – Tallis' horse.

CHOCKY – Dando's jackdaw.

DAMASK – age: 17. Dando's twin sister. Strong-willed girl who rebels against the role assigned to all Gleptish women. Has an affinity with travelling people, particularly the Roma. Is promiscuous.

DANDO (THE LORD DAN ADDO) – age: 17. Second son and heir to the chief of Clan Dan, the most powerful Glept family in the valley of Deep Hallow. A gifted cook with a predilection for reading and dancing. Is in love with Ann.

DANTOR (THE LORD DAN ATTOR) – age: 21. Dando's spectacled elder brother who will become the next Dan when his father dies.

DOLL (ADELAIDE AGNETHA GOODHOUSEN nee APPLECRAFT) – age: about 50. Attached nibbler (Nablan). Potto's daughter. Wet nurse and substitute mother to both Dando and Ann and also to many of the Dan's other children.

DUKE – age: 19. A gypsy boy. Damask's first lover.

ANN (HILDA HANNAH ARBERICORD) – age: 17. Tom's daughter. A servant and attached nibbler (Nablan) at the Justification Inn. Shared a wet nurse with Dando. Has inherited *The Gift* which means she has the power to work what is commonly known as magic. Is in love with Dando.

FATHER ADELBERT – age: 42. Foreign priest and teacher at *the Orthodox Academy for the Sons of Gentlefolk* in the town of High Harrow.

FLORENCE FENELLA BIDDERWADE – age: 61. Attached nibbler (Nablan). Ann's maternal grandmother. Lives at the Justification supported by Ann.

FOXY (EVERARD TETHERER TROOLY) – age: 27. An unattached nibbler (Nablan). Found in the wild - a feral infant of unknown origin. Raised by a goatherd on the borders of Deep Hallow. Works at the Justification.

GAMMADION – age: about 50 when he enters the Land-of-the-Lake. A powerful but corrupt wizard. The stealer of the Key.

GREGORY GUYAX – age: 42 when a 15 year old Tallis encounters him. The leader of a commune who comes to the aid of the boy when he is in dire need and provides him with shelter for several years soon after the start of his journey.

MILLY – age: early teens. Damask's maid. A little black girl, a former child prostitute, rescued from a Gateway brothel by Dando. Idolises the one who ransomed her.

MOLLYBLOBS – Damask's pony *borrowed* by Dando.

MORVAH – age: 30 when Tallis starts his journey. His mother.

MRS MAEVIS HUMPAGE – age: about 40. The proprietress of the Justification Inn.

PHYLLIS – A very old donkey.

POTTO POTUNALIUS APPLECRAFT – age: about 70. Attached nibbler (Nablan). Dando's manservant and surrogate father.

PUSS – Dando's three legged hare.

RALPH – Tallis' dog.

TALLIS (PRINCE TALLISAND) – age: late middle. A lonely man who has spent most of his life on a quest for a mysterious object known as *The Key*. A musician.

THE DAN – age 48. Head of Clan Dan. Dando's father

THE GREAT ONES (AIGEA, PYR, ROSTAN, BRON ETC.) - alien immortals of mainly hominid origin whose original purpose in coming to earth was to retrieve the Key and return it to its intended place in the cosmos but who, once here, were seduced by the notion that, with the Object in their possession, they would have absolute power over the planet and its inhabitants.

THE LADY TRYPHENA – age: 41 when she and the Dan divorce. The Dan's wife. Dando and Damask's mother. Her adult life is occupied with the bearing of children.

THE OLD ONES – alien immortals of mainly non-hominid origin The original visitants from deep space who brought the Key to the earth.

TOM (THOMAS TOSA ARBERICORD) – age at his presumed death: 36. Cobbler and attached nibbler

(Nablan) to Clan Dan, but also the high priest, the Culdee, of the Nablan race. Ann's father.

VALENTINE – a goatherd. Foxy's substitute father who takes over his care and raises him.

YANTLE (THE LORD YAN COTTLE) – age: 29. Third son and heir to the head of the Yan Clan. Sexual pervert who wants to take Ann as his *pet* (concubine).

OTHER CHARACTERS WHO ARE REFERRED TO IN BOOK ONE BUT WHO DO NOT APPEAR

AZAZEEL (THE DARK BROTHER) – alien immortal. Unnaturally conceived offspring of Pyr and Aigea. Originally one being with his sibling Pendar.

JUDD - A Nablan hero

MARTHA BERINGARIA ARBERICORD nee BIDDERWADE – age at death: 19. Attached nibbler (Nablan). Florence's daughter. Tom's wife. Ann's mother. Died in childbirth.

PENDAR (THE BRIGHT BROTHER) – alien immortal. Unnaturally conceived offspring of Pyr and Aigea. Originally one being with his sibling Azazeel.

Unfleshed for all time,
In the regions where the stars wheel,
There the dance is.

Chapter one

"*So wife, shall we declare a truce? It seems as if our reign over this insignificant satellite is about to be challenged and we may need to cooperate to counter the forces ranged against us.*"

"*What are you talking about husband? The place is not worth all the trouble we've taken on behalf of its inhabitants over the course of time but our positions are totally secure. We're worshipped by the fleshed ones throughout the length and breadth of the land!*"

"*But surely you've looked backwards down the time-lines. Haven't you seen him coming – the one who, although he is unaware of the fact, may hold our fate in his hands?*"

"*Pooh! He's just a child – ignorant, inexperienced – he hasn't even known a woman! I can soon deal with him!*"

"*Don't be so dismissive wife – It's no secret that you've tried to dispose of him on one occasion already and failed. Our powers are limited and the Prime Mover may not think as we do. It might be as well to sink our differences and work out a strategy...*"

Meanwhile, along one of those time-lines already mentioned...

There was a man once on a journey of many years; Tallis was his name. *Tallisand, Prince of the Lake Guardians, Keeper of the Key* were the titles his mother claimed for him in days gone by. To a listener of sufficient understanding the grand words would have rung hollow, for if he was a prince it was a prince without a people, and as for the Key that had disappeared long ago. When we take up his story he is sitting on a large spare horse overlooking wide spaces. This is a grey man on the big horse, grey all over as if the dust of the road has worked its way into his pores and between the warp and weft of his clothes; both man and horse appear as dried up and dusty as old leaves. By the horse's hind quarters a lean dog, worn to a shadow yet vigorous still, awaits his master's command. Dog and horse show no curiosity as to their situation or what has kept their feet on the road for so long. They stand patiently while the man gazes down as if in a dream. Some birds, probably rooks, spiral leisurely in an upward air current. Beyond the birds are pale indistinct patterns of fields interspersed with darker areas that must be woods. *Fields beyond birds? How can that be? Unless the fields have somehow broken loose and swum up into the sky!*

The man on the chestnut horse sways suddenly forward in his saddle. His helmeted head nods drunkenly and the next moment he almost loses his balance before every muscle obstinately stiffens, refusing to allow his body to fall, while the dizzy spell runs its course and slowly lifts from his brain. For a long minute he remains motionless, hands gripping the saddle-bow, eyes closed. Then with studied calm he forces himself to survey the scene once more. This time he understands. The birds are between himself and the fields because he is perched high on the south side of a deep valley. The small black shapes are wheeling some way below him, and below them again lies the fertile valley floor.

There's not much time left, he thinks with concern. *Two days without water is not long, but that wilderness seems to have eaten into my bones. What a place to take a horse! Poor Carol; it required all my powers of persuasion to keep him on his feet. Once I could have left him behind without a murmur. God grant there's some hamlet at the foot of this hill. I must get down as soon as possible.*

Despite this urgency he makes no immediate move. The landscape below appears to draw his eyes. There it lies, the valley he has been promised, stretching its length across his path. For many days, weeks in fact, he has been creeping north through inhospitable country, eking out his rations, until he began to suspect that the barren plateau he was traversing concealed no secret hollow, snug among surrounding uplands, where waters flowed and the earth brought forth abundantly. So he had been advised (although with an undertone of doubt) by comfortable stay-at-home folk far to the south who had watched him begin his climb up the lonely northern path with much shaking of heads. Now his faith in the rumours is vindicated. As his brain clears, a sweet breath hinting at warm grass and passing summer ripeness tantalizes his senses, while born on the fragrance, sounds, loud at their point of origin, come to his ears like the piping of insects, all but lost in the hush of distance. An answer to prayer it seems, this peaceful valley, yet the watcher feels a twinge of unease. Down there folk are going about their business as yet unaware of his coming, and Tallis, who asks nothing more than to be left alone to pursue his own ends, will be forced to involve his life with theirs, perhaps to throw himself on their mercy. Well it cannot be helped, it is inevitable. By hook or by crook he must descend.

Here, halfway along the southern margin (the valley runs from west to east), the walls are steep and high. Westward they grow still higher and curve to meet the northern perimeter so that the valley narrows, its upper regions hidden from the eyes of the newcomer amongst the skirts of mountains. Ahead of him and to his right the sides are less imposing, the valley spreads itself, becomes flatter based, there are glimpses of water that may be a river or marshy ground. Yet all around the walls hold with no opening as far as he can see unless it is to be found at the extreme eastern end. Tallis calculates a drop of about three hundred feet between himself and the rest and shelter he seeks. With a sigh he straightens his back and shakes the reins. Carolus the horse starts forward on his feathered hooves, treading the stones as lightly as a girl. As the trio emerges into sunlight from beneath some pines where they have been standing the strong light betrays things that were not visible when the three were little more than silhouettes on the skyline. Tallis' long cloak, his britches, finely woven shirt and leather jerkin are slashed in places as if by a knife, and round the slashes spread stains of dried blood. Both animals also appear to have been wounded, their hides carry a number of lacerations. The water bottles hanging from the saddle bob weightlessly, gaping holes telling their own tale.

The gradient of the hill falls away in a series of steps; trees cling to the slopes while the flatter areas are grassy, perhaps kept clear by grazing. The path swoops to and fro, choosing the easiest route downwards. A delicate translucent haze hangs over the lands below, trapping the light of the lovely autumn afternoon and rendering it palpable, so that the whole valley, eight miles across at its widest point, brims with sunshine. Bees purr contentedly over the open hillside meadows, while inside the stands of trees an occasional bird, rousing from a drowse, stabs the still air with the piercing sweetness of its song. The valley appears filled with luminosity. Tallis' sensations as he makes his way down to it are of a creature of the upper atmosphere venturing beneath the surface of a strange land-locked sea. Could it be a sea of illusion, a dream-locked land, the denizens of which are wrapped, swathed, drowned in self deception? The name of that place - as ancient and mysterious as its origin - is Deep Hallow.

And so, with the mise-en-scene established and three characters introduced, the narration can proceed...

His surroundings, warm and still, were under the spell of evening by the time Tallis reached level ground. As he emerged from the last belt of hillside trees the sun had already dipped behind the southern rim high above. Ahead, always slightly unnerving to someone of a reclusive nature, lay the jumbled shapes of human habitation. It was not a large settlement this life-saving village, just a few cottages at a woodland junction, plus one substantial structure with a look of public use about it. There was no one about outside to ask but Tallis took this to be a wayside hostelry. It stood on the right-hand side of the track at a place where it was crossed by another way following the valley wall. As he drew near he could make out its name, a strange one, painted in faded lettering on the frontage – *The Justification Inn.*

The ground floor of the building was built of stone, the superstructure timber: a crazy mixture of eves, gables, tiled roofs, chimneys and latticed windows, which seemed to lean over the traveller as he approached the archway to the inner courtyard. But this might have been the product of weariness, for Tallis' head was swimming. Now that safety was in sight his iron self control had snapped and his strength was draining away; weakness and fatigue reasserted themselves with a rush. A final effort to turn Carolus' head into the dark entrance and then his limbs were as water; in one gulp he was swallowed whole by the building. Hooves on cobbles started strange echoes inside the passageway, at the end of which flared lights and moving shapes. Above he sensed floors and ceilings, a honeycomb of hollow rooms. For the first time in weeks he had a roof over him and it crowded down crushing him with its weight.

His nerveless fingers lost their grip on the reins and, while the world turned a cartwheel, he slipped sideways out of the saddle as the earth rose ungraciously to receive him.

"Steady now! Tottie, you useless creature, take the genn'lemun's legs, can't you? Do you really need to be told what to do? Hey up! Somebody come and hold the horse there. I can't attend to everything at once."

Tallis never lost consciousness completely. He was aware of arms lifting him, carrying him through into the courtyard of the inn where he had a square of sky over him again, deep purple with the approaching night. He was placed on the ground and surrounded by what seemed to be a prodigious army of legs and feet while voices slammed against his ears. Feebly he tried to beat them away, feeling like a sailor washed up in the intricacies of a cramped port after being out alone on vast waters.

"Shoo, shoo, shoo!" A woman's voice, hasty and short of breath, approached, carrying with it the ring of authority. "What are you a-doin' of Billiard? I don't want no plaguey tramp in this 'ouse, spreadin' contagion around! Take it outside!"

"But it's not a tramp, missus, it's a genn'lemun on an 'orse. Look there's the 'orse, just inside the front there. Green's trying to quiet it."

The crowd around the fallen stranger increased. Tallis felt a pair of hands about his person, searching with eager opportunism for valuables or money. Defenceless for the moment he could do nothing. Then came a welcome diversion. From under the archway bounded a stark grey shape, wolf-like, a growl in its throat. The dog Ralph, usually never more than a foot or two away from his master, had been seduced by the still reflections of the village pond. Nursing a raging thirst of his own, he had been unable to resist breaking those reflections with a running leap followed by a delicious wallow. Now, returning to duty, he found his master apparently at the mercy of a hoard of adversaries. In answer to his onslaught a respectful space rapidly cleared around Tallis, while the dog, in the best traditions of four-footed friends, stood over him dripping protectively. Having been rescued Tallis was now treated to a shower bath which brought him spluttering back to life as Ralph shook himself vigorously. An admiring murmur came from the onlookers.

"Look there – the clever beast. That know what its master be in need of."

The hostess of the inn, for it was she who had nearly had Tallis ejected, was in the process of rapidly revising her first impressions, helped by an aside from a shabby down-at-heel individual at her elbow.

"He's no tramp, woman. There's a fat purse at his belt. Should be able to pay his way." He did not go on to mention that the purse was undetachable and firmly fastened.

"Stand back," commanded the lady of the house unnecessarily, "let the poor man have some air. Oh my! What's that I see? Blood! Blood on his clothes. He's wounded! Green, saddle up at once, ride down to Lanesmeet and fetch the doctor, quick as you can."

"No!" Tallis' voice came out, through cracked lips, as creaky as the sail on an old windmill. "No doctor... just... drink... liquid…"

Within minutes, at least three containers brimming with water were being offered. Tallis swallowed greedily. As he drank, the onlookers, the storied house beginning to glow with light against the approaching night, faded to a dull monotone; his whole being was preoccupied with the sensual delight of absorbing moisture into his parched and desiccated frame. The precious stuff slipped down his throat and once more the blood broke out into his veins like liquid from a dammed up stream. He felt the cells and cavities of his flesh filling and becoming firm, wrinkles smoothing, muscles regaining suppleness. For a brief moment youth itself seemed to have returned to him. He drained two pint mugs and reached for another. But alas, the transmutation had not carried over into this third draft, it tasted not at all like the elixir of life, and Tallis was back to drinking the universal pauper's wine. His belly began to gripe and he shivered, realizing for the first time that his wounds were smarting and that he was deadly tired.

"You are the mistress here?" he enquired, feeling his way back into the habits of speech. The landlady dropped a plump curtsy.

"Mavis Humpage, nee Cockle, at your service sir. May I offer our hospitality? We provide high class lodgin', the best this side of the Great River. I was not raised in these parts," she added confidentially, "I've taught my staff a thing or to about comfort they didn't know before."

"I should like a room for a few nights, perhaps longer," replied Tallis in the formal arms-length manner that was habitual to him, "and stabling for my horse. I should appreciate it if you could have my effects and the horse furniture conveyed to which ever room you think suitable, where my dog will mount guard over them. Be careful with the kuckthu."

"The what? Oh, you mean the guitar – or is it a harp? Never seen one like that before. Perhaps you'll give us a tune when you're feelin' better."

Tallis ignored this suggestion. "I have money and can pay in advance if you require it," he added.

"Oh Lord luv you, sir," cried Mrs Humpage with a high pitched titter, as if the very idea embarrassed her, "by no means, don't think of it. We'll have your room ready in a jiffy, if you'll just wait here a few minutes. Tottie! Shaver! Come and help the genn'lemun to 'is feet.

You Mooney, take 'is things up to the back bedroom on this side. The dear dog ("Don't touch him!" warned Tallis) 'll go with you. And see the maid airs the bed and opens the window. May I know your name sir?"

The surrounding gawpers were sent off on various errands. Tallis gave his name absently, and while the landlady was called away to sort out some managerial confusion his attention strayed to the inn yard which he had the leisure to take in properly for the first time.

It was a far busier place than he had expected, full of moving lights and fugitive shadows. Lanterns were being hoisted to their positions on a balcony that ran round the entire area. In the far right hand corner flaring torches in wall brackets lit up some men hard at work on repairs to a farm cart. On the other side a dark archway led to the back of the building. Judging by the amount of straw that had drifted through onto the cobbles, the stables, where he hoped Carolus was being comfortably installed, lay in that direction. The kitchens were in full production. Delicious smells hung on the air as dishes were carried across the open and through a door on the left which blazed light and cheerful sounds of conviviality into the blue night. The company within was hard at it, judging by the chink and merry clash of cutlery and plate. Outside, the courtyard activity lessened. Moths drifting on the velvety night air rose like ghosts to the steady flames of the lamps. Tallis began to feel hungry.

All at once Mrs Humpage was again at his elbow, apologizing profusely.

"Oh, Mr Tallisand dear, do forgive me. And you near dead on us, not 'alf an hour gone. It's these wretched nibblers, they drive a body to distraction. Why we keep them I don't know. They're lazy as perdition, and stupid's not the word for it. You have to tell 'em something five times before they'll understand you. Come into my office. I've got a cordial there I'd like you to try. I think you'll find it remarkably reviving."

The office proved to be a comfortable little parlour, the cordial sweet and strong, the chair soft. Tallis folded his gaunt length into it feeling obliged to give some account of himself in return for hospitality, yet wishing privately that he could be alone in his room.

"There'll be a meal ready in a tick," Mrs Humpage assured him, "and then something I'm sure you're dying for – a tub of hot water. Can we do you some washing while you're here, or mending?" She looked pointedly at Tallis' soiled clothes.

"No thank you," he replied stiffly, "but I would be grateful if some food could be provided for my dog."

"Ah-ha! We're ahead of you there - all ready taken care of. Now, Mr Tallisand dear, I 'ope you won't think me too nosy if I ask you how you came by your injuries. We're in such a lonely place, tucked away here in the woods, right by the southern wall. If there are any robbers or highwaymen about I shall need to set an extra watch tonight. You've no idea how thick they've become round the valley recently. Only the Outriders keep them at bay, bless 'em."

Outriders? Nibblers? Tallis was used to moving in a fog through strange cultures. He had learnt never to be too curious, and so let the question marks stand for the moment.

"To my mind I think you have nothing to fear." he replied. "It's true I was set on by thieves two days south of here, and although they dogged my footsteps after I had driven them off, I saw no more of them once I entered habitable country. I imagine they are wary of coming too close to the haunts of men."

"Well I never! And you drove them off you say? The wretches! Run-away nibblers I shouldn't wonder. But what possessed you to go so far out into the wild? People here don't usually venture beyond the southern rim, except for a few shepherds after strays."

"You misunderstand me, madam. I have never entered this valley before today. I come from the south. That wasteland has been my home for weeks past."

Mrs Humpage's face dropped in surprise.

"You come all that way? Right across the wild? Well I'm blowed! I never 'eard of such a thing before. Through the Stumble Stones, up the Incadine Gorge from the Great River, that's the way travellers come – not from the south."

There was a pause. Then -

"What never?!" The query hung in the air, perpetuated by its own intensity. Unwittingly Mrs Humpage had hit on something that appeared to concern Tallis deeply. His expression, normally aloof, became animated by a strange excitement.

"Do you mean," he continued, stressing every syllable, "that travellers have never come from the south?"

Mrs Humpage was taken aback. There was nothing unusual about the question as far as she could tell, yet it was as if the man had momentarily opened a shutter into the fortress of his soul. It afforded her a glimpse of passion and singleness of purpose that lay far outside her own experience and made her feel extremely uncomfortable. What was it to him, a stranger, which way people entered Deep Hallow? As if it mattered.

"No I never 'eard of it," she answered almost sulkily, "but then I'm not from around these parts myself."

Now their short interview was at an end. A servant hovered in the doorway announcing that Tallis' meal awaited him in the buttery. He stood up to go and to his surprise the room's fixtures and fittings broke into a dance, whirling and tilting crazily.

I'm ill, he thought, then heard Mrs Humpage laughing as she caught hold of his elbow.

"Whoops dearie! 'Ang on a mo! You'll get your sea legs in a minute."

Disgust steadied him. He saw he had been the victim of a trick. The cordial which had tasted harmless enough when he swallowed it must have contained some insidious local brew. In his present weak and hungry state its effect had been swift. Plainly he was half drunk, a novel and unwelcome experience.

Foolish and darkling suspicions spawned from his ready distrust. What was the woman up to? Did she intend to take advantage of him in some way – rob him even? The quality that had brought him through the wilderness and kept him true to one purpose over all his many years of travel now enabled him to subdue his unruly surroundings and with a freezing little bow turn and follow the servant into the corridor feeling he had escaped from something unpleasant. Outside he floated rather than walked towards the hubbub of the inn's public rooms where lights, smoke and movement burst upon him like a firework display. Someone steered him to a table against the wall and placed a steaming bowl of soup and a crusty roll to hand. He was glad to be sitting down again.

Tallis became absorbed in his meal. As he ate a feeling of mellow lassitude stole over him. The surrounding noise and activity impinged on his senses only after filtering through a charmed screen. His attitude towards the landlady began to undergo a change as his doubts and fears evaporated in a glow of comfortable well-being. After all, the woman was probably innocent of any evil intent, and her establishment could certainly provide first class fare: soup, meat pie with vegetables, stewed fruit and custard, cheese and biscuits to follow; that was a spread worth waiting for! Replete at last hc leant back and surveyed the scene.

The stone vaulted buttery, its ceiling and pillars blackened by the smoke of centuries, was scarcely big enough to accommodate the assembled company. The blame for this rested with a band of rowdy young blades ranged up and down the centre tables whose voices and laughter rose above the general hubbub as they vied with one another to see who could create the most din. The other guests and casual drinkers appeared more than ready to give them a wide central stage to perform on and as a consequence were crammed elbow to elbow around the edges of the room. Normally, these noisy dandies with their plumed hats and beribboned hair, their lace and ostentatiously jingling spurs, would have struck Tallis as an intolerable nuisance. It was thanks to the landlady's beverage that for the moment he was able to regard their antics with nothing more than a mild curiosity, a detached observer before a canvas that had unaccountably sprung to life.

There was a girl in the centre of this throng, a little waitress, frantically busy as she tried to cope with orders amidst the uproar, scuttling to and fro laden with piled plates and handfuls of glass tankards. Hampered as she was by these breakables which she had to lift high in the air to protect them from the odd sweeping gesture or jabbing elbow, she was fair game for any groping hands that came her way. Most girls would not have minded running the gauntlet of such an obstacle course, but this one was little more than a child and Tallis could see that it distressed her. She wore an old grey shawl over her head which kept falling back due to her exertions and which she would rearrange whenever she got the opportunity, but not before it revealed blue eyes and a flushed perspiring face to which clung wisps of pale hair, the colour of flax. Tallis noticed that he was not the only one to be following her progress. In particular a saturnine youth, sitting out of the light beside a pillar, was devouring her with his eyes. He had good reason: the girl was pretty as a spring flower, with a frail grace about her that could tug at the heart strings if you were foolish enough to allow yourself to be moved by it.

A voice separated itself from the melee of sounds, breaking in rudely on his reverie: "'Scuse me mate, can I give you some good advice? It you're going to make eyes at our Hild, try doin' it from behind your 'and like. You're trespassing on private property you know, and it ain't good to get on the wrong side of one of these bully boys."

Tallis found that the unsuccessful purse stealer from the inn yard, an itinerant peddler he took him to be, had apparently materialized out of thin air onto the bench beside him. Slowly, like a sleeper waking from a dream, he collected his scattered wits and tried to frame a sensible reply.

"I ashure you, you're mishtaken," he said with comical deliberation, "I washn't making eyesh at anyone."

"Suite yourself mate, but if you want to know what I'm getting at, take a dekker to your left on the other side of the second table from the end."

Tallis looked in the direction indicated and saw a lonely intense figure holding himself aloof from his companions as if he considered them beneath his notice. It was the young man who had already claimed his attention.

"That's Yantle," his informant continued, "the Lord Yan Cottle, if you likes names with an 'andle to 'em, You don't usually get 'is sort in the Justification. 'E's only 'ere on account of the girl. I don't spose you know much about the set up in these parts, comin' from down south like?"

"The Yans are one of the fifteen families," he went on, "they're the nobs 'ere in Deep 'Allow. That prize specimen is third son to the big Y 'imself, so watch your step matey, and don't get in 'is way if you want to stay 'ealthy. The rest is just run-o'-the-mill Outrider cadets on manoeuvers, but all the same you can't be too careful if you're foreign. The Glepts don't care tuppence what 'appens to the likes of you and me."

The peddler's words caused a sudden chill to invade Tallis' spine. To be warned off in this conspiratorial way, especially by someone who must already have discussed him behind his back in order to have learnt the details of his route, did not please him in the slightest. But the man might have rendered him a valuable service. Tensions in the room of which he had been unaware up to now twanged about his ears, sobering him up. It behoved a newcomer like himself to tread warily and take care not to get involved in something that was none of his business.

"Thank you," he said, with an air of terminating the conversation, "I'll bear your advice in mind."

But the peddler was well launched on a subject that obviously held a great deal of interest for him and was not to be put off.

"Hilda Hannah Arbericord," he confided in a stage whisper, "that's what they call 'er, if you'll credit it; big name for a little tiddler. She's certainly got 'im running round in circles, poor blighter. 'E's been up 'ere everyday for weeks past like a wasp round an 'oney pot. It must be playin' merry 'ell with 'is constitution. 'E wants to take 'er for 'is pet you see, that's their name for it round 'ere, but there's an 'old-up – the girl ain't 'avin' any. It's old Maeve's fault really, the landlady you know, she's too soft 'earted by 'alf. But then she's taken a dislike to this Yantle – there's been one of two funny stories about 'im – and when Maeve gets 'er back up she's stubborn as an ol' mule. She comes from the Delta City like me, and she don't like being pushed around by these pint-sized local tyrants. She can't 'old out much longer though – 'e's made a very generous offer for the girl, and a Yan won't be kept waiting for ever."

"Is that so," commented Tallis dryly, and the peddler, seeing something in his expression, had the grace to look slightly ashamed as he added, "After all, it's not all bad for the likes of 'er: pretty clothes, plenty to eat, no work, unless you count a bit of the 'ow's your father; most nibbler girls would jump at the chance, just to get out from under."

Nibbler - there was that word again. Tallis decided to take a gamble with someone who was obviously an outsider like himself and probably would not be offended at an awkward or ill phrased question.

"Can you tell me," he said, "who or what are nibblers?"

"Nibblers?" the man laughed good-humouredly and then gave a barely perceptible jerk of his head towards the girl.

"Well, that's a nibbler for a start, and 'im, and 'er over there. Look round, you'll soon pick 'em out. Nibblers are the ones who do all the donkey work round 'ere in exchange for sweet fanny adams, which just goes to show 'ow stoopid you can get if you've 'ad your face trodden on for 'undreds of years. To my mind they've got no guts at all and never 'ave 'ad, but if you believe some of the old tales they tell down by the Great River they were once in charge and more."

Tallis nodded; he had met similar situations many times along his route and as a consequence rapidly lost interest in what the peddler had to say, especially when the man switched to discussing the local aristocracy. For these he showed little love, and expounded at length on their arrogance: "...never met such a toffee-nosed lot", their inbreeding: "...faces like 'ot 'ouse flowers", and the resulting high incidence of insanity: "...the Dans are the worst, *Dan-mad* they say locally - all as barmy as each other." Tallis listened with half an ear, most of his attention straying back to the main eating area which was starting to empty as the hour grew late. The little waitress had presumably been sent off on other duties; she was nowhere to be seen. If anyone had told him it was for her he was searching,

Tallis would have denied it indignantly – perhaps a little too indignantly. The peddler had at last fallen silent. Now he slapped a hand to his head with a guilty exclamation.

"Oh cripes – I forgot! I was supposed to tell you that a bath was being got ready in your room. That's the only reason I come back in 'ere in the first place. 'Ere, come to the bottom of the stairs an' I'll show you where it is - that's right – through 'ere – the door to the stairs is out in the yard. 'Ere – are you feelin' all right mate? – you look a bit off colour like."

For the past hour or more Tallis had also been in a forgetful mood: he had forgotten how close he was to exhaustion. Now, coming out into the cool night air he staggered slightly, but testily refused the proffered helping hand.

"I'm quite well, thank you. No need to concern yourself on my account. Just point out my room, that's all I require. I'm not going straight up; I have a previous obligation to attend to first."

The mysterious *obligation* he referred to was his regular goodnight to Carolus his horse, something he would on no account omit, come hell or high water. Once apprised of the location of his sleeping quarters, he doggedly set off to look for the stables, leaving the peddler, secure in the knowledge of his own cosy arrangement with the lady of the house, to think his own thoughts.

Queer stand-offish old fish – bit of a misery really. Bet 'e's got no one to keep 'im warm at nights.

Here and yet not here,
In plain sight but half concealed,
For God's sake get gone!

Chapter two

Backs of buildings often tell you more about the folk that live in them than the fronts. Emerging from the gloom of the rear archway Tallis was faced with a slum-like shambles of chicken coops, sheds, rubbish dumps and trampled straw. To his left a row of rickety turf-roofed lean-tos, built apparently of wattle and daub, propped themselves against the wall of the inn. It was with surprise that he noted that these mean little structures, stuck like martin's nests onto the solid stonework, were being used for human habitation. As he walked out into the open, one or two pale faces peered at him from candle-lit interiors and then quickly withdrew. A couple of mousing cats, also noticing his advance, melted away, and the empty scene seemed to deny their existence. Tallis, always solitary, experienced one of his rare moments of loneliness. The artificial boost given to his health and strength by the landlady's magic potion had finally evaporated, leaving his spirits at a low ebb. In his present mood the building at his back, humming with activity, already seemed set apart. It had cast him out, and he belonged neither there nor beneath the secret night-time woods which huddled invisible and consequently faintly threatening around the perimeter of this squalid sprawl. Something about the evening had dissatisfied him with his own company, something had emphasized his isolation. It was with relief that he identified the stable block and hurried over to it, guided by the odd lantern placed here and there to light the way.

Inside he was stopped short by its magnificence. A double row of stalls flanked a wide sawdust-strewn corridor. There were harness rooms and fodder stores at the far end plus a flight of stairs which presumably led to grooms and stable boys quarters above. In this valley he had certainly stumbled on an equestrian nation, a people that housed their steeds in greater state than their servants. The dim interior greeted him with the comfortingly straightforward smells of wood, leather and dung, mixed with the early-summer scent of hay. As he passed, barely distinguishable heads poked over partitions in the gloom, regarding him dreamily out of their meditative, benevolent eyes. These must be the mounts of the young cavalry he had already encountered. Tallis drew the inevitable comparison: no noise here, no rowdyism, only a calm patient stillness broken by faint sounds of shuffling and munching; nothing to indicate the stored energy that pulsed just beneath the surface and which could break out at a signal into a thundering tidal wave of flying hooves and streaming manes. He had no need to search for Carolus among their ranks; the horse knew his step and had whinnied softly as soon as he heard his master enter the door. Tallis let himself into the stall and examined his friend's surroundings critically. He could find no fault. The horse had been well fed and watered and there was nothing he could do to improve on his comfort. Quickly he looked up and down the rows.

There was no one about. Slipping an arm beneath
Carolus' neck he allowed himself the luxury of pressing
his face against the horse's rough warm hide, sensing life
flowing through the broad body, the great heart on its
steady unceasing task. As always at such times he
experienced peace. Strength and steadiness transferred
themselves, while he clung there, to his own faltering
frame, and doubts and uncertainties which lately had
been plaguing him were temporarily laid to rest by
contact with such monumental simplicity. Trust, loyalty
and uncomplaining service – all these he had known in
abundance while keeping company with this animal, and
with the dog, and with their predecessors throughout his
long wanderings. Who, receiving such gifts, would prefer
the fickle, dangerous, hurtful love of human kind?

To get back into the main yard of the inn he
must pass under the rear portion of the hostelry's upper
story. Somewhere overhead his room was situated. A
distant growl from above advised him that as far as Ralph
was concerned, all was not well. Tallis stood stock still,
listening. A man's voice answered the dog's warning: a
rough musical voice on a note of amusement.

"Shut thee noise, thou stoopid ol' fewl. I bain't a-
gooin' ter steal thee maister's things!"

There was no hope of taking whoever-it-was by
surprise. Although the ground floor of the building
seemed hewn out of solid rock, permanent as the hills, the
dry-rotted timbers of the superstructure creaked like a
ship in a gale at the slightest footfall. By the time he had
climbed the stairs his approach had been well and truly
heralded. A door stood open on his right hand side at the
beginning of a corridor. Ralph could be glimpsed within

the room, his hackles raised, while on the threshold lay an untouched plate of scraps. Outside the door, accompanied by a large bath tub, stood a surly stooping menial, bundled in various shapeless garments, his face half hidden by a hood pulled well forward.

"A nibbler," thought Tallis, remembering how, even in the stifling atmosphere of the buttery, those other underlings that the peddler had pointed out had also been muffled up into a kind of shrinking anonymity. Walking past the man through the doorway he turned to reassure him about Ralph's intentions and found that he was alone. The other returned presently carrying two steaming buckets of hot water which he tipped into the tub after lugging it into the centre of the room. It took several journeys to fill the bath while Tallis stood on the other side of a heavy oak-framed bed, stooping slightly to avoid sagging beams, and staring down through a knee-high window into the back yard where he had been not long before. Ralph tucked into the plate of food that he had ignored while on duty. Not a word passed; the servant kept his head bowed, seemingly determined not to acknowledge Tallis' presence. It was hard to make any connection between this sullen man and the source of the youthful bantering voice that had come, not many moments earlier, from above his head. The contrast in attitude towards his dog and himself struck Tallis as almost an affront. If the fellow had appeared friendly he probably would have seen fit to regard his approaches as impertinence; perversely, confronted by the reverse, he now wanted to draw him into conversation.

"Who lives in these little huts below here?" he asked as the last two pails crashed down on the floor and part of their contents leapt out and drained rapidly away.

For answer he was treated to an unintelligible mutter half drowned by the pouring of water.

"Speak up," said Tallis, beginning to feel irritated, "I asked you who lives down below here. I can't hear if you mumble."

This time he found he was addressing a broad back. The servant had deliberately ignored him, picked up the empty buckets and set off down the stairs. What insolence! Tallis resisted the temptation to demand his return, anticipating that he would not be obeyed. Yet the man did come back. A little later, after Tallis had unbuckled his sword belt and laid it on the bed, had removed his helmet, cloak and jerkin and was in the middle of taking an inventory of his possessions, the doorway was again darkened and there stood the stocky resentful figure, bearing towels, soap, bowl and a jug of cold water. As he put them down Tallis picked up the lamp from beside the bed and stared intently, trying to penetrate to the features beneath the hood, discovering nothing in the process but a firm freckled chin and a mouth with a suggestion of belligerency about it.

Placing himself by the door to block the exit, Tallis said, "I asked you a question a little while ago to which you chose not to reply. Will you give me a civil answer now, or do I have to complain to your superiors?"

The man stood in silent obduracy, head bowed and turned slightly to one side. When Tallis added, "Come on now, I expect politeness when I pay for service – show me your face when I'm talking to you!" he still did not reply in words. Yet as if by making the last command Tallis had stumbled on a magic formula which compelled obedience, the other's head very slowly tipped backwards until Tallis could look full into his face. It

came up slowly, reluctantly, this head, apparently against
its owner's volition, pulled it seemed on an invisible
string, and at the same time, in a gesture that was part
appeal and part child's submission to threatened
punishment, the man stretched out his hands, palms
upward, for Tallis' inspection.

      The traveller had not known until then that blue
was the colour of hate. Blue eyes of an unbelievable
vividness glared back at him, and the look they contained
caused the lamp in Tallis' hand to tremble and the
shadows around the room to shiver and shake. In the first
shock of surprise he imagined he was about to be
attacked. He took a step towards the bed to get within
reach of his sword, while Ralph, sensing his master's
alarm, started up with a bark. But the man just stood there
and did nothing. Tallis began to realize that after all there
was no threat to himself, only an utterly puzzling
situation in which he floundered, completely out of his
depth. Becoming uncomfortable at having to meet that
outraged stare he dropped his gaze to the man's hands
which were still held out inviting perusal. There he saw
something very peculiar. Instead of the usual compliment
of five digits possessed by a normal person, this man had
only four on each hand: three fingers and a thumb. As a
result each palm was exceptionally narrow, scarcely
wider than the wrist, and the whole hand appeared
unusually long and slender. Tallis noticed that he was
wearing a conventional glove of old brown wool on his
right hand, one finger of which was superfluous to
requirements. It looked oddly pathetic, this glove, on the
strange hand, as if an attempt at concealment had been
defeated by poverty and make-do-and-mend. Tallis' anger
evaporated. He realized now, too late, that once again that

evening he was in danger of getting himself embroiled in something that did not concern him. What was it about this place that so easily undermined his cast-iron detachment, and what was he supposed to do about this unknown young man who was apparently forced by some local edict to stand before him on command like a fascinated rabbit, displaying his deformity, while every inch of him blazed with rage against the humiliation? (Had the peddler actually told him that these people were spiritless?) Tallis was suddenly seized by a violent fit of shivering. It was too much to expect him to cope with this baffling state of affairs after all he had been through – to cope when he was almost dead from tiredness and only wanted quiet, rest and hours of blissful oblivion. He shifted away from the exit and turned his back so that he would no longer have to witness the man's mortification, meanwhile shouting hoarsely, "Get out! Leave me alone!" He stood like that, facing away from the door, for a long suspenseful period, and did not dare to move or continue to prepare himself for rest until he was sure the room behind him was empty.

The bath had been taken, his wounds had been dressed, all his clothes except his shirt were folded neatly on top of a chest; prayers had been said, sword, tinder box and candle placed near at hand, and now, the night being warm, Tallis lay to attention on top of the bed, still as a carved figure on a tomb, having felt no need to cover himself. Beyond the four walls of his room someone had been round to douse the lamps and the house had fallen silent. Little light penetrated through the window; clouds had crept out of the west to cover the sky and the man looked up into darkness. Invisible on the floor, Ralph was already far away, his limbs twitching occasionally as he sped hot foot down the trails of his dreams. Soon Tallis' eyes also closed; the tempo of his breathing slackened; he slept.

Within the room's enclosed space something had interrupted the even flow of time. Disturbed, Ralph raised his head, snuffing the air. Again it came: a quick involuntary shifting of position from the figure on the bed, followed by a sigh. The dog's head dropped back to his forepaws, but his eyes under puckered brows peered anxiously upwards towards the master he could barely see, and a small whine started deep in his throat. Every night now, about half an hour after lapsing into unconsciousness, his companion fell prey to an inexplicable perturbation of spirit, and Ralph, his own sleep broken, was forced to witness it with sorely troubled mind. Another sigh, a quick sucking in and out of breath, followed the first, and a faint muttering; then, as the mattress rustled once more, a long moan rose out of the stillness and hung suspended in the air, as if the shadows had momentarily found a voice.

Ralph whimpered and squirmed a few inches nearer, fighting the temptation to thrust an eager enquiring nose into his master's face. When it had first started, this chronic restlessness, somewhere out in the back of beyond many weeks ago, his reaction had been to leap up and sound the alarm, to send packing with a salvo of noise whatever phantoms were attacking his friend. But this, he found, was not allowed. On the third occasion, after Tallis had awoken two nights running, ready to defend himself against a spellbound moonscape where not a mouse moved or cricket chirped from horizon to horizon, the dog had been severely cuffed and called several unprintable names. So now he was banned from interfering, although loyalty and affection urged him to interpose.

Since that day when the solitary traveller had whisked him away from a careless puppy-hood into his own service, one lesson had been rammed home incessantly: *all men are to be treated with suspicion.* Tallis had had no intention of deliberately instilling this way of thinking, it was just that the attitude was implicit in every action he took as they passed from one set of circumstances to another in their passage through the world. Ralph, sensitively attuned, kept his eyes fixed on his leader and took his cue from him, recognizing by minute signs his master's true state of mind. While Tallis imagined he was behaving towards those he encountered with courtesy and restraint, his loyal lieutenant dogged his heels, bristling wickedly or showing a tooth or two; when Tallis greeted an opposite-travelling caravan with a friendly nod, Ralph slunk on his further side, accompanying its passing with a continuous rumbling growl (it was significant that Tallis never rebuked him for these demonstrations of hostility). The dog knew he had to be prepared, at all times, to fly to the defence of his friend, even to sacrifice himself if needs be to save his master's more valuable skin. To find him apparently threatened, as now, struggling in the grip of insubstantial devils that Ralph's nose and ears told him did not exist, and about which he could do nothing, was a torment to him. It was almost more than he could bear to remain detached as his companion tossed and turned under the burden of the nightmare, or whatever it was, until the conflict reached an insupportable point, and to escape it the man tore himself back into full consciousness.

A woman's voice! An argument, and a man and woman's voices raised in anger!

Out of a grave at the bottom of the sea, Tallis flung himself upward to avoid suffocation, rose through fathom after fathom, shot the surface at last and found... himself lying on bare boards with his head half out of the floor-level window and the echo of something he thought he had heard still whispering in his memory. An owl floated a single quavering note onto the still night waters. The outside air barely moved but seemed fresh and sweet compared to the vacuum of his dream. He had no recollection of having crossed the room, only of being smothered and hearing voices. But if there had been anything of the kind it was gone; the only sound now was his own breathing. A damp nose pressed against his hand and he responded with an automatic caress. What time was it? No time. This was the dead hour between yesterday and tomorrow when all things shake loose and nothing is certain. Out there was... what? Impenetrable mystery. He had come to dread these night-time wakings.

Silence and peace. Inevitably, the utter absence of events had a soothing effect on his nerves. His agitation subsided. Yet he did not feel confident enough to return to the dark cave at his back, nor to the stuffy rumpled bed. Trying to ease his prone body into a more comfortable position he sought for an explanation of the malaise that had recently afflicted him: the feelings of panic, of an unnatural and precipitate return, of a body dead, cold and unprepared to receive the wandering spirit. It had not always been so – sleeplessness had not always appeared a curse. Once there had been joy in lying alone, in solitary state, watching the wheeling stars streaming like new creation across the inky flood of heaven. How long ago had he last felt that sense of harmony? Perhaps the wilderness was to blame, or these more northerly climes, where often on clear nights all heat from both ground and air emptied into space as soon as the sun had left the sky. Nature, his own body, had turned against him. The forces which he must combat in order to continue to make progress appeared to multiply, become legion, yet the end seemed no nearer – if there was ever to be an end. Could it be that he was just growing old?

He switched his thoughts back to the beginning of his journey, along the unbroken ribbon of earth, winding over hills, through forests, through and over rivers, each yard of which his feet, or the feet of his horse, had trodden to bring him to this valley. He saw it as a stretched out cord, greatly attenuated, yet connecting him to his place of origin, so that he could still reach back over the years and draw renewal of strength or reinforced determination from recollections of those days, despite the contradictory nature of the words that had launched him, in haste and ill prepared, on the quest that, since then, had occupied practically every waking hour.

"Get gone, Tal! Get gone! Go quickly before they take you from me!"

It was his mother's voice that sounded in his memory, as clear now as when he had first heard the admonishment at the age of fifteen, ringing in the bareness of a high-ceilinged room and breaking through the customary quiet of their existence. He remembered his own words that had called forth the urgency, spoken after two days of troubled silence, and prompted by the sly insinuations of others:

"Mother – have you ever made your home down in the village?"

Each new baby born
Is like a moon just risen,
So where was its setting?

Chapter three

Tallis was no stranger to cold days and even
colder nights. His childhood had been spent in regions
where the breath smoked on the air for the greater part of
the year. It was the chill of altitude he had known, in a
place where lowlanders gasped like fish out of water, and
human dwellings shrank to mere flea-bites on the flanks
of white-maned giants. For want of level ground, villages
there teetered over precipices plunging fathoms into
shadowy crevasses, out of which, thin and far away, came
the distant voice of unseen waters. The rocky streets of
those small towns held ice, like old ivory, far past the
height of summer. Everywhere across the yawning gulfs
massive sentinels shouldered their way skyward; remote,
dream-like summits rose one behind the other, each
familiar unchanging outline a reminder of human frailty.
The men of that country had named the giants, then, as if
awed by their own temerity, had fallen to worshipping
them. In return the mountains walled Tallis' homeland
away from the world, keeping its people simple and
unsophisticated, cutting them off from concourse with
other races, protecting them from invasion. Yet once, his
mother said, many had come that way, a whole nation,

braving the high passes with their oxcarts, droves and baggage wagons, men at arms afoot and knights on horseback, the mighty born in litters of state and old folk, women and children trailing away to the rear.

The conditions were poor and hard for all in that place, no matter who they were, but poorer still, and harder had been the lot of Tallis and his mother. They dwelt not in the village, clinging limpet-like to its broad shoulder of rock, but above it, in an old stone house that had once been a barn, built on the last man-made terrace before the land took a terrifying leap upwards towards the realm of mountain goats and eagles. The terrace walls were crumbling, and the precious soil slid, year by year, down towards the more prosperous levels of their neighbours; Tallis' mother had not the strength nor the skill to build them up again. Nothing thrived on their small patch of ground, neither crops nor livestock. Although the holding faced south, apart from a short spell at dawn and at dusk, the air hung sunless, still and dead all the day through. In his earliest memories a third had been with them in the big dark building tucked away beneath the beetling cliff: an old Cunjor or Wise Man, to whom the villagers brought their troubles when the weight of them grew great enough to conquer their superstitious fears. When the old man died Tallis and his mother lived on alone. The people continued to come; his mother found ways to provide bread for the two of them, but not through her occasional desultory scratchings in the sour and shallow soil, nor her absent-minded wandering in search of nature's grudging bounty.

Morvah, Tallis' mother, did not hold the mountains in awe as did the village people. She looked to the sky and took the one who called himself Lord-of-

Heaven for her deity. She revered everything he claimed as his own: the winds, the firmament, the very day-star itself. Even as a child Tallis found it sad that, considering her devotion, his mother should be denied the rays from the god's most precious jewel for many long hours. He often saw her sitting on the terrace wall, a small shadowed figure outlined against the vast panorama, gazing across at the sunlit view like a prisoner from behind bars. An exile she was true for large stretches of time, yet, on one day of the year, she had her moment of glory. Very early, on that particular morning, when dawn was just a pious hope in the eastern sky, they went out onto the mountainside and made their way to a carefully chosen location where Morvah had installed a little hand-made altar for the use of the two of them alone. Below, the clouds that had come down to sleep overnight in the empty valleys were beginning to stir and writhe uneasily, like interlopers caught on forbidden ground as the true master approaches; in the calm colourless expanses, seeming so close overhead, the stars were stealing away one by one. Light grew like a sustained chord swelling from the pipes of a mighty organ, building steadily until the crescendo reached a pitch of unbearable tension. Then, between two distant peaks, the first fiery spark kindled, a spear of gold leapt the intervening chasms, fast as thought, and smote the exact spot where the altar had been set up. Tallis, kneeling with hands clasped, teeth chattering and body shaking from the intense cold, heard his mother begin the ancient hymn of greeting as the brilliance dazzled and blinded his eyes. Thin and true it floated, the song, one solitary human voice raised in praise, at the brief period when light and dark divide the world and reign for a moment side by side. Afterwards they returned home, Tallis empty and light-headed, feeling as if every last blot had been scoured and chased from his soul, Morvah setting quietly to work to prepare their first meal of the day, her face illumined by a faint echo of the splendour they had witnessed.

Tallis could still bring to mind his mother's face after all these years, constructing it lovingly, feature by feature, like a man putting together a priceless but shattered vase. Her soft dark hair he remembered, and her clear almost transparent skin, showing scarcely a sign of aging. It gave him a pang now to realize – for it was only with his own advancing years that the point came home – how young a mother she must have been when she bore him. Mostly it was her eyes that stayed with him, inward-looking, of palest amber, the colour leeching away during times of deep introspection until they took on the impenetrable greyness of the mists that sometimes curtained the farm. These absences – these moments of *petit mal* – were often of no short duration. The lonely child knew days when he was deprived of his mother's company from early morn until late at night. Although physically present, mentally she had withdrawn to great distances, and was out of earshot of even the most urgent call. Tallis would wait patiently, but with a suppressed excitement, for her return. Morvah, he knew, left him to walk the borders of a golden land, and he was privileged to be the sole recipient of dispatches from those far-off and exotic climes.

On occasions she brought back nothing but a static picture for him to feed on, minutely described, filling his head with petrified images of velvet lawns, glistening marble columns and still pools. But at other times the scenes became animated: leaves flashed light and dark on stooping branches weighed down with fruit or blossom, fountains played, sunlit wavelets lapped a pebbly shore, lush grass rippled like silk or was bent and crushed by the passage of mysterious creatures trailing robes and scent amongst the dappled shadows. But, in actual fact, to catch and pin down the inhabitants of her cerebral vision was an undertaking of a different order. Morvah had to be away long hours before she began hesitantly to sketch the outlines, to define the shapes, of living-breathing men and women. It took many journeys of the mind before she could bring herself to name those happy beings, merely to speak of which wrenched her face with sorrow and longing. There came the day, however, a dark day in the depths of winter, Tallis recalled, when his mother woke from a reverie infused with a radiance that seemed to light up their frost-beset kitchen. From that moment on she ceased to be a grieving ghost, condemned always to view, but never to share, that which she most desired. She had stepped through enchanted portals into a country more real to her than their present harsh existence, and had taken her rightful place among the actors in that glowing tapestry.

A king's daughter she had been – his mother made the claim with pride and apparently no sense of incongruity, holding her work-roughened hands out to the bright eye of the ancient stove, making her fingers glow with their own small interior flames – a king's daughter and an only child in a sunny southern land. *Her* bare feet had paddled the lush cool lawns, had threaded smooth paths winding beneath stained and ancient stone work, had waded in the pools that never failed. *Her* eyes had looked forth from shaded arbours onto distant prospects

of lake shores, where little craft with moon-shaped sails
heeled before a non-existent wind, apparently going
nowhere across blue unruffled spaces. Idling, vaguely
dissatisfied, in the lane outside the back gate of the palace
garden, her own ears had heard, above the drowsy piping
of insects, the sound of quiet voices engaged in desultory
conversation, floating like motes on the surface of a
sluggish stream across the feet thick boundary wall. If,
impelled by she knew not what, she decided to risk a few
bruised toes and chose to follow the empty lane upwards,
leaving behind the palace secure among its army of
cypresses, she knew she would come out at last, above
the orange groves, to a place utterly open to the azure
heavens. This was *his* place, the place of Pyr, the Sky-
Father, where the great white stones that cast no shadows
had been set up, where the strong mellow light of an
afternoon in late summer burned on forever, world
without end.

"One day," Morvah said, "a man came into our
country from without. He came alone, seeming to impose
no threat. As he left the lake road and turned up towards
the palace the route along its entire length was lined with
people. My father, dressed in the robes of the Priest-King,
came to the top of the grand staircase with all the court in
attendance, and I accompanied him, walking at his right
hand. No one alive had ever known such a day before; to
see a face whose lineaments were not engraved on the
mind through familiarity, this was passing strange."

"Where were the borders of our land? It was a
question unasked and therefore unanswered. A barrier
seemed set between us and the world beyond. Our
attention was always inwards, inwards towards the water;
were we not the Guardians-of-the-Lake? Once out of

sight of those dazzling hazy expanses we only knew that the hills closed in and the small wild things became fierce and wary, birds sang less, plants grew coarse and rank, the very face of the sun was dimmed. Now this man, by what means none could tell, had found a way to penetrate the charmed sphere; the surface of the bubble had been breached from without, laying us open to who-knew-what events. But at first it seemed only I could sense that, with his coming, the old ways were gone for good."

"Gammadion – so he styled himself – was given a suite of rooms within the palace walls, above the hanging gardens. Among the stately courtiers, dressed in their flowing finery, he stood out like a marauding crow in a dovecote. For the first few hours I could not look enough at his outlandish clothes and guarded handsome face, its closed expression hiding untold knowledge. He was a dark man, despite his pallid skin: dark dwelt in the harsh lines running from nose to mouth, in the hollow spiral of his ear, in the enclosed space hidden behind his lips. Most of all it lay in the pits of his eyes, burning with a slow fire - I believe we knew nothing of night's true meaning until he came among us. I stood staring, as I said, finger in mouth, eyes wide, until I realized that the cage that should have contained the wild beast was non-existent. Then I took fright and tried to flee, understanding my peril, trembling in every limb, for who amongst those who shared in the slow pavane of palace life was going to break out of the endlessly repeated pattern and come to my aid? At first my infatuation was coloured by fear, but, gradually, that passed. Soon my heart began to leap with joy at the mere sight of him; he became the only real thing in the whole of that dreaming land. His will had wrought the transformation. I sensed this in an uncomprehending way, feeling myself being drawn or pushed in the direction he wanted me to go. It was not long before I was ready to follow him in all things, although when it came to revelations about the curious ways in which a man can serve a woman when the two of them are alone together, I could not help but burst out laughing at the sheer oddness and absurdity of the idea – that is until he took to showing me."

"That was the period of my greatest happiness. We became easy and confident lovers, coming together even in broad daylight with impunity. We might as well have been invisible for all the notice that was taken. Looking around at the empty vapid faces, the bodies frozen in the attitudes of an elegant tableau, I saw myself surrounded by a nation of sleepwalkers out of which only I had awoken. From their midst the whirlwind had plucked me; I had been swept along, bruised, battered, yet glowing with life; I was as full of questions as a four year old child, and like a child accepted all things as new, seeing everything as if for the first time."

"Disappointingly Gammadion would recount little about the wonders of the wide world and nothing on the subject that interested me most – himself. He wanted to speak only of the Land-of-the-Lake, to hear our history and legends, to follow our doings from day to day. Yet now and again, from things he let slip, I began to suspect he already knew as much as I could tell him. Indeed I had this confirmed one morning in a way that made me gasp and cover my mouth with alarm."

"He had taken me to the window with his arm around my shoulders and pointed to where the lake and sky melted into one."

"*Why are your people called Lake Guardians, child? I have left it to you to tell me in your own good time, but now, instead, it seems I will have to tell you: there it lies, hidden in mist, hard to come at – a little rock, placed in the midst of the waters, solely to keep safe the world's greatest treasure.*"

"*Oh, but you mustn't…!*"

"*Mustn't what?*"

"*Mustn't speak so!*"

"He had broken the greatest taboo of all: he had named the holy of holies which only the priest-king was allowed to do, and then only on the day appointed. I waited for the sky to fall. When the birds continued to sing and nothing stirred but flowers in the soft summer breeze, I gazed at the man beside me in awe. Here was someone truly powerful, someone who defied the gods and went his own way without let or hindrance."

"How quickly the gap widens once the dyke is breached. It was like gulping in lungfuls of fresh air to flout the prohibitions one by one, like shedding a load that had weighed me down ever since I could remember."

"*The Treasure! – Yes, it's somewhere out there. No one has seen it, no one knows what it is. The Sky-Lord laid a sacred trust on us many years ago – how does it go? 'Ring the lake, remain vigilant, let no one pass. Keep safe the Thing-of-Power until the last day!'*"

"*So the Guardians don't know what they're guarding,* murmured Gammadion lazily, half to himself, and went on in his laconic, ironical way that made me suspect I was the butt of some private joke: *There are stories in the world beyond that speak of a Key, something of such potency that only those still remaining in the flesh can bear its proximity for long. The tales say that although he who claims it claims it wrongfully he retains the power to prevent all but the king or his heir from coming at the Treasure."*

"These words brought to an end my halcyon days. In the distance I heard the rustling of monstrous wings – an intimation of the doom that was already rushing upon my race – for I saw now what had drawn him to our land. The marvel was that I was able to hold out against him for so long. A fainting dread overcame me each time I thought of what he wanted me to do, and it was solely for this reason that against all his blandishments and threats I continued to deny him, despite promises, pleadings and eventually even blows. To gain possession of something which many people thought of as merely a myth, a fable locked up in old legends, this was his abiding obsession. I meant nothing to him, I was just necessary because he believed I had been endowed with an immunity he could not claim; only I would be allowed to voyage to the very centre of the lake and return with his heart's desire, thereby robbing the Guardians of their reason for existence, thereby flying in the face of the great Lord-of-Heaven himself, from whom it is said all mercies and all bounties flow. Understanding this I chewed bitter fruit but went on loving him, with a love that had passed from sunshine into shadow, giving, instead of gladness, pain alone."

"So it came about that one interminable afternoon we lay together in my bed, the sun peering in on us through heavy net curtains, scattering glowing lozenges of light across the silks and brocades. He began again on the same tack, wheedling and persuading, until, finding me as stubborn as ever, he fell to cursing, me weeping the while. As usual we ended in silence,

Gammadion's expression as stony as if his face were carved out of granite. No timid conciliatory caress of mine could call forth any answering warmth from that rigid frame."

"*I will tell you the truth,* he said at last, a new note in his voice, *I will tell you a little about the rest of the world. Then perhaps you'll learn to be less cruel"*

"This is a very strange place, this Land-of-the-Lake – you don't know how strange unless like me you come to it from without. It's a place where alteration has all but ceased to happen, a place where an hour can seem as long as a day, where a year means eternity. Not so in the country I come from, things alter all the time, people alter. And alteration means suffering; it means births and deaths and partings and disease. And of these diseases there is one common to all – no man can escape it if he lives. Its symptoms are grotesque: wasted limbs, overpowering weakness, a crumbling of the intellect, impotence, incontinence. And when the disease runs its course and at last the sufferer lies abandoned in some filthy corner, forgotten by friends and enemies alike, death comes along like an old rag picker and carts away what's left. That disease, princess, is called Old Age."

"While speaking he had slipped out of bed and now stood naked in front of my full length mirror; naked that is apart from a rather strange piece of jewellery he wore around his neck: a silver pendant in the shape of a jointed manikin that appeared to have been through the wars as it was missing the lower part of its left leg. He gazed at his reflection with all the intensity and earnestness of a doting lover, ignoring me completely for the moment."

"The Key! he growled, addressing himself. *Only the Key holds the solution! The Key which initiates change can also avert it. It prevents the onset of old age, it gives power and, if one owns it long enough, even at several removes, it can grant immortality. No need, anymore, to cling to what is probably a false promise of reincarnation or transmutation of the flesh."*

"Don't you see...! he cried, waking from his self-absorption and swinging round with arms held open wide in an extravagant and slightly comic gesture, *The sickness has already started its work – its mark is already upon me!"*

"Sitting up in bed, I gazed and then turned away. I could see nothing wrong. To me, poor foolish girl, he was perfect as he was; I wanted him no other way. What if his flesh hung a little loose on the bones, and in places showed blotched and darkened? This seemed just a mark of the privations he must have suffered during the hard and dangerous road I liked to imagine he had trodden on his way to our country and only increased his attraction. I suppose at that time he was a man of about fifty years. What I did see, and what, having seen I wanted to forget, was a dew of sweat glistening on his forehead in the smothering dimness. Gammadion the brave, the undaunted, the breaker of taboos, was in terror of the thing he spoke about. To make that fear go away, to pretend it had never existed, I promised to do as he asked."

"We stole a boat from a quiet landing stage about three miles from the staithes below the palace gardens. On the way there Gammadion poured forth a stream of advice. He appeared to have to talk to still his anxiety, and even so his tongue kept flicking in and out,

moistening parched lips. The nearer we came to the
fulfilment of his dream, the greater seemed to be his
dread of failure, and his agitation was painful to see. As
for me, when Gammadion let go the stern and the little
sailing boat I had boarded leapt straight out from the
shore-line like a messenger of fate and was soon far
beyond where our craft were normally wont to go, I felt
nothing at all. To enter the purlieus of that mist, a shifting
magic curtain hanging ahead of me between sky and
water, meant certain death. So I had been taught and so I
believed. I had no faith in Gammadion's talk of a royal
inviolability. But death had been much on my mind ever
since I had begun to realize, that, whether he laid hands
on the Treasure or no, my lover would soon be lost to me
forever."

"The outer limits of the mist filled all my vision;
for a brief second I thought I saw ramparts, bastions, the
defences of a great fortress, looming above; then cool,
damp and slightly perfumed, it enveloped me completely,
without my coming to harm. I heard no voices, was
granted no visions, as Gammadion warned might be the
case, but the waters stood up around me on all sides like
walls of ice, and light from above came down blue and
shining as if the lake had risen and closed over my head.
Gradually the sense of forward motion faded away. A
silence like nothing I had ever known filled the
surrounding vacancy. In a moment that was neither *now*
nor *then* nor any time to come I sat and watched the
treasure house of the Key grow before me out of empty
air."

"Surprise and bewilderment jostled my numbed
senses awake. Was this where the Father had chosen to
hide his most precious trophy – in this little glass-walled

structure – a belvedere or gazebo would have best described it – crowning the summit of a grassy knoll whose roots could be seen going far down into limpid depths? A mere bauble – a clockmaker's toy it seemed, something created purely to delight the eye. Rainbow colours, subtly refracted, glanced between the angles of the walls, and an aura of elusive gold tantalized on the periphery of vision with an endless swirl of dancing flickers of glory. Such fragility! Such ephemeral daintiness! One swing of a hammer and the delicate construction would dissolve into a waterfall of flying fragments. So it first impressed me. Yet the longer I gazed the more I was overwhelmed by the sheer impact of its presence, as if the pretty artificiality was all a semblance and show, and behind it lurked power, energy, intelligence, unimaginable to the human mind."

"Drawn closer to the Lake's centre by no will of my own, I was permitted to set foot on the islet; I was permitted to climb the verdant slope and stand unscathed beside the Sky-King's shrine. With my brain dazed by the beating against it of unseen forces, I was granted a glimpse into the dim heart of the temple. And when with a kind of dread I directed my attention inward, down the endless mirror corridor of a thousand repeated images where the end is forever hidden from view, what did I see beyond those transparent walls? I looked once and looked no more, for within, it seemed, was infinite space – worlds and stars and constellations whirling in a sea of time – the firmament entire."

"I had no need to search for the thing I had come to steal (*No treasure other than the Key, all else is false, all else a deception*), my hand fell on it accidentally as it brushed against the building's half-shut door. Otherwise I would scarcely have discovered it, so tiny it was and in so minute a lock. I pulled it out and, with one quick glance behind, bent to examine what I had found. It lay in the palm like a dragonfly about to take wing, lovely beyond words. What was it and what was its purpose? A key it was, surely, but one so cunningly and exquisitely wrought that its detail drew the eye down, down through numberless layers of ornamentation until from sheer self preservation the explorer had to decline the way and retreat or else be lost forever. A veil of tears suddenly smeared its brightness and hid it from my sight. I would have been a dull fool if I had not recognized a work of the Original Creator in this marvel; it belonged in his hands and should not be profaned by the touch of a mere mortal, or even immortal, creature. Yet Gammadion was right. When it came to the taking - dare I contemplate the blasphemy even for a moment? - I had dominion."

"And so I fled away, my rejection of an intolerable truth driving me from that place just as my refusal to admit another had brought me to it. In desolation of spirit I turned back with the Precious Thing towards my companion, the Lake and mist unrolling before me as I went and the boat needing no hand at the helm to bring it to the point from which it had set out."

"There, on the landing stage under the trees, the light was fading fast. The man was within arm's reach of me before I saw him. One hand gleamed palely as he held it out – his face was completely shrouded – and into it I placed the wonder, the sacred trust of my people. The deed accomplished, at once the clotted shadows before me were empty and the thief was gone. All that remained was a conviction that, in the moment of transference, the

Key had altered under my touch, becoming coarser, heavier, harder, to meet a new and grimmer destiny."

"I had held it for just a brief period in utter ignorance of its nature, yet to be rid of it was already a relief; the persistent dead weight of its proximity to my finite existence had been hard to bear. Now, the trees began to thrash together wildly overhead. Coming to myself a little I turned towards the lake and fell to my knees appalled. A sight met my eyes qualified to freeze the blood. For the first time the farther shore was visible, the divine mist having vanished as if it had never been, and low hills, a long rim of razor teeth on the skyline, stood out with shocking clarity under a turmoil of heavy cloud. There was no wind; the ground itself was rippling like water causing the trees to sway. The lake, still held in the fading dregs of a spell, retained its unruffled purity for a brief time, darkening as the light withdrew – a mirror of silver, a mirror of steel, a mirror of brass, a mirror of copper. But what was that thing on the surface – one fatal flaw in the immaculate expanse? – the god's islet, breaking the smoothness like a monster from the deep, spreading contagion outward from the centre. Pinpricks of black appeared on the surface, grew into blots, contorted, expanded, merged. The water at the marge sank away through the shingle; the stones swallowed it and were dry. One last image followed me into the darkness – something I might have seen or merely dredged from the depths of my own terrified imagination - a vast pit where the lake had been, a gaping wound on the face of the earth, and at the bottom a thousand living dying things writhing in their own slime."

Snow, banked to roof level beyond the massive walls, leant against the house, waiting with the patience of centuries for the first crack, the final capitulation. The child Tallis, hungry for *happy ever after*, stared into the frigid recesses of the lofty room, seeing and not seeing, beyond the stove's small radius of warmth, icicles like palisades of hate, crowding close to the source of the moisture which they sucked so eagerly off the brittle air, and, further into the gloom, a sudden twink and glintle on the floor, betraying the presence of black frost veining the surface of black and beaten earth.

"And then, mother? – What then? – What happened then?" A sad ending is no ending at all. When he continued to question, badgering insistently for a reply, his mother's face turned blank and stupid. She closed herself off so efficiently from his entreaties that he dared say no more, fearing to be left entirely alone within that freezing mausoleum. He had to hold his peace until the following summer before Morvah began to bridge the great divide that lay between the fading of her vision and their present life here on the mountain. And then it was a difficult and troublous undertaking. When she spoke it was without conviction – hesitantly, unhappily, as if groping through a dense fog of years.

The king had saved them. In the midst of roaring blackness, while the rest of his people ran howling and stupid with terror like maggots swarming over a rotting corpse, he intuited the cause behind the devastation and set himself to climb to the place of the stones, going slowly on hands and knees in great pain. There he had spoken with the god and had given and received certain promises, returning a weakened and spent old man. In due time, but not immediately, light had been restored.

The survivors beheld the world's dawn – a remote indifferent star creeping above the horizon, bringing a cruel revelation of total destruction. Thereafter there had been nothing left to do but pack up and leave; to salvage what they could from the wreckage and gird themselves to take to the road, for the Land-of-the-Lake was no more. Theirs was a new calling. The king had solemnly pledged that they would restore the thing that had been lost. This Repository-of-Might, this Potent-Crucible, wandering wild, masterless, at large in the world – they must pursue it now wherever it led, though it might be to the edge of tomorrow, the back of beyond, the uttermost ends of the earth.

At first the path was blazed wide and unmistakable. In its travels the Key and its bearer had trailed cataclysms in their wake. The Guardians, taking signs of despoliation and havoc as a guide, passed through ruined landscapes and later shattered towns, whose stunned inhabitants, their eyes full of nightmares, stared unbelievingly at the grim spectral multitude pacing by whose coming had been presaged so terribly. The hunt was up but soon the scent grew cold – scars had mended, new growth had sprung up from ashes and bare earth; their quarry was leaving them days, weeks, months behind. Report had it that the thief had cut his swathe of violence through the lands of men in a single night, flashing due north with incredible swiftness towards some unknown destination. Troubles multiplied and the way grew hard, leading them into a waste of mountains among which they laboured unavailingly while the old and weak faltered, fell sick and died.

"People began to murmur against me." Morvah went on. "Everyone knew the part I had played; I had cried it to the world, unable to bear the guilt alone. What had happened openly, before their eyes, they now saw through hindsight, as if for the first time, and they recoiled from it, revolted to the core. Gammadion they thought of as a sort of demon, a pure emanation of evil which, through sheer weight of malevolence, forces its way through into the physical world and takes the shape of a man. How else, they asked, could he have had the power to deceive them so utterly? Well – who knows? But to me he seemed a man like any other, what evil there was in him springing from the flesh and not giving rise to it; only a man I think could have got me with child. But they railed and screamed at my father, crying that the miserable slut who had betrayed them by coupling with the devil and who now bore his seed deserved to be done away with; she was bringing them nothing but ill luck; her presence among them called down the righteous wrath of the Lord; the baby would be born a monster and men would go mad at the sight of it. In their eyes I saw a fear, not of me only, but of the forthcoming birth, an unprecedented event in their experience, and beyond that a shrinking from all the body's natural functions, which to the lakeside dwellers were unwelcome novelties, learnt in a single night, as soon as the fire of enchantment had been doused and they ceased to breath its fumes. The old king was a shattered burnt-out shell, a broken reed before the fury of his people, yet he pleaded for me, and for his sake, because of the debt they owed him, they left me behind in the snow, helpless but alive, when they moved on."

At this point in the story Morvah's voice lost its hesitancy. She drew herself up to her full height, chin thrust out, aflame with a kind of tragic jubilation.

"Although I had sinned against him the Lord-of-Heaven would not let me go into the dark! I was saved, Tal, but not by human hand. No – no. *He* saved me, - the Shining One – there on the empty hillside! When the cold had crept into my very bones he came to me where I lay. I saw him here on earth in the shape of a great warrior, striding across mountain ranges as if they were ridges in a ploughed field, his glory illuminating the deepest crevasses, the snow bursting alight wherever his feet touched the ground. He came to *me!* To look into his face is to stare into the molten heart of a furnace where everything is in flux – to see a beast, a flower, a child, one's own image. On his head stood a brazen helm, cloud high; his breath scorched and seared the forests yet to me was sweeter than honey. He reached out the tip of his spear and touched my heart; my body burned and the cold ceased to trouble me. Eventually I found a way to go that few are able to tread in this day and age. It led me to a place where a man had already anticipated my arrival and where the wrong could one day be righted. So I came to this house in which you were born. Here I have waited for my people to return – waited in vain."

During winter snows, or when the ground was soft from rain, mornings often revealed a line of tell-tale footprints coming and going between the village and Tallis and Morvah's habitation. This was when the tongues down below would start to wag. Cold hostility instead of smoke drifted up towards the boy and his mother from the clumped rooftops, blasting their peace, nipping happiness in the bud. At such times Morvah's recollections were everything to the pair, a secure nest into which the woman withdrew like a small frightened animal, escaping the withering ostracism that her night guests only served to emphasise. Her son accompanied her eagerly. In his childish way he wished to be everything to his parent; the furtive scratchings on the door after midnight filled him with rage, he scarcely knew why. In that bright country they walked together, the two of them alone – no one else could follow. Times were though when hope seemed to revive, when the gate to her memories was closed for weeks at a time and Morvah spoke of the future or of passing fancies.

Tallis remembered a day late in their fleeting summer. They were sitting together on the terrace wall, legs dangling in space, while Morvah's fingers flew to and fro, rapidly busy lassoing holes with thread and hook as the shawl she was crocheting grew in length. Her grave youthful profile was at odds with the harsh grandeur of the backdrop against which it was set; she looked more like a serious high-minded schoolgirl, her straight clear thoughts as yet unclouded by experience, than her normal guise as an unlettered mountain woman, a mother of ten years.

"That terrace down there, what colour is it?"

Tallis volunteered the information that it was green.

"And those tiles farther down – what colour are they?"

"Red."

"And the sky...?"

"Blue."

"All right then – now tell me what you mean by blue and red and green."

"You see Tal," Morvah went on after enjoying the boy's fruitless struggle with abstractions, "neither of us knows what the other is seeing. Your blue may not be my blue. We'll never know because we haven't the wisdom to explain a colour. If we could see out of another's eyes, if only we weren't condemned always to look out of our own, we might find the world was a totally different place from the one we believed we recognized."

"D'you know," she continued musingly, "I used to have an odd feeling sometimes when I was a youngster. I'd be walking along through some familiar scene when I'd be struck by a complete sense of incongruity – *What am I doing here? Where is this? What has this house, this landscape – infinitely strange – to do with me?* It seemed almost as if I had been set down there that very moment and all my memories up to that point were quite false, mere paraphernalia of the body I had begun to occupy."

"Why did he save me? Was it the Lord of Heaven who directed me here? As far as I know women mean little to him. If he was responsible, it was for you Tal, that he did it. I think I know how it must be. Most mortals – those down there," her gesture towards the village was contemptuous, "are foolish common people, drifting at the mercy of events, willing to go wherever the currents of life take them until they die. That's the majority. Then there's a swirl and a splash and a glint of silver scales amidst the murk. Something dives into the weedy pools and upsets the equilibrium. The local residents are thrown about by contact with the newcomer or dragged along in the wake of his momentum. I believe there are such individuals, Tal, people who step down from the womb onto a path already laid, their whole life the answer to a call. But not all are recognised: some fall by the wayside or are destroyed. Others – those who slip secretly from birth to death – go unremarked, even by the people closest to them; the far shores their feet have trodden are never guessed at by those they brush shoulders with in the daily round. And then there are the ones for whom a place has been prepared, for whom the cry goes up *This is he!* or *This is she!* because in the moment of glimpsing the unfamiliar face thousands know they have seen it somewhere before, - that out of feelings of great personal and universal emptiness – those dark hours before dawn – it has already risen, like a vision and a promise, within the core of every living being."

"They all hear and answer to a different drum, these special ones. It sounds, and off they go, forging upstream, leaping the rapids, ending at last perhaps in some airless shallow far up among the hills without ever understanding the daemon that moves them with such a burning imperative obsession, beyond all reason. Compared to the mass of humanity they are always swimming in the opposite direction from the rest of the shoal even if it is a voyage hell-bent to destruction or appears as such. What the onlookers don't realize is that for such people this call is their very life-blood, it is the turning away from it that brings death, even though their bodies may still be seen to walk the earth."

In Morvah's face the sun had disappeared behind a cloud. An interior monologue absorbed her completely. Soon she tucked her head down and began to croon to herself in a sly possessive sort of way, as if the song she sang was something precious that had been left in her safe keeping and must be shielded against the malice of the world:

"Transgressions undisclosed,
Me once from joy deposed,
Changing the rose for thorn,
Ere I was born.

A fine and subtle way
Led my poor heart astray,
From bliss asunder torn,
Ere I was born.

Was this the penalty –
That I, no longer free,
True self awhile should pawn,
And so be born?

What was the debt incurred
To quit which I gave my word,
Else should I be forsworn,
Thus to be born?

Through living floods I came,
Naked, without a name,
Woke to a foreign dawn,
And so was born.

Far from the mystery,
In deepest exile, we,
By whom the flesh is worn,
We that are born."

The slender figure bowed over its pain, hands still, work lying neglected. Tallis forbore to interfere, dreading to touch an open wound;. Even if he understood nothing else he knew that this came from very close to the quick. Intimations of a cold misery, a sacrificial renunciation, bound up with his mother's fate, and his, invaded his consciousness like a palpable fog. Over, under, within and without, deprivation seemed to hem him round; the small natural events of the summer morning belonged to him no more; they took on a new significance as an invasion from an unbelievably happy world. Far in the distance the bleating of goats fell on his ears like the voices of the blest.

Abruptly and without warning Morvah turned to face her son and caught his hands in hers, her eyes full of tears. The impulsive movement sent the ball of yarn spinning off her lap. It flew out into space and down towards the next terrace, unwinding all the way, until finding level ground it rolled out beyond the dreary pall under which they spent their days and the end of the thread lay unregarded in the sunshine.

"You are one with them, Tal, I have felt it from the moment you were born! Surely you must be, with the task lying so clear ahead of you – to find your people, to mend what your father has undone, to bring back the Key so that the Land-of-the-Lake can be restored!"

In this manner Tallis first learnt the course his life was to take. It did not occur to him to challenge Morvah's vision for his future, not then nor for many years to come. All he could find to voice his deep dismay and apprehension, his painfully sincere reluctance to assume the cloak of a man of destiny, was the feeble –

"But how shall I know which way to go?"

Morvah replied with a fragment of law, learnt who knows where.

" *The Sun shines on the waters and the waters give back his light.* " she quoted severely, as if Tallis ought already to know the answer, *"In like manner the Lord is revealed in his glory and in his lesser incarnations. But there is also a light that shines in darkness, in the depths of the waters: it is the voice of god within the soul."*

"The Lord-of-Heaven will show you the way if you trust him Tal. He will speak to your heart and point out the road you must travel, for you are his, more so than I could ever be."

Tallis stared hard at his mother, surprising a look of weariness and defeat on her face. One of the foundation stones on which his life was built felt as if it was starting to shift.

"But he speaks to you too," he said in sharp puzzlement. "You have told me so, lots of times – and he saved you as well. Surely he has forgiven you by now for your disobedience!"

"Forgiveness! What is that? I have honoured him and done battle with myself for many years to atone for my fault. But the priests of the Sky-Father were always men, Tal, the reason why I have had to learn stumblingly over the years. In the hall of prayer in the palace by the lake the women sat at the side, their faces veiled. We did not presume to go up to the high table or share in the most sacred rites. Women can never reach the heights determined by the Sky-Father – there is too much of earth in us – too much of roots - we pledged our allegiance elsewhere in an earlier age of the world. The good lord comes to our door – we open to him as to a long-awaited guest – but he stays without, a stranger at the gate. Our bodies are alien to him, moon-oriented, caught up in rhythms that might work him harm."

Morvah sighed, shifted position then gave a small wistful smile. "If I had been born in another place and at another time," she went on sadly, "maybe - because of my feminine nature - I would have invited a different guest onto my hearth."

As she spoke a blindness seemed to lift from Tallis' eyes. He was able to penetrate the woman's surface composure, discovering beneath the mask of calm resignation an unfamiliar hectic cast speaking of long-standing tensions and a continual straining after something that was beyond her reach. Was it possible that Morvah felt herself rejected? Had she offered herself to the god and served his purposes only to be kept in want, her hunger unassuaged? – then a god who thus repaid devotion was not deserving of worship! If in later years he often found himself at a loss, he traced the cause back to those words of his mother's, voiced with such yearning, so long ago. Standing at a crossing with no clear idea which way to take, praying fruitlessly for guidance, he remembered anew the spark of revolt that had kindled in response within himself, a spark moreover which could still be fanned to a faint glow of life, despite every effort of his to stamp it out, when, as at this present moment, the wind had veered and was blowing from a new direction. Sometimes, on such occasions, he began to wonder if the task he had been set really belonged to him at all.

Uphill every step,
That's how it will seem,
And that's truly how it is.

Chapter four

Morvah's trances increased in length as time
wore on. With dread Tallis began to foresee the day when
he would wait in vain for the stir and sigh, the creeping of
blood beneath the skin, which indicated that once again
the wandering spirit had taken up residence inside its
little house. Already that house was suffering from
neglect. As his mother's condition worsened Tallis
became gripped by the notion that it was the trances
themselves that worked the change: *her dreams are*
consuming her! he thought in superstitious awe although
the common-sense half of him knew it was lack of
nourishment, purely and simply, that was hollowing her
cheeks and wasting her limbs. As for food, there was
little to be had about the house. On several occasions
Tallis had sat up in the small hours, Morvah sightless and
unaware beside him, facing the great double doors that
stood between their kitchen and the outside world,
listening with grim satisfaction to the gradually rising
tattoo of frustration being beaten on the exterior panels.
As long as he was in control there would be no more
midnight visitors: no hooded figures would slip in out of
the dark to stoop over signs drawn in the dust while

Morvah's voice chanted words mysterious and obscure; no man would stand with his mother before the firelight glow, two outlines blending into one and becoming vague and changeable as they sank down into the shadows where she had laid her bed. Ever since he had grown old enough to understand the way their life was governed Tallis had resolutely determined not to understand it. Obstinately he refused to see the connection between Morvah's guests and the stocks on their larder shelves. But now as the knocks on the door dwindled, so proportionally did their supplies and the fuel in their fire bucket. Staring famine full in the face it became harder and harder for Tallis to maintain his lofty obtuseness. At last, made both desperate and wise by necessity, he was flushed from his eyrie, and like a starved hawklet compelled by need to take its chance with the sparrows under the market barrows, he spread his wings and dropped noiselessly down to the village.

Oh, the jostling! the pandemonium! the almost physical assault on his senses that knocked the breath out of his body and turned the terrified boy both dumb and foolish, so that those who came running mistook him at first for a natural born idiot, wandering in his wits. They led him into one of their windowless houses, thick walled and sunken floored, with chickens roosting in the roof and dogs and children cluttering the corners, as the whole village came crowding in after, satisfying a long-pent-up curiosity. He almost drowned during those first few minutes. Into the bosom of the human family he had been pitchforked with a vengeance and its representatives were all around him, filling his ears and eyes and nostrils with overpowering, suffocating impressions. Only after managing to win again to the open air could he begin to make sense of the jabbering sea of heads, and then what he learnt caused his courage to revive. They were not going to rebuff or spurn him - from a distance he had once seen them throwing stones at a wildcat, sending it packing, and the memory had hung in his consciousness, feeding his apprehension - no, they were welcoming him after a fashion, offering him food, waving aside a small trinket of his mother's which was all he could proffer as payment. There was no quarrel it seemed between him and them. Whatever they might think of *her up there* he was just a child and could not be held responsible for the actions of grown men and women. And so, after long isolation, Tallis' life opened out and a new phase began.

He spent his nights with Morvah, his days down in the village. In the evenings he never left those narrow streets but with a feeling of relief to be out alone on the twilit mountain, great gulfs of air at his back, climbing the precipitous steps that led towards peace and quiet and the only place he had ever called home; he never reached that haven without the knowledge that the next morning he would be heading the other way, down to a man-sized world, drawn back by vague needs that went far beyond mere physical hunger.

When it came to the gentle art of social intercourse Tallis might as well have been a cripple walking for the first time, a blind man suddenly given the gift of sight. He stumbled about, understanding nothing, barking his shins and stubbing his toes, too simple at first to feel his own pain. The subtleties of intonation, of inferences conveyed by a slight change of expression, meaningful pauses, the trick of leaving certain things unsaid, all were completely lost on him. How could it have been otherwise? In comparison with these gauche untutored villagers he was a new-born babe – they were skilled practitioners with an infinite variety of experience.

Work was found for him when it was discovered that he preferred to give something in exchange for the largess with which he was continually showered. As he applied himself diligently to various menial and sometimes pointless tasks a procession of people came and engaged him in conversation. Gratified by the attention he was receiving Tallis earnestly attempted to follow what was being said. His good intentions were usually doomed to failure. The sense of the discussion always seemed to elude him. It amazed him how people could frequently say two completely contradictory things, sometimes in the same sentence – how they would laugh suddenly, apparently at nothing. The laughter foxed him most of all, he could never get the hang of it; the occasions when Morvah and he had laughed together had been rare indeed.

As the days passed faces became recognizable, names attached themselves to faces. An extraordinary elation gripped him as he realized he was being accepted into the life of the village. Whatever role they chose for him he was willing and eager to fill it to the best of his ability; that it would probably turn out to be a sort of honorary position as local buffoon and nitwit was mercifully far beyond his comprehension. He had no time to think of such things; all his energies were absorbed in coping with the barrage of information – wonderful, disturbing, delightful, shocking – with which he was bombarded every hour that he spent down below. And having learnt that men's chins grow beneath their noses, so to speak, his next impulse was to pass on the revelation. The thrill of discovery becomes barren unless we can share it with someone close to us. At the end of the day Tallis would throw his weight against the doors of the high barn and swing them open, his back loaded with goodies, his head with ideas, exhilarated and half-intoxicated by new knowledge, only to find that the cold dim interior dried up the words in his throat. More often than not he would discover Morvah locked within herself, sitting gazing rigidly ahead like a little wax doll, or slumped across the table apparently lifeless. Occasionally though she was waiting for him in her right mind, and then Tallis would have to endure a look of most eloquent sorrow from those haunted shadowed eyes. No more was needed. He became his own accuser, knowing he had failed her, understanding all too clearly the extent of his betrayal. And so, after a few months had passed, came the inevitable collision between Tallis' mutually exclusive worlds, and with it his last days on the mountain.

He was lying, not alone, in an unfrequented half-empty storeroom - his companion, a wild swaggering marriage-ripe girl, guide on the road to sensual awareness down which he had travelled many miles in recent days. Tallis, full pelt atop his newly discovered sexuality suddenly found himself being pushed off with the climax only moments away, while the girl's body shook with suppressed laughter as she twisted out of his embrace.

"Is it that we should be doing this thing at all, think you love?" she sang in her mountain lilt as he flapped and gasped. "After all, it's cousins we are, don't they say?"

The straw on which they were lying rustled. Within a few yards of their bolt hole the feet of villagers pattered to and fro. Tallis, trembling and trying not to show it, his mouth full of the sour taste of humiliation, rasped "Cousins? What do you mean? Cousins?"

"Why, through Rhoda, silly. You know Rhoda, don't you – my mam?"

He shook his head dumbly. He was being mocked or tested in some way, he felt sure of it, but there was no defence against the cruelty.

"Rhoda and Morvah, Morvah and Rhoda," the girl carolled in her sing-song voice, "sisters see! What tales has she been telling you, love, up in that nasty dark old house? She was always good at tall tales. That's what my mam says anyway; even before she got herself into a fix and Granda showed her the door. There was this fellow – see – not one of us – before I was born – or you – filled her up with all sorts of stories until her head was turned clean right round and she thought she was better than all the rest of us put together. In the family way she was – see – and, although he knew this, one of the Haytor brothers over at Davtah under Rosskill was good enough to say he would take her for his bride – but she would have none of it. None she would have, she said, but that ne'er-do-well who'd run off and left her. There's wicked for you..."

The trouble was that, after Tallis had heard the words, they seemed to have been a part of his understanding for as long as he could remember. He had tried to outdistance them, panting away up the hill, shaking the dust from his feet, but they were with him now, ineradicable. And so after two days of silent misery with the question burning the tip of his tongue he blurted it out at last.

"Mother, have you ever made your home down in the village?" And she had answered with that sentence that rang in his head now as clearly as on the day it was first uttered.

"Get gone, Tal, before they take you from me!"

Not immediately of course. First her lips had parted; she had fought the silence and the stopped breath. He had been afraid for her. Then an inarticulate cry had broken through the paralysis and after that came words. Before he knew it he was being hurried here and there. His clothes were changed, a bundle packed and a last meal set before him. Stupidly obeying orders he stumbled in her wake, trying to ignore the import of this frenetic activity, trying not to believe where it was leading him. Then haste resolved itself into stillness. He was out on the mountain kneeling before his mother's altar and she was offering up a prayer for his safety and the accomplishment of his task.

"But what task, mother?" he cried, his voice rising in anxiety and fear to boyish shrillness, interrupting the devotion. Like a knell tolling his doom came her familiar reply.

"To find your people, to mend what your father has undone, to bring back the Key so that the Land of the Lake can be restored."

The sound issuing from between her lips creaked and crackled as if its begetter were on the verge of disintegration. Soon they were descending a flight of uneven steps which connected the place of the shrine with the track leading from the village. Some of the steps were giant ones, both steep and deep. Morvah sat down to ease herself from one level to the next. Tallis, behind her, waited for her to move. When she did not, he clambered past in sudden concern to view her face. It was a complete blank, a hollow empty room. Fruitlessly he tried rousing her: rubbed her hands, shook her, called her name, even breathed into her mouth as if he could transfer part of his own living fire onto her dead hearth. But in his heart of hearts he knew that this was the last time; that from this absence there would be no return. In desperation he turned to threats. "It's no good mother – I can't leave you like this. We'll have to forget the whole idea of going away. I'll have to take you home – I'm taking you home."

He bent and lifted her, amazed at her fragility and fleshlessness, and as he did so her mouth fell open and he heard a voice which turned him cold all over. It was not his mother's voice, it came from far away, an ancient voice, uncanny, infantile, as if from the long dead or the not yet born.

DO – NOT – CONCERN – YOURSELF – FOR – THE – WOMAN. SHE - EXISTS – IN – THIS – WORLD – NO - LONGER.

Gently he placed her once again on the step, but when one of her arms seemed to cling round his neck he tore himself away, his skin crawling with revulsion. Fear sent him flying down onto the path below and it was not until his birthplace was well and truly hidden behind a swelling in the mountain's flank that he slowed his pace. Even then he did not stop. If truth be told he had not really stopped from that day to this, despite occasional lacunae. Everything from that moment on was part of the same journey, a journey he began to doubt if his lifetime was long enough to encompass. The body finds all sorts of excuses not to continue when the mind begins to waver.

A small hard insistent noise; the springing to life of many scents. Released from his recollections by some barely discernible interruption Tallis stirred, aware once more of his surroundings in the Justification Inn and the bed at his back, and was instantly assailed by pain in his long immobile joints. Gingerly stretching and massaging his reluctant body back to life he temporarily lost the urge to pursue his tale any further along the road leading to the present. Something that, just recently, he had been reliving vividly as if for the first time was drifting away now and becoming lost on the damp air like a whiff of marsh gas. Had what he remembered his mother telling him ever actually happened? Had it? He could ask himself this question quite dispassionately, with the indifference born of near inanition. One thing could not be denied: he had been there in those mountains – now he was here at this hostelry – and in between had passed – what? – his boyhood, his young manhood, his prime, his maturity, and he had hardly noticed the years slip away. He yawned hugely. Rain was falling. That was what had disturbed him. Coming to his knees he turned towards the bed. But with morning just below the horizon, and the feeling that now he could sleep for a week, he was temporarily prevented from crawling gratefully back into oblivion.

A rough musical voice on a note of amusement; he remembered it from the previous evening, now heard it again within the darkness below him. Some people, he fancied there were three, a man and two women, had exited from one of the hovels built against the back wall of the inn and were speaking together urgently in whispers. The voice was no longer amused. Although he could not distinguish words there was no mistaking a note of sharp disagreement and anger. Then in the grip of emotion the man's tone rose and became intermittently intelligible.

"If that *mumble mumble*... If he *mutter mutter*... you mark my words! Ha you forgot who she is? You know *murmur*... the Culdee *further murmurs*... ...I'll see to that!"

"Shhhhhhhhhhhhhhhhh!" One woman was doing the hushing, the other putting in a subdued comment every so often. Tallis had a vague memory of something heard earlier in the night. The voice fell and became less emphatic. Then he was aware of a leave taking and the man, again comprehensible, vehemently insisting, "Think on't, think on't!"

Footsteps made themselves audible and a light was doused somewhere out of sight below. A dim shadow came into Tallis' view beyond the roof of the lean-to, stumping away across the yard, bypassing the stable block. A gate creaked and the sound receded into the distance until it merged with the gentle patter of rain. Tallis was left with the almost certain conviction that this man and the truculent nibbler who had filled his bath the night before were one and the same. As if this small sign of life were the signal for a general awakening, other sounds, tiny, comfortable and domestic began to rise from the interior of the inn and its environs: the chink of a pail, water splashing, a cock crowing, the creak of a door, somebody clearing their throat. Tallis finally returned to the empty bed and lay listening while everything that had happened to him in this place so far processed calmly across his mind's eye as a prelude to the images that would ascend from a deeper level as he lost consciousness. The rain hissed, and sooner or later, when he was apparently already unaware of his surroundings, from within the inn young male voices were raised in song:

> "*The bird stoops on the branch*
> *but cannot fly;*
> *The air has grown thick,*
> *mist lies in the hollows.*
> *In the meadows, under the bowl of night,*
> *Little streams have lost their way.*
>
> *Fires die out on the altars;*
> *the door stands ajar;*
> *Hills shape-shift, forests drift,*
> *slowly the pattern unwinds.*
> *In the dead hours of darkness,*
> *the Old, the First-Comers,*
> *Mount once again their iron earth-bound*
> *thrones.*
>
> *Turn back! turn back! turn back!*
> *turn back Lord Pyr!*
> *The Year Child lies here with us*
> *–see – safe in his cradle.*
> *Deep, too deep to delve,*
> *are the haunted Caves of Bone*
> *That swallowed the Wayward Son,*
> *long lost to the world.*

Stretch out your arms and loosen
the tongues of the birds;
Green the high fields,
fill up the valleys with gold;
Grant us sweet hope,
the song in the blood and the laughter,
Wipe away tears and bring us to
joy in the morn!"

The Night-Hymn to the Father! Tallis recognised it, had sung it himself more than once, and even though virtually asleep, part of his brain remembered it when eventually he awoke much later in the day. But whether the chant had taken place in the primary world or had risen in his mind from memories of the long distant past he had no way of knowing.

Now leave we Tallis slumbering through the hours of daylight and turn we elsewhere, to a place not many miles distant...

The stone skims the waters.
He will go likewise alone,
Deep into danger.

Chapter five

The rain ceased, the sky cleared, light grew in the east; the tide of morning streamed over the land. Before the weak rays of sunlight caught the high ground the toilers were already up and doing; some – the old, the very young, the privileged – slept on and dreamed. Such a one we will find if we go straight as the crow flies, swift as fate, across roads and dewy fields, leaving the Justification half submerged in woods, swooping down into the upper reaches of the main valley, where a small town, High Harrow, stands on a rocky outcrop above the surrounding common land, arranging itself neatly along the brow of a low river-washed cliff, down to the first floor of a house in the finest street, the most select neighbourhood. And there he lies, our dreamer, enmeshed and entwined in his nightmare, dream-prisoned and dream-paralysed, eyes flicking to and fro behind their lids, helpless beneath the great spider-phantasm that crouches over his mind.

Waking fearfully in the middle of the night, that was how the dream always started, with an awakening at ten years old in his bedroom in the south-west tower of his father's castle to find the walls and ceiling bathed in an unnatural lurid light and himself possessed of the notion that the rest of the cavernous pile he calls his home is hollow and dark, he the only scrap of life in the whole labyrinthine edifice. In fear he sits up, straining his senses, while the strange light glows and dies, glows and dies, and from very far off comes a faint rushing noise like a weir, or a huge concourse of people, or a wind through woods, everything nearby remaining profoundly silent. In the stillness a tight knot of dread forms within him as he puts his foot to the floor and this grows into a kind of vague unfocused terror, a certainty that terrible things are being played out abroad lit by that bloody light, while at home where he should have found comfort, there is naught but an empty house, an unlit warren. To reach the window he has to climb on a clothes chest, the pulsing rays streaming over his head. Slowly he raises himself to intersect the beam. His eye-level comes up to the sill, looks across it and across the tops of trees into the distance. A fire, a huge fire is burning! The massy woodland stands out in sharp silhouette against an ominous brightness; farther away, crimson-shot smoke, sparks, bits of flapping blackness swirl into the sky. Yet where there should be crackling and roaring only an insect whisper comes to his ears on the calm night air. The bog beyond the ravine - Hollow Marsh they call it - the bog is ablaze! And in truth he should not have been able to see that far from the tower-room window for a wall of rock stands in the way. But could such a place burn? Not like this. The conflagration must be on the high ground that lies in the midst of the mire, the holy place, the troy-town. He shrinks inwardly at the magnitude of the desecration. To take fire to such a place! And that was the place where once... Despite the

veil of trees and interposing cliffs he suddenly has a
vision of it swathed in flames and in the centre a figure –
a figure that he knows. Tom! Tom Tosa! His ten-year-old
fingers grip the sill and he tries to cry a name, the name
of a friend now seen to be in deadly peril. But being a
dream his throat will not obey him and the most he can
manage is a strangled moan. A rescue! He dashes from
his bedroom down the spinning stair to the outer door,
only to have the sequence of events fracture so that he
plunges through the opening into a deeper darker
nightmare, the malice of the dream turning towards
himself, a trap baited… closing…

　　　This time there was no fire, no light even, but
somehow his dream eyes saw, saw a leaden sky, pressing
down like a roof, saw the grand western avenue through
the park leading away like a tunnel hemmed in by huge
trees that formed a palisade on either side. And here came
the high-point of terror, for it was a tunnel indeed, within
the outer confines of which he stood: a dark shaft, wide
enough for three carriages abreast, slanting down towards
the planet's secret entrails, and out of it blew a gale fit to
chill the blood. Nothing about the vision obviously
threatened yet before that gaping orifice his sinews
melted and his thews became as water. It drew him – he
was caught – reason sagged and crumbled. The vultures
of insanity came flapping from every empty-socketed
window in the fortress behind and flopped down through
black air towards his panic-lacerated flesh. Driven
forward he screamed soundlessly – and woke, soaked in
sweat.

　　　He lay quiet as a mouse beneath the shadow of
an eagle. The dream's after image was so powerful that
for a while he was completely astray. It took a great

rallying of forces to reassert his reality in the everyday world. Dan Addo –he was Dan Addo – Dando – Dando; his own name acted like a calming mantra. Not ten years old, but just turned seventeen, not in the tower at Castle Dan but here in the town house in High Harrow. He was the Lord Dan Addo, a Gleptish nobleman, second son and heir to the Chief of Clan Dan, a family illustrious, powerful, to be feared, afraid of nothing. The summoning of his public persona began to have its effect. The dream was retreating, still occasionally rumbling and flickering, but impotent now, for he gazed on its darkness from the perspective of a room full of the light of morning, light filtering through a fine gauze curtain which waved gently at a half-open window, while from outside came the sweet threadbare song of an autumn robin. He sighed, half relieved, half ashamed.

It was necessary for the moment to allow himself to drift, cocooned in comfort, while his eyes roved freely, taking in uncritically each item that made up the sumptuous landscape of his bedroom. Luxury was the condition in which he lived; he could not help but accept it as normal for himself, although for other ranks and conditions of men he saw that things were far otherwise. The seemly whiteness of the freshly laundered sheets, the multi-coloured tapestries, the soft pile of the jacquard carpet: these were pleasing but ordinary manifestations of Dan wealth, mere Gleptish trappings that had been part of his life from the beginning. Far more interesting to him was the ancient granite house he sensed behind the glittering veneer, smiling its enigmatic smile, waiting out the centuries. It was a fine house this town house of the Dans, already old when they had acquired it many years ago, its streetside walls with their tiny barred and

shuttered windows as thick and formidable as a castle
keep's, its exterior appearance slightly raddled. Within –
warm in winter, cool in summer, cosily protected – the air
held an indefinable but delicious smell hinting at
elegance and mellowness, the manners of a bygone age.
Inside again, enfolded at its heart, lay the simplest yet
most beautiful little garden you could hope to find in a
treeless town. Dando, comparing its appointments with
the overblown flamboyance of his ancestral home, found
them admirably understated, but liked the house chiefly
for the fact that, despite the furniture, it was devoid of the
presence of his family. Though their image might
usefully be conjured to exorcise night-time demons he
was not sorry to be out of their ambience for a while. The
Dans had not created this house, had barely left any
impression on it during their comings and goings, for it
was considered just a necessary pied-a-terre, handy when
business forced them into town. Now, since he had been
banished from his familiar haunts in disgrace the previous
autumn it had become, by happy chance, his temporary
abode.

Eleven momentous months he had been living
here – away from family and friends.

"This is your last chance," his father had told
him. "Go and study book-keeping with the priests in High
Harrow, then you can help your brother run the estate.
Otherwise…"

"Yes Father," he had answered dutifully. And so
he had spent the time trotting to and fro across town
according to instructions, sitting at the feet of his
teachers, trying to absorb extremely dull facts, and
backsliding only occasionally when the call of summer
became too great to resist. He had grown an inch or two,

thought a lot and learned more than intended. The period
had passed with the illusory stillness of a sown seed.
Then in the last few weeks that damned dream –
childhood dream – not once but five times now – had
come back to haunt him.

Abruptly he turned on his side breathing a barely
audible "Shsh…T!" So – alright – he was going to have
to do something about it. As usual he felt disappointment
and disgust that he was being forced to take cognizance
of an aspect of his life he did not wish to acknowledge. A
smell of coffee brewing warned him that in a few minutes
Potto, his manservant, would be coming to wake him
with his long-ingrained mixture of bossiness and
deference. The morning routine had already started and
soon he would be expected to rise and attend to his toilet
and then go through the small rituals that devolved on the
head of any Dan household, be it that grand ménage
hidden in the north-west corner of Deep Hallow, or the
immediate small satellite establishment. As the only
member of the family in residence at present, the bustle
of the household was focused solely on his own person,
its purpose, to launch him into the world this bright
morning as a worthy representative of his clan. Clothes
that had been laid out for him last night would be
receiving a final meticulous inspection; in the marble
bathroom next door the marble bath would be brimming
with hot water; warm towels and perfumed soaps, tooth
brushes, hair brushes, shaving brushes (a recent
innovation) would be awaiting his use. When later he
emerged gleamingly clean into the breakfast room he
would find boiled eggs in porcelain egg cups, as many as
he could eat, piles of buttered toast prettily arranged on
silver salvers, conserves in china bowls, the afor

mentioned coffee. Besides these, the sideboard would be loaded with an amazing range of goodies: mutton chops, grilled trout, pickled salmon, potted hare, muffins, provided as always in the prodigal Dan manner though very rarely sampled by himself. He had also heard there would be grapes on offer this morning, along with the usual apples, pears and plums, the first bunches of the year having been gathered from the house's ancient vine.

Yes, before all this started he must decide what to do, although in reality he knew there was no decision to be made. After the second recurrence of the dream, the way he had to take had been plain to him, and after the third he knew there was no escape. He must do what he had done last time, when, much younger, he had sought to free himself from a year of anguished nights by bearding the monster in her den. Last time he had found the den empty and the persecutions had ceased. But could he work the same trick twice, and why, why had the dream returned now, this dream of his childhood, at the moment when he was leaving childhood behind?

He stretched cat like and swung his legs out of bed just as Potto, attached nibbler to Clan Dan, entered the room.

"Up already, Lord, m'dear? You do well to start early. Town'll be chooked up with all sorts of hobble-me-downs today because of the celebrations; un'ttached nibblers, stry gents, such-like squits. Best you don't goo through the square this mornin' – best you ride Motley and goo round edge of town."

The voice of authority! With amusement Dando noted that Potto also flourished away from the uneasy cross-currents and boudoir conspiracies of the Dan power base. *One day I'll have it all to myself*, he resolved, meaning the town house, a life here briefly appearing more inviting than the many other avenues into the future waiting to be explored. He bent forward to allow Potto to tug his nightshirt over his head. Together they launched into their morning rite, made smooth by long practice, Dando raising his arms and lowering them, revolving slowly, stepping here and there on command, submitting passively to being stripped, cleansed, anointed, clothed, thinking meanwhile, *the fair! They'll guess I've slipped my leash and gone to the fair!* Out loud he said,

"W-what an old woman you are Potto. I w-will ride – but I'll take Attack, not Motley. Let them know – please – when you go down." (His slight stammer always came to the fore when he was a trifle unsure of his ground.)

The administrations stopped and did not restart. Dando felt himself silently condemned.

"I know what you're thinking Potto, but Dantor isn't going to be here 'till this evening. If I take him out today what difference will that make to the show tomorrow?"

"That hoss don't goo to stay quiet all day with them priest fellows. Him's hully bustlin' out of his skin with peevishness. What they gonna do with him whilst you're book-learnin'?"

"It's b-because he's so fresh that I want to take him. If he don't get some exercise he'll be the very devil to handle tomorrow when they put him on parade. You know what he's like."

"Them priest-fellows'll make a hash of it. Best leave him with those that knows him."

"Well, the truth is," Dando, sensing he lacked conviction, decided to capitulate, "I'm not going to school today."

The servant who until that moment had been exuding complacency, a king in his little kingdom, fell apart comically into doubt and uncertainty.

"You ain't a-gooin'? Oh, but my Lord…"

"No, I *ain't a-gooin'*. So you see Attack won't be left with *them priest-fellows*. I'll give him a good ride and bring him back as gentle as a lamb."

Potto looked dour, his lower lip thrust forward truculently.

"Where be you a-gooin' then?" To ask was to step out of line. Dando smiled sweetly, ignoring the lapse.

"That's my business."

Their relationship was complicated by the fact that they loved one another, Potto with anxious paternalism, Dando impatiently, slightly irked at knowing he was the apple of the old man's eye.

"You gone missing six times already."

"Not that much." But it was probably true. Potto kept tabs on him and even might, under duress, be reporting to headquarters.

"Six times you gone a-wandering when you should 'a' been at your book learnin'. Now this un'll be the seventh. I be a-feared for 'ee Lord, m'dear."

"Oh *come on* Potto!"

Potto bent close to his young master's ear.

"Those that cross him stumble and fall, Lord. Some have fallen and never got up no more."

"Absolute tripe!"

Dando turned away in distaste feeling trapped by the old man's concern. That he should need to mistrust his own father! He could not be reconciled to it!

"Well, I'm going, so that's all there is to it. Go and tell them to saddle Attack." And when the servant seemed about to demur further, "*Do it* Potto." with an edge to his voice.

Thus an hour or so later we see Dando standing just within the house's main entrance, a tall slim silhouette against the outer brightness, waiting for his horse. It was the first day of the two-day, once-a-year, hiring fair. This explained the presence of the Dans' black pearl of great price in High Harrow. Four years earlier they had imported the great stallion from beyond the rim of their small world to improve the faltering blood-line of their native stock. Attack had blown up the Incadine Gorge like a hot wind off the steppes to sew his seed among the local mares and fillies, the dust of the Kymer flood plain which he had traversed still on his hooves. Since then he had won the seven league circuit, the annual steeplechase, three years in a row and had become the king horse of the valley. Until his own children reached maturity he would be unmatchable. On high days and holidays when the Gleptish nobility, the fifteen families, chose to display themselves, Attack took his place in the parade, demonstrating the Dans' pre-eminence, flaunting their superior wealth. Astride his back in recent times, now that the Dan was rarely seen in public, would be Dando's elder brother Dantor, serious and middle-aged at twenty-one with responsibility and secret knowledge, eye-glasses perched on nose, hating every minute of it. *A waste* thought Dando, who in his place would have enjoyed the opportunity for histrionics and showing off.

His descent from the first floor apartment into the high dim space which was the house's covered courtyard was sure to have been noted. The fact that Attack had not yet been brought through from the back meant that he must be leading his grooms a merry dance this morning. Dando, whose timekeeping was of the vaguest, felt no sense of urgency, of the morning slipping away. He was content to idle, examining his fingers, experimentally stretching his hand out into the sunshine to admire the glisten of flesh and the glitter of a ring, an heirloom traditionally worn by each successive second son. Although the brief shower that had passed by just before dawn had brought with it a clean feel to the air, a fine haze like the thinnest of veils had already been drawn across the sky's blueness, and the heavy languor of the last few weeks was seeping out of every wall and paving slab. The autumn had been strange so far, the nights full of overblown moons, the days of weak suns, the atmosphere stifling, smelling of smoke, threatening fog. In this golden setting the valley stuck like a fly in amber. The untypical season had the air of a woman preserving her beauty into old age – at first admired, then marvelled at, - after that just the faintest hint of vampires and the blood of virgins.

A disturbance in the street outside, distant but coming nearer, grabs Dando's attention. Curious, he steps through the archway to investigate. And now, as he enters the sunlight, behold if you please the Gleptish nobleman in all his glory, blazing abroad in baroque splendour. See, if you can avoid being dazzled, the mirroring leather, the antique silver, the glowing velvets and brocades. Notice the slashing and the dagged hems, the odd scrap of lace glimpsed through a calculated dishabille, also the carefully tousled hair arranged to appear as if caught in a hypothetical romantic gale. Such a theatrical style had held sway for a short while many years ago in the Delta City, Vadrosnia Poule. Decades after the fashion had become history in its original home its influence had percolated as far as this high valley. In its dotage it had struck roots and put out exotic growth, nourished and sustained by the self-image of the race that lurked here as if in hiding from the rest of the world. In so doing the transient had achieved a sort of immortality. Dando however was not thinking about his clothes which were no more than his everyday wear and none of his concern. He was more interested in the minor riot that was approaching down a side street. A moment later a noisy crowd of young men rounded the corner and he was greeted by familiar faces. Recognizing friends, he slapped his hand to his brow and staggered rearwards, groaning dramatically. The new-comers literally fell on his neck as if reclaiming a lost leader.

"Oy–oy–oy – look who it isn't!"

"It's the bloody Dandyman – skiving as usual!"

"Where've you been all summer, you turd?"

The babbling rabble crowded round with obvious delight, good-humouredly man-handling him, lugging him to and fro, re-establishing contact with someone who had been absent from their ranks for sometime.

"Hey Dando, we're on our way to…"

"Two whole days of…"

"Jenny's place, remember?"

"Pax, pax," moaned Dando, extricating himself as best he could but grinning the while.

"Where have you been Sonny Jim? We've missed you."

"We're only in this godforsaken hole for the fair – come back down to Gateway with us tomorrow."

"Hey ho, come to the fair…"

"With a little bit of this and a little bit of that…"

Two of the clowns were executing a clumsy dance, taking up most of the roadway and impeding other passers by. With a thought to the reputation of his house, Dando pulled them out of the way.

"Shut up you madmen. I c-can't come – I'm going up country – there's something on…"

"Up country!" The words were spoken in unison and with immense scorn. On a scale of places which were worth inhabiting, the upper reaches of the valley came bottom. For a young blade desirability of location increased the closer one approached to the outside world.

"No, old man," Dando was seized by one individual and addressed eye to eye, with great intensity, "you don't want to go there, you want to come with us."

"Painting the town red," the others chimed in.

"And after we've painted *this* ol' town red we may just bugger off down the Incadine Gorge and do the same to Drossi, oh."

"To the tarts down by the harbour."

"We'll show 'em that we know a thing or two that the blokes off the ships aren't up for."

"We'll show 'em before you c'n say *knickers away!*"

"An' when we're done they'll be lying on their backs, feet in the air, yelling for more!"

"Come on you old bastard, we need you."

Drossi? – they would never go to the Delta City, they would never get beyond the end of the valley. Dando found he was facing a silent audience. He sighed and flopped back against the wall.

"Look fellows," gently, "I need you like a hole in the head. I'm bunking off in order to lay a ghost."

There was a pause, then a shout of laughter.

"To lay your pet more like!"

"Who is she Dando?"

"...lay an egg!"

"The lay of the ancient minstrel – ha ha."

"Yeah, that's what he is – I don't think!"

"C'mon baby let's get laid."

"The ancient mistral!"

"A windy old fart you mean!"

The noisy discourse broke into several strands of repartee. Undercover of the row, one of the boys, a particular friend, spoke close to Dando's ear.

"Are you coming back next term?"

"Depends..."

"They say you refused to take the oath. *Why* Dando?"

Dando shook his head, smiling with tightly buttoned lips. Over the last year he had begun to avoid awkward questions when they were asked by those wanting to understand his recent behaviour. It was a bad but necessary habit, this reticence, but charm usually saw him through. This time it did not.

"You're falling behind Dando. It's serious. If you don't become an Outrider what are you going to do? You'll be up the creek without a paddle." The other waited for confidences. When none were forthcoming he looked nonplussed, then cold. Something had ended.

For about five minutes the group wheedled and cajoled, reluctant to give up on this once leading light within their ranks. Then, finding him immovable, they grew suddenly bored and began to straggle off along the road, making their farewells. Within a few yards their gadfly minds, as signalled by the increasing racket, had already turned to other things. Dando, watching them go, felt a sharp stab of isolation, almost of panic. *Up the creek without a paddle* – perhaps he was. He had a sudden urge to run after them, to fall into step, to throw an arm across someone's shoulders and be merged once again with the crowd. Left behind and on his own he was all at once aware that some time ago, almost without thinking, he had taken a divergent track that would lead him farther and farther away from the route his peers were following. Not normally one for introspection, it was only now that he saw, in a flash of illumination, what he had relinquished: the blessed comfort of good company, bosom pals, mutual support, like-minded cronies tucked around one like a blanket. As a result of his actions these things which he hardly realized he valued were slipping from his grasp. Yet it had never been his intention…

Beneath the portico sparks squirted in the dimness at ground level. A stable boy emerged from the archway, seeming to draw darkness after him. A monolithic image – water over a black rock – filled the shadowy entrance. Ears pricked forward, whickering a greeting, the king-horse stepped into the sunlight like an idol from his shrine. Dando turned to him with a lift of the heart. Here was a friend to whom there was no need to say goodbye. Of all the joys of horsemanship what can bear comparison with that first heady moment when you spring from the ground to board the living creature, landing lightly in the saddle, matching your movements to his, man and animal together as one, sweet music, beautiful symbiosis. Along with elation went a remembered pride that once he had been the only rider privileged to achieve this exalted position. Attack and his grooms had not hit it off on first acquaintance. The horse, wild and nervous on his arrival after the stresses of his journey, had reacted violently to clumsy and insensitive handling. Dando, coming many times to the stables, just to admire and keep silent, gradually found that he could do what others were denied. The next season, when it was again time for the Seven League Circuit to take place Attack had still not fully relented. Being now his second year in the valley it was unthinkable that he should not run. For the first time the race's spectators were treated to the spectacle of one of the Fifteen Families, and not just a member but a first ranker, leading the field home. It had started a fashion. At the time Dando felt that even if he lived to be a hundred and twelve he would never know a day of such unalloyed joy. Now as they pirouetted and side-stepped down the street (the horse was *very* fresh) he was swept by a sense of his own felicity. He loved the world, the world loved him. Anything he turned his hand to was within his grasp, be it wealth, fame or fair lady.

Encouraged by admiring glances, maybe he made more of the struggle of wills between rider and mount than was strictly necessary. The street was already filling up with fair-bound merry makers and the town's young ladies were out in force. Although not aware of it, Dando looked all of a piece, in the blacks and browns of

Dan livery, his sword and dagger by his side, with the great black stallion he rode. One fair opportunist, making haste slowly out of his path, collapsed in a graceful heap among her giggling sisters, feigning terror at her nearness to the horse's clattering hooves. Dando observed the little melodrama with a grin but refused to be drawn, understanding full well the transparent subterfuge. He passed on but not before his eyes had met those of the prostrate damsel in a glance of mutual challenge and surmise. The incident sparked off a rueful train of thought. So, the merchant's daughter would like to set her cap at the lord's son. It must seem the stuff of fairy tales. But what would be the fate of such a girl if he turned up at Castle Dan with her as his prospective bride? As an outsider she would be barely tolerated and permission for the union might be long in coming. She would disappear into the women's realm under the thumb of a fearsome phalanx of aunts, the guardians of Dan tradition, hardly seeing her fiancé from one week to the next. Certainly not the happy ending she might have envisaged. It needed a bold spirit to rebel against the suffocating conventions of Gleptish society. Damask, even Damask his stout-hearted twin sister, had vanished into the same female maw at the onset of puberty. For the first month or so there had been ructions, screaming rows that penetrated the thick walls and raised the hairs on the back of his neck. After that silence. Next time he saw her she was strapped into the confining garments worn by all Gleptish women, with her usual cloudy fuzz of chestnut hair tamed in an ugly bun. She had refused to meet his eye. It was a while before, by mere chance, he managed to make a contribution to her day to day existence that greatly improved her situation.

The crowd flowed sluggishly onwards toward the centre of town, impeding the progress of horse and rider, spreading out when it reached the main square and then funnelling into a street on the west side; Dando was perforce compelled to go with it, as his way lay in that direction; Potto was right, he should have gone round the edge of town. And now the throng was lapping against the walls of *The Orthodox Academy for the Sons of Gentlefolk*, the establishment that would in normal circumstances have been enjoying his patronage this bright autumnal morning. Dando shrank into himself, trying to appear inconspicuous (an impossible task). His scalp pricked and he imagined numerous pairs of accusatory eyes gazing down at him. The school was run by a group of priests from outside the valley and, despite its name, catered mainly for the middle classes, the children of merchants and tradespeople who were the backbone of the small valley towns. But Dando had seen little of his fellow pupils. The arrangement made by his father was for one on one tuition. At this very moment he should have been sitting in a stuffy room with his first teacher of the day, sweating over maths and economics. In an hour or two's time he would have been with cleric *numero due* pursuing a course on estate management and book keeping; and then this afternoon instructor number three would have attempted to enlighten him on business studies. At least he would have done if both master and pupil had not come to a tacit agreement, a few weeks back, that such an attempt was doomed to failure. Dando's opinion of the intelligence of this sleek, very secular priest had gone up several degrees in consequence. A foreigner, belonging to some order devoted to river worship, the man, with his exquisite

urbanity and worldly cynicism, was a type quite outside
Dando's experience up to that point. He was both startled
and fascinated by the reverend gentleman's sceptical
erudition. Father Adelbert's presence in the valley was
explained by a comparative religious study he was
engaged upon.

"...and so my footsteps inevitably led me in this
direction. Nobody has ever attempted such a wide
ranging investigation before. When finished my book will
become a standard work of reference. Unfortunately, this
research is a slow business. When dealing with the sacred
one meets with so much secrecy, so many taboos. The
best policy is to gradually win the trust of a single
individual and, through them, to gain entrée into
whichever arcane world one is hoping to explore."

He looked enquiringly at Dando at this point, but
Dando, evidently labouring under an excess of secrecy
and taboos, or rather acute embarrassment at the thought
of speaking in cold blood on such an emotive subject,
declined to volunteer for this tricky position.

Having, for the moment, abandoned the
proscribed syllabus they spent most of one lesson
exploring the enormous but eccentric collection of books
that constituted the priest's travelling library, and it was
here that Dando made a discovery that for him was little
short of a revelation. He had pulled out a bulky but
nondescript-looking volume from the pile and begun
leafing through it.

"Wait a minute!" he cried, "What's this? What's
this supposed to be?"

The priest took it from him and read.

"Oh that – how on earth did that find its way
here I wonder? It's a book on household management, a

house-keepers' bible, published about fifty years ago and so thoroughly out of date."

"But this – this page. It has instructions for constructing meals – no, I mean dishes – for the table!"

"Yes recipes."

"And there's more – look – masses of them!" Dando could hardly contain his excitement. The priest gave him a quizzical glance.

"Have you never seen a recipe book before?"

"No – never!"

"Well – that doesn't surprise me in this benighted place." The priest spoke feelingly. From his comfortable corporation and glossy embonpoint he looked like a man who enjoyed his food. "However I can assure you that there's a plethora of the things at large in the world for the sole purpose of tormenting us poor mortals. No amount of reading of recipe books will produce a good cook unless the talent is there in the first place."

In a blinding flash Dando saw his opportunity and seized it with both hands.

"Would… would you like to c-come for a meal? I mean… could I invite you to dinner," he stammered, "one evening… whenever you're free? It would be better… better than you get here." He ended lamely.

Consequently, a few days later, they were both to be found suitably dressed, sitting at the Dans' dining table in a strangely quiet and empty house, being waited on by a cheerful girl, not one of the regular staff, who seemed to be suffering from some nasal complaint, judging by the suppressed snorts that occasionally escaped her. As the meal got under way Dando's acute nervousness evaporated, while at the same time his guest relaxed from his initial wariness and set himself to be entertaining. Two or three courses later he became more thoughtful, and once or twice after a particular mouthful his finely arched eyebrows rose slightly.

"Well, what did you think of the food?"

Post prandially they were sipping the sweet fortified wine which figured as one of the valley's exports to the world beyond and Dando could not keep away from the subject any longer.

"Extraordinary."

"What do you mean? – Is that good or bad?"

"I mean these dishes are quite remarkable – completely outside my experience. Good – I mean good – but it's the originality that is the surprising thing. Who…?"

"It was me - I thought them up – I did the cooking," confessed Dando, the blood rushing to his face with the enormity of the admission. There was a long silence while the priest refrained from asking all the obvious questions.

"Well then, my Lord," he remarked dryly at last, "if you were ever in a position to leave this place - this valley of Deep Hallow - you would have a great future ahead of you."

As he started to descend towards the outskirts of the town Dando's face broke into a huge grin just to think of it. The priest's endorsement of his craft had filled him with joy, and the man's suggestion, for one dazzling moment, had seemed like the solution to all his problems. The fact was that he had been a closet cook from almost before he could walk, from the time he had followed his wet nurse into the kitchen and had lifted a mysterious cloth to find beneath it a pale billowing mound of proving dough, an undifferentiated living entity awaiting the hand of a master to give it form. As an important member of the household he had been indulged and allowed to cover himself in flour. It was soon acknowledged below stairs, with some astonishment, that Dando could make better pastry than anyone else in the place, and sometimes, because of this fact, he was allowed, without his involvement being disclosed, to impress important guests by producing the tart cases for some dinner party that the Dan was throwing.

He had picked up information like a magpie, not only at Castle Dan but from the kitchens of any other premises in which he found himself. Later, accompanied by Damask, he had made the fortuitous discovery of an abandoned cottage, complete with range, below a waterfall in a corner of the Dan estates. Here, when he could get away, he put into practice what he had learnt, and gradually, through many hair-tearing disasters, evolved a technique and some ideas of his own. By necessity it had always been a covert operation, but there had never been much danger of these deviant practices being exposed. He had discovered early on that, when away from the castle, he could go quite openly into the servant's quarters of any of the large valley mansions, and while the kitchen maids fluttered and the cook smiled archly, discuss with insouciance and amiability the making of such things as baguettes and game pies. For a Gleptish nobleman to interest himself in food preparation was so aberrant as to be beyond the bounds of credibility, so he was always credited with an ulterior motive. After all, as the novelist says: *you cannot possibly be genteel and bake.* Diffidently he told some of this story to his teacher, and, as a sophisticated man of the world, the priest explained that in contrast to the valley where all the cooks were women, male chefs were held in high esteem in the towns along the shores of the Middle Sea.

"Should you wish to try your luck in the Delta City I could supply you with a letter that would give you a foothold in the right establishment."

Oh how tempting had been this prospect when it had first been glimpsed! To be a full-time cook would be like waking up in paradise. Cooking had always been a refuge from the two agencies that ruled his life: his overpowering family and the strange occult forces that, dating from a particular occasion in his early years, had invaded his world. It had been a comfort, an escape, and the only thing in his existence which seemed to have no shadow attached. But the Glepts clung to their foothold in Deep Hallow like a hunted fox to its earth. Not a single one of his people, to his knowledge, had ever ventured beyond the valley's boundaries for any length of time. To leave familiar territory, to abandon his kinsfolk, to go alone into the world - did he possess the courage?

The houses came to an abrupt end. The holiday-makers had melted away already, vanishing along a lane to the right which led across a high-level bridge over the watercourse and down some steps to the meadows where the fair's booths and sideshows had been set up. Dando gazed after them wistfully. There was a strong temptation to become one of the flock, afoot and anonymous, and eagerly descend into the midst of those exotic delights. It hardly needs to be mentioned that such a goal appeared far more congenial than the hazardous one he had set himself. Already, though, the turning had been left behind and Attack, now the way was clear, progressed from a walk to a trot, from a canter to a gallop, his pace opening up with every succeeding stride. The road continued on in the form of a paved downward-sloping ramp which met the grass of common land beneath a lonely arched gateway and then became a well-trodden dirt track leading westward on the south side of the River Wendover. Dando made no attempt to rein the horse in but put his hand in his pocket and pulled out a handful of coins. The gate marked the town's limits in this direction and was a site where beggars were allowed to gather and solicit alms from those entering or leaving the settlement. There would be few, none but the truly needy, beneath its shade today; the rest would have gone on a merry with their fellow citizens. As they thundered towards the opening a silver shower flashed briefly from Dando's hand and dispersed in bouncing, ricocheting confusion amongst a small number of huddled figures for those to grab who could. In such a way was the largess of the Dans distributed. Then they were through and the horse joyously flung himself forward along the ribbon of road as the boy, rising in the saddle, tried to bend his long body into a jockey's crouch.

The way extended straight and unobstructed for about three miles. Attack being Attack went to the limit as usual, his hooves beating an agitated drum roll across the plain. Horse and rider paid scant heed to the few lumbering farm carts coming in the opposite direction. Going like the wind Dando was unable to hear the odd heartfelt curse his headlong passage engendered. Eventually though the common came to an end, they were between hedges and fields, and the road began to twist and turn. Although the horse had barely broken sweat Dando tactfully suggested that it might be wise to moderate their pace somewhat. The animal fell into an easy canter, a gait he could have maintained almost indefinitely. Accompanying the neat *clipita clipita* which altered in resonance from one moment to the next according to road surface and passing scenery a strange tuneless threnody ululated and echoed its way along the lonely track: it was the sound of Dando singing.

The Outriders: the Outrider College in Gateway. Little Gleptish boys, when they reached the age of ten years, joined one of the Watchdog units which collectively formed the junior arm of the military training establishment. They played at scouting, competed for badges, went on summer camps. At fourteen they became Outrider Cadets and began their instruction, most of them in Gateway. Then at sixteen they took the oath of allegiance and graduated to senior level, but with four years of schooling still to come before they could be enrolled in one of the Gleptish regiments. Most boys from the nobility, the fifteen families, avoided the hurly-burly and levelling effect of the Outrider College; instead they submitted to tutoring from a member of their own family, and were taught privately. Such a practice meant a fast-track route to officer status in their chosen regiment. Dando however, going his own way as usual, opted for the journey to Gateway. He had pressing reasons for leaving Castle Dan and the area in which it was situated. Besides, to relocate to the town at the eastern end of the valley through which passed all the traffic between Deep Hallow and the Kymer Levels would be a fine adventure and a new start away from his clan. And so he bade farewell to his father and mother, to his sister Damask, to Doll his nibbler wet nurse, to Attack in his stable, but not to Potto. Limits were set as to how far he would be allowed to go towards becoming a lowly proletarian cadet; even in Gateway he was to have his own apartment and manservant. On leaving, he gave away his pets to his younger siblings with a vague sense of betrayal. There were three: his jackdaw Chocky which he had found half fledged while on a climbing expedition with Damask over the roofs of the castle, his big old ginger tom-cat Asbo, and Puss a three legged hare. It may be significant that none of these creatures survived his departure by more than a few months. Asbo the cat turned semi-wild after he had gone and disappeared one day, never to be seen again, Puss, unsupervised, was taken by a dog, and Chocky - Chocky sat hunched on his perch with ruffled feathers for hours at a time and died in the end, it seemed, of a broken heart.

With his cheerful and easygoing disposition Dando soon had a circle of friends around him at the Outrider College, a very necessary protection against the harsh manner in which the new intake was dealt with by the older boys. Initiation rites amounting almost to torture were regularly handed out to vulnerable youngsters and even group solidarity was not always a guarantee of exemption. Dando however had an extra layer of immunity; most of the persecutors knew who he was and which family he sprang from. No one wanted to offend the Dans. If he had been on the receiving end of this maltreatment he might in his turn have become a perpetrator. This was the case with a lot of the victims, who, having been *beasted* as the process was known, enthusiastically passed on the punishment in their second year that they had suffered a few months earlier. As it was he usually contrived to be elsewhere when such unpleasantness was taking place, although he had an uneasy feeling that this was the coward's way out. A vision of his sister Damask would come to him, as she might have behaved in similar circumstances, wading in with all flags flying, her typical reaction when confronted by something that offended her sense of justice.

What were the Outriders *for?* No-one ever asked this question. Why all this intensive military training when the only apparent enemies the Glepts had to face in the valley were the wretched nibblers? And unquestionably it was as an enemy they were regarded, albeit a conquered one; an enemy inexplicably still to be feared. If the Outrider cadets were hard on one another, with their culture of dog eat dog, then heaven help any members of the subject race who fell within their ambit. Abuse, beatings, violations; all were carelessly handed out as if by right. It seemed that you had to prove that you held these unfortunate creatures in utter contempt, and that there could be no feeling of common humanity where they were concerned. It was not long before Dando discovered that unless you could claim that you had forced at least one nibbler girl (preferably a virgin) by the end of your first year you were not considered a paid up member of the Outrider fraternity.

Most boys at the College knew Dando's identity, but by no means all, especially in the early days. He never played on his connections or asked for special privileges, preferring to adopt the fiction that he was a run-of-the-mill student. And so, one day, sitting with friends in a tavern, having a convivial drink, he heard an individual at a nearby table, a man in his fifth or sixth year, holding forth on the subject of his (Dando's) family. The gist of the peroration was far from complimentary.

Dando felt the blood rise to his face. His companions looked at him with a mixture of sympathy and embarrassment. It was obvious he was going to have to do something about this; there was no getting around it. After a few minutes he got up and walked over to the other table.

"Did I hear you discussing the chief of Clan Dan just now?" he asked.

The man frowned blearily and tried hard to focus on this young wipper-snapper who had suddenly appeared before him.

"You mean that nibbler-loving aristo? What's that to you?"

"I'm curious."

The loud-mouth regarded Dando uncertainly. Part of his mind was advising caution, but it was not the part that was uppermost at that particular moment. He had enough drink taken to make him reckless and besides he had a good story to tell.

"Sit down – I'll let you into a secret."

Dando sat.

"When he first came to Gateway as a cadet, the Dan as is (he was one of the toffs who chose to slum it down here at the College) was bowled over by this nibbler girl and took her for his pet. Did I say pet? No – partner – in all but name. They went through a ceremony – you know that just isn't done. Nobody could say much – he was one of the top-dogs after all. Then at the end of his senior year, when he went back to his castle, he took her with him and built her a dwelling up a side valley - of course he couldn't bring her into the castle proper. They say a child was born and *allowed to live!"* The man suddenly became aware of Dando's gobsmacked expression. "Yes – I know it's hard to credit – but that's what I've heard. At the time the Dan as was, that's his elder brother – their father had died - was away with the fairies, so nothing came of it. Anyway, then his brother killed himself – you know about that? Tried to fly off the battlements – and he had to assume the leader's role. Things got awkward. He was expected to take a wife like every head of clan, a proper wife I mean. But fate stepped in. The nibbler woman was found dead in the pool by the cottage. The child had disappeared. They say the Dan suspected that her own people had done away with her but he had no proof. Anyway the whole thing was hushed up as you'd imagine."

The man sat back with a smug, self-satisfied expression, pleased to have passed on this juicy piece of gossip to a newcomer not in the know. Dando stood up and looked coldly down at his informant.

"You might be interested to learn," he said, "that my name is Dan Addo, and that's my father you've just been slandering." And turning on his heel he walked away.

Out in the street he realized he was shaking with fury. He was not sorry that the spinner of tall tales was going to spend an uncomfortable few days wondering what retribution was about to descend on him from the all-powerful Dans. For a few moments he indulged in lurid fantasies of revenge, but as his anger abated somewhat he understood that he would do nothing.

However, over the ensuing weeks, try as he might, he could not get the story he had been told out of his head. It nagged at him like a toothache. The Dan as nibbler lover? In his experience the clan chief had always been a harsh master to the semi-slaves in his household, thinking nothing of doing such things as separating married couples if the whim took him. That had happened to Doll, Potto's daughter, when the father of her expected child had been exchanged for some prime cattle and packed off across the valley to the Grant mansion. And then there was Tom… He shied away from the thought like a startled colt. Yes, the whole idea seemed absurd. And yet… For the first time Dando was being forced to think of his parent not as the commanding authority figure he was familiar with, but as an adolescent, wet behind the ears, not unlike himself. Had he really done his training at the Outrider College? This was easy enough to verify, and a few cautious enquiries confirmed that it was indeed the case. And yet nothing had been said when he expressed his own preference for such a course. The parallels were obvious. It seemed that several years before another Dando, *'the spare to the heir'* as second sons were often called, had cut himself loose from his family and thrown in his lot with the rank and file of Gleptish youth.

His thoughts turned to the matter of the isolated cottage on the Dan estates, below the waterfall, beside the pool. He knew it well. It was the place where he had taught himself to cook. Here was something solid and tangible to back up the senior's story. Funny how during all the time he had spent in that idyllic spot he had never asked himself who its former occupants had been. Now he had a picture in his mind of a lonely woman and a little child, a nibbler woman, a woman a man had once adored.

For many days Dando's brain was a whirl of conflicting emotions. It took him a while to sort out how he truly felt. At first indignation was paramount, and also a squeamish distaste for the more sensational aspects of the story. But gradually, dominating these and becoming the prime sentiment as the other feelings faded, came a sense of solidarity with this ghostly young parent who he no longer doubted had lived and loved in Gateway. For Dando nursed a secret that had long stood between himself and his peers, creating barriers of loneliness and isolation. It was something he feared he could never admit to without incurring an avalanche of scorn and disgust. The awful truth was that Dando also loved a nibbler girl.

Time at the Outrider Academy passed quickly and Dando came back to Castle Dan for the second of the long summer vacations, the first time he had set foot in the south-west tower for two years, previous holidays having been spent with friends in various parts of the valley. But now his bedroom seemed a refuge of sorts where he could shut himself away with a few good books and forget about the future for a while. That autumn he would turn sixteen, his birthday fell three days after the equinox, and he would be expected to take the Outrider Oath. It is easier to rebel by inaction rather than action. On the day he was due to return to college, Dando stayed in bed, while the smell of the coming season seeped into the room with its promise of fresh beginnings, of unpredictable outcomes, of journeys to far off places. He thought that his continuing presence in the castle would soon be challenged, but it was nearly two weeks before anyone of influence noticed he was not where he was supposed to be. Dando had not set eyes on his father all summer; the Dan had become remote and unapproachable during the time he had been at college, surrounded as he was these days by a bodyguard, nay almost an army, of mercenaries, recruited from outside the valley. Now however Dando was sent for to offer a reason for his strange conduct.

"Why are you still here and not down in Gateway? Are you ill?"

"No father,"

"Then why are you playing truant?"

This was an almost impossible question to answer, because he could not explain his actions even to himself. He remained silent.

"Come on – stop sulking boy. Why haven't you gone back to college for the autumn term?"

"I don't know father."

"Then in that case you'll get your things together double quick and be off tomorrow first thing. I won't have a slacker in the family."

Back in Gateway his friends found him preoccupied and uncharacteristically subdued. He performed his allotted tasks like a sleepwalker, and went through the motions expected of him, but when it came to the day of his majority, his sixteenth birthday, those that waited for him in the Hall of Oath-Takers waited in vain. An account of this non-attendance eventually percolated to the upper reaches of Deep Hallow, with the result that a few days later the Dan came storming through the door of Dando's apartment in person, raving about filial duty and obedience.

Together they stood in the Oath-Takers' Hall - father and son, side by side - each holding a tablet with the words of the pledge written on it in elaborate script.

"I will retake the oath," his father had instructed earlier, "a soldier can do this at any time, and then you will do so after me."

Slowly the Dan sank to his knees, raised his right hand, and read out the sonorous words.

"*I call on all here to bear witness that before Heaven and its Maker I vow to hold this valley of Deep Hallow against all manner of folk, to protect my people and to obey without question those in authority over me. I will regard the lives of my fellow Glepts as more precious than either my own or that of any member of a foreign race I may encounter and if challenged I will maintain such a belief with the last drop of my blood and by fire and by sword on the bodies of my enemies. Thus may it stand until the King shall return. So help me God.*"

The clan chief needed assistance as he struggled back to his feet.

"Now it's your turn, boy. Get down on your knees."

But Dando remained standing, fractionally shifting his head from side to side as if communing inwardly with himself. A long silence ensued. At last the Dan could contain himself no longer. He seized his son by the shoulders and shook him violently.

"Who put you up to this?!" he almost screamed, with a gleam of pure lunacy in his eyes. "It was that dead man, wasn't it! It was that dead man put you up to it!"

Demons and hobgoblins
Can be deterred for a while,
But they will return.

Chapter six

Dando had stopped singing. He did not like the direction in which his thoughts had taken him. So now he was deliberately trying to *think of something nice* as his wet nurse and substitute mother would have put it. The point for which he was making was hidden at the western end of the valley. To get there, following the most direct route, would have meant crossing the river in order to reach the highway on the north side, but that took him far too close to his home, Castle Dan, which at present he was anxious to avoid at all costs, so he stayed to the south, threading a network of tracks near the steep terraced hillside that Tallis had descended the day before. He would inevitably have to enter Dan land, that was unavoidable as his family held all the territory towards the head of the valley, but in these rarely frequented deep-cut lanes he was unlikely to meet anyone he knew, unlikely to meet anyone at all.

Two passions ruled Dando's life. Cookery came in at number one, but running it a close second was his addiction to books . This was an unusual and unexpected obsession for a member of the valley's aristocracy; the upper crust gave the three Rs a pretty low priority, and most blue-blooded boys grew up with a minimal understanding of academic subjects. As far as the young women were concerned the picture was even bleaker. Dando was allocated a tutor for a mere four hours a week, and that not until he had reached the advanced age of seven. Damask, his twin sister, insisted on sitting in on the lessons, until the man complained that it was beneath his dignity to instruct a female. Even so the little girl did not give up. She bullied Dando into passing on what he had learnt, which at least meant that he was forced to pay attention in class and to rehearse everything a second time.

And thus the situation might have remained, except that on a windy and rainy winter's afternoon, confined to the huge and rambling pile that was his abode, the boy had wandered down a little-used corridor somewhere in the castle's tangled inner regions and come upon a low carved door. Incised into the woodwork in primitive lettering was the legend *The King's Vault*. The door was locked, but he had enough curiosity to persevere in sifting through the hundreds of likely keys in the Key Room until he found the right one. Even so the lock proved troublesome; it must have been years since it was last turned. With the help of an oily lubricant he finally got it undone and, lamp in hand, pushed the door open. Immediately he was seized by a fit of sneezing. Dust lay thick in the room, completely undisturbed until that moment, providing proof of its neglect. Lifting the lamp he surveyed the murky interior, casting hither and thither before him, and the first thing that caught his eye was a faint glint from a huge heap of metallic objects piled in a corner, so tarnished that they were barely distinguishable from one another. But these valuables were soon forgotten as he became aware of shelf upon shelf, tier after tier of books in all shapes and sizes, large, small, worm eaten, ancient, utterly mysterious. He reached up, gripped the spine of one of them and tugged. It disintegrated under his hand. More carefully now he eased the damaged volume out from amongst its neighbours creating a space. Now he could move the others sideways and lift them down without exerting any force. He opened a book at random and found himself gazing at a language he thought at first he did not recognize. Only gradually words began to jump out at him and take on a certain familiarity. It was the common tongue after all but in such an antiquated form as had not been spoken for many years.

He carried it back to his room and set about deciphering the script with a great deal more application than he ever gave to his lessons. In this tome, as in others that followed, what wonders were revealed: tales of gods and heroes, elves and dragons, battles and quests, love stories, tragedies, sagas and ballads. At first he read painfully slowly, finger following the lines, lips silently forming the words, but quickly his skill increased and he devoured volume after volume, until Damask complained that he was no longer any fun to be with because he always had his nose in a book. In this way, almost by accident, Dando acquired the great facility of existing both in the primary world, the world of everyday, while simultaneously inhabiting the secondary world, the sublime world of the imagination It enriched his life immeasurably and for all time.

Yes, that was definitely *something nice* to think about. Dando was smiling as he turned Attack into a neglected path which led to the right and slightly downwards. At this point the river made a wide loop towards the southern wall. Trees crowded thickly on either side of the track and soon met overhead. The light, having been cut off in one direction, filtered in from another as the meandering Wendover was glimpsed slipping silently by, illuminating the branches from below with its silvery gleam. Then the path left the water and began to climb towards the head of the valley leaving the river to follow an alternative descending course eastwards. The fields were now behind them and extensive woodland bordered the road they were following. Leaves were beginning to be shed, creating a carpet underfoot, but there was none of that glorious autumn colour that a colder season might have brought. Occasionally, deep within the forest, Dando glimpsed something that looked like an untidy heap of straw or mound of turf. These were the dwellings of unattached nibblers, sited illegally in this unfrequented spot, forever in peril of being torn down around their occupants' ears. Unattached nibblers, belonging to no one, with no legitimate means of support, were the dregs of valley society, yet the boy's eyes were unerringly drawn towards the shelters that he passed, searching with fierce eagerness for signs of life.

Here under the trees the air was stifling and his back was soon trickling with sweat. Because of the dimness, he was almost on top of it before he became aware of the wall that cut across the path and made off into the woods on either side, stretching as far as the eye could discern. It was high this wall, about fifteen feet, brick built, and held an iron door, closed and barred. It was also very ancient and much repaired, the repairs being of coarser work than the original. But now even the repairs were crumbling, and beside the door which once straddled the main track a gap had been broken, so that the path took a swerve and carried on uninterruptedly. There was something both sinister and impotent about this man-made barrier in the lonely woods, and the state of decay which reduced the stern command KEEP OUT to a futile gesture. Dando rode the horse through the gap, knowing as he did so that he was entering on the lands of his own family.

The trees marched ahead seemingly for ever. This land had once been farmed, but the Dans had allowed it to revert to its original state for the benefit of hunters, trappers and other stalkers who were under their dominion, so that now the newly-established forest teemed with game. Attack's hooves ate up the furlongs and Dando, lulled by the monotonous rhythm, became preoccupied with his favourite daydream: planning the layout of the perfect kitchen. They had just ridden into a clearing and for a short distance the way stretched bright ahead, but beyond the sunshine stood a wall of shadow, and within that shadow something more intensely dark. Attack suddenly bunched and staggered, attempting to stop, slid sideways, reared, and then slewed round a hundred and eighty degrees while Dando clung like a monkey to his neck to avoid being thrown into the ditch. They finished still upright, facing in the direction they had just come, the boy reining in fiercely in order to stop the terror-struck animal bolting back along the track. A grey mist had swept across everything within his field of vision; black night hung amongst the trees. As he dismounted a sharp migraine gripped his scull and hollow nausea seized throat and stomach so that for a moment he felt deathly ill. A hissing noise filled his head. The source was behind him and he felt pretty sure of what he would see if he turned around; there was little room for uncertainty as to the *frightful fiend* that was causing his heart to beat at twice its normal speed. Instead of turning he led Attack back across the clearing and tethered him to a sapling. Then he retraced his steps towards that which awaited him, only pausing a moment to cut a long wand-like stick from a bush. A dog stood barring the way, calamitous, catastrophic, creating its own time, a time ancient beyond imagining. It was the Hell Hound himself, the Bartgeist, Snarliyow, Blackshuck, jaws salivating, eyes blazing, huge. Such an apparition is humanity's common inheritance.

"Get out of my path," said Dando quietly to himself. The dog's darkness rippled and pulsed, sustaining itself from one moment to the next. He raised the stick and, walking slowly forward, recited as he went:-

> *"Kymer, Kymer, Kerigillum.*
> *Caught a rat but couldn't killum.*
> *Bought a cat to kill the rat,*
> *Cat killed Kerigillum.*
>
> *One direction, two direction, three directions,*
> *four...*
>
> *Hickory dickory dock,*
> *The crocodile swallowed the clock...*

Avaunt! Avaunt!"

The image faded; daylight blinked back on. Dando swallowed hard. A taste like bitter aloes filled his mouth and a scorching smell whipped by on a wind that had suddenly arisen. He walked across the spot where the thing had manifested swinging the stick from side to side as if brushing away cobwebs. Then he threw it away and leant against a low branch, putting his hand to his brow. He stood like that, still as a statue, for a few moments, barely breathing, before going back to fetch Attack and continue his journey.

There was no way, however, that their expedition could proceed in the same happy-go-lucky manner that they had adopted up to that point. The horse had been thoroughly spooked and took to shying at every unexpected marker-stone or mysterious rustle. Dando too had been spooked in his own way, and felt both unnerved and dismayed. He asked himself for the umpteenth time why he had been chosen, why these creatures showed themselves to him, for as you might have gathered, this was not the first time he had been through such an experience. At seventeen, Dando's dearest wish was to appear normal, to be simply a regular guy, one of the fellows. All this supernatural nonsense – he hated it with a vengeance; yet ignoring it was not an option, he had tried that, it did not work. And now here he was in the thick of it yet again, on his way to a rendezvous the outcome of which he could not predict and which might prove perilous.

Most of these unwelcome visitations came to him through a particular channel, he had learned. A certain low level of watchfulness in that direction was enough to block them off. His technique was almost perfect by now, but it had to be maintained by willpower. Specific circumstances, for instance significant times of year such as the equinoxes and solstices, a lack of concentration or just inattention to detail could deactivate the barrier. All three pitfalls had combined just now. Illness too could break down the wall. Of course he knew his family's reputation. Often he had asked himself if he was not just plain crazy. But he had evidence that these visitations had a separate identity rather than being just a product of his imagination. The shoemaker, Tom, had been able to perceive them if he chose, and after all, back down the track, Attack had seen the very same thing that he had seen, and to prove it was carrying on as if scared of his own shadow. It was Tom who had taught him what to do when threatened – Tom, one of only three people to whom he had dared unburden himself. The first necessity was to be brave and steadfast: you must betray no fear. You must walk directly towards the vision, fixing it with your gaze and point at it with your hand or a wand. Then you must recite a spell of some kind. "Don't matter what," said Tom, "but certain words can give control to the beast. Better stick to sums." Times tables, however, were an alien concept where Dando was concerned: he was lucky when adding two and two if he got the same result twice running. Nevertheless doggerel from the nursery stood him in good stead, and he was prepared to risk the possibility of a spectre waxing powerful on hearing *Ring a Ring o' Roses* or *Old Mother Hubbard.* Tom Tosa, - how he missed him, and how at this present juncture he could have done with his wise counsel! He was suddenly startled to realize that he had allowed the cobbler back into his thoughts without the usual feelings of panic and dread that normally overwhelmed him. Perhaps it was time to face up to what had happened to Tom and also confront the memory of other painful events that he spent most of the time trying to forget. Tom's place in his story was vital because Tom had been there right from the start...

Thomas Tosa Arbericord was the attached nibbler who made and mended footwear for the Dans' people. He could turn his hand to anything in the shoe line, from crude but serviceable boots for the lowliest farmhand to the dainty embroidered slippers of a Gleptish lady. His cottage, some way from the main house, held a sizeable workshop, filled to the brim with a chaotic mess of tools and materials; Tom was not the tidiest of mortals. At the back of the workroom - the entrance concealed behind a substantial dresser - lay a smaller room containing a curious and significant object. A block of stone, four feet high and about sixteen in girth, was carved into the gross distorted image of a woman with pendulous breasts, a huge pregnant belly and tiny head. The idol dominated the cramped space, as it would have done a much larger room. In fact this small stone had once held sway over the main valley of Deep Hallow in its entirety, for it was a primitive image of Ga-Tum-Dug; Innini; Aigea: the Mother-Goddess herself. That it still existed after all this time was due to the foresight of a former priest who had hidden it away as soon as a multitude of strangers had entered the valley from an unexpected direction. Now Tom Tosa kept it safe in his turn, for Tom was also a priest, namely the Culdee, the high priest of the Nablan race. To embrace the religion of the Earth Mother was a capital offence in Deep Hallow. Sorcery, necromancy, witchcraft were the labels the Glepts put on such worship and feared it exceedingly. There was not a single member of his people who did not know of Tom and what he represented, and there was not a single member who would have whispered the truth, even if their life depended on it. Petitioners continually came to his door with problems seeking an answer from the eternal female, but they came in secret, under cover of darkness, and he laid the concerns they brought before the statue on their behalf. In like manner the oppressed nation had practised their creed throughout the whole of their servitude.

Tom had had a wife, Martha, and soon after their marriage she had become pregnant. When her time came to deliver she went into labour and died giving birth. He had been warned by his teacher, the previous Culdee, that the Mother was a jealous mistress, but he had hoped against hope that this time she would show mercy. When this was not the case he bowed his head in submission and took the baby, a little girl known familiarly as Ann, to Doll, Potto's daughter, who at the time was lactating. The Dan's lady had also recently been through a pregnancy - her fourth. She had already presented her husband with a son and heir, thus fulfilling her side of the marriage bargain. Now she was brought to bed with twins – a boy and a girl. The noblewomen in the households of the fifteen families did not breast-feed their own children. They were too valuable as breeders to experience the long period of infertility that such a practice might entail. Doll had been selected as one of the wet nurses to the twins and her own infant, which was the reason she had milk and to spare, was packed off to a baby farmer in Low Town in the centre of the valley. The supply from her ample breasts should have been reserved for the boy twin alone, but because the bereaved Tom had asked if she would suckle his motherless child, out of the goodness of her heart she could not reject the little girl. And so she fed one baby openly and one in secret.

The Glepts had a curious attitude towards nibbler children: they treated them like lap-dogs. Up to the age of about eleven, maybe because they looked like little cherubs with their fair hair and blue eyes, they were tolerated, even indulged. No one objected to flawless little Ann, at age three or four, flitting around the corridors of the big house, either below or even above stairs. She spent a large part of her day in the castle but went home to her father's cottage at night. Because Doll, her stand-in mother, was at the centre of both their worlds, she inevitably found herself in company with the boy twin, the Dan's second son, Dando, for it was indeed he who had been her companion at the breast, and also with his sister Damask. People got used to seeing the three children together, the intrepid Damask always the leader in their games and adventures, the quiet Ann and the dreamy Dando being content to follow. Upper-class Gleptish parents were also inclined to be indulgent to their own offspring and only imposed real restrictions when they reached their teenage years.

Although, in the early days, Damask spent most of her time with her sibling, by the age of six she had begun to forge an independent existence. Every spring a tribe of Roma visited the valley and because of their expertise in horse flesh the Dans let them camp on their land. Besides horse trading the gypsies worked metal, making cutlery, kitchen equipment and garden tools; they played music for balls and weddings and practised palmistry. While they were in residence a caravan usually came up to the big house to repair farm, stable and cookery appliances. Driven by her insatiable curiosity

Damask investigated and soon made the acquaintance of two boys about her own age. Their wildness and exoticism fascinated her, and when they returned to camp she followed. Here she was found by worried adults from the house, sitting at the feet of one of the gypsy mothers. The upper echelons' indulgence did not stretch as far as allowing a member of their own race to fraternise with these footloose didicoys and Damask was told off in no uncertain terms. But being thoroughly scolded did not deter her; given the opportunity, she would still slip away to join her new friends so that Dando saw less of her and more of Ann. His sister only returned permanently to his side after the gypsies had decamped in the autumn and left the valley.

During the winter when the sun shone, even if it was cold, the twins were out and about around the castle, but at the onset of bad weather they normally confined themselves to the south-west tower. As well as the big circular play-room which they loved, there was plenty of space for a bedroom each and accommodation for the bevy of servants assigned to wait on them. They could be found here on wet or snowy days along with little Ann, raising a rumpus as they acted out childish fantasies. Occasionally Ann returned the compliment by offering them hospitality in her own home. She was proud that she could entertain the two noble children at her father's cottage where Tom greeted them with a dignified politeness, gave them refreshments and a fascinating demonstration of the mysteries of boot and shoe making. It was while he was out on his rounds though and Ann was unwise enough to let them into his workroom unsupervised that the harm was done. Damask, forever curious, poked her nose into the dim recesses of the shop

and discovered that a massive dresser did not stand flush
against the wall. Slipping through the narrow gap behind
she pulled aside a curtain and was confronted by a small
lamp burning before a looming presence that radiated
power. She backed hurriedly away.

"What's that in there?" she demanded of the
horrified Ann who covered her mouth with her hands.
When the little girl did not reply Damask called Dando
over to have a look. The two Glepts peered nervously
through the opening at the ugliest thing they had ever
seen.

"What is it?" Damask demanded again.

Ever since Ann could understand, it had been
dinned into her that the hiding place of the image must
never be revealed. That the children of the house had
discovered it was a disaster of the first magnitude.

"It be what we say our prayers to." She faltered,
"You mun't tell!"

"You say your prayers to that?!" sneered
Damask with immense scorn. "To a stone?!" Although
she would not admit it she had been severely frightened
by the toad-like statue. "It's the Sky-Father that answers
prayers, not a stone!"

As Damask became more intimate with the two
Roma boys she had met the previous spring she found
that all was not well in their cramped caravan-sized
world. Their mother was ill, had been ill for months, and
all the potions and herbal remedies in the gypsies' vast
pharmacopoeia had been unable to effect a cure.
Although the woman tried to carry on as normal there
was no disguising the fact that she was gradually fading
away before their eyes. Her husband sadly explained this

to Damask as he bent over his metal work. It seemed to relieve his mind to talk, if only to a child.

"We pray for meeracle, deo volente. You say prayer, too, sorella; you say prayer for my poor girl."

The conversation fired Damask with ambition. She did not know what sort of gods the Roma worshipped but she imagined some sort of minor insignificant deities. Surely the god of the Glepts, the powerful Glepts, would be more capable of answering prayers than those pip-squeak divinities; she envisaged presenting a miraculous cure to her new-found friends. The Dans' chapel and priest's quarters lay in the basement of the castle. Damask had no intention of involving the house chaplain, a man she cordially disliked. Yet in her experience the intercessor between a petitioner and the Sky Father had to be male. She cast around for a suitable candidate: Dando - it would have to be Dando. The little boy – used, by now, to being recruited to his sister's lunatic schemes - rose to the challenge and composed a supplication not unlike those employed in the few rites at which, up to now, they had been required to be present. The two of them crept into the chapel when the priest was not around and went through the ritual. Damask was left with a feeling of doubt. Surely there should have been some sense of the presence of the god. All she had been aware of was an absence, a negation.

Nevertheless a few days later she enquired hopefully after the health of the sufferer. Their mother was no better, the older boy admitted; in some respects she had gotten a little worse. This was a blow and destroyed at a stroke Damask's faith in the Gleptish religion. However she was not one to give up in a hurry.

She suddenly remembered the grotesque totem at the back of Tom's workshop.

"I want to say a prayer to your stone." She announced to the appalled Ann.

"That's for Dadda to do."

"No, we're going to do it. You can show us how."

Neither Ann nor Dando could withstand the force of Damask's personality for long. Ann soon capitulated.

"You must bring an offering and some oil."

"What sort of offering?"

Ann wrinkled her brow and thought hard.

"Something precious," she said at last.

Dando stole some oil from the kitchen and brought pretty sweetmeats that he had gone to a great deal of trouble to make. Damask contributed an ancient dagger that she treasured. Although Ann assured them that the Mother was unconcerned about the sex of her priests Damask was not prepared to run the risk of failure; Dando was again delegated to conduct the ceremony. As far as they knew, on the chosen morning Tom would be away several hours. The three children crowded into the small annex as Dando self-consciously placed the offerings at the foot of the effigy. He was aware of a tremendous sense of watchfulness, and for a moment felt like a baby deer hiding in a thicket and being stalked by a ravenous predator. Damask handed him the phial of oil and with his breath coming thick and fast he poured it over the statue. Then, following Ann's instructions, he touched the stone and, with moistened finger, touched his own brow. Straight away a light appeared to leap from the statue and smite him between the eyes. The light was inside him and seemed to pluck words out of his brain.

"Hello boy," came the greeting and then, *"I see you, I see you, I see you…"* endlessly repeated like the tick of a clock measuring out eternity. *"Well met my lad, lad, lad, lad… You will soon be mine, mine, mine, mine… Come to me, me, me, me, me…"* The words echoed on forever within the hollow of his skull, a cacophony of words.

But then Tom was at the opening.

"Ann, you crazy mawther! What d'you think you be adoin' of?"

The two girls turned guiltily, but Dando did not move. Tom bent over him anxiously.

"My young lord – come you away. This be no place for thee." He picked the child up and carried him outside. It took over an hour for Dando to return to himself, and even then he was confused and at a loss, not understanding what had happened. Somewhere at the back of his mind he could still hear *"I see you, I see you, I see you…"*

He wept.

Summer faded into autumn. Life went on. The Roma prepared to depart and Damask's friends rejoiced because the boys' mother was showing signs of a steady improvement.

"Next time you see me," she smiled at Damask, "I will be A-OK, top notch."

Damask was pleased, as, for one thing, it meant the family was intending to return next year. Also, although Dando had not had time to voice any of the prayers they had prepared, she still felt that her intervention had born fruit. What the experience had meant to her brother lay completely outside her understanding.

Damask, Dando and Ann were now at the start of their seventh year. Tom, displaying a natural authority that no Glept would have credited to a nibbler, lined the brother and sister up and lectured them about confidentiality, hinting at the grave consequences to Ann and himself if they told anyone about his double life. Dando listened with solemn attention, Damask with impatience. Who did this man think she was? Did he think she would betray her friends? In actual fact the cobbler's secret was safe in the twins keeping. As often happens with such close siblings, events that occurred during the course of their mutual exploration of the world were considered to be their own business and no one else's. Damask would not even have told the Roma.

The mid-winter festival, with its celebration of the most recently elected year child, came and went. Soon the second moon following the New Year rose above the hills and it was nearly spring. At this period the Hunter with his belt of stars had already entered the eastern sky while the west still held the sun's after glow. Tiny leaves from spring bulbs were showing through the cold soil, but, from day to day, there was the possibility that they might yet be checked by an iron frost or buried inches deep in snow. This was the danger time, when the Mother's power waxed, having fed all winter on the quiescent, slumbering fields, but had found as yet no outlet, no release, no dissipation in the season's great unfolding. She lay coiled in seeds and buds, a runner in the slips, while a deep soundless throbbing invaded the cold crackling air and everything waited with breathless anticipation.

Very early one day, Dando, having been involved in some disagreement or other, refused to eat his breakfast and ran outside into the pure morning light just as dawn was breaking. There he met a representative of the castle's pack of hounds, also truant, and they led one another on, wandering far from the house. Garrulous skeins of wildfowl arrowed outward from their roosts across the opalescent spaces above. The faint scream of a distant fox came to the little boy's ears, born on small puffs of freezing air which slyly fingered through his indoor clothes. In time he and the dog reached an out-of-the-way part of the castle grounds where a track called Spring Road came down a hill from a grove known as Lady Wood, and as he stepped onto the path Dando saw that a woman, a beautiful woman, was descending the slope. The dog let out a low growl and fled but the boy stood rooted to the spot before falling to his knees as if hamstrung. The vision was wearing a garland in her hair along with a loose pale garment and seemed immensely tall. She glided rather than walked in his direction, then, drifting level, turned on him a look of piercing sweetness.

"Well met my lad." The words came from within his own head. She passed him by, and then, looking back, extended a snowy arm.

"Come," she said.

Later, and for a long time afterwards, Dando thought he retained no memory of what had happened during the subsequent hours, up until the moment when he awoke, a poor shivering little thing like a half-drowned kitten, in the arms of Tom, the cobbler.

Another month passed and, as Dando eventually discovered, Tom went to talk to Potto, needing someone to whom he could open his heart - a sympathetic ear to assuage his loneliness.

"She led him to walk the Wynde, a child of that age! She hooly want him dead, I misunderstand why. When I hear they were looking for he, I went to the back 'us and made the oblation. I suspicioned he were with her. She warned me to stay away, but by then I knew where he be: he was with her up at the Midda – all those miles. She warn me, but I went there all the same. I found him halfway through the Wynde, curled up on the ground. I thought at first he were a gonner: his eyes were turned back in his head an' he weren't breathin'. An' he were cold – so cold! I picked he up an' when I did that she waxed hooly wrathful. It came from deep down in the crust, but she couldn't stop me. I carried him off the hill and across the causeway and laid him down in the soft grass. I coaxed he and give him my breath and after a while he were alive again."

"I knew I mus' get he back into familiar surroundings as soon as possible so I carried he through the Clough alongside o' the rapids and, on the way, he stare into the river and say, *Look!*"

"Says I, *What do you see?*"

"*Ladies in the water!*"

"*What sort of ladies?*"

"He puts his mouth close to my ear an' whispers, *They don' have no clothes on.*"

Tom laughed. "I saw them too then – water sprites, human-shaped Old Ones, sky clad. That's when I realize something had torn a hole in his mind. He has the open eye now, but without the power. Very dangerous."

Tom stopped speaking. The older man remained silent. Both were lost in their own thoughts. At last Tom rubbed his hand over his face and heaved a heavy sigh.

"Her don't forgive, Potto. I know I be in for it, sooner or later. Maybe not just yet, but someday – not too far off." There was a prolonged pause. "But I'd do it again!" - angrily - "she took my Martha, but she won't take this little ol' boy!"

With the resilience of youth, Dando would have banished the memory of his encounters with the paranormal to the back of his mind, had it not been for the visitations that began to plague and terrify him. Strange creatures from the spirit world , mainly non-human in shape, suddenly invaded his life, and seemed to lurk in every odd corner, even within the castle walls. They were not all hideous and ghastly, some were beautiful, noble and wild, but without exception they appeared to have no purpose other than to scare the pants off him. He tried talking to them, but if they had ever understood language it must have been in a tongue long since dead. Unlike in the stories his nurse told him they never granted him three wishes, and as far as he knew he could not bind one to be his magic-working vassal. Sometimes they were as thick in the air as summer hail or a flock of winter starlings. They left him with a permanent sense of loss, through showing something that no longer existed in the present era – a sort of ferocious innocence.

Eventually, reluctantly, he turned his feet in the direction of Tom's cottage, to one of the few individuals in whom he felt he could confide, and even then he was afraid he would not be believed. But Tom seemed to be expecting him and proceeded to deal with his problem in a matter-of-fact way that was a tremendous relief to the little boy.

"You incomers, you sing about them, you know." explained the cobbler. "How does it go? ...*In the dead hours of darkness, the Old, the First-Comers, Mount once again their iron earth-bound thrones.* And, after the Old Ones arrived, the Great Ones soon followed."

"The Night Hymn to the Father," said Dando, recognizing the words of the anthem.

"That's what they are – Old Ones; old because they were here afore - or so I was told."

"Before what?"

"Afore everyone else that come from outside. But they don't have much power now except at the dark of the moon and at the dark of the year; not much power except perhaps to drive a man mad."

Yes, Dando had seen evidence of that. Taken into High Harrow to be measured for some new clothes, he had noticed a poor distracted woman roaming the streets of the town, screaming and gibbering, talking into the air, occasionally abused but on the whole tolerated by passers by. Dando had been perfectly well aware of the unseen partner in her ravings that led her on and tormented her: a curious little imp-like creature that rarely left her side except occasionally to go and play tricks in the crowd. He had seen the result of these tricks – possessions dropped or mislaid, sudden pains or itches. He had been forced to laugh, despite the infantile or rather senile nature of the jokes on offer. The thing had looked at him, delighted that someone had recognised its cleverness; the only time he felt any sense of connection with one of these gremlins.

"Does being mad mean you can see more than other people?" he asked Tom.

"You're not mad, my dear - never you fear. I'll show you what to do so they don't bother you no more," and he was as good as his word.

Coming to the cottage another time, Dando stopped by the door and inadvertently eavesdropped on the cobbler speaking rather severely to his daughter.

"…I didn't bullyrag you then, girl when you shew them the image, although you deserve it. Now do what I tell 'ee an' we'll call it quits."

"But why do she want to hurt he, Dadda?"

"I misunderstand why though I hev my suspicions, but it misgives me that she be out for his blood. Be a good girl and stick close to he when I can't be there. Look after he for I. If that Old-Woman come a-sniffin' round you make the call. I've shown you how."

Troubled, Dando slipped away without announcing his presence.

After that Ann followed him constantly, coming to heel like a little dog, much to his annoyance. He hated the thought that he was being mollycoddled, and, besides that, he resented the possibility that Ann only sought out his company because she was obeying orders. In the thoughtlessly cruel way of the very young, he asserted his Gleptish dominance by calling on her to *show*. Ann would stretch out her three fingered hands in the gesture of subservience. Then Dando would slap one of them up from below, shouting "You're *it!*" and gallop off down the road laughing, leaving her to follow.

During the summer months Damask was off at the gypsy camp most of the time, but Dando had promised to vouch for her being at his side, if questioned. He and Ann were often to be found in the vicinity of the abandoned cottage up the tributary stream that he and Damask had discovered the year before. While Dando experimented in the kitchen, Ann kept house or dug in the garden she was establishing outside the back door. They would sit by the pool as they ate his concoctions, in silence at first, but pretty soon talking animatedly, as his resentment faded and was soon forgotten.

Young as she was Ann proved to be a mine of information when it came to the valley and its people. For a start Dando learnt that there were no such things as *nibblers*; this was just an insulting corruption of the true name for her race – *Nablar*. And the Nablans, who had lived in that place time out of mind, had once played host to a great influx of pilgrims coming to pay homage at the shrine of the Earth-Goddess in the upper valley, the Midda as her people termed it, although it was far from resembling a meadow. At that period the main valley was occasionally known as The-Lap-of-the-Mother as it also contained a focus of power: the stone idol that now lay hidden at the back of Tom's workshop. As such, wayfarers approached with a sort of devout terror, overwhelmed and exalted at the thought of the dread deity that lay in wait to bless or ambush them either there or within its western extension. People came from many miles away to worship, and those who had endured years of spiritual training - the Adepts - set out to Walk-the-Wynde, that is to thread the maze which was to be found atop Judd's Hill in the midst of Hollow Marsh and meet the goddess face to face. The custodians of the shrine were known as *the Seed of Erde*, the Children-of-the-Earth.

"All manner of great folk came to pray at the Midda – kings and queens and princes, all dressed in beautiful clothes and bringing presents." Ann waved her hand in the direction of the mountain barrier with its one gap through which the river came tumbling.

"But that can't be true," argued Dando, "w-we wouldn't have allowed it. We don't let anyone foreign go to the upper valley."

"You weren't here."

"What do you mean?"

"You weren't here – you ha'n't arrived."

"Where were we then?"

Ann shrugged. Dando frowned and shook his head. "That's nonsense."

"Afore that we kept the Key for the Earth until the Sky came an' stole it."

"The Key, what's that?"

Ann wrinkled her brow. "I'll ask."

If she was stumped by a question that Dando put to her, a few hours later the little girl could usually supply an answer. Dando realised she was acting as a conduit for her father's knowledge, and that the quiet shoemaker was the source of most of her tales.

"The Key opens doors," she told him next time they were together.

"Well so do most keys. You say you kept the Key for the Earth until the Sky stole it. This is just a story, right?"

"What do you mean?" Ann was not aware that many in the modern world believed there was a distinction between myth and reality.

"I mean it's not actually true, it's just a legend."

"O' course it's true!"

Dando was left with much food for thought from these tetes-a-tetes, and wished he could question the cobbler directly about the history of his people, but a certain diffidence held him back. Had the Glepts always occupied the valley and, if not, where had they come from? He became aware, as if for the first time, that the ruling race never talked about the past, that the status quo was assumed to have always existed.

Sometimes Ann could not come to the cottage.

"Dadda be teaching I," she told him in order to explain her absences.

"Teaching you what?"

"Oh, you know," she replied evasively, "Nablan things."

When she was not there he missed her.

But Dando's life also led him in other directions. Often he was to be found keeping company with boys of his own age in the local Watchdog troop, learning to drill or conducting mock battle manoeuvers. A few times, impelled by curiosity, he followed his sibling down to the travellers' encampment where he was soon swept up into the lawless escapades of the young gypsies. Tolerated for his sister's sake, he was grudgingly allowed to participate in their sport, and now, on one particular occasion, it was Dando's turn to be left behind. Not sure of his welcome, feeling slightly superfluous and suffering from a really bad summer cold, he trailed Damask and most of the older children through a warm spell-bound evening, the only things seeming to move in that somniferous landscape being themselves. On, on, on, on – during the time they spent in the valley the romany youngsters were always in pursuit or flight, waging fierce campaigns against other wild spirits, poaching, thieving, constantly under threat of some well-deserved punishment, and now, in echoing back their voices, the very hedges and thickets, lanes and woods assumed a role in their drama, and took on an aura of unbearable moment. Having thrown in his lot with the outlaws, Dando panted after until his sore throat burned, his chest felt like an aching void and, as a result, he lagged far to the rear. Damask, becoming aware of his plight, fell back and remained with him as he doubled over, trying to recover his breath. The rest of the gang disappeared into the distance.

"I don't think you're cut out for this at the moment, Do-Do."

"I think you're right." he wheezed, grateful that she had stayed behind to assure herself of his well-being when she could have been far ahead in the vanguard of the tearaways; normally she was extremely intolerant of frailty. They retraced their steps to the gypsy camp, where, feeling a good deal better, he spent a fruitful hour or two picking up tips about pungent food dressings known only to the van-dwellers' womenfolk and learning the intricacies of such a dish as rabbit flavoured with fungi and herbs, wrapped in leaves and cooked over a slow fire.

The Roma's name for Damask was *Principessa*, spoken with respect and admiration. As her brother, Dando became known as *the Gorgio Prince*, but with a faint hint of mockery in the title, especially when the males of the tribe found that his passion was cookery. Food preparation in their culture was entirely woman's work and was not something that any real man, or self-respecting boy, would admit knowledge of. The wives looked on him rather more kindly however and taught him about the wild bounty that could be gathered from woods and fields. They also instructed him in open-air cooking methods. From one, whose late mother had been a fellow enthusiast, he received a treasure with a price above rubies: an ornate box which contained many small bottles of herbs and spices that the Roma had brought from lands far away.

"Come and have your fortune read," urged Damask.

At the periphery of the camp stood an elaborately decorated wagon, the home of the tribe's matriarch, a great, or even great-great-grandmother. Too ancient now to often leave her van, the old lady still exhibited a formidable intelligence, and ruled her large clan with a rod of iron. She was well known as a clairvoyant, with a reputation for second sight. Many came to consult her. Dando was reluctant.

"Oh for crying out loud! don't be such a wimp! I'm going to marry a king so I've been told, and have lots of children. All you need to do is cross her palm with silver."

The interior of the caravan was so dark that at first, coming in from the bright summer's evening, Dando could see very little. Gradually he became aware of a tiny fairy-like figure sitting at the far end, wrapped in a gaudy shawl, with piercing jet-black eyes that shone in the gloom.

"Come here," he was ordered.

The money was presented and he held out his hand. The grandam took it in hers but, for a long time, stared into his face as if plumbing his soul. Then with a movement like a caress she stroked his hand open and dropped her gaze. Her eyes filmed over like a kingfisher's as it takes its plunge and she looked not at his palm but through it. Her jaw moved rhythmically. For a long moment even breath seemed suspended. Then abruptly she pushed his hand away.

"I cannot read it," she said.

"But..." began Damask, astounded.

"I cannot read it." the old woman repeated with a note of hostility, even fear, in her voice. "Here..." she held out the coin that Dando had given her. "Go... go..."

Dando and Damask were unceremoniously ejected from the caravan and walked away with their tails between their legs, not understanding what they had done wrong.

The three children, the two Glepts and the Nablan, passed their tenth birthdays. Once again, after her summer absence, Damask joined the others at the cottage, but for the first time, to her chagrin, felt like an interloper; by now, Dando and Ann were so obviously an item. Later, when she had her brother alone and spurred on by vague feelings of jealousy, she asked, "Do you want people to call you a nibbler- lover?"

"What are you on about?"

"That girl – why do you spend so much time together? Are you sweet on her?"

Dando opened his mouth for an indignant denial, then suddenly got the sensation that he had been hit over the head by a ton of bricks. A huge blush started in his toes and swept up through the whole of his body ending at his hairline. He was remembering how Ann would slip her hand in his when they set out on the long walk to the cottage; how, falling asleep in the shade, side by side, one hot afternoon, they had awoken to find themselves in each others arms. He was remembering the warmth of her body and the smell of her hair, the beautiful azure of her gaze. The scales fell from his eyes and at a stroke his innocence was gone for ever.

"I should let her alone for now," advised the worldly-wise Damask, "otherwise people will start to talk. Hang on 'till you're fourteen, then take her as your pet – nobody'll object to that."

For three days Dando stayed in his room and Ann waited at their usual rendezvous in vain. Then on the fourth day he went in search of her and found her standing outside her father's workroom. "We can't do this anymore," he barked abruptly and saw that she caught his drift. She ducked her head and seemed to diminish and cower, her pale hair falling forward to hide her face.

"No wait…!" He reached out but did not quite touch her. "When I can get away I'll put something in the window – something in the tower room window – something blue. When you see that, you come to the cottage by yourself and I'll be waiting for you. We can still be together up there - no one will know."

She looked into his eyes - a long searching look - then gave a tiny smile. "All right." she whispered brushing her hair aside. Impulsively he pulled her towards him and planted a quick peck of a kiss on what was supposed to be her cheek but which in fact turned out to be her nose. Then he whisked off into the distance, shocked at his own temerity.

The new arrangement did not last long. They met under the new scheme on three separate occasions, but the old easy camaraderie had vanished. Too young to handle what were in fact adult emotions in embryo, Dando was left wallowing in a sea of awkwardness and inexperience. After the third encounter the *something blue* did not appear in the window again.

Dreams are sent
From gates of horn and ivory,
Some to deceive and some for warning.

Chapter seven

The upper extremity of Dando's homeland was now not far off. His route continued to climb slightly until he had gained enough height above the flood plain to get a view over the roof of the forest through which he had just passed and see a wide panorama to the north and east, in the midst of which he could make out the four towers of Castle Dan, each flying the Dan flag. Above the castle a fine mackerel sky spread itself, suggesting that the weather was about to change, while beyond, an ugly scar was carved into the northern hills. This quarry was the source of the family's wealth and influence. An exceptionally pure deposit of ironstone had been discovered on the Dans' land and, because there was a great demand for the mineral in the towns along both shores of the Middle Sea, they had set about excavating and refining the ore, exporting it in huge lumbering wagons down the Incadine Gorge. Next to the quarry stood an iron works pouring smoke into the air from its charcoal furnaces; the sound of water-powered hammers echoed between the valley sides. Quite soon after beginning the operation the clan members heard that a certain respected wise woman from down on the plains had warned that they were doing Deep Hallow a great disservice by indulging in this activity. Rather defensively they dismissed the report, branding it an example of fake news, before carrying on regardless as if no-one had questioned their process of enrichment.

Thinking of these things Dando turned away, preparatory to continuing his journey, but then looked back, looked back longingly, at the sky over the castle. It was when he was struggling with his sums at the age of nine years or so under a tutor named Pearling-Proctor that he had first been initiated into certain mysteries. This newly-employed pedagogue often turned towards the window during the lessons they shared, away from his pupil, in stark contrast to Dando's previous tormentor who had always fixed him with an accusatory glare.

"Sir – please sir," he finally asked one day, "what is it? What can you see?"

"Clouds, my Lord," the man had replied and, abandoning the maths they were presently engaged upon, set about teaching the boy the many names (*cumulus, cirrus, stratus* etc.) for the celestial mists which, as far as he was concerned, hugely enhanced the attraction of the outside world. Dando became an immediate convert and from then on scarcely an hour passed without his glancing upwards. Every cloud type that he identified turned into a personal triumph, the new discovery either fascinating or awing him in equal measure, apart, that is, for *stratus nebulosus opacus* which, on the occasions when it stretched overhead from horizon to horizon, cast a pall across both the landscape and his developing mind. Now, as a farewell to childhood, he labelled the present formation *cirrocumulus stratiformis undulatus* before heading once more towards his ultimate goal.

The road ahead now followed the lower contours of the valley side, weaving in and out, until it took off across the mountain blockade at the western limit and, meeting the main highway, disappeared into the only opening in the barrier, the defile known as the Clough which connected the two areas that made up Deep Hallow. Through this gorge the track climbed, steep but negotiable, wide enough to take a farm cart, which he knew it had done on at least one occasion, while beside it the river fell by a hundred feet or more, descending in a series of rapids and cataracts to emerge eventually into the lower valley. But now he hit a temporary set back, for Attack refused point-blank to enter the couloir. It took all Dando's horsemanship to win the battle of wills with the stallion and persuade him to continue. In taking Attack to the Midda he was defying a ban imposed by his own family: no horse or pony was permitted to travel up the narrow ravine. If he had known the reason for this veto he might have been more inclined to pay attention to the prohibition. Inside the clough, climbing the uneven path, his ears were beset by the noise of rushing water, amplified between rocky walls. A fine spray filled the air, dampening his hair. He was now on the last leg of his journey and would soon reach his destination and what awaited him there. He was anxious to get it over with – whatever *it* turned out to be. But first – now that this latest delving into the past had reached his second decade - he must deal with what he thought of as the *dark time*, a time occasionally bathed in a lurid glare.

Dando and Damask, like many aristocratic youngsters, were raised by servants. They gave their love to these surrogates and rarely made contact with their real parents, except, in their early days, for the Dan, who had taken an interest in them up to the age of three or four – it amused him to play with toddlers. As a tiny tot Dando had rehearsed a party piece, and his father had stood him on a table at one of his dinner parties for the performance. When he finished, the unexpected applause caught him unawares. He had shyly retreated until he toppled backwards off the table only to be neatly retrieved in his father's arms. From then on it became a favourite game of theirs: both he and Damask would fall backwards off various high places to be unfailingly caught after the delicious moment of maximum uncertainty. By the time they reached their fifth birthdays however the safeguarding arms were no longer present; the Dan had transferred his affections to younger offspring of whom there seemed to be an inexhaustible supply.

The Lady Tryphena, the Dan's wife, was continually occupied with carrying and giving birth to new additions to the family and had no energy left for older child rearing. The twins saw little of their mother after the first few months of life, the only time they were in the same room being for formal religious occasions. It was through Doll and Potto that they learnt that the baby born after their ninth birthdays, Dan Septor, the seventh son, was giving his parents cause for concern. This charming little boy, known affectionately as Daisy, had been chosen as the year child, and had been carried through the dark house at the mid-winter festival. But as the months wore on and the year grew old, he failed to thrive, a bad omen for those of a superstitious nature.

Damask was feeling contrite. Having interfered between Dando and Ann and broken up their cottage idyll she now sensed that her brother was deeply unhappy.

Although not normally given to remorse she had an uncomfortable sense that she was partly to blame for his misery. Well, she would have to do something to cheer him up. Over the years Damask had involved the two of them in a variety of hair-brained escapades. There had been the night-time climbing expedition up the outside of the castle walls, from which they were lucky to return alive. Then there was the occasion when she had managed to purloin a flagon of wine and they had drunk themselves insensible. Now she had a new idea. Every so often news came up the Eastern Drift from that river-girt, jewel-bedecked old dowager, Vadrosnia Poule, the city on the Kymer delta, of music and dances, trends and crazes, all well out of date by the time the rumour of them reached Deep Hallow, but seized upon hungrily by the novelty-starved young. One fashion that had come to them by this route and which was taken up for a short while in the valley was that of body art, otherwise known as tattooing. Damask came back from a visit to friends at the Grant mansion primed in the technique. "I know how to do it," she told Dando, "We can do the double D. I'll do you first and then you can do me." The Dans wore a large capital 'D' on their escutcheon. Dando and Damask had added a second reversed D to the left of the main one, thus creating a circle bisected by a vertical line; it was their secret sign, Damask and Dando, the terrible twins.

Dando endured the pain stoically as Damask jabbed him with her needle, knowing that any sign of weakness would be met with scorn. It proved to be a much messier and more difficult business than she had bargained for and by mutual consent they agreed to postpone the return match until the morrow.

Unfortunately, through some oversight, Damask had not been taught about sterilizing her equipment. That night, in the small hours, Dando suddenly brought up his supper. By morning he was feeling feverish and sweaty and had paid numerous visits to the privy. By midday he was unable to get out of bed. By evening the bogeymen that he had learned to keep at bay came crowding around, shrieking and squealing, beating their scaly wings. A dark chasm opened beneath him and he fell down into it pursued by unspeakable horrors.

How long was it before he was once again in command of his senses? Two weeks? Three? He was not sure. All he knew was that when he emerged from the coma into which he had sunk everything was *changed, changed utterly*. In the first days of his long haul back to health he felt so light, irresponsible and helpless, so lacking in continuity of thought that he seemed to have regressed to babyhood, the world appearing new made and extremely strange. As he passed this acute stage these feelings faded, but the strangeness remained; things around him were completely out of kilter. He soon learnt that the whole castle was in mourning. His youngest brother had died, soon after the onset of his, Dando's, illness, in mysterious circumstances. The household was exhibiting a peculiar reticence on the subject. More extraordinary, his mother had evidently left the Dan mansion and gone back to her father's house. There was a coming and going of lawyers; the Dan had put in train proceedings that would end in divorce. The servants, particularly those of the Nablan persuasion, were creeping about the castle like frightened mice, and a small band of foreign soldiers were strutting around as if they owned the place. His sister Damask, in deep disgrace after the tattooing fiasco, seemed to have lost her tongue and would not answer the most innocent of questions. Even Doll, his comfortable nurturing Doll, doyen of the nursery, had committed some heinous crime that no one would name. He was horrified to hear that she had been beaten and sent away to do hard labour at the quarry. On top of this, when he tottered the half mile or so to Tom's cottage to get some clarity on the situation, he found it not just deserted but demolished, only the foundations remaining.

"Where are Tom and Ann?" he asked his sister, a small knot of anxiety growing in his chest like a tumour. She shook her head. When he persisted she replied impatiently, "You'll have to find out for yourself – I'm not going to tell you." This was unprecedented. Throughout their short lives they had never held any secrets from each other, Dando had always shared everything with his twin, even his supernatural encounters, although he was not surprised when she dismissed these as nonsensical fancy. "Where are Tom and Ann?" he asked Potto. The Nablan stared at him with haunted eyes and made a gesture indicating that he was unable to speak.

"Where are the cobbler and his daughter?" he asked of whoever came within his orbit. Those interrogated looked at him uncomfortably, then patted him on the shoulder, telling him not to bother his head about such things but to concentrate on getting well.

This was easier said than done. At the current stage of his convalescence old age seemed to have claimed him prematurely. He was always cold and tired, creeping to bed at an early hour, waking exhausted after nights in which cinders and glowing coals streamed across the sky of his dreams, spewed from some smouldering volcano of the unconscious. It was nearly six months before he could stretch himself as formally, before he could run and jump and wrestle without fear of the consequences, before even a trace of his natural joie-de-vivre began to reassert itself. Only then did they tell him that in the first days of his illness he had been to the very gates of death.

Something shocking had happened while he was out cold, that was patently obvious. As soon as he was physically able he set out on the long walk to the lonely cottage up the side valley, accompanied by his jackdaw Chocky, not knowing what he expected or hoped to find. Chocky, seemingly attuned to his friend's angst, sought to divert him with aerial clowning, expressing his devotion in the only way he knew how.

All for you, master, all for you – this soaring through the air, this twirling, this tumbling towards the ground. Watch me! I will bring you food as I would to a mate, as the beloved EGGS I will cherish you. Take my feathers master – for your hat, for your pen. Pluck me master as I lie on my back in your hand. Use me as you will – I am yours forever! Dando watched him and could not help but smile despite his troubles.

He sat in the kitchen of the cottage staring at the cold range and thinking about Ann and the time they had spent here together. All of a sudden he heard footsteps coming along the path. With a leap of the heart he rushed to the door, but it was Potto, his manservant, Potto Potunalius Applecraft, puffing up the track with a knapsack over his shoulder. Dando took him indoors and offered him water from the stream, the only refreshment currently to hand, surprised that the elderly Nablan should have followed him all the way to this remote place. Potto, after he had sat recovering for a while, delved into the bag and, like a magician with a rabbit, pulled forth a fine pair of brand new walking boots, stout and well made, their leather softly glowing. "These are yours." He announced.

Mystified, Dando took them from him. "But they're much too big." He demurred.

"They won't be in a few years time. You'll be needing them, he said. You got to keep them oiled."

"Tom made them! Potto, where is Tom?" and then catching the expression on the other's face, "is he...?" He found he could not put his apprehension into words.

Potto turned his head away. After a pause he muttered, "I come to tell you the truth. I couldn't tell you down there."

Dando felt his own face lose its colour. He steeled himself. This was going to be bad, he knew that much. "Go ahead," he said with great trepidation.

Potto began by recalling the conversation he had had with the cobbler three or four years earlier, already reported. "He reckon she would take her vengeance on he for gooin' agin' her will. I reckon he were right from what my poor girl tol' me before she were sent away. This is how it were…"

During his first year of life Daisy, the Dan's seventh son, had become increasingly poorly. When he set out to crawl, although he always started out gamely enough, even a small effort would leave him breathless and panting. Sometimes his little face would become contorted and grey as if with pain. The spasm soon passed but while it lasted appeared alarming. Tryphena, the clan's first lady, was taking more of an interest than usual in this baby because she realized that probably after this one there would be no more. The Dan, whom she loved, had always been cold towards her except when he considered she was ready to produce further progeny. If this last child died she would lose both baby and husband at a stroke. It was when things had progressed thus far that Doll, once again the wet nurse, spoke up to her mistress as they sat by the baby's cot.

"Oh lady, if you would let me have him, just for a little, I think I could help."

Tryphena was astonished. "What do you mean *have him*? For how long?"

"Oh, not long lady – less than a day."

"And to what purpose?"

"To make he better."

"And how would you do that?"

"Oh, not me my lady - another…"

"*Another*? Who is this other?"

"I cannot say."

Of course the mother was not going to trust her baby out of sight in the care of a stranger, so there things rested. But the child grew worse.

"Doll, when you said that someone might be able to cure Daisy, did you mean a doctor?"

"No, lady, not a doctor."

"Well who then? Can't you see I must know who it is, and what they do, before I could even think of it."

"Oh lady, I know they say it be wrong and wicked and mun't be allowed, but it ain't, we know it ain't, an' the baby might be helped."

A suspicion began to form in the mother's mind. "Doll, this person, is he a conjurer?"

"Yes lady, but please don't take on. It ain't wicked, we know it ain't."

"How dare you suggest such a thing! I would never let Daisy near such filthy practices! Never speak of it again or I shall have to tell the master!"

But the child got worse.

"Doll, who is this conjurer? Do I know him?"

"He be a good man, lady, an' they say he ha' the power. He's done wonderful things. The baby might be helped."

"But who is he? Can't you see I must know who he is."

"Well you mus' promise never to tell a livin' soul. No incomer mus' know, otherwise he be in mortal danger."

"Very well then, I promise."

"Tom Tosa – I reckon he know what the baby be a-needin'."

"You mean Tom Arbericord, the cobbler?"

"Yes, his little girl play with the twins. He be a good man – he ha' the power…"

The two women, carrying the baby, made their way to the shoemaker's cottage. It was night and within the small dwelling a dim light burned. The interior smelt of leather and resin and oil. A small figure was curled up asleep on a mattress in the corner. Tryphena had never actually exchanged words with the cobbler before. She saw a youngish man with a quiet tired face. He had an air of listening about him.

"The baby is dying," she said in a shockingly matter-of-fact manner and gave Daisy to him. The cobbler sat down on a stool and began a careful examination of the child, feeling it, smelling it, pressing his ear against its body. The infant did not object, in fact it giggled appreciatively and then went to sleep. At last he finished and looked up, straight into her eyes, as no nibbler had ever done voluntarily in her life before. "There is no sickness." he said, "He were wrongly made."

"Yes," said the woman eagerly, "That's what I thought. But can it be changed? Is there anything you can do?"

The cobbler gazed at her quietly for a while.

"It might be unwise," he said at last," to bring this child to the attention of the Mother."

"But is there the possibility of a cure?"

"Yes, there is the possibility."

"Then you must try!"

The man inclined his head slightly by way of assent and shut his eyes. Tryphena looked uncertainly at Doll who pressed a finger to her lips. They stood awkwardly as the long minutes ticked away. Inside the room a space began to grow, a space filled with stillness. Outside, in the night, small sounds made themselves shockingly audible. Soon the very breath of the people in the cottage seemed an intrusion. Then a tiny noise broke the web of silence. As it lay on the cobbler's lap the baby gave a faint trembling sigh after which it appeared to compose itself into a sounder deeper sleep. Tom Tosa, the shoemaker, also stirred and looked up. Something in his face made the mother step forward sharply. "What has happened?" she cried.

"Aigea saw he were not fashioned properly and has arranged for him to be taken."

"Taken? What do you mean? He's all right isn't he?" But even as she reached for the child, she knew, and

Doll, who gave a sudden cry, also knew, that he was dead. The young cobbler, with untroubled calm, put the little body into her arms.

"He will be remade." he said. "Where there is wrongness then the making will begin anew. He will live again, many times, but not in this body."

"Oh heavens!" wailed the Lady Tryphena, "What shall I do? How can I tell him? He'll never forgive me!" She was thinking, not of her child, but entirely of the husband whose heart had always been withheld.

"That's what Doll tol' I." said Potto.

"And Tom...?" asked Dando.

"The lady and Doll tried to hide what had happened - the way the baby died - but somehow word got out. Next morning the Dan's sheriffs took Tom and locked him in a cell in the punishment yard. He were there for days wi'out food or water."

Potto paused as if having second thoughts about continuing his account.

"Go on," said Dando with gritted teeth.

"I got in to the yard to see him. I took the place of the pot boy carrying ale to the guards. I spoke to he through the grill in the cell door."

"*Look after my gel, Potto,* he say, *keep her safe.*"

"*I hev, Tom, I hev,* I say, *she be down with her granny at the Justification.*"

"*Good,* he say, *an' keep an eye out for the little ol' boy.*"

"*What little ol' boy be that, Tom?* I say."

"*Why, the Dan's second, o' course. Your little master.*"

"*But he be none o' ours, Tom,* I say."

"Never you mind. You look arter he, and if he take a mind to goo a wanderin' later on don' ee stan' in his way. I got a present for that boy; they're in the cupboard under the work bench, some boots. Tell him to keep 'em oiled. Then someone come by an' I had to leave."

"Did you manage to talk to him again later?" asked Dando.

"I never seed him arter that – to speak to," said poor Potto, and his eyes filled with tears.

The Dan could not find any volunteers among his own people to do what he required; the Glepts, despite their customary bravado, were afraid to tamper with the Mother's territory. That was why it had remained undefiled for so many years, apparently abandoned, but surreptitiously maintained and tended by unknown hands. There was, at that time, a platoon of masterless soldiers in Gateway. They had climbed up the Incadine Gorge looking for employment, and were about to return the same way, having found no one who needed their brand of naked aggression. These the Dan enlisted to carry out his purposes. On the day appointed half of them traversed the clough to the upper valley and there cut brushwood which they piled feet thick over the whole of the turf maze atop Judd's Hill. The rest took and bound the prisoner and set him in a tumbrel which between them they manhandled up the defile beside the river until they came to the causeway across Hollow Marsh. They carried him to the centre of the maze, the troy town, and nailed him to the ancient tree that grew there, the roots of which were reputed to go down many miles through Aigea's domain until they reached another realm entirely. Then they retreated and set the brushwood ablaze. Crowds of people stood on the edge of the marsh to watch - Nablans, Glepts, travellers, townsfolk, many others. They stayed there silent until the last flame had died and then melted away. Several hours later, when it was cool enough to approach the centre, the mercenaries collected what they could find of the body and threw it into the swamp. They demolished the causeway and departed. Back at the castle they went down to the shoemaker's cottage and smashed up the stone idol they found there with sledge hammers; then they tore down the little dwelling until only the foundations remained. In one fell swoop the Dan had executed the Nablans' high priest and desecrated the Mother's shrine. He had had his revenge for the death of his son.

Dando sat gazing unseeingly into space, the tears rolling down his cheeks. Potto wanted to put an arm round the boy's shoulders but was prevented by the habits of a lifetime. Instead, by way of comfort, he said, "Don'ee fret, lord me dear. It's over now. They can't hurt he no more." But two terrible facts were hammering at Dando's brain. The first was that his own father had done this deed which was bad enough; the second, worse, was that the cobbler had originally defied the goddess and thus incurred her wrath, just to preserve Dando's own wretched hide. The awful fate that had descended on Tom could therefore be laid entirely at his door. He did not know if he had the strength to bear such a weight of culpability. At this juncture Chocky suddenly plumped down onto his shoulder and began to fondle the edge of his ear with his beak. Dando put up his hand and caressed the bird, and in so doing realized that he could and would go on. He would find a way.

"Thank you, Potto," he said quietly, "no one else would tell me."

A few months later, to all intents and purposes, Dando appeared to be a completely normal eleven year old boy. He laughed and joked, he fooled around with his friends, he argued with his sister. He had *found a way,* and the way he had found was complete denial. The memories of the terrible, traumatic events that Potto had described, and his own involvement in them, were pushed down into the furthest recesses of his mind. On the rare occasions that they surfaced, because of a chance remark or other evocation of the past, he plunged desperately into some displacement activity, mentally twisting and turning to avoid facing up to unbearable reality. The boots he had been given, because they acted as a reminder, were put away in a cupboard and quickly forgotten. But this effort of will came at a price. When asleep he was no longer in control. The vague fiery dreams that had afflicted him during his convalescence coalesced into a specific reoccurring nightmare, beginning with a night time re-enactment of the maze burning, misleadingly happening within sight of his tower room window, and ending with the alarming vision of a tunnel under the world. The dream occurred two or three times each month, and always left him weak with terror. After a year of this he had had enough.

"I'm going to the Upper Valley," he told Damask

His sister opened her eyes wide in surprise, but was not about to be outdone in daring by her brother.

"OK," she said, "I'm in. When do we start?"

One bright windy morning, having put it about that they were visiting friends, they set out, Dando carrying a knapsack containing food and drink which he had had the forethought to provide. It took them about three hours to cover the distance to the extreme west end of the main valley, climb up through the clough and reach the hidden combe at the head of the ravine. Silent and watchful the Midda awaited them, a cliff-girt arena filled with light, the theatre in which the first part of his dream was enacted. The upper valley took the form of a completely circular space, a bowl with vertical sides. Facing them, about three quarters of a mile distant across the basin, they could see the top half of a waterfall, the Maidenhair Fall, where the river, called Windhover in these upper reaches, spilled from a higher cleft. The base of the waterfall was hidden behind a flat-topped central mound rising above the surrounding marshland - marshland in which the river lost itself. This was Judd's Hill, or, as it was sometimes known, Juddering Hill, the holy of holies, the goddess's sacred place. The two children stood and stared, overawed by the quietness and the mysterious aura of this open-air chamber.

"Look," said Dando, almost in a whisper, "what's that?"

Clouds were scudding overhead and a steady breeze was blowing. Pouring off the top of the mound, on the wind, they could see a wide continuous stream of what looked like snow – snow in summer.

"Let's go and find out," said Damask. They walked forward until they came to the edge of the marsh, but as they were too low down to see over the brow of the hill they were none the wiser.

"There must be a way to get across." said Dando. Damask seized his arm.

"No, don't do that. If we go over there and climb up the cliff a little way we'll be able to look down on the top."

They went to the bowl's perimeter, at a point where the sides were not quite sheer, and scrambled up about thirty feet. Now they could gaze across at the flat summit of Judd's Hill, and an astounding sight met their eyes. Where once you would have found the intricate convolutions of a grassy maze, traced out over the whole area in an elaborate pattern, there was now a sea, a rippling ocean, of pink flowers covering nearly every inch of level ground.

"I've got to go and see," said the boy.

"No, Dando!" The girl's voice held a note of sharp anxiety.

"I must," he said simply.

The twins had never learnt to swim. Glepts did not swim, although they had some boating skills, and, as far as nibblers were concerned, any public watercourse or lake was out of bounds. How was he to negotiate the swamp? But something about this spot was familiar. Of course, he had been here once before when lured by the Mother to her killing ground and he realised now that he did have a sort of dream-like memory of the place. There had been a causeway then and he thought he could remember where it was situated. Although the Dan had tried to destroy all means of approaching the shrine, the remains of the ancient pathway, as Dando quickly discovered, were still to be found beneath the water. With a lot of splashing and wallowing he waded across and arrived safe but wet on the side of the hill. Here he stood for a long time, gradually summoning up the courage to climb the slope and venture onto the level platform above.

Images of the time when he had been brought here as a seven year old now began flashing on his inward eye. He saw the Wynde – the maze - as it had looked to him then: a tortuous path carved out of green turf, leading those who dared, to and fro and round about, but always closer to the centre, the Mother's seat of power. He could also recall the oppressive hush that had hung over the place. Things were slightly different now: small intermittent drones, rustles, flutterings interrupted the general stillness, reminding him that he was not entirely alone. As he stood there, looking back across the marsh, his five senses sharpened and he was able to pinpoint more and more accurately the living creatures that shared his solitude. There was a rabbit on the opposite bank, watching him suspiciously, a lizard basking on a stone in the full sun, blackbirds anting, mice and shrews in the grass forest. Finally he detected some small predator crouching quite still and out of sight but betrayed by a bird's sudden anxious call. After a while the sounds, while still present to his awareness, were stripped of their meaning, and became merely a frame to emphasize the huge vacancy growing within him. In the end he became lost to himself and drifted on the tides and currents of the universe, a mote floating slowly closer to the centre, but safe as yet from being sucked in. When he returned to the prosaic everyday world, sometime later, it was as naturally and with as much refreshment as from a long sleep. How simple things were when he and the valley were left alone together with just the earth beneath him and the ineffable sky above. He made his way to the top of the rise.

The forest of plants that met him there was higher than his head. The tops of the stems bore pink flowers which were waving and bowing in the breeze, but lower down the flowers had developed into narrow pods, and lower still these had burst apart and curled back, and it was from here that the fluffy white seeds they had seen born on the wind were issuing. Soon, as he pushed his way through, the down began to cling to his wet clothes and hair. Not being a gardener or a botanist, Dando was unaware that this was a species variety known as *epilobium angustifolium*, the fire weed, the first plant to colonize burnt ground. Towards the centre of the hill the growth thinned and took on a stunted appearance, and all of a sudden he stepped out into a clear circle of scorched earth. In the middle of this open area he was confronted by something that resembled a piece of sculpture symbolizing Torment or Affliction. Apparently frozen in an attitude of grotesque agony, he realized that this frightful object, gesticulating wildly into space with the immobile stumps of truncated limbs, was in fact the blackened carbonized remnant of a large tree. Another flash of memory showed him the tree as it had been in its pomp: squat but of huge girth, its gnarled branches growing horizontally from the trunk. This was the ancient entity, here maybe even before the advent of the Mother, which was reputed to draw its nourishment from the bowels of the planet. It was in this place that Tom had met his end; man and tree had been consumed together. The after-echoes of that baleful event were strong all around him and for a moment his sixth sense awoke. He felt the heat of flames, he heard the roar, and he smelt the abominable stench of burning human flesh.

No, no – he must not allow himself to think like that – that way madness lay. He looked about him for a diversion and something caught his eye. Walking forward to within touching distance of the ruined trunk he found, astonishingly, that encircling the base of the charred relic there was new growth, weak and spindly it was true, but incontrovertibly alive. The tree was not dead! To his great mortification the sight of the green shoots brought tears once again streaming down his face. He struggled for control, ashamed at his emotional fragility. A new thought struck him. Here he was at the centre, at the very heart of the mystery, and yet still unscathed. Where was *she*, that *old woman*, as he had heard Tom call her? If she was still present it was somewhere deeper than deep, somewhere far below the surface of things. It was as if a great beast had been beaten into temporary submission and cowered in the shadows with eyes gleaming and muscles coiled, chastened but wild and dangerous still, ready to spring upwards at the first sign of weakness on the part of its persecutors. He would be ill advised to linger.

Damask had been watching the hill anxiously while her twin was out of sight within the pink forest. She was greatly relieved when he reappeared but managed to disguise this fairly successfully. "You took your time," she complained.

Dando shrugged. "Whatever," he said.

"Did you find anything?"

"Oh, just an old dead tree."

They spread out their picnic and set to work polishing off the goodies, both realizing they were ravenous. They ate in silence for a while until Dando remarked, "What I don't understand is why she allowed them to destroy the maze."

"Dark are the ways of the gods to the children of men," quoted Damask unhelpfully.

"Perhaps the maze was unimportant to her; after all it must have been made by ordinary people in the first place. Or maybe she's not as strong as she once was. Maybe there's something stronger. Or maybe…"

"You think too much my brother. Anyway, it's about time we got a move on, otherwise someone's going to start asking questions."

No-one discovered that they had played truant for a day and they slipped seamlessly back into their normal routine. The trip had been for a purpose and the strategy seemed to have worked: the dreams ceased and Dando was able to resume the pretence of being a simple straightforward young man with no hang ups and no psychological complications. To start with, however, he at last nerved himself to go to his formidable parent and argue Doll's case before him.

"Think how good she has been to us, Father: Dantor, Doris, Dinah, me and Damask, big Donnie, little Donnie, Daphne, Dymphney, Douglas, Dothric – the whole lot. We couldn't have got by without her; she's been a real brick. A-and that thing… the thing that happened… i-it wasn't her fault… she thought she was acting for the best… well, how could she have known…? S-she loved him… the baby…"

The Dan frowned and brusquely dismissed the boy, not wanting to hear more of his faltering pleas for clemency, but a little later the bruised and ill-used Doll returned to the house although in a very menial capacity.

Dando tried to find out what had happened to Ann. Despite having had no contact with her for over two years she was always within his thoughts. At the start of his quest he made the mistake of alerting Potto to his intentions. "Potto, is Ann at the Justification?"

"Oh no Lord, I don't think that be likely."

"But you said she was – you said she was with her grandmother."

"Oh no Lord – I misremember saying that."

Dando realized that, despite Potto's affection for him, his trustworthiness was in question because he belonged to the ruling class. He saddled up his pony and rode down to the inn, armed with an elaborate fiction that would allow him to thoroughly examine the premises.

"The Castle Dan Watchdog troop is thinking of mounting a scouting expedition in this part of the valley early next year and we're not going to camp because of the season. Can I look round your inn to see if it's capable of providing suitable accommodation for the members over two or three nights?"

Mrs Humpage, for it was our old friend, had to hide a smile when confronted by this very young ambassador.

"Certainly, m'Lord. I'll show you round meself. Where would you like to start?"

"Well, the kitchens I suppose, and then the bedrooms of course… and the stables…"

The inn seemed to be overrun with a plethora of servants, amongst whom were several attached-nibblers, and some that appeared to be more in the nature of casual workers. One particular individual, a red-headed fellow who was busy forking fodder down from the hay loft, caught his eye. Stocky and powerful, with an air of

167

bellicosity about him, this retainer lacked the usual
Nablan's cringing humility, so much so that for a moment
Dando doubted that he belonged to the valley's drudges
until he caught a flash of brilliant blue as the young man
shot him a speaking resentful glance. Dando felt that a
challenge had been issued and was puzzled and
disconcerted. Mrs Humpage droned on and he followed
her in and out of doorways, up and down stairs, out to the
yard at the back, where he noted the nibbler shacks
attached to the wall. His eyes darted to and fro looking
for a complexion with the delicate transparency and
luminosity of frosted glass, for hair weightless and
colourless as marsh mist, for eyes like shadows on snow
and for that unexpected smile which illuminated the
rather pensive little face so that sunlight seemed to be
burning its way through haze, turning it warm and golden
from within. But Ann was nowhere to be seen. They
ended in Mrs Humpage's parlour where he was given
refreshment.

"Well m'Lord, I can offer lodgings a cut or two
above what you'll discover in the rest of Deep Hallow. I
come from down around the Great River meself and can
teach the people in this locality a thing or two about
hospitality. We'll do our best for your Watchdogs, I can
guarantee. What do you say?"

"I must report back to my troop leader," said
Dando uncomfortably, and then in desperation, "we're
looking for a nibbler named Hilda Hannah Arbericord,
she's run away from her service at Castle Dan. Is she here
by any chance?"

Mrs Humpage's expression changed subtly and
her face took on a closed look. "We don' 'ave no run-

away nibblers," she said, and with that Dando had to be content.

Because he could not forget Ann he found it hard to move on. Over and over he recalled every minute of the time they had shared, and he then went on to construct new narratives, new dramas, starring the two of them. As he grew older these fantasies became more sensual and erotic, causing him excitement and shame in equal measure. He remembered Damask's advice to take the little Nablan as his *pet*, his concubine, which he was legally entitled to do at the age of fourteen, a time that was fast approaching. To have a subordinate sexual partner, chosen from the valley's underdogs, was considered a healthy move for a boy of the dominant race, and he believed that if he expressed the wish, his family would do their best to find this particular girl for him, whether she was beneath a Gleptish roof or within an unattached-nibbler's dwelling. The temptation was strong to use this route to discover her whereabouts but he rejected it with revulsion. How could he even contemplate such a thing! *Oh, Annie, Annie!*

A few weeks before he was due to join the Outriders he asked his elder brother if he had any idea where the girl had gone. This was a question he had posed to many people by now, in a could-not-care-less, not-really-bothered, hardly-worth-your-answering manner.

"Well," said Dantor, from the vantage point of his eighteen years, "she was a pretty little hussy. I reckon she might be down in one of the cat houses in Gateway."

Dando almost stopped breathing. He had never considered such a possibility and was shocked beyond measure. The idea was so disturbing that he had no choice, as soon as he opted to take his military training in the border town at the head of the Eastern Drift, but to try and find out if it could be true. As a consequence he soon got the reputation amongst his fellow cadets of being a bit of a lad, of pushing the plough around as they termed it. His friends were puzzled however.

"Why fork out good money for what you can get for free?" they asked.

"I'm looking for someone," he replied mildly. This was met by a series of derisive raspberries, but was no more than the truth. Systematically he paid a visit to every Gateway brothel, dropping in at the Mares Nest, the Horny Hen, the Rising Sun, the Spread Eagle and all the rest. He described Ann, giving her age, telling them he wanted this particular girl. Never did they turn him away, despite his youth. As he waited in one of the business-like little rooms a girl always came in to him. Sometimes she fitted the description, sometimes she was nothing like; some were much older, some even younger, none of them was Ann. He talked to them, learned their histories, where they came from, paid them, went away without touching them. "This isn't her," he said before he left, "are you sure there's no one else?" Some were mere children.

At last one of the madams took pity on him and made her own enquiries.

"I've asked around and I don't think the person you describe has ever been part of our profession, no, not even as somebody's pet. Several of my ladies say quite emphatically she's not on the game. It's odd, the nibblers in particular seem so sure; I think they must know something about her. Tell me again, where was it you last saw her...?"

Dando puzzled sombrely over his predicament. Who was this wraith he was in thrall to? She had grown with him - fourteen, fifteen, sixteen, seventeen. After all this time he no longer felt hopeful of finding her. She might well be dead for all he knew, and yet she lived, an inner reality more tangible than any flesh and blood girl, because she had been part of his own substance since birth, the other half of him. He had remained true to her - *Mine own true love*.

It was in a melancholy mood that he reached the top end of the clough and stood looking out having gained his objective.

There's eternity,
And below it the circling world,
Turning in time's shadow.

Chapter eight

The valley's remote western extension was not
the light-filled bowl that Dando remembered from his
previous visit. The day had clouded over and was
threatening rain. It was long past noon and he was
starting to feel hungry, but, on this occasion, he had
omitted to bring any food. He slipped from Attack's back
while still within the mouth of the ravine, noticing, as he
did so, the changes that time had wrought. A
transformation had occurred that made him realize how,
in its heyday, the hand of man had been largely
responsible for the appearance of this circular adjunct to
his homeland. When he and Damask had visited the holy
place at twelve years old it had been deserted for only
two years since the Dan's intervention. Now another five
years had passed and wild nature was rampaging over the
terrain. Trees had begun to grow, mainly alders and
willows with a few pines interspersed. Contours were
blurring, dark thorny bramble bushes had created a dense
tangled barrier, barring the way. There were no pink
flowers waving in the breeze any more; there was no
breeze, everything was quiet and still; the hush had

returned. He listened anxiously for signs of life, but heard nothing, apart from a solitary caw which indicated that there was at least one bird somewhere in the vicinity. Attack sidestepped restlessly, his perturbation adding to the general sense of unease, and, as Dando stood there straining his eyes and ears, the earth moved. Through his feet he felt a vibration, and this shudder was accompanied by a low rumble, almost below the threshold of hearing; it was like experiencing thunder underground. At the same time a flock of rooks exploded into the air from amongst the few mature trees in situ squawking loudly. Somewhere this tremor must have an epicentre and it seemed that Juddering Hill might be living up to its name. Attack gave a terrified neigh and bolted forwards into the open while Dando hung on grimly to the reins, getting severely scratched by passing briars for his pains as he was dragged along. When he finally managed to bring the horse to a stop they were some distance from the clough in a small clearing by the southernmost part of the cliff. He hitched Attack to a branch and stood recovering his breath, thinking hard.

The nightmares were plaguing him again. He wanted to free himself from the persecution. It seemed logical to presume that what had worked once would work again. It was on this premise that he had set out that morning, intending to repeat the tactic that had had a successful outcome when he was much younger. As with the tremor, the source of the first part of his dream appeared to be the goddess's shrine - ergo, the solution to the problem, the cure for the malady, would be to go straight to the heart of darkness and confront the one who lurked there. He was asking the same question: *How can I rid myself of this incubus?* and therefore the same

answer should suffice: *Face your demons*. But time had
passed. During the earlier trip he had found the Midda
apparently deserted; if there had been something to fear it
had been driven into the depths, and he had been well out
of reach of its claws. Now he was not so sure of his
ground. He put his hand in his pocket and pulled out a
small strap that he could fix tightly round his arm if
necessary by means of a buckle, and he felt for his sword,
secure in its scabbard at his belt. Yes, if things turned
nasty he thought he knew how he could escape. After all,
he remembered hearing Tom say, many years before, *It
misgives me she be out for his blood*. He returned the
strap to his pocket and plunged into the jungle of new
growth, making for the marsh and, beyond that, the hill.

A short while later he climbed, wet and muddy,
onto the mound's southern side and then scrambled up to
the level summit. Saplings and immature shrubs obscured
his view across the wide expanse that had once been a
sort of open-air temple in days long past. As no brambles
had gotten a hold on this isolated island he could have
slipped easily between the vegetation and made his way
to the centre. He knew immediately however that this was
out of the question. His skin had been invaded by goose-
bumps, warning him of danger, and his sixth sense was
again working overtime, because s*he* was here, he had
never been more certain of anything in his life, he could
detect her aura, the atmosphere seethed with menace as if
lightening were about to strike. Standing at the margins
of the flat area he felt horribly vulnerable and cursed
himself for his foolishness in approaching so close to the
focus of power. An urge to flee possessed him but he
resisted it, guessing that this would be courting disaster;
instead he determined to see things through as best he

could, letting the devil take the hindmost. But how? What was he to do? Slowly an idea began to form in his mind that would necessitate his attracting the attention of the demiurge, even of communicating with it.

When I was led here at around seven years old, he thought defiantly, beginning his campaign, *I was defenceless - you manoeuvred me into the Wynde and I would have perished had it not been for Tom. But things are different now, old girl, we're into a whole new ball game. You may get a surprise.* He waited to see if there would be any sort of response to his non-verbal provocation and yes – there it came – an unaccountable restlessness which could only be satisfied if he took a step away from the perimeter, and then another step… and then another… Obstinately he thrust out his jaw and erected a mental barrier to block the alluring temptation. He grasped the hilt of his sword and pulled it from its sheath. Holding the naked blade between his hands upright before him, he said aloud, "If I can walk round the edge of this hill and back to my starting point without straying, the dreams will cease for good and I will go free."

He had flung down the gauntlet; now he waited with his inner receptors on full alert, to see if the challenge would be accepted. For a long while all he could detect, coming from the centre, was an undercurrent of rapaciousness tempered by cunning. At last, very faintly, he seemed to hear within his skull the words, *"So be it."*

Immediatcly, but perhaps unwisely, he laid the sword on the ground to act as a marker and, turning to his right, began to walk eastwards, following the rim of the hill in an anti-clockwise direction. How far did he have to

go? It should be possible to work it out. He actually
remembered having been taught by his tutor that the
formula for the circumference of a circle was two pi r. So
the radius, the distance to the middle? – it was probably
about a hundred feet. And pi? – that was three point
something. Therefore to find the answer one would
simply have to multiply three point something by one
hundred and then again by two... er... um... He gave up.
Well, it was quite a long way anyway and it was not
going to be easy, it might take every ounce of
determination that he possessed, but as long as he stuck
to the path... Path?! What was he on about? There was
no path! For the last few minutes he had seen it clearly
stretching ahead of him. Now he wrenched his mind back
to reality. The path disappeared and he found himself
already several paces nearer to the centre. He hastily
regained the edge of the hilltop, his heart beating wildly.
That was sneaky! That was really sneaky to deceive him
like that! But it taught him a valuable lesson, he must be
constantly alert, on his guard at all times.

He had been hungry; now he realized he was
absolutely starving. His stomach began to churn and to
make matters worse a delicious smell was floating across
the flat circular summit which lay on his left-hand-side.
He stared in that direction and beheld a sort of low tripod
on which was placed a metal bowl within which were
pieces of glowing charcoal. Over these a rack had been
laid supporting chunks of meat and vegetables spitted on
skewers. Beside this odd-looking brazier stood a table
holding sauces, bowls of salad, bread, butter and empty
plates. Dando's mouth watered and at the same time his
curiosity was fired by this strange cooking device; he had
never seen anything quite like it in the kitchens he had

visited. The temptation to investigate was strong and hard to resist, but resist it he did, and the vision faded along with the smell.

He smiled ruefully. *How come you know me so well, old woman?* he asked himself.

He half expected the next illusion. After food comes drink. He had heard the expression *a raging thirst*, now for the first time he understood what it meant. His tongue swelled and clove to the roof of his mouth; his saliva vanished; he felt his lips harden and crack. Even his eyes started to burn because the tears had dried up; there seemed no moisture left in his entire body. He was lost in a parched desert and felt he had not drunk for a week. He realized he had never really been thirsty before. At this point the bushes and trees on the flat area vanished and were replaced by a limpid pool. Just a few feet, a few paces to the side, and he could fall to his knees and plunge his face into the precious liquid, ending the torment. *No, no, keep walking, keep walking, it's just a will-o'-the-wisp.* This time the phantasm faded only slowly. Even after time had moved on his mouth remained dry and he suspected it would continue to do so for several hours.

All the same he was making good progress. Already he had passed the easternmost point of the circle, closest to the clough, and was covering the distance to the northern extremity. But something was accompanying him on his circuit: it was a little black creature, flopping and scrambling along to his left, a few yards distant. He recognized a bird with a broken wing, he recognized Chocky. But Chocky had died while he was away in Gateway, Chocky was dead! All the same it was difficult to ignore the little jackdaw, struggling to keep up with him, and in obvious pain and distress; however much he denied its existence the image persisted; it was not easy to harden his heart and reject his little friend. A single step towards the bird though would probably result in the creature fluttering out of reach, and then, pursuing it, one stride would lead to another until before he knew... He guessed that he would never be allowed to effect a rescue.

The northern point was gained and passed and he was more than halfway round the ring when his foot seemed to catch in something, or rather his foot was caught and held. He fell forward onto hands and knees – no, not his knees – he was *standing* on all fours, on all four feet! There was fur on his front limbs, grey fur, he sensed that his scull had changed shape and his eyes had altered position in his head. He felt the weight of a tail and the twitch of a whisker. To his ears came an eager whimpering – did it come from his own throat? Before his long dark muzzle he saw the rump of a female wolf with the tail obligingly cocked to one side and everywhere the overwhelming, acrid, irresistible scent of a bitch on heat. He moved to cover her, he arose on his hind legs, rose up on the neat tip-toe hind legs of a wolf and took two mincing steps, like those of a circus dog, forward; and in regaining an upright stance he recovered his human form. His brain reeled. The whole metamorphosis had come and gone in a flash; he had been delivered from something terrible, but not through his own resourcefulness; he had escaped, it seemed, by a mere fluke. And if he had remained in wolf shape and had united with the female, what would have been the result? He was not sure how this story had been meant to end but he could guess. His fertile adolescent imagination immediately supplied a lurid plot. He had watched dogs mate and seen the difficulties they sometimes got into, clamped together and unable to part for more than half an hour at a time. It seemed likely that the objective had been to trap his willy inside the female and then to haul him off to the centre of the shrine with the intention of separating him both from the bitch and from his manhood. Did goddesses suffer from penis envy, or was she hoping for a brainwashed gelded slave? He knew his own people believed that some of her priests had actually undergone this mutilation. He shuddered. What was she going to turn him into next, and would he be so lucky on another occasion?

He hurried forward, rounding the section furthest from the ravine and passing the western compass point. So far most of the threats and lures had come from the area to his left. He looked that way and was surprised to see that a stockade had appeared circling the centre of the maze with a gate opening directly towards him. Why should that serve as a temptation to leave his chosen route? Suddenly he detected movement in the corner of his right eye and, turning, reacted almost too late, for boiling over the edge of the hill, rising up from the marsh, came a scurrying army of vermin: rats and mice mainly, but with a fair scattering of reptiles and huge insects. His hand flew to his sword but found it absent, he turned to run to the stockade, but instead flung himself flat on the ground with his head buried in his arms. Then they were on him, suffocating, burying him. "It's not real, it's not real, it's not real!" he gabbled, and indeed it was not, for the multitude passed over and vanished. When he raised his head there was no sign of them and only the stinging of his exposed flesh proved that he had felt their sharp little claws.

Now he was nearly home. Ahead of him, not far off, he thought he saw a gleam half hidden in the grass - his weapon - marking the finishing point. He relaxed a little and his pace slackened. Someone was coming across the level ground, someone small and fair with a smile of greeting exclusively for him. The girl came to a stop and held out her hands. He gasped and tried to speak, until eventually the word emerged as a strangled croak - "Annie!" It was shock that rooted him to the spot, not any caution or awareness of danger. She nodded and beckoned for him to come to her, and he would have done so, except that as he looked he glimpsed something not quite right about her face, something invisible unless seen through the eyes of love. For a moment he was back, at seven years old, in that late winter dawn, watching a beautiful woman floating down Spring Road from the fastness of Lady Wood. "Y-you're not…" he faltered, and as he did so the girl changed and became that woman, and then she changed again and he glimpsed the bloated idol from Tom's workshop, and then a crone, old beyond imagining, and then something totally alien, hideous and terrifying. "No!" he yelled. The apparition sank into the earth and was gone. He leapt forward along the edge, flying onwards across the last few yards, until he could stoop, snatch up his sword, and hold it aloft in victory. "Made it!" he cried.

Why did he think she would honour her side of the bargain, a goddess renowned for her treachery? There was an explosion of anger on the psychic plane, an eruption of fury. For a moment he stood there, battered by the storm, and then it was as if the ground shot upwards while his legs buckled under a multiplication of G forces. Crashing backwards onto the earth, the breath was expelled from his lungs and all his limbs trebled, quadrupled in weight. There was just one thing he knew for certain – he was going to die. But by some foresight, some premonition, he had made provision for this moment, for Tom had said *she be out for his blood.* His hand still clutched his regained sword, and in the position in which he had fallen it lay across his body and athwart his left arm. It was almost impossible to move, but by some huge physical effort he dragged the blade a few inches to the right and the sharp edge cut into his wrist. Bright globules of blood flowered along the incision, grew, merged and flowed down unstoppably into the black soil beneath. Now he had burnt his boats. The strap that he had brought along to use as a tourniquet was in his pocket, but it might as well have been on the moon for all its usefulness at this present moment. If this did not work he would die anyway, the only difference being that he would have killed himself rather than succumbing to the malignancy of the goddess. Centuries, aeons, seemed to pass as the lifeblood leaked from his body; he felt himself growing weaker, while a black veil descended across his vision. Then the force dragging him earthwards lessened slightly, the first indication being a slight easing in his struggle to breathe. His right hand crept towards his pocket, he found the strap and managed to loop it round his wounded arm. He lay panting for a few moments and then with a tug which took all his resolution, pulled it tight and fastened it. The bleeding ceased. By no means could he get to his feet, or even onto his knees. He turned over and, inch by inch, with many pauses to recover his strength, dragged himself to the hill's edge before allowing his body to half tumble, half roll down the steep incline towards the boggy bottom where he came to rest half immersed in mud.

How he got across the marsh would forever remain a mystery. Having gained the bank on the farther side he lost consciousness, perhaps actually falling asleep from sheer fatigue, whether for a few minutes or more than an hour he could not be certain. When he came to, it had started to rain and he immediately thought of Attack. He had left the horse tied to a tree with scarcely a backward glance; now he was filled with remorse at his neglect. Cautiously, with the aid of a convenient branch, he pulled himself upright and tested his limbs, finding that, after all, he was able to stand. He felt weak, debilitated and inclined to faintness but with staunchness and determination believed he could overcome these handicaps and press on. Slowly retracing his steps through the confusing copses and thickets of the glen's margins he eventually came to the place where he thought he had abandoned the horse, but Attack was no longer there. One clearing looks much the same as another, and he imagined, at first, that he had come to the wrong place, until he saw the snapped off tether still attached to the tree. A considerable amount of force must have been used to break the leash and a sense of apprehension began to grow in his breast. He roamed to and fro whistling and calling, his ears attuned to catch any reply, for normally Attack would answer him when he heard his voice, but the horse did not respond and his search became more and more desperate as a rising tide of anxiety overwhelmed him. He was at least half a mile from his starting point, and beginning to loose hope, when he stumbled over his mount wedged in between a dense spinney and the rock face at the periphery of the valley. The animal was standing completely still, his head drooping almost to the ground, his normally gleaming coat caked with sweat, and some ugly gashes visible on his side. He gave no indication that he was aware of Dando's presence. The boy fondled his neck and mane, caressing him, trying to produce a response by babying the huge beast.

"Poor old fellow, what's up? What's happened to you? Are you hurt, my beauty? Never you mind old chap, I'll look after you, you'll be alright. Don't be frightened."

The horse's eyes, normally so expressive, stared sightlessly ahead as if haunted by invisible demons; there was no recognition in them at all. When Dando tried to lead him out of the crevice in which he had taken refuge he discovered something equally bad if not worse. As Attack put a hoof forward one of his front legs almost gave way; he had sustained some traumatic injury and was desperately lame. This was a calamity of the first water: the Dans' once-in-a-lifetime investment damaged, perhaps, for good and all and he, Dando, entirely to blame. Now he began to see why horses had been forbidden to enter the upper valley. He ran his hands carefully down the maimed limb, trying to ascertain the extent of the injury. He was no expert horse doctor, but he had spent a lot of time around the castle's stables, and his gut instinct told him that there were no broken bones; as for the horse's broken spirit, that was another matter entirely. But now he had to decide what to do for the best. It was obvious that Attack could not stay here while he went for help; the Midda was inimical to the horse's well being. The nearest refuge was Castle Dan itself, and that lay miles away. All the same there seemed little alternative. He would have to lead him down through the clough and over the intervening distance, however long it took. They would go slowly and take frequent rests.

As the day wore on towards evening, boy and horse made their way across league after league of dark desolate country, through steady relentless rain, until they arrived, both equally soaked and exhausted, at the Dan mansion. The grooms were just retiring for the night, but one glimpse of the great horse's condition was enough to set them working to try and rectify the harm done as best they could. Dando worked alongside them. No questions were asked, and he did not feel up to giving an explanation; his privileged position protected him for the moment. When he was satisfied that everything possible had been fixed that could be fixed, he slipped away and stood for a while under shelter in the stable yard. He knew that now it was his duty to report to his father and face the music, but after all that had happened that day he did not feel he had the resolution for this final ordeal. It was undeniable that the skies were going to fall on him very soon - the Dan would hear what had happened by morning - but meantime he needed a breathing space in which to prepare himself. So, weary, wet-through and weak from loss of blood, Dando set out to walk the miles to High Harrow - there was no way that he would have dared borrow a horse. It was around the hour of two the next morning by the time he made it to the town house, looking like a drowned rat and, having muttered to the ever-faithful Potto, who had waited up for him, that Attack was at the castle and could not be put on parade, groped his way to his room.

It seemed only minutes later that his servant was leaning over the bed and telling him he was late for school.

"Go away, leave me alone"

"But it be time to get up Lord."

"Leave me alone."

"But Lord, me dear, you missed yesterday as well. What will become of you? I be afeared what your father will say!" Dando heaved an enormous sigh and spoke patiently to the concerned old man. "Potto, stop doing my worrying for me. I'm in the deepest of deep doo-doos as it is. Going in today won't make a wit of difference, one way or the other. Now let me sleep."

In his heart of hearts he knew quite well he would never be attending the school again. He turned over and fell into a slumber which lasted several hours.

Hounds may lose the scent
If they track their prey over the brook
And on towards the stars.

Chapter nine

Everard Tetherer Trooly, unattached-nibbler,
alias Captain Judd, alias the Fox, notched an arrow to his
long bow and slowly and silently pulled back the string.
Before him, in a clearing in the forest, lit by the early
morning light, lay a charming pastoral scene. A group of
hinds, knee deep in mist, grazed beside their fawns,
completely unaware of the man who stood like a statue
within the margins of the forest. Carefully he selected his
target, an immature doe, paused long enough to be sure of
his aim, then loosed the arrow, straight to the heart. The
animal fell as if pole-axed; the rest of the herd leapt into
motion; the idyll had been destroyed; death had come to
the glade. Foxy walked forward to examine the illicit kill,
having first looked carefully around before leaving the
shelter of the trees.

Foxy: although this was how he was known to
his people, his name spoken with a mixture of awe and
apprehension by most of the Nablar, with a kind of
incredulous hope by a few of the more rebellious young,
he did not welcome the soubriquet; he would have
preferred to be known as Judd, after a legendary hero of

his people who had been instrumental in cementing their unique relationship with the Mother, or so it was believed. However, he was stuck with the title, there was no help for it. He had been born to be a fox, the outcast animal, because of his elusiveness, because of his crafty flouting of the rules, because of his red hair. Fox he was called and fox he was by nature, fiercely independent, stealthy, quick to give hunters the slip, a sniffer out of traps, a sly stealer.

He picked up the deer, hoisted it onto his shoulders and set out for his base, a small cave hidden in a defile on the south side of the valley. The journey would take about an hour. There he would butcher the kill and distribute the meat to others like himself, living beyond the pale, before adopting his servile guise and making his way to the Justification to work his shift as a general dogsbody covering the dirty jobs and the heavy lifting - lifting such as climbing the stairs with buckets of hot water in hand as he had done the previous evening when their new guest had required a bath. The landlady, being from down around the Kymer river and therefore unconcerned with local politics providing the current situation did not impinge on her business, was not particular whom she employed as long as they were reliable. Foxy had haunted the Justification for a number of years, drawn there like a moth to a flame, the flame in question being a young Nablan girl know to the inn's inhabitants as Hild. Foxy had appointed himself her guardian, for he was one of the few frequenters of the hostelry who knew that this was the Culdee's daughter, the Culdee who to all intents and purposes had been merely the Dans' cobbler and yet had been so ruthlessly slain at the same time as the Midda was desecrated, and that, as such, she was of huge significance to the Nablan race and to Foxy's plans for his people. Foxy had travelled outside the valley and had learned a thing or two in foreign parts. He had returned to his homeland with intoxicating ideas of rebellion and revolution.

To reach his refuge he did not follow a track but took a direct route through the woods, his sharp fox's nose leading him in the right direction. Across his path on the long walk ran several deep cut lonely lanes that he must cross in order to reach his destination. It was extremely unusual to meet anyone in this unfrequented part of the valley, and as he slid down the embankment onto one roadway he was not paying sufficient attention to his surroundings. Only as he reached the middle of the track did he register the sound of hooves approaching from around a bend. It was a mad scramble to get himself and his booty up the bank on the other side and into the concealment of the trees. Then, curious, he turned to discover the identity of the solitary horseman, travelling at speed through this lonely place. As soon as they came in sight he knew both the steed and its elegant and richly dressed young rider: this was the Dans' great black thoroughbred, the winner of the Seven League Circuit and absolutely unmistakable; on his back, sitting easily in the saddle, a member of the elite, the crème de la crème, the Dan's second son. Quick as a flash Foxy again had an arrow fitted to his bow and the string pulled back. The moment to loose it came and went but he did nothing. Although a masterful hunter who had made drastic inroads into Gleptish game preserves, he had never, as yet, slaughtered one of his own species. The horseman disappeared round another bend and the sound of hooves died away into the distance.

Foxy hated all Glepts, but most of all he hated the Dans; and of all the members of Clan Dan, glimpsed occasionally from a distance in their despicable magnificence, he resented, in particular, this boy who had just passed him by. The girl at the inn, the Culdee's daughter, was his especial concern. One day he dreamt of seeing her reinstated as the high priestess of her people, the focus that would draw his race together and unite them in a glorious uprising. Nablan priestesses, with a few notable exceptions, normally remained chaste throughout their lives, for the general feeling among their fellow countrymen was that to be the consort of such a one would be to commit a sort of blasphemy. As she reached sexual maturity he guarded Hilda jealously, suspiciously watching any men who came near her, trying to shield her from lascivious glances. But there was a fly in the ointment, the girl had a heart, and that heart was already spoken for, by this Lord Dan Addo in fact whom he had just had within reach of his bow. She had never confessed as much, but Foxy thought he had sufficient proof.

In his early days at the hostelry he had occasionally found himself carrying out tasks in the kitchen as the girl and her grandmother Florence prepared food for the evening meal, and while he worked he listened in to their conversation. Curious about the structure of a noble household, something completely outside his experience, he was all ears as the older woman drew the reluctant girl out to speak about her childhood, that happy time which had eventually come to such a painful end. Foxy listened avidly; after all, any information was grist to his mill and might prove useful when *The Day* came at last. Hild had spent her early years at Castle Dan, where her father had been one of the attached-nibblers in his role as cobbler. He learned that, as was often the case, Nablan and Gleptish children had played together, and Hild, or Ann as she had been known at that time, had made friends with a pair of twins, a boy and a girl, offspring of the Dan himself. She and the boy had had the same wet nurse. It was in speaking of this boy that the girl's expression had softened, her eyes moistened, her voice took on a note of yearning. Foxy was both disquieted and disgusted; as far as he was concerned his virgin priestess should harbour tender feelings for no-one, least of all for one of the usurping persecutors of his people; she should be without affections; cold; pure; inviolate.

Soon after Hild had come to the inn to live with her grandmother, and had arrived, lost and afraid, traumatized by terrible events, the boy had paid them a visit. Foxy had seen him touring the watering hole and its environs, accompanied by a deferential Mrs Humpage, his eyes swivelling hither and yon, looking, he was sure, for the girl. Fortunately Mr Applecraft had warned him that someone might come from the Castle, and he had spirited Hilda away, only letting her return when he was sure interest had died down. And now, just for a moment, he had had this obstacle to his ambitions at his mercy and had failed to act. He would probably never get such a good opportunity again, and yet he had let it pass him by. Why? What was wrong with him? Had he not got the guts to kill one of the accursed Glepts who deserved far worse than death for their crimes? When *The Day* came at last there would have to be lots of killing, he knew that much.

Shouldering the hind once more Foxy stumped off into the trees, kicking angrily at things that got in his way to relieve his frustration. When not under observation, our poacher walked with a swagger. At five foot seven he could not impress by his height, but his stocky frame was tremendously strong. He went barefoot. Living out of doors for most of the time, he had become impervious to wind and weather, and rarely, except at the inn, wore more than a pair of buckskin breeches and a sleeveless leather jerkin lined with goats' hair. Round his throat hung a necklace of boar's teeth, trophies from his hunting, and at his back were slung his quiver and bow, while on a belt at his waist he carried a knife and small axe. The skin of his upper body was covered in freckles, and freckles all but obscured his round pugnacious face with its prominent brows and lashes and piercingly-blue Nablan eyes. His hair summed up his personality: thick, short and fiercely curling, it flamed red as his own passionate, rebellious nature. To have to act the servant at the Justification, to shuffle and bow and cast down his eyes, to have to bear the suffocating walls and roof over him (yet, on occasions, he slept in a cave!) was a constant trial, but he endured it for Hilda's sake and for the rest of the Nablar whom he longed to awaken.

Arriving at his base in the late morning, he cut up the deer and then went on his rounds, having first kept a portion of the venison for himself (he ate some raw before setting out, not having time to put it over a flame) and making sure to save the choicest cuts to give to Florence for Hild's supper. In the valley of Deep Hallow attached-nibblers were expected to work their fingers to the bone on the minimum of nourishment. The food with which they were provided was of the poorest quality and came in desperately small amounts; they were grudged even the bare necessities to keep body and soul together. Mrs Humpage was meaner than most, and thought nothing of starving her servants, while giving as an excuse the need to economise. For years Foxy had been bringing Hilda a portion of his kill, and standing over her while she ate it, haranguing her meanwhile about Nablan rights, about injustice, about the coming apocalypse. It was thanks to Foxy and the provisions he brought, that she had reached puberty and was entering womanhood. Without him she would probably have remained a gradually fading child until the final collapse.

Most of the meat from his trophy he left at the doors of masterless men, either unattached-nibblers who had not the skills to hunt for their sustenance, or ageing members of his race who had been cast adrift to fend for themselves after a lifetime of service in one of the great households. Foxy was always on the lookout for Nablans whose spirit had not been completely crushed, people with enough foresight and optimism to be able to glimpse his vision of a day when they might cast off the hated yoke and be a free nation once more. But recruiting volunteers for his secret army was uphill work. Most of his kind regarded him as slightly mad, and anticipated a time, not far off, when he would be caught and subjected to the rigours of Gleptish law. The penalties for stealing the *King's beasts* were harsh: flogging, a slit tongue, the loss of hand or ear, even hanging. Foxy however knew the lay of the valley inside and out and the location of all the coverts and bolt holes where, if pursued, he could go to earth. One of his favourite pastimes consisted of slipping through the undergrowth ahead of a Gleptish hunt and, by his mere presence, clearing the nearby woods of all runnable game; he would do this despite the danger of himself becoming the quarry. In the absence of allies mature enough to stand shoulder to shoulder with him in a common cause, for the past year he had been waging a one man guerilla war. He had tried his hand at rick burning and cattle rustling, as well as dabbling in highway robbery and burglary, but was clear-sighted enough to see that he was just acting as an irritant to the valley's rulers. What he needed were men and weapons, and he had neither. Sometimes he felt daunted and depressed at the task he had set himself and wondered why so few of his fellow Nablans dared to share his dreams and ambitions. The reason in fact was staring him in the face; it lay, as was patently obvious, in his very different upbringing, for Foxy had never been taught to grovel or cringe, to believe he was less than a man; if he was a nibbler it was one without a normal nibbler's mentality. His early memories took him back to a time when, at the age of four or five, he had been a wild child, a small feral creature roaming unclothed and alone on the periphery of men's abodes. Even earlier than that there had been a woman, a nourisher, a mother; but one hot day she had gone in the water and he never saw her alive again; there had been a cottage, but after the woman left him the supply of food dried up. In order to carry on living he had had to go where there was food.

A goatherd from somewhere beyond the valley had an arrangement with the Dans which allowed him to graze his flock on the upper slopes of the hills at their northern perimeter during the winter months in exchange for hides, milk and meat. In the summer he drove his goats up lofty canyons which climbed into the western mountains. There he lived without sight of another

human face for months on end. One hard winter, while on
the Dans' land, he surprised a naked shaggy-haired
urchin rooting among the rubbish outside his back door.
He enticed him into a byre - he would on no account
come under a roof – and fed him there throughout the
winter until in the spring the waif took himself off just
before the goatherd made his usual summer migration.
On returning to lower pastures with the bitter weather he
found the child waiting for him, apparently ready to
accept a certain amount of domesticity. The boy had no
language to speak of, communicating mainly by whines
and barks. Valentine, the goatherd, wondered if this was a
sign that he had spent part of his brief life among wolves.
The man decided he needed an appellation.

"By your looks you're one of these here nibblers.
They go in for these fiddly long winded names. So, let's
see now - how about Egbert – no, Everard, that's a good
name – belonged to my brother, the one who went for a
soldier – haven't seen hide nor hair of him since. Everard
Tetherer – that was my grandma's name on my mother's
side – the one that came from Pickwah. And then there's
Trooly. Gave me my first two goats did Sid Trooly.
Everard Tetherer Trooly – sounds like a nibbler."

Slowly he tamed the fierce little creature,
persuaded him to wear clothes, coaxed him into his hut.
He trained him as he would one of his dogs, with a
mixture of discipline and kindness, and like a dog the boy
began to make himself useful, searching out straying
animals, keeping watch for predators. The next summer
Valentine took the lad with him when he made the
journey to his mountain fastness; it made a change to
have someone to talk to. And Foxy, for of course it was
he, soon began to talk back. After the first few words his

194

acquisition of language came easily and fast, seeming more like something recollected than brand new knowledge. From the start he spoke with a Nablan accent.

As a consequence of this upbringing Foxy had spent his childhood either among the western mountains or on the slopes of the valley's northern hills, seeing few people apart from fellow herders and an occasional bird catcher. His adoptive father, the goatherd, imposed a prohibition on venturing down into the valley proper. "That ain't a good place for the likes of you," he warned. "They don't treat nibblers as they should down there."

For several years Foxy obeyed this stricture, but as he approached his final adult height, his chest filled out and his muscles hardened, he became restless. He was bored with his own and Valentine's company, bored with the dogs and most of all bored of the goats. He wanted to see more of the world. One mild winter's day he dressed himself in his best and slipped away early in the morning, making his way along the hills and then down into the centre of the valley where lay the settlement of Low-Town, a vast metropolis in the eyes of the simple goat boy. He walked past the Broad, the lower valley's shallow lake, through the burg's outskirts, through its more densely populated inner regions into the centre and straight into trouble. He was standing halfway down the main street, looking in the window of an outfitters which displayed a dummy decked out in all manner of silks and brocades, jewels, feathers and slashed sleeves. At first he presumed this costume was intended for a woman, until he looked more closely and noticed, beneath the jacket, black velvet pantaloons with white lace ruffles at the knee. Were there men in Deep Hallow who actually wore such effeminate clothing? Suddenly he was presented with just such a one, as a gaudy individual appeared next to him and attempted to elbow him aside with a gruff, "Move over nibbler!"

Foxy, indignant at the rudeness, stood his ground and replied, "Move over y'self. I be here 'afore yew!"

The other's mouth fell open in surprise and he was struck dumb for a moment. Then recovering himself he expostulated "What insolence! How dare you! It's about time you knew your place! Show, damn you!"

Foxy was baffled.

"Show what?" he asked

"Show, damn you, show!" the man yelled

"You don' have to shout," admonished Foxy, "I c'n hear."

The man turned and stared down the street.

"To me, Outriders! To me!" he called.

In a trice Foxy was surrounded by a group of similarly dressed foppish youths who seized him and, despite his attempted resistance, strapped his arms behind his back. Then, in a matter of minutes, he was dragged around the corner and into a building where the local sheriff's court was holding its weekly session. A complaint was laid.

"What's your name nibbler?" the official at the top table asked. Foxy did not reply. "He refuses to give his name," the man said to the scribe who was taking notes.

"Who is your master?"

"I don' hev no master."

"He confesses he is masterless, and is therefore living outside the law, but he is still subject to the process of law. Do you have anything to say nibbler?"

Foxy glared but remained silent. He sensed a collusion amongst everyone else in the room to convict him of some crime, but of what he had no idea. The sheriff scribbled on a piece of paper for less than a minute and then looked up.

"For showing insolence to his betters and failing to make the obedience – twenty lashes – next!" He smashed down his gavel.

During the following half hour Foxy received a harsh lesson in what life has to offer the powerless and unfriended. He was taken to a yard behind the courthouse where he was stripped and tied to a post, following which he was mercilessly flogged by a huge man who seemed to get great satisfaction from his work. Afterwards he was released to lick his wounds, dress himself and creep away, suitably chastened. But it was far too late in the day to teach Foxy either subservience or humility. As he left the town, his shirt sticking to his bloody back, he could scarcely think or even walk straight for the fury and outrage that were churning in his breast. From that moment on the Outriders, and by association all Glepts, acquired an implacable enemy. He vowed in his heart of hearts to do everything in his power to get even with his persecutors and to avenge the brutal act that had been committed against his person

This experience did not stop him from going down into the valley, but from then on he was far more circumspect. He acquired clothes that looked like the sort of homely outsize garments with which the Nablar commonly swathed themselves, and a hood to cover his flaming hair. He found out what *show* meant, and would even, when it was demanded of him, stretch out his three fingered hands in the deferential gesture, although his whole being revolted against the indignity. The purpose behind these expeditions was to discover more about the history of the valley and about the Nablan race, but it was a difficult task he had set himself; most of the underdogs were afraid to speak on such matters. In the end he discovered more from outsiders who had learnt things by hearsay. He observed the relationship between the two races, the Glepts and the Nablar, and confirmed what his foster father had told him: *They don't treat nibblers as they should, down there.* His personal feud expanded to encompass a vendetta on behalf of all his people.

Every so often the goatherd decided to turn some of his animals into cash and he knew he could get a better price for them down on the Kymer Levels, where their silky coats were highly prized, than in Deep Hallow. His habit at such times was to bring the entire flock back to Dan land and hire someone to keep an eye on the animals that were to be left behind while he set off through the valley and down the Incadine Gorge with one of his dogs, driving the goats and kids that he intended to sell before him. There was a large livestock market held once a month in a settlement just beyond the Stumble Stones, which was the name given to the place where the ravine disgorged travellers onto the plain. On the last few occasions Foxy had been the one delegated to act as stand-in back in the Valley, but when he was around nineteen - he could never be quite sure of his age - he asked Valentine if he could accompany him.

"I'd like to take a peek down 'long the Great River, Dadda, and with me 'long you won't be needin' Towser. If I'm on side I reckon us'll do pretty well – us might manage a few more beasts between we."

Valentine thought it over and agreed that Foxy could become a member of the party. There were some purchases he wished to make in a town a little further north; perhaps the boy could deputise for him and save him a journey; his lumbago was making long distance walking a bit of a trial. They set out at high summer and arrived in good time at the bottom of the Eastern Drift where Foxy got his first glimpse of the plains. He had not realized the world was so large. They obtained a good price for their animals and Valentine put some of the money into Foxy's hands.

"Tell me what you're going to buy again."

Foxy rehearsed the list he had memorized: mainly chemicals for tanning hides and preserving meat, plus sugar, salt and goat medicine.

"Good boy. Buy something for yourself while you're about it. I think you'll find everything you need at Millfield. Keep to the main road and don't linger. Once you've got the stuff come straight back. I'll go up to the cabin and we can have a nice meal when you get home."

Foxy grinned and embraced the older man but with no intention of doing what he was told. Millfield might be a few miles away, but his plan was to travel much farther, to the end of the road in fact, because at the end of the road lay the Delta City, the great water-girt metropolis of Vadrosnia Poule. Drossi, a free trade port, was the town where a multitude of ways came together and mingled, a meeting place for peoples of all nations. *See Drossi and die* was a common saying in the country round. Foxy had no intention of dying but he did want to see.

He hitched a lift on a mail coach which crossed the plains in a matter of days. It seemed no time at all

before he arrived at the beginning of the Green Dolphin
Avenue, part bridge, part causeway, which formed the
only paved access into the renowned city by land. Drossi
had been built on a series of islands at the point where the
Kymer River split into many channels before flowing out
to sea. The city's symbol, a dolphin, could be seen in all
parts of the town, carved into walls, on flags, inlaid into
sidewalks; even the bollards on the quayside at East
Harbour and at the Armornia Dock were in the form of
dolphins. Now Foxy walked between the long rows of
similar monolithic statues on the approach, gazing up at
them goggle eyed, while at the same time dodging the
continuous streams of traffic entering and leaving the
City. On passing through the Land Gate it was hard not to
appear the complete yokel when confronted by
magnificence such as he had not imagined even in his
wildest dreams. Foxy had come a long way from the
naïve adolescent who had been overawed by the little
hamlet of Low Town, but nothing had prepared him for
Drossi's splendours. He gawked at the palaces, some
seven stories high or more, decorative as wedding cakes,
lining the pungent-smelling water courses, at the soaring
temples and churches and at the great sea-going tall ships
in the Poule. He stared at the skyline with its gold-plated
roofs and domes and at the pavement beneath his feet
embellished with intricate mosaics. Everywhere he
looked he saw glorious colours: azures, aquamarines,
turquoises, violets, the blue water reflecting the blue sky
and the sun sparkling back off the water onto the
buildings in rippling patterns of light so that even the
coolest darkest corners became bathed in a mysterious
deep sea glow. And the people, the people: every skin
colour imaginable was represented, from alabaster to blue

black, while a multitude of languages assaulted his ears! The city's gloriousness was so impressive that it took sometime before he began to notice the shanty towns, built over water, rimming the more prosperous areas and the beggars haunting the side alleys.

Foxy had intended to stay only a day or two, just long enough to make his purchases and give the place the once over, but two days stretched to four and then to a week and then to two weeks. The claustrophobia that this crowded city engendered in him made it necessary to take periodic breaks from the teeming streets and go to a place with quiet skies and wide horizons. And so sometime after midnight he would set off along one of the dykes on the edge of town until he came to a rickety wooden bridge that led to a small eyot where he had set up camp. Here he would snatch a few hours sleep before heading back to the cafés and specialised restaurants, to the vast taverns and tiny dimly-lit bars, to the shopping arcades, to the markets and piazzas with their tumblers and street singers, and to the theatres, the floating outdoor stages and the music halls.

One evening, sitting and drinking a libation at a pavement café he fell into conversation with a shifty-looking individual who offered him sex at a price. Feeling flush, and with vague notions of loosing his virginity far away from his usual haunts, he took up the man's offer after first making sure his weapons were all present and correct. The pimp conducted him to a slummy quarter of town, to damp tenements filled with a warren of small rooms. Here he was introduced to a woman, not in her first youth, but judging by her highly-educated voice, surprisingly well bred. She resignedly submitted to Foxy's extremely inexpert and puppyish

advances, guiding him through the experience and
ensuring that his first foray into the world of sexual
intercourse was not an unmitigated disaster. Foxy, to his
surprise, found the encounter not greatly to his liking, but
curiosity drew him back several more times, until the
whore, thinking he had succumbed to her charms, began
to refer to him as *my little backwoods bumpkin.* But Foxy,
on that first visit, had heard hints of a sad story in which
she had been involved that to him did not seem sad at all.

Along this part of the Middle Sea's southern
coast lay a number of city states, linked together in a
confederation entitled the Seven Sisters League. The
treaty between them had been drawn up giving equal
weight to trade and defence, and they had all benefited,
from Pickwah in the west to Kingscauldie in the far east.
But Kingscauldie was now misnamed for it was no longer
a monarchy. The citizens of that small realm, incensed by
years of bad government and corruption, had risen in
revolt against their rulers. The army had deserted en
masse and joined the insurgents and the dynasty had been
sent packing. Incendiary phrases had been bandied about
such as *the rights of man, equality for all* and *power to
the people.* They sang about the mythological progenitors
of their nation:-

When Darren delved and Sophia span,
Who was then the gentleman?'

The prostitute trembled as she recalled her terror
at hearing the mob baying outside the windows of her
house, for she had been one of the nobility who had had
to flee, and had escaped with just a few jewels to her
name; many of her friends and relatives had not been so
lucky. Now the royal family, their lords and ladies and
any members of the upper classes that had managed to

cross the border had thrown themselves on the mercy of the governments of neighbouring cities, and were living as refugees in various places up and down the coast, coping as best they could. She had been reduced to espousing the oldest profession of all and goodness knows how long that would remain a viable option.

"I'm not as young as I was," she sniffed self-pityingly.

The revolutionary council of the new republic had issued a proclamation insisting that the state's foreign policy had not changed, that they would honour the pacts made with the rest of the League members. But the other cities were looking askance at their little sister at the end of the line, uncomfortably aware, for the first time, of injustices within their own systems.

Foxy lingered on in Drossi, excited beyond measure by these revelations, wondering whether to make the journey to Kingscauldie in order to meet the instigators of the uprising. By listening in to conversations in the eating and drinking places he frequented he made the acquaintance of a group of young people who he discovered were keen for a similar revolt to take place in their own city. They met in each other's houses when their parents were away, drank wine, partook of various exotic substances, and discussed strategy, adopting impressive revolutionary names to disguise their identities. As a fellow subversive Foxy kept them company for a few evenings until he decided that this proposed insurgency was all talk and no action. Besides, these nicely-spoken youngsters belonged to a social stratum that, as far as he was concerned, would be the first up against the wall when *The Day* came at last. Then his money ran out. He was brought back to earth

with a bump. Where were the goods that he had promised
to purchase? But Foxy was nothing if not resourceful. A
few late night expeditions to the part of town where the
supply merchants kept their stores and he had purloined
most of what he needed. He beat a hasty retreat from the
city, his swag over his shoulder, and set out for Deep
Hallow.

As soon as he returned to the valley with his big
idea, Foxy began to plan how he might transform it from
a remote hope into something more concrete. How could
he rouse the Nablar into throwing off their oppressors and
seizing back their freedom, as the citizens of the little
sea-girt kingdom had done? Who must he enlist to his
side? Who recruit? Who had enough charisma to fan a
faint spark of revolt into a raging fire? There was just one
person known to all the Nablar and esteemed by all that
he was aware of: their traditional high priest, the Culdee,
the latest in a remarkably unbroken line of shamen and
wise-women going back to the great days before the
Glepts came to the valley. Foxy had never met Tom Tosa
Arbericord, but he knew how reverently he was regarded,
the respect and affection with which his name was
spoken. Foxy was not naturally religious. His foster
father, being a herdsman, venerated the spirit of the
woods and fields, the horned god Bron who had all four-
footed creatures under his care. Foxy paid lip service to
the cult, asking permission to kill before setting out on a
hunt, thanking the god before eating, but it meant little to
him. That the valley had been known far and wide as the
Lap-of-the-Mother and had been regarded in foreign parts
as the most important centre of worship for the earth
deity was a matter of pride to him but also of puzzlement.

He had been to the upper valley, the Midda as it was known, and approached the edge of the holy of holies. He had climbed a hill with a large ancient tree in the centre of its flat top and a design incised in the turf. Out of respect he had not ventured far from the periphery but, as he stood there, had felt nothing unusual, nothing of the numinous. If this was where Aigea resided, then it was plain she did not choose to speak to him.

Preparatory to attempting to enlist the man to his cause, Foxy found out all that he could about the Culdee. What he learnt made him realize that enrolling such a one in his army of liberation might not be easy. He sensed a great gulf between his approach to life and that of this person whose acquaintance he had yet to make. Every candidate for the priesthood spent many years of arduous training under the tutelage of the existing shaman. The succession was commonly, but not always, handed down via a close relative, as the gift of mana often ran in families. It was necessary for the raw talent to be moulded and disciplined if it was not to become a wild and destructive force. The student priest normally had to give up much that ordinary people took for granted: family, companionship, love; becoming less than human in order to become more than human. The Culdee's task had always been to restore balance and harmony to individual lives and to the world in general; what Foxy advocated, violent disruption, was the polar opposite of the cleric's raison d'etre. He became aware that if he explained his cherished dream too crudely he was likely to give the impression that he was a reckless hot-headed firebrand. From month to month he put off approaching the master, trying to work out a form of words that would prove irresistibly persuasive. He delayed and delayed and then, in the end, it was too late

----------.

Each summer, while he was away in the mountains, Valentine left four nanny goats with the Dans' kitchen staff to provide milk for the delicate digestions of the Castle ladies. In the winter, however, Potto Potunalius Applecraft, attached-nibbler to Castle Dan, would regularly trundle an empty churn on a hand cart up to a hillside rendezvous in order to exchange it for a full one. Foxy, carrying the full churn effortlessly on his shoulder, went down to meet him, and discovered the man wide eyed with momentous news.

"They've taken the Culdee! They've found him out! The Dan's youngest ha' died and they say it were all his fault! I be afeared they be a-gooin' to do away with he! My girl led him on they do say."

In a moment Foxy saw all his hopes and aspirations dissolving in front of his eyes. "What can we do?" he cried in distress.

"You mus' help we to get she away," replied Potto.

"To get he away? An escape you mean."

"No, no. He be in a cell in the Punishment Yard, and there's all these out-of-valley squits round he. No hope o' that at all. It's her, Tom's girl. We must git her down to the Justification before they think to do her harm."

Foxy had not even known there was a daughter. It was Potto's plan to send the little girl on her way alone, as less likely to attract attention. "But I need folk to watch out for she – see she don't take a wrong turning, see she come safe to her granny's"

And so Ann, bewildered and slightly rebellious (*Dadda wouldn't want I to go, I want to wait for Dadda*) overcome with dread at mysterious events that no one had the heart to explain, set out on her own to cover the miles to the inn where her mother's mother was in service, her head in a muddle over instructions concerning the route she was supposed to follow. But every time she hesitated at a junction or dithered over whether to turn left or right at a lanes'-meet a voice would come from within a bush or from behind a nearby tree: "'Long this way, Tom Tosa's girl, 'long this way." Foxy shadowed her throughout the whole journey, keeping pace just within sight of the road, until he saw her arrive at the Justification and fall weeping into her grandmother's arms. Then he returned to the environs of Castle Dan where he hid himself away in order to await the inevitable.

That the High Priest of the Nablar was about to have some draconian penalty imposed on him for his alleged misdeeds, the denizens of Deep Hallow were in no doubt. But when the nature of this punishment began to be rumoured along the highways and byways, both Glepts and Nablans were thunderstruck. The condemned conjurer was to be put to the fire and in the Goddess's ancient shrine, the place open to the sky that had been venerated time out of mind by people across many lands! The Dan must have truly gone mad to order such a thing; it was courting disaster to put such a dangerous deed in train; it would bring down a curse on the valley!

Came the appointed day, and despite this universal feeling of dismay, crowds followed the creaking tumbrel up the Clough, Foxy amongst them. He tried to get close enough to the cart to obtain a clear view of the prisoner, but he had left it too late to be in the forefront of the voyeurs. He was struck by the contrast between the meagre number of guards round the wagon - the foreign mercenaries the Dan had hired - and the huge multitude dogging its wheels, many of them Nablans. If they had so chosen his people could easily have overpowered the soldiers, despite what Potto believed, and effected a rescue, but nothing was done. With deep anger in his heart Foxy set out to watch the hideous spectacle by climbing to a vantage point on the cliff side once the Midda was reached where he could obtain an uninterrupted view, but then found he was unable to see anything clearly. Throughout the hours that the fire raged the victim, pinned to the ancient tree, never uttered a sound. Because smoke veiled the sides and the top of Judd's Hill, even onlookers at a higher elevation were unable to witness his suffering. How long his agony lasted was known only to the tinder and the leaping flames.

Afterwards, Foxy went, not back to the northern slopes and the goats, but down to the Justification to look for work. Mrs Humpage, presented with a strong likely-looking youth, took him on immediately and never lived to regret her decision. Foxy gave good value for money, but the real purpose of his presence there was to safeguard the Culdee's daughter. He saw now that he was in for the long haul before the girl reached maturity and could lead her people to victory, but he had the ability to be patient when circumstances demanded it. He would yet live to see the Glepts, the Outriders, and in particular the members of Clan Dan, the tribe guilty of perpetrating the obscenity at which he had just been present, brought to book.

When Foxy returned at last to the cave after having shared his illicit kill with several Nablan unfortunates he hurriedly donned his nibbler clothes, securing them with a rope around his waist, gulped down some more of the venison followed by a drink of water and then set out. When toiling at the hostelry he always left his bow, arrows and axe behind, but took with him the small dagger, concealed about his person, from which he was never parted. He had left the Justification before first light that morning and, on this occasion, he was especially anxious to return, as a situation was developing there that worried him considerably. Stepping out into the warm afternoon sunshine he raised his head and sniffed the wind - rain was on the way and it would not be just a shower this time - perhaps the good weather was coming to an end at last. To reach his destination where he was due to cover the evening shift would take some time and in consequence he set a cracking pace, feeling that the sooner he arrived the better.

Hilda had been a beautiful child, a rare flower of perfection, and she was now in the process of becoming an even more beautiful young woman. Working in the public rooms she was bound to attract attention. On his visit to Drossi Foxy had noticed some females enveloped head to toe in garments that only exposed their eyes. He sometimes wished that he could conceal his little priestess within such robes, away from prying glances and speculative leers. He had seen the way they ogled her, the Gleptish men that frequented the inn, and in particular the young apprentice Outriders who were presumably on the lookout for a quick lay. Foxy was fairly confident, however, that he could keep the girl out of harm's way as far as they were concerned. But now there was this Lord Yan Cottle, Yantle for short, a scion of one of the Fifteen Families, who had been prowling round the inn for weeks past, slumming it on account of the girl. This was an entirely different kettle of fish. Top people were not accustomed to being denied what they most desired, and the majority had enough clout to get their own way under any circumstances. Foxy understood that money had been offered, a considerable sum, but for some reason which he did not fully understand the landlady had declined to take it; perhaps her attitude had been influenced by the nasty rumours that were circulating concerning this particular Glept: it was whispered that he had had two pets already and that they had both disappeared; nobody had any idea what had become of them. Now he was looking for a third. Foxy had never felt his powerlessness more keenly; what could he do? Nothing it seemed. To make matters worse he knew that, despite Yantle's reputation, many would consider that Hild was being offered a great opportunity. A lot of people, Nablans amongst them, thought a nibbler girl lucky if she became the mistress of one of the aristos. Hilda's grandmother seemed to be of this persuasion and as a result had crossed swords with him on a number of occasions. Early that morning, standing arguing outside the old woman's little lean-to shack which was situated below the window of the room taken by the new guest, they had come perilously close to falling out permanently on the matter. In the grip of emotion Foxy's voice had risen.

"If that duzzy rascal come anywhere near her, if he lay a finger on her, he'll be in far deeper than he bargained for, you mark my words! Ha' you forgot who she is? You know who her father were – the Culdee that were your girl's man. She be the next in line. No squit is gooin' to lay his filthy hands on her be he ever so high up - I'll see to that!"

"Shhhhhhhhhhhh," hissed Florence, and then in a stage whisper, "Yes, my Martha married the Culdee, an' a lot o' good it do her. Don't talk to me about priests! I tol' her it would come to no good, but her wou'nt listen an' look what happen. Better to forget all about priests; better to let the mawther take her chance in town and live like a lady!"

While this was going on the girl in question, the object of their argument, stood next to the quarrellers, ignored both by her grandmother and her notional protector.

The rain had already set in as Foxy came over a slight rise and gazed across at the Justification where the lamps were just being lit. In actual fact, looking at things from a practical point of view, he reckoned he had three options where Hild was concerned: he could leave things as they were and trust that Mrs Humpage would continue to refuse to give in to the Glept's blandishments - the trouble was he had no faith in her will to resist if the sum of money being offered went on increasing; secondly he could spirit Hild away from the Justification; but where could he conceal her? The valley, which he had once thought contained the whole of the civilised world, was in actual fact quite small. When it came to playing hide and seek with the powers that be, vanishing into thin air when on the point of capture or leading pursuers a merry dance across country, all of which he had done himself in the past, he realised that the girl could not be expected to emulate him, and that wherever he hid her, a determined troop of Outriders had the ability to seek her out. If they adopted the third course of action - that the two of them should leave Deep Hallow and venture into the lands beyond - it would be the end of his dreams for the salvation of his people; he had a hunch that, under such circumstances, they would never return. As he passed through the archway into the inn's courtyard Foxy had a frown on his face, which caused someone to remark, "Look out - the Larrikin's in a bad mood tonight," (*Larrikin* was yet another nickname by which he was occasionally known). He went down to the stables in order to discover what tasks he had been allotted that evening, and to gird his loins for the several hours of hard and dirty work ahead. He knew he would not finish until two or even three in the morning. After that he must sleep for a while, probably on the floor of Florence's shack, unless he had been banished from her good books for keeps, before going hunting once more. In his mind nothing was resolved. Should all else fail perhaps he would have to resort to a fourth and final option, that of killing the man, and, if so, he would make sure, this time, that he did not waver.

Life makes promises
Concerning love, joy, fulfilment,
But then reneges.

Chapter ten

"Ah, there you are wife – no wonder you've been hiding yourself! As I originally anticipated, your latest attempt at coping with the current situation has been a complete farce, just like the last. I should have known better than to take notice when you told me you'd finished him off. I was stupid enough to believe you until I looked down from above and there he still was, large as life and twice as ugly!"

"Yes – but I nearly had him, didn't I and if I'd continued... Unfortunately, when I tasted his blood I was sure he must be dead so I stopped paying attention; how was I to know it was all a trick and that, somehow or other, he'd been clever enough to wriggle out of my grasp."

"Well, there's a simple lesson to be learned, wouldn't you say? You failed because you underestimated your opponent. You've got to try harder – you've got to use greater subtlety, greater cunning – greater, perhaps, than you possess..."

If a polite knock had not come on his door in the late afternoon to remind him that the outside world still existed, Tallis might have gone on sleeping for several more hours. It seemed that the staff at the Justification were becoming impatient. They wanted to remove the chamber pot and the bath left from the night before and to find out if Tallis intended to eat at the inn that evening. It was Ralph's bark that woke him and, as he began to move, muscles and joints which had seized up yet again during his long period of immobility came to life like the hinges of an old iron gate. Having given the two servants permission to enter he waited until they had finished their chores, then climbed painfully out of bed, let Ralph out to do his business, washed (what a luxury it was to have even cold water for his ablutions), and began to dress himself. He performed his toilet in a methodical, even obsessional, manner, superstitiously doing everything in a set order from which he did not allow himself to deviate for fear of incurring some unspecified misfortune. His clothes were really in a shocking state. The damage inflicted during his fight with the robbers three days earlier had been the last straw for garments that were already ragged and filthy dirty; it was time to look round for some new ones. His customary procedure when dealing with this aspect of life on the road was to replace his outfit every time it became offensive to his senses, laundering and mending not being practices with which he had ever become familiar. In his pack though, neatly folded, lay the richly embroidered gown which he used in his performances when he carried out a proper pre-arranged recital; he went to great lengths to ensure that that was kept in pristine condition. Kneeling down he repeated his daily prayers to the Lord-of-Heaven and then, from beside the bed, picked up the kuckthu, a many stringed instrument, sat down on a chair and prepared to begin his regular daily practice session.

He started with a few scales and arpeggios to loosen his fingers, and then continued with some exercises, which quickly segued into a lively jig followed by a reel. He hummed along feeling his way into the music. The increasing stiffness in his joints had not yet affected his playing to any great extent, but he was apprehensive about the future. His skills as a musician were what paid his way through the world and he wondered how he would manage if he could not earn money this way. On entering a new village or hamlet his usual first task was to offer his services to the local hostelries and taverns, or, if he detected a more sophisticated audience, he might hire a hall and put on a concert. It did not take long for people to realize they had a virtuoso in their midst. Sometimes though he found himself treading on the toes of local musicians and once or twice he had been run out of town by jealous rivals. Now he moved from up-tempo dances to slower and more introspective pieces: an aubade, a nocturne, a beautiful berceuse to which he was inspired to sing the words. Gradually he became lost in the music and his mind drifted back to the time when he had been handed the kuckthu at the tender age of fifteen.

Most individuals when they go among mountains are struck by a sense of their own insignificance. For Tallis, mountain born, his first sight of the plains as he looked down through a northward facing gap from a great height, conveyed the same sensation. Dotted with settlements, veined by highways, they stretched with eye-wearying, two-dimensional monotony into the far distance, a vast stage on which millions of interlocking human dramas were being played out. After his precipitous departure from the old house above the village, finding his way through the giants of his native country had been a difficult task for the ill-prepared youngling. By the time he set foot on a lowland road and had left the great ranges behind he was dog tired and virtually starving. Nevertheless, minded to stay true to Morvah's aspirations for her son, he began knocking on doors with a tentative enquiry: –

"Did a lot of people, a host of people, come this way about fifteen years ago? And before that, was there a man carrying something that caused destruction as it passed by? I'm trying to discover which direction they took."

Even as he asked the question he was struck by how foolish it sounded, especially when the response he got was invariably incomprehension and a shaking of heads. Lonely and with a feeling of total abandonment he rapidly began to loose heart and sink into depression. It seemed no time at all before he was washed up in a grubby corner of some anonymous small town, hopeless and forlorn, totally ignored by the local citizenry who could not have cared less if he lived or died. He probably would have died from simple lack of nourishment, and sooner rather than later, if a man, passing through, had not recognised his pitiable state, lifted him out of this slough, and brought him back to the strange commune that he called home.

Gregory Guyax, a big boned, bearded, energetic individual, was the leader of a community that encompassed both a large farm and a small village. To this settlement he returned with Tallis in tow, a second Mr Earnshaw accompanied by another Heathcliff; and, truth to tell, in due course Tallis did fall in love with his benefactor's daughter. Meanwhile Gregory explained the situation regarding his colony:

"...I'd just reached these conclusions about how we ought to live, when out of the blue I heard that my father had departed this life and had left vacant the farm I hadn't seen since I ran away from it in boyhood. Determined to adopt a new type of existence, I packed up all my books, scrolls and papers and carried along with me my wife and children and any friends who were mad enough to listen to my wild ideas and fall in with my plans. After weeks on the way we reached the ancestral home to find the whole place disintegrating, the land going to rack and ruin and the villagers disaffected. I set about putting everything back into good heart. My idea was to build a fraternity from the indigenous population along with my own people. I gave the method much thought, and in the end based everything on one simple stratagem: the encouragement of nosiness. No one was allowed to keep themselves to themselves; all the people gossiped and interfered to their hearts content, and then the gossips were gossiped about and the interferers investigated. Everyone was goaded into speaking their minds about everyone else and doing it at the tops of their voices. We had a noisy few years, I can tell you, also one attempted murder, one suicide and several defections to the outside world. After that things began to settle down, and, although I hardly dared to believe the evidence, people seemed to be getting quite fond of each other, not just of their own parents, husbands, wives and children, but of their neighbours and the fellow down the road. That was quite a while ago now, but most of us are still together. What do you think my man? Would you care to join us?"

Because of his debility Tallis had little choice, at first, but to go along with this suggestion. However, even when his strength returned he felt no great urge to move on, his will to act had deserted him. In the end he remained a member of the community for eight years, from the age of fifteen to twenty three. At the start Gregory put the beautiful old kuckthu into his hands.

"Our main minstrel is thinking of retiring – joints getting a bit arthritic, you see. Perhaps you'd care to take a few lessons; might stand you in good stead."

In the tradition of the place everyone wanted to know his back story. Tallis attempted a token resistance, afraid of being laughed out of court; but the matter was not allowed to rest, and in the end they dragged from him the reason behind his wanderings. To his surprise his mother's account of the stealing of the Key was treated with respect.

"But it couldn't have happened as she told you," Gregory informed him. "There is such a legend of a theft, but it took place thousands of years ago. Could she have read it in a book?"

"She couldn't read," replied Tallis.

"You neither? I'll teach you. And she told you that you were the son of the stealer of the Key? My word! This Key - it's mentioned in the old sagas. Every time the Key is turned a new age is ushered in so they say, but as for it granting immortality, I've never heard that one before."

Tallis learnt to read and eagerly perused Gregory's books and scrolls, finding oblique references to a myth of grand larceny, but nothing like the vivid

personal account of the purloining of a treasure that
Morvah had given him; the mystery was deepened by his
researches rather than clarified. As he became accepted
into the community, and doubt having been sewn in his
mind, the urgency of his quest faded and then was almost
forgotten. By the age of eighteen he had an understanding
with Prudence, Gregory's daughter. A rustic marriage
ceremony was performed, with his mentor's blessing, and
the couple moved into one of the farm cottages together.
Sharing a life with his new bride Tallis was simply and
uncomplicatedly happy; it was the first and last time in
his life that he achieved this blessed state. The only thing
needed to complete his felicity would have been a little
one, but this was not to be. Soon after he turned twenty
three he began to sense that something was amiss. For a
week or two his wife had seemed remote and
preoccupied; he wondered if these moods were the first
signs of pregnancy and hopefully awaited the outcome.
Then, one morning, he awoke to find her gone; a man
from the village, a young tearaway who had rubbed a lot
of people up the wrong way, disappeared at the same
time. Tallis was devastated. Furious and bitter at being
cuckolded, the warm and generous side of his nature took
a hard knock; coldness, cynicism and suspicion of his
fellows gained the upper hand. He was also overcome by
a feeling of remorse; if his trust had been betrayed then
he was also guilty of a betrayal. By leading this static
existence he had proved unfaithful to Morvah's plans for
his future. Angrily he blamed the commune members for
his dereliction, forgetting that nobody had forced him to
stay. Gregory pointed this out to him.

"You were free to go at any time. There was
nothing holding you here apart from your own heart.

Take your leave now if you wish, but I believe that you will be on a fool's errand if you follow this path; what you seek is nothing but an illusion that vanished from the earth many years ago."

Tallis shut his ears and refused to listen. Gregory, being the leader and also Prudence's father, was the main focus of his ire; he was indifferent to the man's own loss and he had forgotten that this individual had been his rescuer and had probably saved his life. He made his preparations for departure. Ignoring Tallis' hostility Gregory found him a quiet reliable horse.

"You'll do better to go mounted than on foot. Your musicianship will be the key to your survival. You are a fine instrumentalist now, and your voice isn't bad either. You'll be able to earn your living with the kuckthu."

"The kuckthu?" said Tallis, surprised. He loved the instrument but had not imagined that he would be allowed to keep it.

"It's yours, my man. You know its ways better than anyone. Treat it kindly."

"Thanks," replied Tallis ungraciously.

"And here's another thing that might prove useful." Gregory handed over something that looked a bit like a pocket watch but with a swinging needle under the glass. "It's called a compass; the needle always settles to the north. The few stories that have survived about the Key say that it's to be found in the north."

As he left the commune, most of the people who had been his companions throughout the last few years gathered to wish him well and wave goodbye, but Tallis, after returning Gregory Guyax's handshake in an indifferent manner and making his way down the path to the main highway, did not look back. Disregarded, behind him, Gregory sighed and shook his head.

With his renewed purpose at white heat Tallis refused to accept that the events his mother had recounted belonged in the dim and distant past. If that was the case it meant that her story would have been just fantasy, and, although the tale might have had some elements of truth, the role she claimed for herself: king's daughter, and for Tallis: son of the Key-stealer, heir to the royal line, were pure make believe. On the contrary, his rationale demanded that he give credence to her account. Again Tallis began to ask his foolish question, "Do you remember, have you any record of a travelling people, a nation on the move, who may have come this way? And before that, was there a man carrying something that trailed havoc in its wake?" Communication was not a problem. Throughout the lands that he was slowly traversing most people were bi-lingual, speaking the common tongue alongside their own language, with individuals and places often having two names, one in each vocabulary. Getting the answer he sought was more difficult however; a few people, a very few, thought they knew what he was talking about. Yes, there had been a time of trouble: the time of the earthquake, the flood, the pestilence, etcetera etcetera, when a large host had passed through their country, if you could believe the old tales, but it was long, long ago, lost in the mists of time. Tallis seized on the confirmation of events and ignored the vast period his informants insisted had elapsed since they occurred.

As he crept northwards, following the sun, through many months and years, his eyes were always

scanning the distance ahead. When he came round a
corner his glance would dart to the next bend as if he
hoped to be in time to see a stray traveller, a lagging child
perhaps or an errant dog, from some company journeying
ahead of him. At the top of a hill he would sweep the
view looking for camp fires or moving specks on the
ribbon of highway. Sometimes he would glimpse
something that made him spur on his horse and ride
swiftly forward. But always, when he came up with it, he
would find merely a gathering of locals making their way
to a monthly market, a row of lumbering farm carts, a
religious procession, a band of wandering shearers. All
the time his mind was making strenuous efforts of the
imagination, trying to picture this narrow bridge over the
pretty stream bearing the weight of mountainous baggage
wagons; these overhanging trees brushing the plumes on
the helmets of an array of knights; this ford, scarcely
more than a water splash, and now overgrown with
meadow sweet and bog asphodel, churned to a mire by
countless hooves, wheels and feet. Could the muddy path
leading down to it, presently marked with just two faint
ruts, once, within living memory, have been widened to a
bare brown swathe by the passage of a multitude?

After a night of wind and rain he would stand in
the naked, new-born morning, gazing over a tumbling
river or through a narrow pass where the glimpse of lands
yet to be crossed was all blue distances and bird inhabited
air, and slowly, first on the mind's eye and then on the
inner ear, the vision would come of a marching host, a
monstrous earth-bound leviathan going ahead of him,
forced to slide along on its belly and adapt its shape to the
contours of the land through which it travelled. In his
imagination the unwieldy creature rolled its ponderous

bulk forward, seeming, despite continual fluctuations and tremors throughout its length, to be hardly progressing at all. When the country allowed, pseudopodia would ooze out sideways, only to quickly lose their impetus and melt back into the main body, while at the back a straggling tail, varying in length, and always longest on upward gradients, trailed after. Subsequent to leaving Gregory's collective, Tallis' aim in life had become an all-consuming obsession, unleavened as it was by companionship or other human contact. It possessed him constantly, and, even when he rested, weary, in front of a lodging house, sitting on the top step of a mounting block with his head in his hands, his eyes, bent downwards, would still be searching for footprints in the dust.

He came to the end of a long and difficult piece of music that had kept pace with his thoughts and laid the kuckthu aside. Then he picked it up again and, as a coda, played and sang a simple intercession that he had composed himself:-

> *"Dear Lord of Heaven grant I may*
> *Walk safely through the world this day.*
> *Pray I heed no tempter's call,*
> *But guide my steps what ere befall.*
> *And if peradventure I should die,*
> *Straight to thy bosom let me fly."*

The words demonstrated that normally he held no truck with the idea of reincarnation, a notion he had encountered on his travels. However, when he thought of the story his mother had told him, he sometimes began to wonder if it could be a memory from a previous life.

During his long journey he had not always been on the move. Now and then, as at the commune, he had been forced to rest, occasionally for an extended period, but unfailingly, in the end, he took up his burden and set forth once more. In this manner, with great singleness of purpose, he had traversed half the length of a continent, while each day the sun climbed ever higher overhead and his shadow shortened. Eventually he came to a region of forests with jungle trees hundreds of feet high. Below the canopy all was deepest twilight, the haunt of immense beasts that prowled silent and invisible. The men of that country had skins as velvet dark as the shadows through which they slipped, and all went naked. They lived beneath thatches of leaves in clearings: wells down which, at midday, the sun would briefly strike the forest floor. Sometimes, however, a cloud, many miles thick, hung over the tree tops, and from its belly spears of lightning lanced into the woodland, rending branches, kindling fires. A raging wind sent sparks flying far and wide, while the great trees bent and threshed like a bed of rushes. As the conflagration grew, red flames leapt from branch to branch, and glowing debris rained down igniting creepers and vines below. Just as a violent inferno seemed about to devour the jungle, there came a greater holocaust; the heavens opened and the world vanished behind a wall of living water. Strong enough to beat you to the ground or to drown you standing was this deluge; afterwards ruin, desolation, every leaf stripped, huge trunks splintered and laid low; yet, in a few weeks, three months at most, phoenix-like the forest renewed itself and no scars remained. The jungle marched on for hundreds of miles, only the largest mountains heaving their shoulders above its green mantle. When Tallis left it behind at last he found he had also outpaced his guide, the sun, which now hung in the sky at his back. From this point on he could date the return of his doubts and uncertainties, a fatal irresolution that try as he might he could not shake off.

Having brought his recollections almost up to date, he laid the instrument aside, got to his feet and took a turn across the room, then stood staring down through the window into the back yard and across at the stable block. Winter was coming, a season to be wary of in these latitudes; a time when it was best to stay indoors. He had accumulated enough gold to pay for his own and his horse's accommodation for several months. Besides this he saw the opportunity that such an oasis of civilization presented for earning more. He was inclined to wait until spring before travelling on, and even then he felt reluctant, for the first time in his life, to go alone. The encounter with the robbers had taught him a valuable lesson: that because of his advancing years he was becoming weaker, more vulnerable; he needed someone with whom he could stand back to back in a crisis, a useful servant who would handle some of the strategy of survival along the road. Strangely enough his mind kept coming back to the resentful underling who had brought him his bath the previous evening. Although Tallis had been dismayed at his hostility, the man had had health, strength and youth, qualities that he felt he himself could no longer lay claim to and which, if regained at second hand, could prove useful adjuncts.

A gong sounded from somewhere below; dinner was being served. He realized that he had not eaten since the previous evening and was extremely hungry. With a

last glance over his possessions, and promising Ralph,
who was once more at his side, that he would have some
food sent up to him, he left his room intending to descend
the staircase to the inn's ground floor. But, as he set out,
he found the way partially blocked. Just above a bend in
the flight of stairs a small figure was seated, head
propped against the wall. It was the little nibbler waitress
he remembered from the night before. The girl's body
was slumped sideways and completely still. She appeared
to be asleep and Tallis realized that, probably before she
dropped off, he had had an audience for his playing. He
hesitated, not sure what to do. All he could see of her face
was the soft child-like curve of her cheek, half obscured
by her waterfall of pale hair. The coarsely woven grey
scarf with which she usually chose to hide it had fallen
down around her shoulders. Her posture was one of utter
weariness and exhaustion. Tallis, normally insensitive to
others' predicaments, felt a traitorous stab of pity. For
how many hours was she made to work each day, this
child-woman, that she should collapse like this in the dim
stairwell? He looked down on her with something
approaching compassion, an emotion foreign to him in
recent years, and, bending, laid his hand gently on her
shoulder. Nothing prepared him for what happened next.
One minute the girl was a huddled pathetic figure dead to
the world, the next she had metamorphosed into a wild
animal crouching at bay on the step below, gazing up at
him with pale blue eyes that held an unmistakable threat.
At the same time something like a flash connected the
two of them and he felt as if he had been struck a blow in
the solar plexus which flung him backwards onto the
stairs as a wave of heat whipped past. He gasped and
struggled to sit up, only to find he was staring, once

again, at a trembling mouse of a child who directed at him a look of mixed terror and appeal before scuttling down to the exit into the courtyard. All this took place in a matter of seconds leaving him shaken to the core. Had he been assaulted? Thinking back he would swear that the girl had not touched him yet he had reacted as if he had been hit. Tallis retreated to his room and subsided onto the bed, where Ralph, sensing his master's distress, whined and came to lick his hand.

As his breathing slowed, he forced himself to think rationally and calmly, and quickly arrived at the most obvious explanation: he must have had what his mother would have called a *funny turn*. It would not be the first time this had happened; there had been a few dizzy spells over the last few months. He had merely been taken temporarily ill, he decided, and this time it was not because he was intoxicated; if he could just lie quiet here for a minute or two he would recover. After a while his equilibrium began to re-establish itself. He inhaled and exhaled quietly, gradually stilling the fluttering in his chest, and things started to appear more normal. Nevertheless this episode confirmed what he already suspected, that having suffered a number of such indispositions in the recent past he would have to take a break from his journey and overwinter in the valley, this place in which he had already discovered two races coexisted so uneasily and unequally. Nibblers and Glepts. The word nibbler in this context meant nothing as far as he was concerned, but Glept was familiar; it was an epithet that had often been applied to him personally as he moved through foreign cultures; in the languages of lands far to the south it meant simply *stranger*. There was a puzzle here that he felt almost on the brink of solving.

A revelation hovered just out of reach; he drowsily grasped at the explanation but instead drifted into sleep.

Sometime later he awoke with the smell of food in his nostrils. Time had passed. If he did not make a move immediately he was going to miss out on his dinner. He hurried down the stairs into the yard to find that it was raining, and was crossing to the buttery when a hand grasped his arm and pulled him to a halt. He recognized the peddler, one of the few people to whom he had spoken since arriving at the inn. The man was lurking outside the window of Mrs Humpage's office, a conspiratorial grin on his face.

"Ol' Maeve's on 'er 'igh 'orse," he whispered. "Just listen to 'er!"

Angry words came from within the room.

"...an' I'll thank you not to patronize this 'ostelry again, mister. You ain't welcome."

An equally irate voice answered.

"You won't get rid of me that easily, woman! You know who I am! This isn't the last time you'll be hearing from me or my family!"

"Go on, get out! Glept scum!"

"I'll go, but I'll be back!"

"Goodbye and good riddance!"

The door opened and a furious and vaguely familiar figure swept past them.

"It's the Yan's number three, the one 'oo I tol' you about," confided the peddler. "'Im as is after our 'Ild. Maeve's surely given 'im the 'eave 'o and no mistake."

When Tallis entered the buttery most of the company had already dispersed and plates were being cleared away. His request for food did not go down too well but eventually an adequate meal was provided. As he ate he noticed three war-like figures at one of the centre tables, lingering over their supper, impervious to the waiters' impatience. These were not the foppish young cadets of the evening before. Idly he wondered who such millitary-looking personages might be with their practical leather and mail, their shields and weapons within easy reach on the benches beside them. As he came to the end of his repast, he discovered that the peddler, with a full glass of stout, had arrived once again at his elbow.

"Night cap," the man confided, raising his glass.

Resignedly Tallis turned to him, deciding that as long as he had to endure his company he might as well make use of his local knowledge.

"Where do these soldiers come from?" he asked. "Is there a garrison in the vicinity?"

"Oh, they're foreigners like you an' me – not from Deep 'Allow. They work for the Dan, 'e's the big noise at this end of the valley. 'E's got a regular army of 'em up at the Castle. Them bein' down 'ere is all to do with 'is fear of witchcraft – you know, sorcery and suchlike – 'e's goin' a bit doolally if you ask me. Someone tol' 'im that a witch had been heard of in these parts – spells s'posed to have been cast and that sort of thing - so 'e sends three of 'is 'eavies 'ere to investigate – Maeve's not too 'appy about it I can tell you. Lot of nonsense if you ask me, this magic stuff, but to the Glepts it's deadly serious – they've already burnt one supposed sorcerer in this valley."

This was a whole lot more information than he had asked for and it left Tallis feeling slightly uncomfortable. He thought again about what had happened on the stairs and for a moment saw the little nibbler girl in an entirely new light. After all, according to his mother's accont, the supernatural was at the root of his own life-long pilgrimage so he could not dismiss the idea out of hand. But here, in such a commonplace domesticated setting? No – surely not. As the peddler had said – *a lot of nonsense.*

When he finished eating he once again went outside, intending to go for a short walk before retiring, probably in the direction of the stables, but then noticed there was still a light in the office. Although normally reluctant to ask for help or advice, he made an exception in this case and went to the door and knocked. Mrs Humpage was sitting at her desk bent over several large ledgers.

"Ah, Mr Tallisand, dear, 'ow are you gettin' on? Is there anything you need? Don't be afraid to ask."

"Everything is quite satisfactory, thank you. But I wonder if you can assist me? When I continue my journey I'm considering employing a servant – a sort of man at arms, someone who understands a bit about self-defence and can also help with the practicalities that have to be met with along the way. Do you know of someone who might be suitable?"

"Oh dear, you're not thinkin' of leavin' us already, I 'ope. No, I can't think of anyone off the top of me 'ead. But I'll tell you what – there's a 'irin' fair goin' on right now up at 'Igh 'Arrow. It's on today an' tomorrow. You go along to that, you'll stand a good chance of findin' somebody. You 'ave to go to the Town 'All first off an' tell them what you want. Then they'll give your message to the Crier oo'll call it at the fairground and in the town square. Meanwhile you go to one of the pubs an' the interested parties'll come along to you an' you can give 'em the once over. 'Ow about that?"

Tallis thanked her and took his leave. Was it too premature to be looking for a companion, now, when he did not intend to set out until the spring? He thought not. If he came across a likely looking man he had enough money in his purse to offer him a retainer, and over the winter he could get to know him and set him to work preparing for the journey. Being such a confirmed misanthrope, accustomed to maintaining self-sufficiency and his own personal space, he would find this a huge leap in the dark, but one to which he was not wholly averse - strangely enough he even felt intrigued at the change in circumstances that it would bring. Slightly more hopeful about his future than he had been when he arrived at the inn he turned his steps once more towards the stable block and a reunion with his horse.

Not play with gypsies?
And certainly not in the woods?
Well, you can stick that!

Chapter eleven

"Your brother's in a whole heap of trouble. He took Attack out without permission when he should have been in school, and then he rode him so hard, they say, that he's brought him back broken-winded. There's a horse doctor down at the stables right now trying to sort out the mess. Just thought you'd like to know."

The Lady Damask, twin sister to the second in order of succession within the Clan Dan hierarchy, had not long retired and now, rudely awakened after having only just dropped off, came groggily back to consciousness. The speaker, holding a candle, had appeared around the bedroom door within her apartment and she recognized the pale, resentful, slightly faded face of Demeter, a second cousin. The message was delivered with undisguised malicious glee. As Damask showed signs of putting her feet to the floor her informant beat a hasty retreat; the Dan's third oldest daughter was credited with being a formidable opponent and had even been known to resort to physical violence on occasions. "That's impossible!" Damask shouted after her, convinced that such a diagnosis could not be correct; she knew a thing or two about horses. The time was nearly eleven at night. Damask lay down again and stared at the dark ceiling while the clocks struck the hour. Then exclaiming angrily, "Oh for pete's sake!" she abruptly got up, lit her own little lantern and throwing a robe over her nightdress, slipped her feet into some pattens and quitted the apartment. Was Attack really at the Castle? As far as she knew he had been sent down to High Harrow for the autumn parade. Traversing various passageways and descending a couple of flights of stairs she came to a side door and slipped out into the rainy night. At the stables she found that the story did indeed hold an element of truth. Yes, Attack was in his stall, but there was no sign of a horse doctor and his wind was sound. All the same things were far from satisfactory: he had been seriously lamed and was acting half crazy as if he had been frightened out of his wits. Yes, it was the Lord Dan Addo who had brought him in. The man she questioned explained that the grooms had done their best for the horse and were now preparing to keep watch throughout the night. "Only time will tell," he added gloomily, shaking his head.

"But where *is* Dando? Where's my brother?"

The man looked around vaguely.

"He were here, jest now. Mayhap he's gone to report to the boss; he'll have to know what's happened sooner or later."

Damask retraced her steps, determined to discover the truth concerning Dando's whereabouts despite the fact that to do so she would have to trespass on territory within the mansion's living quarters normally barred to unaccompanied females. Entering the house by a different access point she threaded the elaborate interior, a wasps' nest of complexity, before eventually arriving outside the Dan's apartments. Two soldiers sat in the foyer.

"Has the Lord Dan Addo been here recently? Is he inside?"

"No m'Lady," replied one, eyeing her boldly up and down. "The commander-in-chief's retired for the night. He turned in about an hour ago and is not to be disturbed."

Damask became suddenly acutely aware of her state of undress. She pulled her robe tightly around her and swept haughtily away, but not before she caught a smirk on the face of the other soldier - news travels fast it seems and she guessed that these door-keepers had already heard something of her brother's recent history. Setting out to visit the south-west tower, her old stamping ground, where Dando still lived when he was at the Castle, she sidled through the cavernous entrance hall situated to the left of the main bailey. Here she was in time to speak to a Nablan watchman returning to sign off after completing his shift at the gatehouse.

"Have you seen my brother, the Lord Dan Addo, this evening at all?" she asked, with a sort of sinking feeling as if she already knew the answer.

"Yes m'Lady, I saw he go out past me down at the gate, not half an hour since. I wished he goodnight but he di'n't reply."

"Was he on horseback?"

"No Lady, he weren't a-ridin', he were afoot. If he be intending to take the road along the valley I mistrust he'll be hooly drenched by the time he git where he be a-gooin'."

Damask made her way back to her own suit of rooms. Her clothes were quite damp. Not wanting to disturb her maid she went to the closet in the anteroom, stripped and then shrugged on a clean nightgown, leaving the wet one, and her robe, on the floor, all the while turning over in her mind the unpalatable facts that had been presented to her. So Dando, for reasons best known to himself, having put the valley's most valuable horse in jeopardy, had brought him back here in a lamentable state, after which he had cleared off, shown a clean pair of heels, run away, like the worst kind of coward. Oh boy, *was* he in trouble! She found a towel and rubbed some of the moisture out of her fuzz of chestnut hair, made more frizzy by the damp, all the while repeating over and over to herself "Bloody hell, bloody hell, bloody hell…!" After which she got back into bed and lay wide-eyed with her brain in turmoil.

Was there any way she could mend what had been done? Perhaps if she went to her father early the next morning, before he had heard anything from his sidekicks, and was the first to break the news about Dando's misdeeds, maybe she could soften things up a bit for her brother. But she might not even be allowed in to see the clan chief; it was a long while since he had paid her any attention. These days there were many barriers to be surmounted before you could approach him, not least that of his personal bodyguard. An atmosphere of paranoia surrounded the family head and he was becoming increasingly remote. He might not even acknowledge his own daughter. Dan females had little influence over the castle's affairs. From the age of thirteen, or from the start of their menses, whichever came first, they were banished to a form of purdah in the women's section of the great building and were largely ignored, only regaining a modicum of freedom and influence when they were given in matrimony to an appropriate suitor. Damask mentally addressed her brother wherever he might be: *Oh Dando, Dando; what are you playing at? Don't you see that this is the end as far as you and he are concerned? You've been handed chance after chance and the way he is nowadays he'll not allow you another fresh start. Why couldn't you be a bit more like me and at least present the appearance of conforming?*

The trouble with Dando was that he had not the guile to disguise his oddness, and it had been glaringly obvious for some time that her brother was stark staring bonkers; there had been too many examples of his insanity to put the question in doubt. She went over them in her mind. There was the time he claimed he was receiving visitations from the spirit world - that had been weird enough, and then he had gone and fallen head over heels in love with a nibbler girl, a sure sign of madness. He was a cook, god help us, and he had refused to take the Outrider oath – what could that be about? To cap it all, to the best of her knowledge, he was still a virgin, something utterly unnatural in a boy of his age. Yes, he was quite barmy and you could see it a mile off, whereas she was a master of subterfuge.

She had learnt quickly at a very young age, and in a school of hard knocks, that if she wanted to go her own way she would have to lead a double life. To conceal the fact that she was pursuing a parallel existence required a great deal of bluffing and ingenuity. When, rather tardily, the powers that be tumbled to the fact that she had reached puberty and she was banished to the region of the Castle's sisterhood, the subterfuge became well nigh impossible to maintain, until a serendipitous intervention by Dando (yes, he had his uses) brought about a change in her fortunes.

It had all started at the age of five when she was forbidden to keep company with the two gipsy boys who came up to the Castle with their parents. Scolded and punished for disobeying orders, she had had to become sly and secretive in order to achieve her ends. She had found ways of playing truant without being found out. As a result she deserted Dando for a large part of the year and he obviously missed her company; nevertheless he always covered for her throughout the long hot summers. Those in authority took it for granted that when she was away from the house it was with her brother, either in the park or up at the cottage, whereas in reality she was much further afield, running wild with the lawless pack of travellers' children. Gypsies, peddlers, tinkers, tramps – all the members of this footloose tribe had her heart in thrall. Something deep within her felt a kinship with such outcasts, maybe because, unlike Dando, she had had a freelance peripatetic wet nurse. That they tended to be emotionally unstable, flying into passionate rages that ended in violence, that they waged feuds, were often cruel to their young ones and animals, sometimes lived in squalor and were faithless and inconstant in their relationships was unimportant to her; she shared their wholesale free-spiritedness, and when those that visited the valley left in the autumn she longed to go with them. Life at the Castle after they were gone seemed a poor shadowy affair.

She had been ten when she heard the news from the Roma.

"They go to burn witch up at ecclesia – you come see?"

Her informant was Duke, who, along with his brother Boiko, had been the first of her original gypsy friends. Could this possibly be the case? On returning to base from the travellers' camp, having fled there in order to escape the universal condemnation that had come her way when it was discovered that her stupidity had been the root cause of Dando's illness, she found her brother still under the supervision of his carers and therefore unavailable for questioning. It was with some difficulty that she discovered, to her shocked surprise, that the tale was indeed correct, and that the condemned man was to be found on her own doorstep, languishing at that very moment in a cell in the Punishment Yard. It was with a sort of incredulity that she heard that the prisoner was Tom Tosa, Tom the cobbler, Ann's father. Her mind flew immediately to the stone idol, hidden at the back of his workshop. Had a stray word from either Dando or herself betrayed him? No, no, that was ridiculous. Although no one wanted to tell her, she found out that the crime for which he was condemned was that of using necromancy to bring about the death of the Dan's seventh son. At that time, because she was in deep disgrace after the blood-poisoning debacle, her every move would normally have been strictly monitored, but in the highly charged atmosphere permeating the Dan mansion during these days of waiting no one was taking much notice of her comings and goings, so she returned to the Roma and stayed several nights.

On the morning of the sentence's enactment the gypsy camp emptied, most of the adults making their way to the upper valley. The children were left in charge of two young mothers whose primary concern was the welfare of their own babies; it was easy enough for Damask and her friends to slip away. Damask had put on boy's clothing and hidden her long hair under a cap. She rubbed dirt into her face. It was a disguise she often assumed when away from the castle. If Boiko and Duke were going to attend this spectacle she was not going to be left out, although a twisting sensation in the pit of her stomach warned her that she might not find it pleasant. They hung around with others at the entrance to the clough until they saw a tumbrel coming from the direction of Castle Dan, a great gathering of people trailing along behind. The prisoner was standing, bound, at the front of the cart, supported on either side by two soldiers. Despite her view being partially blocked Damask caught a glimpse of his face; he seemed to be gazing afar off at something beyond the bounds of common or garden reality. It was a long way to the head of the ravine taking into account the pace at which the wagon travelled, pushed along by main force, and the three children were crowded and jostled as they tried to keep their feet in the midst of the throng. When the Midda was reached the multitude surged forward until it came to the edge of the marsh, the boys and Damask finding themselves squashed in amongst many older and bigger bodies. Judd's Hill rose up out of its watery surroundings and they could see no further than the rim at the top of the slope as they tried to squint between the broad backs of the people in front of them. Damask could not see, but she could hear, and what she heard was the sound of hammers. She turned to Duke, two years her senior, and the fount of all knowledge.

"What are they doing?" she demanded.

"They go nail 'eem to tree," he replied, a wild look in his eye.

Damask listened for a few more minutes until she detected a whiff of smoke on the air, after which she abruptly turned and fought her way out of the crowd behind her. As she entered the clough she passed a few late comers, then found herself alone. She ran as hard as she could down the steep path beside the rapids, and as she ran she sobbed, while her mind seethed with anger and disgust. She felt sickened by her family and in particular her father for ordering this abomination, anger at the mercenaries for carrying out such orders for money and repulsion at the morbidly curious crowd for lapping up the horror. She was even disgusted by the apparent compliance of the victim: if he was such a great sorcerer, as everyone, both friends and enemies, claimed, then why did he not blast his persecutors to smithereens? It was from the day of the execution that she could date her determination to leave the valley. Her mind was set. With or without permission, either sooner or later, she would go for good and all, and no ties of affection, no loyalty to her race, would have the power to stop her.

The twins' halcyon days in their childhood haunts were coming to an end. As mentioned previously, on reaching thirteen, whether she had entered puberty or not, Damask was destined to join the women in what was known as the gynaceum, and at fourteen Dando would become an Outrider cadet. Since his illness, he had returned to his sister somewhat changed - he seemed more mature somehow - and although to all outward appearances he was still the cheerful, easygoing, gregarious boy he had always been, Damask knew him too well not to notice a difference. She sometimes detected a melancholy cast to his features which became more marked when they were alone together and he knew no-one else was watching. This mood was not the same as the acute misery he had displayed when she had interfered between the two infant lovers, but she imagined it arose from the same source.

"I shouldn't go on looking for that nibbler girl," she advised, "She could be dangerous – I was told recently that she's some sort of witch, just like her father."

Dando blushed. "Absolute tripe!" he countered. "Anyway, told by who?"

"The Roma."

"And I suppose they know everything!"

"Almost."

There was a moment's silence.

"You would think that, about her being dangerous," added Dando, "it's pretty clear you never liked her."

"That's not true. I just didn't feel she was good for you."

At the Castle nobody spoke of Tom, or the manner of his death. A conspiracy of silence reigned. She knew Dando had been having nightmares but she did not add these to the list of his eccentricities because she herself was also having the occasional bad dream; a lot of people were she imagined. Then brother and sister played hookey and paid their visit to the upper valley after which Dando seemed a mite happier.

All too soon Damask started her periods. At whatever age this milestone occurred menstruation should have been the signal for her removal from her old haunts, but if it was humanly possible she was going to delay the evil day for as long as possible. By dint of Dando's connivance she managed to conceal her condition for several months, and it was not until much later when she was, in fact, approaching the cut-off year that one of the servants discovered her secret. Meantime she thought long and hard about the future. She made up her mind that she would quit the valley on her seventeenth birthday; she would be a woman by then, wise in the ways of the world, well able to fend for herself. (Yet here she was, a day, or was it two days by now, after that significant date, and she remained at home, unprepared for departure.) During the respite she had gained by her subterfuge she spent more time with her twin. It had at last been brought home to her that she and Dando would soon be parted. In the absence of parental love she had always been able to turn to her brother in times of crisis, and she realized now that with him gone she would find life a lot harder. A sudden feeling of panic assailed her. How was she going to cope without him? She had always taken it for granted that she was the stronger of the two, the one who provided a shoulder to cry on. Now, for a brief moment, she wondered if it had really been the other way round.

On a certain morning in early winter, they were both confined to the south-west tower, while Damask fretted and fumed and paced to and fro in front of the window.

"Oh, if it would only stop raining," she moaned, "then perhaps we could *do* something!"

Dando looked up from where he was sitting sprawled in an easy chair, cat on lap, book in hand, and stared out at the misty hills. "It looks a bit brighter over there," he said mildly.

"You're just saying that," she complained. "It doesn't mean anything. It's so depressing. If it isn't raining, the wind is jabbering away all the time, and no one around for miles. I really hate this time of year!"

"I quite like it," said Dando.

Damask gave a snort of despair. "How can you say that? What do you mean? - Tell me."

"Too difficult to explain," answered Dando.

"Try."

"You wouldn't understand."

"Who says! Try me!"

"Well, it's sort of to do with stillness. The wind outside makes the inside of the house seem extra quiet – there's a sort of heart of stillness somewhere," he waved his hand vaguely behind him in the direction of the vast warren of rooms that constituted his home, "p'raps in a storeroom, p'raps in a cupboard, but it's the centre of everything. And then also in here," he pressed his fist against his chest. "An' the rain, - that sort of connects everything together: the trees, the clouds, the sky, yourself if you're out in it and you get wet."

Damask looked at him with a kind of exasperated fondness.

"You're the first person I've known," she said, " to get off on the weather."

"There you are, I told you you wouldn't understand."

This exchange made her realize for the umpteenth time the huge gulf that existed between the two of them. In the scheme of things they could not have been more mentally dissimilar: it was plain that although born under the same star they came from two completely different planets. Neither could entirely fathom the other, but in the final analysis she was beginning to realize, late in the day, that, despite their disparate characters, there was no one, emotionally, to whom she felt closer. "You will come and see me sometimes when I'm gone?" she asked anxiously.

"Of course, as often as you like."

Ensconced in the women's realm Damask tried her best to retain some sort of personal integrity. For several weeks she fought tooth and nail the attempt to make her conform to what she considered to be a stupid, restrictive regime, but in the end realized it was hopeless, the opposition was just too strong. She gave in and bowed to the inevitable, allowing herself to be coerced into dressing and behaving in a way that was completely alien to her.

Damask had her own kind of beauty. She was a honey-coloured child, her soft wavy tresses, several shades lighter than Dando's shoulder length raven locks, falling almost to her waist. Her eyes of burnt almond and firm oval face, smooth as a cream egg shell, singled her out for admiring glances, while her determined chin and full voluptuous mouth gave her visage its own individuality. She was tall for her age - there was little to choose between her and her brother at this stage of their development – and she always carried her height proudly, staring down her strong finely-boned nose. But now she was subjected to a process of uglification. Her thick eyebrows were plucked and her hair pulled back into a bun; her skin was anointed with various, to her, foul smelling unguents while garishly-coloured paints were dabbed on her face and nails. Application and removal took up hours of her maid's time, morning and evening, during which Damask almost died of boredom. Another ritual consisted of lacing her body into rigid corsets that limited her movements. Thus hobbled and constrained she was expected to sit for hours either reading insipid and sentimental novels chosen by the local female mafia - *Oh Dando, if you could appreciate the plight of this latest slave to the written word you might not think that books were always such a good thing!* - or working on a piece of embroidery which became spotted with blood from the pricks she inflicted on her clumsy fingers. As third and fourth alternatives she was allowed to go for short walks on the terrace outside the castle walls or take part in a ladylike game of croquet. Damask, who, up to now, had been the possessor of a frank direct gaze, became ashamed to look anyone in the eye.

Dan women were not a happy bunch: time was on their hands, their social situation was fraught with frustration and they were expected to conform to an ideal of unworldly, passionless femininity. No wonder Glept ladies were great sufferers from the ills of the flesh, while neuroses and psychosomatic disorders bred like flies. The aunts, who had been ceded sovereignty in their area of the household, governed with imperious authority and feuded with deadly vituperation amongst themselves, (each had their own territories, defended to the last ditch), but they also spent a lot of their time consulting faith-healers, fussing over their diets, being pummelled by masseuses and swallowing foul-tasting cure-alls. The women's section was run to a rigid routine of meals, family prayers, ritualistic socialising etc., the staff having to steer a perilous course between the conflicting demands of the various old autocrats. The size and complexity of the establishment was self-generating: servants waited on servants, tradesmen and craftsmen were employed full time, their needs necessarily catered for. The aunts spent every hour of the day administering, or rather wielding, this rod they had created for their own backs.

The portals of the female ghetto were well guarded; those entering and exiting were continually vetted. The women themselves, when unmarried, normally only emerged under supervision, in order to make routine visits to relatives or to attend formal dress balls and religious ceremonies. Anyone desiring admittance had to have a very good reason for doing so; casual calling was not encouraged, as Dando very soon discovered when he tried to be true to his word and drop in on Damask in her new situation. There was a certain urgency in his wish to see her. He had been made anxious by the shrieks, the muffled bangings, the voice pouring out anguished words just beyond the threshold of understanding, that had reached his ears when he first eavesdropped outside the place where he understood her rooms were situated. Snooping around the outside of the castle, trying to find an alternative entrance, he came across a small unwatched side door. It was firmly fastened, but through his familiarity with the Key Room, he eventually ran the right key to earth, had two copies made, and, one day, crept up to her apartment when there seemed to be nobody else about. As luck would have it he found Damask in residence and her maid absent. Damask leapt up with a cry of joy at the unexpected arrival of her brother, before stopping abruptly, embarrassed by the knowledge that she must look a complete guy in his eyes. Then, as he explained how he had gotten in, she became concerned that he would be discovered.

"You can't stay," she warned. "Therese'll be back any minute, she's just gone to fetch the laundry. If she finds you here word'll be all over the place in no time, and there'll be the very devil to pay. I'll have to give you some sort of signal to let you know when the coast's clear."

"Put something blue in the window; I'll keep an eye out. Here – this is for you, (Pressing one of the spare keys into her hand). Goodbye sis." He planted a kiss on her cheek - she looked as if she needed it - and hurried away.

Damask was right to be afraid of the sharp eyes of her maid. This grade of servant, usually consisting of daughters of the middle classes with some pretensions to gentility, formed the aunts' spy network. The girls were bullied by the old dragons into revealing their mistresses' most intimate habits, and were encouraged to spill the beans if one of the Glept females stepped out of line. They were expected to act as the aunts' eyes and ears and to inform on any of the quarters' inmates regardless of status. Menials caught showing loyalty to someone other than the presiding viragos were instantly dismissed. If she wanted to avoid an even more stringent regimen, the sort of treatment designed to break her spirit, Damask had to appear above reproach in her dealings with Therese. The maid was rarely further away than the next room and only took a single day off a month to visit her family. Waiting through the intervening weeks for this one occasion when

she could spread her wings a little Damask almost
screamed with frustration. "Why was I born a girl?!" she
lamented.

Dando came to see her whenever possible,
which was not very often. Then they both turned fourteen
and he set off for Gateway to start a new chapter in his
life. Left behind in the purdah that had been imposed on
her, her patience strained to the limit, Damask seethed
with envy. "I shall go mad!" she threatened under her
breath and almost welcomed the prospect. However, even
the most static situation is bound to undergo a change
sooner or later. A few months passed and it became
apparent that she might soon be in need of a new maid.
Therese, always somewhat poorly, was being laid low by
frequent headaches. The local command had decided that
her intervals of sickness were occurring far too often and
her employment was to be terminated. A replacement
would be sought. It was during such a hiatus that a
surprising apparition stood in Damask's doorway: Dando,
whom she had thought miles away, appeared before her
one evening grinning, apparently very pleased with
himself.

"Dando, what are you..." she was going to add,
doing here? but instead bit her tongue and took a deep
breath, not sure whether what she was seeing was real or
an hallucination. A small black girl, barely taller than her
brother's waist, was peering from behind him with an
expression half wary, half eager curiosity.

"Who on earth...?"

Dando reached backwards and gently pulled the
youngster round in front of him.

"Hi sis, - meet Milly. Say *hello* Milly."

"'Allo,"said the immature female, in a surprisingly hoarse and deep voice.

"She's about twelve or thirteen we think, although she may well be more and she could be a lot less. She's had a tough life. Can you look after her for the time being?"

"Time being? What do you mean? How long's *time being*? What's your game?"

"Sorry, can't stop. Must put in an appearance before I'm missed." To the girl, "Stay here like I said, Milly," and to Damask, "See you." He was already halfway along the corridor.

"Wait," cried Damask,"Come back! What am I supposed to do with this brat?" She pursued him as he made his escape down the stairs, reaching the top just as he arrived the bottom.

"Dando!" she thundered, "Come back here!" The only answer was the slamming of the outside door. Frustrated she returned to the apartment to find her brother's protege standing in the middle of the living room. They stared at each other for a minute or two.

I ain't a brat," remarked the urchin gruffly.

Damask realized she was going to have to make the best of things.

"No, I don't s'pose you are. Sorry. Your name's Milly, right? Where are your parents, Milly?"

"Ain't got none."

"Well, have you some place to live?"

"I got a room at the Spread Eagle, - I'm a working girl." (said with pride).

Damask began to get an inkling of where Dando was coming from.

"There's some food left over from my supper, - are you hungry?"

"Yes please, your majesty!"

Damask put meat and drink in front of the new arrival and was surprised to see how rapidly they vanished.

"Where were you born, Milly? I mean where did you start from? You're obviously not from the valley."

"I b'longed to Colonel Quatre, 'im 'oo owns the circus, - we travelled around. But then 'e sold me to Madame La Tour at the Spread Eagle. I liked the circus (wistfully), - I would 'ave liked to stay wiv the circus."

By ten o'clock Therese had still not appeared. In her absence Damask put Milly to bed in the maid's room where she was within calling distance, and then went through a much abbreviated beauty routine before climbing into bed herself. One question was nagging at her - had Dando paid money in order to rescue the girl from the Spread Eagle brothel? She thought he probably had. It was not in his nature to steal, even from someone engaged in trafficking minors for sex, although that would have been absolute anathema to him. If saving fallen women was going to become a habit, then it would probably turn out to be a rather expensive pastime; she hoped he would not take it up permanently, otherwise he might bankrupt the whole family. A little later she heard whimpering coming from the adjoining room. Relighting her lamp she went to see what was up.

"What's the matter Milly?"

"It's dark."

So far the little girl had displayed such bravado and sang-froid that Damask had been regarding her as a miniature adult. Now it was brought home to her that

Milly was no more than a child under the tough-guy exterior, and a child who had probably been through unspeakable traumas.

"Here, you can have my lamp," she said, "I'm just next door – don't be afraid."

"I ain't afraid," said Milly.

The next morning Damask woke to a smell of smoke. She opened her eyes to see a faint haze drifting in from the next room. Understandably perturbed, she crossed to the doorway where a remarkable sight greeted her. She found her guest sitting up in bed and with great insouciance smoking a clay pipe which she had lit from the lamp that was still burning.

"D'you 'ave any more shag?" the child inquired, "I ain't got 'ardly none left. 'E di'n't give me no time to get me stuff together."

"You'll have to put that out," Damask warned, rather taken aback. "If they get even a hint of something that goes against the rules you'll be in trouble and you'll get me into trouble too. Come on – get up. I've got to think of a way of explaining you to the authorities."

She returned to her room to face the prospect of carrying out the elaborate washing and dressing routine expected of her without assistance. "Where's that wretched Therese?" she complained loudly, picking up a comb. "She's never been away this long before."

Milly, who had followed her, watched her start to try and tease out the overnight tangles from her unruly mop.

"I c'n do your 'air, your majesty." the nymphet offered, "I done it for lots of the girls, an' I c'n do it for you. An' I c'n do your nails, an' your face, an' I c'n give you a good rub down too, if you wan' it."

Damask looked at her appraisingly, then wordlessly held out the comb. Milly set to work. In a very short while Damask's body had been washed and anointed, her usual fuzz of nut brown hair persuaded into some quite respectable curls and now Milly was occupied in applying make-up, a little pink tongue poking out between dusky lips as she concentrated on getting it just right. Damask surveyed the result in her mirror.

"That's very good, Milly. It even looks half decent - not the usual fright, the way that Therese does it." She was suddenly struck by a brilliant idea.

"Hey Milly, how would you like to be my maid? It's not a bad life. You'd get food and lodging, and a bit of pocket money every week too. You'll still be a working girl but it'd be a different kind of work, and you won't belong to anyone except yourself. I know you're very young but there are other girls around your age in the section. I think we might persuade them. What do you say? Would you like to stay?"

"Will 'e be comin' back 'ere agin?"

Damask saw where Milly's priorities lay.

"Maybe," she replied. "Did he just bring you here or did he ask you if you wanted to come?"

"'E ast me, but 'e di'n't 'ave to. I said I'd go wherever 'ee went." The moony expression on the little girl's face spoke volumes. "Will 'ee be comin' back agin?"

"Sooner or later he will. Dando's my brother; we're twins; born on the same day. If you're here long enough you're bound to see him again – sometime."

"Orl right your majesty. I'll stay – 'till 'ee come back." Damask gave a short laugh; she wondered if Dando knew what a conquest he had made. Later she discovered that Milly held an utterly scathing opinion of men. Basically she regarded the sex with wholehearted loathing mixed with fear. Even poor old Potto was not above suspicion. Only Dando was exempt. It seemed that the girl's devotion to her twin had started from the moment when, in the guise of a client, he had met her at the bawdy-house for the first time but had not laid a finger on her; an unprecedented phenomenon in her experience.

Damask explained the situation as clearly as she could to the prospective maid.

"I can't decide if you'll be accepted or not. It's up to you to persuade the people in charge that you're the right one for the job. You have to agree with everything they say – make them think you're on their side; do you understand?"

Milly nodded solemnly.

"I'll take you along to them and introduce you. I'll tell them you used to work for my dressmaker in High Harrow, the one who's gone down to the Great River to nurse her mother, and that you know all there is to know about serving a lady. Then you're on your own."

It was a lot to ask of a child of Milly's age that she should carry out this subterfuge and outwit the old harridans. Damask, having returned to her room, held her breath for what seemed like ages, until, eventually, the girl came bursting through the door. One look at her face informed Damask that their ruse had succeeded.

"I tol' 'em I'd do their business for 'em – I said I'd let 'em know what was goin' on. I tol' 'em I was a good girl. They said I could stay an' the other one would 'ave to go!"

"Good, good!" laughed Damask. She hugged the little girl fiercely to her. "You know what, Milly, I think you and I are going to have some fun!"

If she flouted the conventions and went her own sweet way, as she fully intended to do now that she was no longer under the gimlet-eyed surveillance of Therese, Damask realised that there was yet a chance that Milly would betray her. After all she had known the girl for less than twenty four hours and Milly's life up to now had probably contained little of either trust or loyalty. Nevertheless she had an irrational confidence that the waif would not let her down. In Milly she thought she recognized a comrade in adversity, a natural rebel, who given half a chance would kick against oppressive authority and fight to the last ditch to preserve her independence. For most of her time on this earth, it seemed that the little girl had been just a piece of property to be used and abused according to the whims of whoever claimed ownership of her; now she had the opportunity to take responsibility for herself and Damask guessed she would seize it with both hands. First though she had to convince her that the old dispensation was over for good; not easy for someone such as herself who, because of her nature, was not the most tactful or sensitive of mistresses.

One day, soon after the child had taken up her new duties, they were both in the bathroom going through the usual elaborate toilet ritual when Milly dropped a pot of salve which shattered, splashing oil and glass all over the floor. Damask had got up in a foul temper that morning, her mood matching the gloomy weather outside the window. As Milly gasped at the catastrophe she spun round with her hand raised shouting "You idiot! Look what you've done!" Quick as a flash Milly crouched down as if expecting a blow, her arms flung up to protect her head. Damask dropped her hand, feeling ashamed and walked out of the room. It was a fact that she had not hit a servant since the day when, at four years old, she had smacked the motherly Doll in a fit of babyish pique because a treat had been withheld and the Nablan woman had turned on her a sad patient look, more eloquent than mere words. She would not have hit Milly, but the girl was not to know that. All day the child crept around with a defeated slump to her shoulders, the light in her eyes extinguished. Damask, cursing herself for a fool, watched her anxiously and was hugely relieved when the next morning the apprentice maid was back to her usual perky, defiant self. This episode brought home to her the fact that Milly was indelibly marked by her experiences, and not just psychologically. When she first witnessed the girl naked she was aghast to see that her body was covered in scars.

"Milly," she cried, "What are all these?!"

Nothing loathe, the child launched into an enthusiastic enumeration of the origins of the injuries which ranged from the hazards to be met with in a travelling circus, through the uncertain temper of Madam La Tour, to the occasional strange preferences of clients. Damask shook her head dumbly in admiration; - Milly was nothing if not a survivor!

At the first opportunity following the girl's acceptance onto the gynaceum's staff, she let them out of the door Dando had discovered, using the copy of the key that he had filched, and they made a beeline for the Roma camp. There she had a joyous reunion with Duke that rocked his caravan on its axles. Meanwhile Milly explored the site, falling into conversation with people she met and discovering she had a lot in common with the travellers. When Damask went in search of her later she found her squatting down beside an old woman, comparing the relative merits of camping grounds down by the Great River.

"What did you think of that, Milly?" she asked on the way home.

"It woz nice," replied Milly. "It woz like the circus."

"Well, we'll go there again – we'll go lots of places." In her bag she had a suit of Duke's clothes that he had outgrown, and also a gypsy-girl's outfit for Milly. These she concealed in a hollow tree inside the castle's outer wall that she and Dando had discovered when they were small. Now she and Milly were all ready for whatever adventures they chose to embark on.

As they began their new life the girls were usually careful not to be seen, undisguised, beyond the gynaceum's purlieus. Most of the time when they wished to set out on an expedition they left secretly by the side door, but occasionally Damask had another means of escape. Aristocratic Gleptish ladies were encouraged to pay decorous social calls from one privileged family to another in order to strengthen the ties that bound their class together. She began to cultivate the friendship of a bovine, rather stupid girl in the Webb household that she remembered from the days of childhood parties. This old acquaintance was one of those females whose god is their stomach, and provided Damask took her an offering of fruity meringues or lemon drizzle cake made according to recipes that Dando had concocted she was prepared to turn a blind eye to the fact that her visitors were absent for many long hours during the days they were supposed to be spending with her. Damask, accompanied by her chaperone Milly, looking demure and dressed in her best, drove a dog cart out of the main entrance of Castle Dan, with their change of clothes hidden in a bundle under the seat, en route for the Webb mansion. And once they had checked in with Wilhelmina and exchanged the usual pleasantries, who knows? - the whole of Deep Hallow was their oyster.

It was Damask's firm resolve, now she had regained her freedom, to go for a walk on the wild side; disappointingly the sort of places she had in mind seemed few and far between in the valley. A further brake to her ambition was the fact that she now had Milly at her elbow. Damask considered herself to be fairly worldly wise, but in Milly she recognized someone far her superior; sometimes she wondered if the girl had really been in need of rescuing at all, she seemed so street smart. The child, three years or more her junior, took command when they ventured among the fairground booths of High Harrow, the seedier alleys of Low Town or the red-light district in Gateway. She would not let Damask get involved with anything she considered risky, and lectured her in her broad Drossi patois on the dangers of unprotected sex and the side effects of certain dodgy intoxicants. Damask paid attention to this diminutive martinet most of the time, but nevertheless had twice to drink one of the gypsys' bitter brews to bring on her period when it was late starting, before she finally learnt her lesson and put Milly's knowledge into practice.

They did not always go to the towns or the gypsy camp. On a certain occasion the two of them drove the dog cart down the Eastern Drift which ran alongside the River Wendover through the Incadine Gorge until they came to a point just above the Stumble Stones where travellers from Deep Hallow caught their first glimpse of the lands beyond. Damask brought the little carriage to a halt and sat gazing through the gap between the ravine's walls for a very long time. There it lay, the wide world that awaited her, stretching far, far into the distance, its siren call urging her onwards. But as yet she did not feel ready to cut loose completely and take the plunge into the unknown; another year or two would have to pass.

"One day, Milly," she said, "one day soon."

She turned the cart and headed back up to the valley.

The summer holidays arrived and Dando made his first official return to the Castle in two years. The brother and sister were fast approaching their sixteenth birthdays. Dando soon came visiting and Milly was in seventh heaven on seeing him again; her little face lit up with pleasure and she sang about the apartment in her hoarse gravelly voice. Dando's attitude to his small admirer, once he had assured himself of her well-being, was one of cheerful indifference. Damask marvelled at his obtuseness.

"What are you going to do about Milly?" she asked.

"What do you mean?"

"I suppose you realize the girl's potty about you?"

Dando looked at her in astonishment.

"But she's just a kid!"

"And I suppose you weren't in love at her age."

As usual Dando reddened when reminded of Ann.

"That was different."

"How come? Anyway, she's crazy for you. She'll follow you back to Gateway in the autumn when you go – you mark my words – unless you say something."

"I couldn't!" said Dando, horrified.

In the end he did not have to. Having been apprised of the situation he became acutely embarrassed in Milly's company and tended to avoid her whenever possible. The girl could not help but be aware of this and suffered accordingly. It was Damask who, eventually, taking pity on her unhappiness, felt she had to intervene.

"When we were little," she told Milly, "we had a friend called Ann. We used to play together and go to that cottage I showed you, up under the hills."

"'E woz in love wiv 'er!" said Milly, immediately seeing the light.

"He thought he was. And then when we were ten Ann had to go away. Dando missed her."

"'E's still in love wiv 'er!"

"He thinks he is."

"Mm."

Damask was surprised when Milly took this news with equanimity. That her beloved was carrying a torch for some unattainable ideal seemed to enhance his stature in her eyes. The girl apparently decided to settle for hero-worship at a distance and resigned herself to staying at the castle when Dando returned to the Outrider Academy.

It was about three weeks after they turned sixteen that Damask learnt that her brother was back home in the middle of the autumn term and in bad odour with their father. She was shocked to hear that for some inexplicable reason he had refused to take the oath that would have promoted him to full Outrider status, and was now awaiting a final interview with his parent which would be undergone after it had been decided whether to send him down to High Harrow to serve a two year suspended sentence for gross insubordination or to inflict on him an even more draconian punishment. In the end the first option was adopted. This meant that he would live at the Dans' town house and begin business training at the local school which would fit him to fill some sort of lowly position as clerk to his elder brother. When Damask managed to make contact she was surprised to find he was in quite a cheerful mood, or maybe he was just putting a brave face on it.

"It won't be so bad," he assured her. "I'll have the house to myself most of the time. When I'm not at my lessons I'll be able to get into the kitchens and produce something really worth while; I couldn't do anything like that down in Gateway. And anyway, I won't be far away; I'll come and see you most weekends." (In fact, as things turned out, he was unable to abide by this pledge, although he made a few surreptitious forays. "You're not to show your face at the Castle," his father had shouted after passing judgement, "until you've proved to me you're not a total waste of space – do you understand?" "Yes father," he had answered meekly.)

Damask shook her head pityingly.

"I'm sure they've got perfectly competent cooks in High Harrow without you sticking your oar in."

"No honestly – it'll be good and I won't even have to do the washing up like I did at the cottage."

"Lazy bugger," she replied affectionately.

She noted that despite his positive attitude her twin was paler than usual. He might deceive most people, but he could not hide from Damask that his confrontation with the Dan in the Hall of Oath Takers had been an ordeal that had greatly disturbed him.

"But why did you do it – why didn't you take the oath?" she asked. "You know what he's like; he was bound to blow his top."

"I don't know."

He did not know! If it had been anyone else who had given this answer she would have presumed they were prevaricating, but Dando... She had to accept the fact that her brother was prepared to turn himself into a pariah despite not really understanding his own motives.

The first year of Dando's exile passed slowly. Damask worried about him. She felt in her bones that something worse might be about to happen. Dando would never settle for being a clerk; even if he made a stab at conforming he was constitutionally incapable of taking on the role; the Dan was trying to create a sow's ear out of a silk purse. It was at this time that she had promised herself that she would start preparations for leaving the valley, but how could she go when her brother seemed to be riding for a fall and might be in need of saving from his folly? Now in the last few hours the *something worse* had happened and she could not see how she could help apart from pleading his case before her father. She yawned. The next thing she knew Milly was standing over her and it was morning.

"Milly! What's the time? I must go and see the Dan!"

She leapt out of bed and, without even washing, began to throw on her clothes as soon as Milly brought them in, meanwhile giving an account of what had taken place the night before.

"Why d'n't you wake me up?" cried Milly. "We could've stopped 'im leavin'"

"No - by the time I heard about it he'd already gone. There's nothing you could have done, nothing I could do; but I must try and get in to see the Chief now."

She set off once more for the Dan's suite only to be met by a brick wall. The Commander was busy – she would have to make an appointment – perhaps he might be able to spare her some time tomorrow – if she gave her name they would see what they could do.

"You know my name!" shouted Damask at the soldier blocking her way, incensed at the man's arrogance. "If you don't let me in I'll have you cashiered!"

In reply the other spat on the ground and grinned at her. Damask had no choice but to retreat with as much dignity as she could muster. As she re-entered her room Milly grabbed her arm and dragged her over to the window.

"Look!" she cried.

They watched as four armed men rode away down the drive leading a spare horse - there was something ominous in the sight - perhaps the head of clan had already been apprised of the previous day's events.

"Do you think they're after Dando?" asked Damask uneasily.

"They'd better not be!" replied Milly balling her fists and sticking out her chin. Damask smiled despite herself; she was reminded of a little hen bird preparing to do battle in defence of her chick. The Dan's establishment would do well to think twice before it tangled with Milly!

Earth-bound or Dancer?
The age-old question repeated
At each lifetime's end.

Chapter twelve

Ann had been slaving away since dawn. It had been an unremitting slog without a break, and now the light was fading. Her tiredness was made worse by the worries that were playing on her mind, the chief among which being her concern over the thing she knew she must never reveal at any cost: her battle to rein in the power that was growing and growing inside her. It was always worse at the time of the new moon, as was presently the case, and the astral phenomenon often coincided with the immanent onset of her monthlies, another peak of potential. A gift Dadda had called it, this capacity, but to Ann it felt more like a scourge, an unwanted destructive force that if discovered would put her life in danger. "You've inherited the talent, sweetheart," Dadda had said, "but it won't start to show 'till you're a bit older. Then you must learn to use it aright."

But who was going to teach her how to use it now? When it waxed powerful it appeared to be using her, not the other way round. It was as if she contained in her breast something explosive that might go off at any

moment. Once or twice in the past year, when it had
gotten too potent to be supported any longer, she had
slipped away into the woods for a brief period and,
stretching out her hands towards some unfortunate tree,
had allowed the energy to fly free. Lightning had
streamed from her fingers and the leaves and branches
had burst into flames. Simultaneously the recoil knocked
her flat on her back. But oh the relief to be rid of the
pressure, the same relief she felt when her bleeding
started.

Having at last finished her afternoon chore of
cleaning the upper floor she was on her way to the
kitchens to help prepare the evening meal when she
passed the room of the *knight errant* as she had heard the
new arrival called. This was, in fact, just one of the
misnomers that ill-wishers at the inn had applied to their
rather haughty guest in order to reduce his prestige in the
eyes of the remainder of the residents by turning his
standoffishness into a joke. To Ann, however, such was
the man's austere old-fashioned air, that the term seemed
a very appropriate way to describe him and not an insult
at all despite the fact that the age of chivalry was long
past. As she hesitated she realised that sweet sounds were
issuing from behind the door. In her present state of
exhaustion she saw no harm in sitting down on the stairs
where no one could see her and listening for a few
minutes. The music was temporarily soothing and
enabled her to think more rationally and calmly about her
plight. Why could she only destroy? Dadda had been able
to create beauty with just a graceful gesture: from his
fingers had blossomed a flight of tiny brightly coloured
birds, a blizzard of rose petals that scented the air, a
spring of crystal-clear water erupting from nothing. He

had worked the magic purely to delight her and amuse himself. He had also been able to put sick people on the road to recovery and mend broken minds. In their lessons together he had taught her a few simple charms such as a spell for sleep, basic thought transference, an invisibility incantation, but these were things anyone with the aptitude could learn. He had not told her how to control this wild beast within that was at one and the same time part of herself and totally barbaric; she had no idea how she could become its master and turn it to good. And now she was feeling especially afraid because she was under threat. Twice the Glept Lord, Yan Cottle, had grabbed her arm as he passed her in the corridor and dragged her into a corner.

"How about I take you out of this place, nibbler?" he had grunted, his eyes glinting in his intense saturnine face. "I could show you a great time, we could get it on together – we could push the plough around."

And, when they next came into contact, after he had pulled her to him and run his hands down her body: "Come on girl, you know what's good for you, don't make things hard on yourself. You realize I've only got to say the word..."

"No, no!" Ann had cried, shaking her head violently, terrified at what he might force her to do. The gift must never, never be used for personal gain - Dadda had insisted on that - neither for advancement nor profit nor even for self preservation; those who did so use it would lose their way and end up in a psychic blind alley for all eternity. So her father had believed and so he had practised right to the bitter end.

Granny Florence had urged her to go with the Glept.

"Take your chance girl – you'll never get an offer like this again! What be you a-waiting for? That Trooly ain't the one for you."

Ann was so weary most of the time, so worn down, that she was almost ready to follow the line of least resistance and go along with whatever was being asked of her, but there was that in Yantle's physical presence, a sort of slow-kindling smouldering fire, that gave her a glimpse of something not right, something warped in his make-up that frightened her exceedingly. And besides there was Foxy...

Her mistress, Mrs Humpage, had called her into the office a few days previously and shouted at her to *show*. When Ann lifted her head to meet the angry gaze and opened her hands, a piece of paper was thrust into one of them.

"Orlright – now tell me what that means?!"

Ann peered at the words.

IF HE TUCH HER YOOD BETER WOCH OWT!!

"I can't read it," she whispered. The landlady looked as if she might strike her.

"It says – *If he touches her you'd better watch out.* Does that mean anything to you? Does that mean you?"

"I don't know."

"Did you write this?" snatching back the paper.

"No madam."

Mrs Humpage took a turn about the room, her expression taking on a self-pitying droop.

"You've got to understand girl," she complained querulously, "I've refused 'im for almost as long as I can. I don't want to lose you but 'e's quality – you can't bargain wiv toffs of 'is sort forever. I won't be threatened – not by 'im, nor 'ooever this is," shaking the paper, "but I'm beginning to think it'd make things a lot easier for everybody if you'd just agree to go along with what he wants." Ann looked down at the floor, her hands now hidden in the folds of her skirt, while her hair slipped slowly forward until it formed a curtain in front of her face.

"I can't." she murmured.

"So - although you say, *I don't know,* you <u>do</u> think it might be you that's meant?"

"I – I... It could be..."

"Flippin' 'eck!"

There was a long silence

"'Oo is it then? 'Oo wrote it?"

Ann shook her head dumbly, dry eyed but with an ache in her throat. The landlady mulled over the problem.

"Well if you won't tell me, you won't, but I got me suspicions. Go on – scram. You'd better work a couple of extra hours tonight to make up for the trouble you've caused."

Throughout her life at the Justification, the seven years she had spent here under her first name Hilda, because it had been decided that in this way she would be less likely to be identified as the disgraced Culdee's daughter, (she had not been consulted), Foxy had been a constant presence. He had been there right from the start, watching over her, attempting to guide her, providing her with food, glaring jealously from the sidelines when she formed relationships with any of the other denizens of the place. He had acted like a possessive elder brother and for a while she had accepted without question his bullying proprietorship. It was only as she entered her teenage years and the gift began to manifest itself that she became oppressed by his determination to appropriate her existence for his own ends. She was dismayed when she understood what he was asking of her. It was extremely unlikely that she could be what he wanted her to be, that is to fill Dadda's shoes, to become the next Culdee and lead her people out of bondage. She had tried to make this clear but Foxy had ridden rough shod over her reservations. He paid not the slightest heed when she demurred, giving the impression that he regarded her as just a useful tool to be employed in achieving his angry quest for justice. Passionately stumping in and out of her dreary existence, day after day, he was quite oblivious to any thoughts and feelings she might have. Despite this total insensitivity she took comfort in his solid proximity. His physical strength gave her the illusion of being shielded from what she most dreaded. All the same she could not help but be aware, in her more clear-sighted moments, that this confidence was misplaced. When it came down to it Foxy was just as vulnerable as she was, just as much at the mercy of those in higher authority, and twice as likely to put himself in danger. She feared for him if Yantle made a move to take her by force. Foxy would not just stand by and let it happen; he would intervene and bring down ruin on both of them. But what could she do? What could she do?

She sighed, leant her head sideways against the wall and closed her eyes. Her weariness won out and she nodded off. Abduction; rape; retribution; burning; all her waking nightmares were still with her in sleep but the controlling mind was absent. When a hand was placed on her shoulder she lashed out in a flash (literally!), action coming a long way before thought. The next moment her consciousness came back to life and she took in the situation. A man, the stranger, was lying on the stairs above her. As she gazed horrified at what she believed she had done, he struggled back up into a sitting position with a stunned puzzled expression on his face, looking down at her stupidly as if she might provide the answer to a question he had not yet formulated. Briefly she stared into his eyes, tempted to throw herself on his mercy, before turning, scuttling down the bottom flight into the yard and through the passage that led to Granny Florence's lean-to where she crouched trembling, glad that, for once, the old lady was not at home. Now she had well and truly cooked her goose: she had used the gift in her own interests which Dadda had warned her she must never do and had thus revealed herself. She waited for the hue and cry to start; there were soldiers in the saloon, she knew, rumoured to have been sent by the Dan to root out witchcraft. Time passed and all remained quiet. Perhaps the stranger had not told anyone what had happened; perhaps he was incapable of doing so. After about half an hour she emerged from the hut and crept to the entrance at the bottom of the stairs. Cautiously she climbed up until she came to the bend. The man was no longer a step or two above her; he had disappeared and the door to his room was closed. She wondered whether to go and knock but could not summon the courage. Instead she retreated to the yard where she was immediately seized upon and berated for not being at her post. Dispatched to the kitchens to join in food preparation, it was not until much later that she caught a glimpse of Tallis in the buttery and satisfied herself that he seemed to have sustained no permanent injury.

Foxy was back at the inn now, working the long evening shift, fetching, carrying, doing the dirty jobs in the stables. Having toiled into the early hours he would spend what was left of the night with Florence and herself in the shack, unlike tomorrow when he would start at lunchtime and be gone by midnight. She preferred the nights that he slept with them. Lying on her small pallet she was always reassured by the dim hump of his body on the floor inside the doorless entrance, lit by wan starlight, a barrier against the threatening world. She knew from experience that he was not interested in her physically, in fact he was determined to keep her inviolate at all costs. All the same she resented his assumption that she was his to command when it came to affairs of the heart, his unthinking tyranny. She remembered in contrast her father's gentleness and sensitivity, and also recalled the boy, whom she hardly dared think about now she had come into her power, for fear of causing him harm. Later, starting to make inroads on a huge pile of washing up, she brought to mind what Dadda had told her about high priests and love.

"My teacher warned I," he had said, "but I wou'n't listen. I thought I knew better. I were besotted wi' her and we were barely eighteen. I took her to wife, your ma, an' everything seemed well at first. After a while she were in the family way 'an we were very happy. But child-bed be a time of danger. That Ol' Woman, she can take the danger an' make it deadly, an' that's what she did. I lost her, your ma. Remember that my maid an' don't 'ee do the same if you find yourself in my situation. Even if you be in love, don't 'ee lie with the man, an' don' 'ee confess to your feelings even within your own heart, for it will be he that she hurts, maybe more than you. Remember, she be a jealous god, an' she be most vengeful when the woman be expecting – if a Culdee fall pregnant that's when the danger be at its greatest. All the same there were those that bore children, the women I mean; what happen' to their menfolk I couldn't say."

Tom explained about a gifted female's magic to Ann: how it is most powerful before she has known a man; how she is pure and perfect then, her blood flowing with the phases of the moon. If, despite everything, she takes a mate and she is fertile, her blood flow ceases, she gives birth. At that time she has no magic for anything but passing on life to her child. But later if she is a true mage she may learn a new magic, earth magic, the magic of all fruitful things.

"You stay away from men, my hinny; don't 'e bring sadness on yourself like I did."

When Ann thought about her childhood at Castle Dan it seemed as if she was remembering another life entirely, a life that had happened to a completely different person. That person had not been, as this one was, constantly reminded of her worthlessness, she had not been engaged in continual toil for which she was never thanked. It was during those golden days that she had known the boy, they had been companions, sweethearts in all but name, although still only children; she could wonder at it. Her memories of that period in her life, her memories of him, were indissolubly linked to all the things she longed for and was presently denied: independence, fresh air, the chance to walk freely and unburdened under the wide sky, to plunge her feet into some cool stream, to sing, to laugh, to go bare armed and bare legged, to drink in beauty in order to nourish her starving spirit. He must have forgotten her long ago, her one-time friend, born as he was now on the wings of his privileged existence, and she must not even dream of their days together in case the Mother got wind of it and somehow used the memories to hurt him as her father warned her she might.

"Why do 'ee do it Dadda?" she asked one day, after her father had finished speaking of his mistress, meaning: *why have you dedicated your life to serving this ruthless, duplicitous deity?*

"Well my hinny," he replied, "I live in this place that were once called the Lap-of-the-Mother and the people need someone to stand between her and they. An' I be Nablan and the Nablar hev always fancied that they were her people. An' I be gifted. There's really no choice. You'll understand when you get a bit older."

"But Dadda, does the gift come from her?"

"Ah," said Tom, "that's a good question."

He mused quietly for a while, frowning and gazing into space. Ann waited patiently.

"I used to think so. That's what the ancient, the old Culdee, taught me, an' o' course I believed he. But she were angry wi' I for savin' that little ol' boy, she still be angry, yet she ha'n't taken the gift away. I can still mend people's ills, I can still stand between her and they when the need arises, an it's my hand that touch they as the healing come. I don't know if she can work that sort of enchantment wi'out me; she certainly can't prevent me playing a part. Sometime I think that I could do it wi'out *her.*"

"I thought a lot about this, my love. It seem to me they can't make something from nothing, the Great

Ones, it was another did that right at the start. What they do is *convert* things, and, often, harmfully when I'm not there to put my spoke in. The whole world, let me tell you, is like a cloth, made up of the warp an' the weft; the Great Ones can convert the warp, the aspect, but they can't convert the weft, the essence. An' what's true of the world is also true of people: they can influence the warp, that's people's minds, but they can't transform the weft, that's people's natures. Do you understand, my maid?"

Ann looked at him mutely, hurt and confusion in her eyes.

"I'm very sorry sweetheart, but I have to pass on these things now because later I may not be here."

Ann was surprised. "Where be you a-gooin', Dadda?" she asked

"Nowhere I hope, my love."

This was just one of the many sessions she shared with her father during her last days at the Castle. *Whereof one cannot speak thereof one must remain silent* says the philosopher, but she realised, much later, that Tom had been engaged in a race against time when he spoke of the ground-breaking ideas whirling in his brain, desperate to communicate the discoveries he had made since his falling out with the goddess before the chance vanished, searching for words that a Nablan's normal vocabulary would not have encompassed. He was attempting to convey knowledge both handed down and acquired from an abundance of experience which had recently been dramatically modified, to a recipient who was no more than a ten-year-old child.

"They come from outside. It's what I long suspected but now I'm sure of it because I often hear her voice - she think I be worth talking to since I crossed her

- it's hard to bear. The earth were here 'afore they come, she tell me, even the Old Ones who were originally alien creatures with mainly animal-like bodies before they made the transformation. I used to think the Old Ones were here 'afore everything but that's not so. They came, these forerunners, thousands of them, across space from another source, maybe not that different from earth and they found a Treasure circling our sun not far from this very world,. Once they had it in their possession, because this world were a good world, they decided to take a step backwards in their life's journey an' come down to ground level, not realising that if they became surface dwellers once more for any length of time they would be trapped here for ever. They made their homes in rivers an' streams, in the mountains, in the moors an' forests, even in the depths of the ocean, an' they demanded to be worshipped by those beings of the flesh that were here already – our ancestors. But once here they quarrelled over the Treasure an' it passed from han' to han' during damaging battles because none could keep it in their possession for long wi'out sufferin' hurt. It changed its form according to who held it, an', as it changed, something happened which caused it to become bound to the earth an' the earth to it so that now it rules the fate of our world. In that time of strife a link was forged between the Object-of-Power and anyone who carried it so that their destinies and the destiny of the Thing were ultimately connected. However it's not so well known that the physical and mental maturation of those in the flesh who hold it, however briefly, is often brought to an abrupt halt so that they are incapable of moving on. They therefore remain fixed at whatever point they have reached and live extended lives, sometimes for many thousands of years. Close behind these first arrivals came some that we call the Great Ones, but I'm beginning to believe they are little different from us and only earned that title because of their greater experience of the unfleshed state. These were lookin' to retrieve that which had been stolen and carry it back to the region where its intended destiny lies, whatever that may be; that's the purpose for which they were sent here. What I've just told you applied to them as much as to those of a lesser degree, an', when they saw our world, they also saw that it were good, an' as they believed they would be all-powerful here if they could possess the Treasure, they forgot about returning and claimed a portion of the planet for themselves. Amongst their number were the two known in this valley as Pyr and Aigea and they took the air an' the earth's surface as their domains. Because the female were closer to the heart o' things she discovered where the Object lay hidden an' carried it off, deprivin' the Old Ones of most of their power. By this time it had assumed the likeness of a Key so she were able to turn it an' unlock the second age, the Age-of-Essences and of the Heart. Some say though that it was one of our precursors, a primitive human, who turned it for the first age, the Age-of-Beginnings, before it fell into her hands and that therefore it was a member of our own race that brought down the curse upon mankind which presently we labour under."

"You say the gods come from other worlds Dadda," interrupted Ann at this point, her mind having wandered a long way from her father's narrative which she barely understood. "Will *we* ever be able to sail to other worlds like now people sail across the sea?"

Tom, becoming aware of her lack of comprehension, fell silent for a while before smiling and attempting greater clarity.

"Who knows sweetheart, who knows. Men of the future will have to build boats that fly for that to happen – it may come to pass – perhaps it already has. Yet there's a surer way to go outside. They are a spirit people, entities of pure energy, those that come from afar, able to inhabit matter or not as they choose, but they once had fleshy bodies like ours which they shed long ago. We can think and reason like them, in our minds we can stand outside ourselves and speak of who we are like them, we can tell the difference between good and evil. By rights we ought to have the ability to become as they are, immortal, unfleshed, free to dance among the stars. Instead most of us are tied to the world of creatures and things, increasing in numbers with each new generation, forced to suffer birth, death and rebirth in bodies that are cousins to the lowliest of the living. In the old days people believed that after death you went permanently to either a good place or a bad place according to how you'd lived your life on earth. People still often speak of heaven and hell. But because of certain pre-birth memories and occasional eavesdropping on those that claim to be gods we now think things are far more complex and uncertain than what was once supposed."

"But do we really get borned again Dadda an' live lots of lives?"

"That is what is now understood, my love. And why should we be so punished? - for punishment it is I have no doubt. Could it be due to the Key's connection to the earth as some of the stories have it or is it because of the first turning? She won't tell me. An' that's not the only thing she won't tell. When I ast why she want that little ol' boy dead she waxed hooly wrathful and roared at me so that my head nigh split. You know who I mean – the one who suckled from the same breast as you when you were babes. It shows that in some ways her power be not so great, for he still lives. Mayhap he has a well-wisher watching out for he, a well-wisher that tol' me where he be that day. I get the feeling that he is special in some way and there is a task – a task that was laid down many years ago and which is at present the preserve of another - that he was born to perform. If I can no longer do my bit to protect him when the time comes it will be up to you to stand between he and those that intend he harm. It misgives me that he has a hard road to travel an' a dangerous."

"But, Dadda, what would have happened if the Key had not come to earth?"

"Without the Key mankind would have taken a different path through the centuries and might have been more sure of reaching the final goal that all thinking creatures are meant to attain."

"But what different path would that be? I don't understand."

"My hinny, no-one here understands. Until we speak with others who come from outside we won't know the true way." "But you said that the Great Ones come from outside. Couldn't the Mother tell you?" "No, I doubt it. Because Pyr and Aigea forsook their duty and threw in their lot with life here on earth it seems they prefer to forget what went before."

The washing up done Ann moved on to her next job which she shared with the other Nablans: cleaning and tidying the public rooms now the clientèle had departed; after that came the kitchens, scrubbing and mopping, and then the dirty task of cleansing the latrines. Finally she was deputed to sweep the yard, by which time the night would be well on its way towards morning. The work did not require much mental effort and her mind was free to return to recollections of her father and another piece of information he had placed in her keeping.

"No, as I told you, they can't create from nothing," he had repeated, "although they can create the illusion of form; but even so they can take up station within matter and change things; they could possess you or me if they so chose. And as they can only create from existing substance they also find it hard to destroy; often they have to get others to do their dirty work for them. Either that, or if Aigea want someone to die, she would look into the future and find a remote time-line down which that particular result is fated to take place and then attempt to arrange for it play itself out in the real world bringing about the misfortunate outcome. But I mistrust that she be turning things to bad more often now when they could be brought to good, because she be vexed wi' I. Also you must realise that although she can't kill directly she can put people in the way of hurt so that they may perish. When that little ol' boy near lost his life in the Wynde where she led him it were the earth that were doin' away wi' he not her; the earth magic were just too strong for such a baby"

"But I thought she were the earth, Dadda."

"No sweetheart, she choose to be connected to the earth that's all, to rule the upper levels, an' to dwell within things that spring from there: the root, the bud, the

flower. O' course if you get too close to one of the Great
Ones your mind can give way; that's why we need years
of training before following the Wynde to the centre. I
can't tell you what that be like,"

"But what about the Seed of Erde Dadda, when
she made us from the grass. That be true surely?" All
Nablan children were taught the legend, at least those
whose parents were able to attend to their upbringing, of
how the Mother had given birth to their race by creating
them from seed husks filled with her breath, following
which she had taught them the ways of the world.

"Surely that story must be true, Dadda," said
Ann, "cos it tell us who we are and where we come from
and why we're important to she."

"I'm sorry, my maid, but, although I used those
words myself when I was instructing you, I think now
that it's just a pretty fable to make us feel special. After
all, when the Mother first came here - when her rule
began - she would have known little of this planet, so
how could she explain to us how it worked, and if we are
her chosen people and her hand be over us, why do we
now live in servitude? No, it seems clear to me that the
Nablar are no different from the rest of humanity: we
come from the great pool of life on earth same as each
and every fellow creature, although what the story say at
the end about the valley being at first land-locked and
then later opened to others so that pilgrims began to make
it their goal I believe has some validity."

"But what about when we looked after the Key
for the Mother, is that just a fib too?" That was what the
boy had suggested and she had indignantly denied it; now
she wondered if he had been right all along.

"As the deathless ones become damaged quicker than those in the flesh if they hold the Periapt for any length of time I believe she passed it on to us for safe keeping until she might need it, although, in those days, our species had little more understanding than the birds of the air or the fish in the sea. Such a tale is not part of the much bigger history that the Incomers tell."

"You mean their story be true and ours bain't?"

"No, I mean their story can stand beside ours because both hold an element of truth, although they tell theirs a little differently from us when it comes to speaking of the gods. They tell it as if it's a tale about people like us, men and women, who are creatures of the flesh, instead of about the Great Ones who are creatures of the spirit. Nevertheless, because the immortals' natures are closer to ours than they would like to admit, I think we may accept it as true."

"Tell it to me then, Dadda."

"Well, as I've already recounted, the Mother found the Key and turned it for the Age-of-the-Earth, the Age-of-the-Senses which is another way of describing the second epoch. But no age lasts for ever, although a thousand years may pass, mayhap ten thousand years or more before the end arrives. Eventually a point in time comes round when it must be turned again if the world is to continue. When that day came, Pyr, the Lord-of-Heaven, decided that this was his chance to take possession of the Treasure an' so he went a-wooin' the goddess with the intention of persuading her to give it to him. Our Lady, beguiled by his sweet words, yielded her immaterial body, and yielded also that which he was seeking, the Key, whereupon he carried it off in triumph, forgetting the protestations of love he had been pouring into her ears only hours before. He fitted it to heaven's door and turned it to usher in the third age, the Age-of-Air, the Age-of-Thought, and so yet another era began to wear away."

"The Mother was weakened by her loss and by this new turning, but not so much as she would have been if the Object had been wielded by a complete stranger. She retained most of her power over the earth's surface – the fertile layer. Understandably her fury knew no bounds at being so deceived by her consort, especially as they had set about the creation of a child between them during their courtship – an unprecedented act considering it would be constructed purely of spiritual substance. A plan of revenge and retrieval hatched in her seething brain, using the infant as instrument. When it was fully formed she took hold and struck it in half, bringing into being two male offspring where there had been just one - one child all light and the other all darkness, one positive, one negative, one image and one reflection. The bright child she cosseted and indulged, preparing him carefully for his role, while the uncomely one she abandoned on a hillside and believed him to have perished. But at the turn of the year an inhabitant of the night crept out of the depths and took the little lost creature down into a part of the underworld that is to be found beneath a lonely mountain and there he grew and flourished. Meanwhile, once her favoured child had also grown, the Mother put it about that she had born a son, and the Sky-Father, learning this and pleased with the notion, went to meet the bright one, hoping that the child would have the strength to assume the task of guarding the Key on his father's behalf. (The Mother of course intended that the boy, in his new role, would retrieve the Priceless Thing and return it to her). Their offspring, by this time a young man and disgusted with his warring parents' schemes, refused to do as either desired. He veiled his spirituality, assuming a physical aspect, and went among humankind who so far had been little regarded. He walked to and fro across the world and up and down the years instructing men in understanding which would enable them to form complex communities and later nation-sized states that nourished learning and progressive development. Meanwhile Pyr, through necessity, had also handed the Treasure to fleshly custodians." Tom paused, then broke off his narrative in order to switch to a related topic. "As you may have realised from what I've told you already," he said, "the spirit people don't live as strictly within the present moment as those with earthly bodies are forced to do; they can visit both the past and the future, seeing what is most likely to occur and what least, understanding what fate holds in store for them and us if the present time-line is allowed to take its course."

"Anyway," he continued, "the demonic son, Azazeel, having grown to maturity in the netherworld, and hearing the story of the Key, also determined to possess it. He ventured abroad on the earth looking for someone to be his emissary and found him in a great and subtle wizard of overweening ambition who had strayed from the correct path. This wizard, yclept Gammadion, having been lured beneath Azazeel's mountain, learned that possession of the Thing-of-Power froze the ageing of the body. Because of this he went eagerly to retrieve it from the keepers Pyr had appointed but with no intention of surrendering it once he had it under his hand for he believed that the longer he possessed it the longer he would live. He seized it and fled."

"It must have been sometime before this that the bright brother, Pendar, began to suffer from feelings of incompleteness, a sense that he comprised only one half of what made up a normal life-form's psyche. Eventually, unable to stomach this inadequacy any longer, he directed his steps downwards into the subterranean regions in the hope that his sibling would agree to unite with him in order to recreate a single whole and rounded individual with both a light and a dark side, like every other living creature. He travelled under the mountain into the haunted Caves of Bone where Azazeel dwelt, never to be seen again beneath the sun. What he desired to achieve I assume did not come to pass. Each winter it is believed that the Lord-of-Heaven ventures into the abyss in search of his son and at each midwinter festival the year-child is chosen and dedicated to the god to persuade him to return. And meantime the Key's whereabouts are unknown and the day intended for the next turning has come and gone."

"Those are the words that the Incomers, the group of Glepts that stayed in the valley instead of travelling on, use," said Tom, " an' from the time of the wizard's theft I believe their people have understood more about the gods' doin's than we have my hinny. But when they speak to the Sky-Father in these latter days I don't think he answers them anymore because they have abandoned the task he set – this despite the fact that, along with the other Great Ones, Pyr is similarly guilty of reneging on a promise. As for the Key it meseemeth that the world has been in thrall to it for far too long; the land is sickening and starting to die, the decline quickening since the most recent turning was missed. In my bones I feel the end approaching and unless something is done soon to destroy it or banish it from the earth I fear for the future of all life on this planet."

Ann tipped the final pan of dirt that she had swept from the yard into the dust cart that was waiting to leave, hung up her broom and went to report to the major domo, hoping against hope that her labours were over for the day. She felt dizzy with fatigue yet it was on the cards that another job might yet be found for her. She was almost too weary to care when told she could stop work and go to her bed. Granny Florence had long since retired by the time she entered the lean-to. The older woman turned over on her pallet and yawned.

"Your meal be on the stove," she muttered, "Foxy brought some meat. Don't make a noise – I be asleep."

Ann took the dried-up offering and sat down on the one and only chair with the plate in her lap. It was the first time she had had a chance to eat since sun up and now she no longer felt hungry. Florence started to snore. Ann wondered what her grandmother did out the back here all day. She had come to live with her at ten years old and by the time she was twelve and was strong enough to scrub floors and wash clothes Florence was pleading incapacity due to ill health and suggesting that her granddaughter should not just work alongside her as she had done so far but take over her position entirely in order to become the sole provider. Ann had had no choice but to comply if she wanted to keep a roof over her head, and in this way her life of toil and drudgery had begun in earnest. So long ago now it seemed when she had first arrived at the inn, and how distant was the time before that, the time at the Castle, which had come to such an abrupt end.

"You'll mayhap have to go an' live wi' your granny for a spell," Tom had told her. These were almost the last words she had heard him say. She had fallen asleep on her bed in the corner of the work room that night only to half-wake later with the vague understanding that there were other people in the cottage, but midnight visitors were nothing strange to the cobbler's daughter and she thought nothing of it. She ultimately surfaced well on towards mid-morning to find the little dwelling deserted; this certainly was unusual: her father never normally started his rounds without first sharing breakfast. Later Potto arrived, an expression of both dread and resignation on his face, to tell her that she must make her way to the Justification. From that point on a terrible feeling of impending doom assailed her. She protested loudly against leaving, hoping against hope that if she remained at the cottage, sooner or later Tom would come back and everything would return to normal. To go felt like an abandonment at a time when he might be in need of her.

"You won't be seeing your father again," granny Florence had announced a few days later with a sniff. She seemed to be both afraid and angry at the same time, her anger inexplicably directed at Dadda. A veil of sorrow descended over Ann at the words - a sorrow that was with her yet. From that day onwards she had forgotten how to laugh; it was only after time had elapsed that she realized she had also forgotten how to cry.

Now, having picked over the food, she disposed of the leftovers, removed her clothes and went to lie down. A little later Foxy's burly form filled the doorway.

"Are you awake?" he asked in a hoarse penetrating voice that was his version of a whisper. Florence groaned and covered her ears. Foxy entered the hut and deposited a sack of oats that he had pilfered from the stables. "Ha' that cheeky varmint been here again tonight?" he continued.

"He were here but he done somethin' to rile the mistress an' she sent he packin'. She tol' he not to come back."

"Good for her."

"But Foxy, there were three soldiers in the saloon." She lowered her voice to a whisper. "Someone say they be lookin' for witches."

"Soldiers, what soldiers?" Foxy had spent all of his time with the horses that evening and had been unaware of events in the public rooms.

"They come from the Castle. I be afeared. The power, it's been very strong today. I don't know how to hold it down no more. What can I do?"

"Did they see you – were you servin'?"

"No, I weren't in the buttery cept when the mistress call me, I were in the kitchens and upstairs. But Foxy, I be afeared I be goin' to give myself away - it be so hard to hide."

"Don' 'ee fret girl – I'll look after 'ee. No-one's a-gooin' to hurt 'ee while I'm around."

Ann sighed wishing she could believe him. All the same she felt soothed. Just to have someone before whom she did not have to dissemble was a relief, despite the fact that she was sure he did not really comprehend what she was going through.

Not withstanding their disagreement the night before Florence had also left a cooked meal for Foxy. He ate it with indifference and then, wrapping himself in a cloak he took from a peg, stretched his length on the floor just inside the opening to the stable yard. Sounds from the inn gradually faded and the quietness of deep night reigned for an hour or two. It would not be long before the first light of dawn began to banish the darkness. Ann knew she must get some sleep, she was desperately in need of it, but she had reached that pitch when she was just too tired to sleep. In the silence she was aware of a ringing in her ears and a tiny voice seemed to be repeating her name over and over again: *"Ann, Ann, Ann, Ann, Ann..."* When she came to the Justification she had lost her Dadda, he had gone out of her life, but not long after that someone else had entered it. On approaching puberty she had become aware that the Mother was interested in her. *That Ol' Woman had come a-sniffin' round* as Dadda would have put it. As her power increased so had her sense of this incorporeal presence: eager, curious, greedy, predatory, hovering on the margins of her consciousness. If Dadda had been alive and she had been recognised as the Culdee's heir, ready to set forth on years of arduous training, there would have been a formal ceremony, carried out in the utmost secrecy, to dedicate her to the Mother. At that rite she would have been pledged for all time and would have spent the rest of her life serving the Goddess. But without it what was she supposed to do and to whom did she belong? She had prayed hard for guidance, for help in understanding the gift, but all she got in return was an increased sense of alien emotions, of jealous possessiveness directed towards her that was extremely frightening.

"Go away," she pleaded silently. "Go away please and let me sleep."

To try and distract her mind she went back for the last time to her memories of her father and to a day they had spent together when happiness had been the normal tenor of her existence. Dadda had come home early one morning from measuring feet and fitting shoes and instead of getting down to work at his bench had suddenly said "Come on, it's a hooly nice day, let's take a walk." They left the castle grounds by the rear entrance and climbed silently and companionably into the hills. When they were well above the valley floor Tom had stopped and turned to look back, the whole of Deep Hallow spreading its length below them. From up here it looked a green and tranquil place, a place of deep woods and still water. He had stood for a while with his arm around her, gazing across wide spaces, seemingly lost in thought. At last he broke the stillness.

"How beautiful the valley is," he said sadly. This idea seemed to occupy him for some time and then his hand gripped her shoulder.

"When the mind get strong enough it should be able to leave the body – that be our ultimate destiny," he reiterated. "The person who has reached a certain stage in life comes to a conscious decision and then transforms by abandoning the flesh and the wheel of reincarnation. But a certain thing, which I think now must simply be the Key's nearness to our earthly existence, prevents us on this planet from becoming *dancers* as the immortals are called. I know we're well an' truly fit to go because, despite everything, there are some among our people who, on extremely rare occasions, can still make the change if they be wise enough and on the brink of death.

There be an' ol' verse I hear once which say that one day we'll all go free and when that happen ...*the great rocks will sing and the little rocks frolic like lambs*. It's all music an' numbers - remember that my maid - music an' numbers for all eternity." He stroked her neck and then pulled her to his side, whistling under his breath. Ann realised that the tune was *Over the Hills and Far Away*.

   "You have far to go sweetheart," he added a little later, "far, far to go. Be brave, be steadfast, be true to yourself. Don't forget what I've told you." He bent and kissed the top of her head. Ann waited to hear more but nothing was forthcoming. She looked up at his profile and saw that he was already deep within himself. They had walked back down the hill as silently as they climbed it, Tom rapt in contemplation. That had been not long before the end. Ann heaved a deep sigh and turned over. What she realised now, perhaps for the first time, was how lonely Dadda must have felt, estranged from the goddess and with only one other gifted individual – his young daughter – to confide in. If she had been a little older, besides passing on his newly-acquired knowledge, he could have explained the danger in which he stood but, because of her extreme youth, he did not share what he most feared and therefore went to his death without the comfort of knowing that at least one person was with him in spirit. It was so sad. Her eyelids drooped, her breathing deepened and became more even. She slept.

Each man an island?
No – however much we might wish it
We have to relate.

Chapter thirteen

Tallis was up betimes for his expedition to High
Harrow. As usual he knelt by the bed to say his morning
prayers, but cut the devotions short after a few minutes. It
was the fourth time he had invoked the god since entering
this valley and each time he felt as if he were addressing
a vacuum. Throughout his life he had prayed every day to
the Lord-of-Heaven although never with any sense of
personal connection to the deity. Here though he noticed
a difference. Elsewhere his supplications had gone
winging heavenward, but in this place they seemed to
leave his lips directionless, to hang on the wind and then
gradually fade away like a thin plume of smoke
dispersing on the waiting air; he felt as though there was
nothing at hand ready to receive his petition. This gave
him a new insight into his previous experiences. Perhaps,
after all, the Sky-Father had been with him on his
journeyings, although he had often doubted and been
discouraged, especially recently, now the days were
shortening as he made his way farther into the north.
Here, in this valley, however, the god was definitely
absent, he felt certain of it, and he experienced a novel
sensation of nakedness and vulnerability which made him

realise that previously he had been clothed and protected.
This was a god-forsaken place, forsaken by Lord Pyr at
least, yet he had heard the Night Hymn sung in this very
inn, or so he thought. There were people here who called
on the Lord-of-Heaven for guidance and worshipped him,
so why had he thus forsaken them?

After washing and dressing, Tallis opened the
window and looked out. The prolonged spell of rain had
passed, but so had the warm weather: there was a late-
autumn nip in the air and the sun, hanging in the south-
east, was half hidden behind a thin veil of cloud. Tallis
thought that the great life-giver, regarded throughout the
lands as Pyr's chosen emblem, appeared very distant and
remote, far removed from and indifferent to the dwellers
in this valley of Deep Hallow. Another ruled here it
seemed.

An hour later, he and Ralph having breakfasted,
he had seen Carolus saddled and led out of the stables, so
that all three were ready to set out for their destination.
He nerved himself to ask for directions and was told to
follow a path leading down to the crossroads at
Lanesmeet and from there to turn left up river along the
banks of the Wendover. When, after tracing this route, he
reached the little burg's outskirts he found High Harrow
crowded with folk taking a day off to go on the town,
while in the distance he could hear the sounds of the fair
wafting across from the water meadows. He had no
trouble in locating the main civic building or of finding
temporary stabling for Carolus, but was somewhat
dismayed on entering the hall to discover that, within, it
was thronged with people. If he wanted to have his
message put onto the Town Crier's itinerary it meant
waiting his turn. Tallis was not good at waiting. He could

have made the most of the time at his disposal by starting a conversation with the man behind him in line, an elderly Nablan who seemed prepared to be friendly, and by so doing discover more about the nuts and bolts of this society in which he found himself, but as usual he preferred to keep his own council. At last he managed to discharge his business and went out into the main square where the Crier would make his first appearance at twelve of the clock. He awaited his arrival with a certain amount of trepidation.

"A knight of the road is looking for a companion at arms," yelled the Crier (judging from this opening gambit it appeared that our traveller's arrival at the Justification had already been bruited about). "Who wants to try his hand at a bit of squiring? Wages ten shillings a day! Apply to Mr Tallisand at the King's Head Inn before the hour of five this afternoon."

Tallis was not happy. What was all this about knights and squires? All he wanted was assistance along the way: a simple menial for practical support. And this idiot had got the money side of it wrong: it was ten shillings a week he was offering! He tried to push his way through the crowd in order to set things straight, but the Crier had moved on before he could get to him. In the circumstances he had little choice but to go in search of the hostelry in question so as to be on the spot if anyone decided to apply for the post.

At this late hour, only a few streets away, Dando was also getting dressed. It was shortly after midday. When he had awoken in the town house about half an hour earlier, having slept the morning away, it had been into a state of blissful amnesia which had lasted for several minutes until he discovered that someone, presumably his faithful man-servant, had bandaged his left wrist; then everything came flooding back. Ruefully he rehearsed the events that had led up to his present situation. Firstly there had been his decision to play truant and visit the Upper Valley, after which came his determination to ride Attack, followed by his long mental journey into the past and his perilous encounter on Judd's Hill. Through his own negligence the horse had been injured, which had led to his decision to return to the Castle, and finally, last night, there had been his crazy notion to come back here instead of remaining to face the music. Yes, he was way up shit creek, and no mistake, without any hope of making an about turn. He rang for Potto.

"Have they sent for me from the Castle, Potto?" he asked.

"No Lord."

"If I don't hear anything I shall have to go back tomorrow. Will you come with me?"

"O' course Lord," replied Potto, amazed that his company was being sought in this tentative manner instead of his being ordered about as usual. He had lots of questions concerning his master's recent doings that he knew it was not his place to ask. Soon Dando showed signs of getting up and Potto tactfully suggested that he still had time to have lunch and go to school that afternoon if he got ready quickly enough. When the boy rejected this idea out of hand the old man relapsed into a disapproving silence. So now, as they went through the ritual of the toilet, the onus for carrying on a conversation fell to Dando.

"Come on Potto," he admonished, "snap out of it and tell me what's been happening while I've been snoring."

"The Lord Dan Attor were here overnight," replied Potto reluctantly, "but he went home this morning 'acos he cou'n't take part in the parade wi'out the horse."

"No, of course not. And what have you been up to?"

"I were at the Town Hall getting a licence for our wine-making."

"Oh yes, you need a separate one for here, don't you. And did you go on to watch the parade?"

"No Lord, I were too long at the Hall; there were a whool heap o' folk in front of I, all in High Harrow 'acos of the fair but doin' their business at the same time. An there were furriners as well: the gent next to I - he weren't happy wi' the delay - he had a message for the Crier, somethin' about needin' a packman and porter. I reckon he wanted someone to fetch and carry for he 'acos he be feelin' his age. From what he said to the pen-man behind the desk it seem he were on a long journey."

"What was he like," enquired Dando intrigued.

"Well, mayhap he were a good man, or mayhap he were a scallawag, I cou'n't tell, but what were plain to I were that he were no natural man for sure, the sort that likes a settled life wi' a wife an' childer aroun' he. You be too young, Lord me dear, but I've seen his like before, many times. They come up the gorge to this place, drawn here 'acos o' what it were 'afore times, young men, old men, always men, an' they never find what they be a-lookin' for, an' I'll tell you forwhy – 'acos they never look close enough: their eyes is allas on blue distances an' they never see what's under their very noses. So off they go,

south into the wilderness or west into the mountains or
north on the Shady Way, an' they hardly ever return.
What happen to they I cou'n't say, except that the Fellow
with the Scythe get 'em in the end, same as for all of us."

"And you say he had come a long way?" said
Dando wistfully. "I wish I'd had a chance to meet him; I
would have asked him about the lands he's travelled."

Potto glanced anxiously sideways at his master,
hearing the tone of longing in his voice.

"You don' want to be like that, Lord. It be a
great sorrow to be out alone in the world wi' no roof over
your head an' no bed an' no-one to know your name – a
fearful thing. Keep a hold on what you got here, an' stay
where folk have you in their hearts."

"Easier said than done," replied Dando a mite
sadly.

As usual the Lord Dan Addo emerged from
Potto's administrations looking the very model of a
Gleptish nobleman, a credit to his family, a contrast to the
bedraggled waif who had come to the door in the small
hours. Physically he felt very few after-effects from the
traumas of the day before: a little stiffness perhaps, a
slight weakness as after a mild illness, but mentally he
was bearing a fairly heavy burden of guilt on account of
Attack. As he had heard nothing so far from Castle Dan,
he decided to visit the fairground where perhaps he could
forget his troubles for an hour or two.

"I'm going across the river, Potto," he called as
he left his room and passed the servant sorting dirty
washing in the linen closet.

"But you ha'n't eaten, Lord," protested Potto,
attempting to detain him.

"No matter, I'll get something over there."

In fact his normal objective when attending this type of festivity was not to see the main crowd pullers such as the bearded lady, the two headed calf, Punch and Judy, the boxing and wrestling booths where locals could try their skills against professionals, the Aunt Sallys, the magic lantern slides, even, last year, a moving picture show; no, what drew Dando irresistibly were the food and drink stalls, and not just the ones selling gilded gingerbread men, sweetmeats or mead and punch; he was always eager to investigate any foreign delicacies on offer and if possible winkle out of the stall-holders the ingredients used and the method of preparation employed. It was not always easy to get them to reveal their secrets; he often had to use all his charm and tact to achieve his end. Dando, in truth, was becoming known to the travelling fast-food fraternity as an up and coming practitioner of their arts and therefore a potential rival despite his apparent disguise as a seed of the valley's most illustrious family. However they were not ungenerous; he certainly would not go hungry.

Crossing the bridge over the Wendover he met a steady stream of merrymakers coming away from the revels with their *kiss-me-kwick* hats, their tawdry booty won on the hoopla or nine-pin bowls, their bags of sticky candy. The fair was into the afternoon of the second day, the parade had gone by and people were starting to leave. None the less the din from the site - the sound of mechanical organs accompanying hand cranked carousels, the clack of skittles, the cries of barkers, the lowing, bleating and neighing of live animals being traded - could still be heard from several miles away. Dando followed his nose and was soon deep in conversation with a woman selling honey-soaked layered pastries filled with chopped nuts, a type of patisserie he had not encountered before. When the Town Crier took up his stance right beside that very stall, rang his bell and embarked on a long elaborate spiel which drowned out Dando's informant, he at first regarded him as an exasperating nuisance. As the itinerant cook broke off in the middle of her explanation in order to listen to what was being said he was also, perforce, compelled to turn his attention to the Crier and all at once his interest was caught.

"Oyez, oyez, oyez," the man was yelling at the top of his stentorian voice. "A gentleman traveller, Master Tallisand by name, intends to make a journey next spring and is looking for a companion-at-arms to accompany him. The wages will be ten shillings a day plus gear and vittals. Retainer to be paid immediately. Now come on all you likely lads – who'll go adventuring? Who's game for a bit of shield-bearing - a bit of squiring? The gennlemun's a musician – I dare say he'd throw in a few lessons on the banjo for good measure."

The crowd which had gathered to listen snickered and stirred but no-one came forward. After a pause the Crier lost interest and hurried on: "Applications should be made to Master Tallisand at the King's Head or after market hours at the Justification Inn down beyond Lanes Meet. Thankin' you." Clang, clang, clang went the bell. "Hear ye, hear ye, hear ye, good people! Latest fashions and furbelows on sale now at fantastically reduced rates – get your winter wardrobe from Messrs Pinchkin and Batty's emporium – hurry, hurry, hurry..."

Dando walked away deep in thought having forgotten about the pastries. Surely this must be the man

Potto had described seeing at the Town Hall, this stranger, Master Tallisand, a *gentleman traveller* as the Crier described him, on a journey that, inspired by the choice of words in the pronouncement, he romantically imagined might prove to be some sort of lifelong quest such as knights of old undertook. And he was to be found at the King's Head. Perhaps this was his way out? Dando's constant crie-de-coeur was to be allowed to merge with the mass of his contemporaries, to become one of the crowd. *I just want to be normal,* he pleaded silently, *I'll never be allowed to be normal while I stay in this place.* What normality entailed he could not quite decide; it was just a vague concept to him, an insubstantial abstraction that other people possessed and he did not. Father Adelbert had assured him that he had the makings of a chef. All he needed to do was get himself down to one of the cities on this side of the Middle Sea and find an establishment that would be willing to employ him. There perhaps he could fit in, there he might be able to discover his metier and become *normal* at last. It seemed to him, suddenly, that if he could say goodbye to Deep Hallow for good, every one of his problems, but in particular the awful fix in which he presently found himself, would be solved at a stroke. Well, here was an opportunity to leave staring him full in the face; he would be a fool if he passed it by. With this in mind he recrossed the river and climbed to the centre of town where the famous old tavern, the King's Head, was to be found. He nursed an intense curiosity about this foreign wayfarer and was eager to meet him. All the same he approached the possible encounter with a certain amount of caution. The man at the desk inside the door of the inn came rapidly to attention as he caught sight of the Dan's second son entering his establishment.

"Have you got a Master Tallisand here at the moment?" asked Dando. "Is there anyway I could catch a glimpse of him?" The receptionist took his meaning immediately.

"Yes Lord, 'e's in the snug; been 'ere for some time. Not much of a drinker. You c'n 'ave a gander if you come through into the wine-waiter's cellar. Just look through 'ere. You c'n see wi'out bein' seen."

Dando, obeying orders, peered through the indicated spyhole at the figure walking to and fro in the small room beyond and was immediately struck by the fact that he did indeed bear a certain resemblance to a man with some predetermined purpose, or at least how he imagined one might look. What he saw was a sort of *eminence gris*, a spectre at the feast, a phantom in the little paint-box town. The man's head was neat, scull-like, with hollows under the cheek bones, a lipless mouth and lifeless skin, drawn and ingrained. Dando stared at his calf muscles, occasionally visible as he moved, knotted like old tree roots, and at the long emaciated hands with spatulated fingers and joints like knobs of old ivory. His stance was erect and his clothes hung on him gracefully, A leather jerkin covered a finely woven shirt, knee britches beneath, while over all he sported a huge collared cloak of some thick but dull grey-brown stuff, the collar overlapping his shoulders and the garment reaching almost to the floor. Dando was fascinated by his footwear, its very strangeness speaking of foreign parts, composed of a supple yet strong leather tapering at the toes to elongated points like fashions of bygone days. The shoes were gathered up around the ankles with what appeared to be purse strings, the material displaying a defeated long suffering look, speaking of countless buffetings on roads that have no ending. All his clothes showed signs of damage and wear; could those dark stains be patches of dried blood?. On his head he wore a close-fitting helmet reinforced with steel bands round the rim and across the crown which he was obviously reluctant to remove even though he was in a non-threatening environment. When he looked up his eyes were almost colourless, as were the few wisps of hair that escaped from his headgear. Nearby, unaffected by his master's restlessness, lay a large wolf-like dog, also grey in colour. Dando had never seen anyone remotely like this individual before and was instantly smitten.

"Have you got a place I could use," he asked the attendant, "where we could talk?"

"Yes Lord, through 'ere. Nice and quiet – you won't be disturbed."

"All right. Now go and tell him I've come in answer to his cry and I'd be happy to meet him if he'll be so gracious as to wait on me."

Having arrived at the King's Head, explained his business and paid for the privilege of using the hostelry as a rendezvous for the next few hours, Tallis had found himself at a loose end. To while away an extended period in a public place with nothing whatsoever to do was a species of torment for someone as unsociable as himself. He had no desire to interact with any of the inn's other customers nor to partake of a meal, and, where drink was concerned, he was extremely abstemious. He sat for a while in the small bar he had been shown into, ignoring anyone else who happened to enter, then got up and strode restlessly to and fro, sat again, fiddled with his weapons, directed a word or two in Ralph's direction, counted the age marks on the back of his hands, got up and paced once more. It was not until halfway through the afternoon that the receptionist came and told him that his message, conveyed by the Crier, had produced a response.

"There's a lad 'ere 'oo wants to see you about your wanted ad. But I'd better warn you, this ain't your usual riff raff – 'e's gentle-born, this one. You'd better watch your step. Follow me – 'e's in a room at the back."

Tallis, who had imagined that any applicants would come to him rather than he to them, felt rather disconcerted and put out to be summoned in this manner. He also asked himself why, after having paid a substantial sum, he had not also been offered a private room in which to conduct his business.

"End of the corridor," instructed his guide, "you can't miss it," and hurriedly returned to his deserted post. Tallis walked on silent feet along the passage, accompanied by his dog, and peered through a half-open door. The occupant of the room had not heard his approach and Tallis was able to examine him at fairly close quarters without his being aware. The stranger before him was a tall slender youth with luxuriant sable-coloured hair, dark eyes under finely drawn brows and an expressive mouth, although with something secretive about it. His rich clothes and impeccable grooming singled him out as one of the quality. Tallis remembered the peddler's remark about *'ot 'ouse flowers*. This boy had one of those curious androgynous faces that would have looked good on either sex and, because of that, and because of a sort of unwitting air of upper-class superiority, appeared quite striking in his own peculiar way. At this particular moment he was standing looking downwards with his weight mainly on his right leg, one arm across his chest, exhibiting the interesting spiritual pallor that often, in youth, follows a night of dissipation.

Scarcely more than a child, was Tallis' first thought. He chose to ignore the fact that, remarkable to relate, considering his normal enmity to strangers, for the last few minutes Ralph's great plume of a tail had been swinging slowly to and fro.

Dando – who else could it have been - looked up, and catching sight of this prospective employer came forward eagerly in order to seize Tallis' nerveless hand and shake it vigorously. "Pleased to meet you," he said.

"I beg your pardon," replied Tallis, "I must have come to the wrong place; I was expecting to find an applicant for the position I advertised through the Town Crier today."

"Yes," answered Dando eagerly, "that's me – I heard your message – I heard you wanted a squire – I think I might suit you."

"That was just the Crier's pipe dream – I never said anything about squires. All I need is a servant to carry my baggage – someone who could be useful with the sword if necessary."

"Yes well... it's the same thing really, w-whatever you call it," replied Dando, sobering up slightly, "I can fetch and carry for you – and I don't need to be paid – and I've had plenty of fencing lessons." He displayed the weapon at his waist.

They say that you form an opinion of someone within the first few minutes of meeting. Tallis had very occasionally come across individuals such as this boy on his travels, types with the effortless self-assurance that comes through being born into privilege. Although, many times, his mother had claimed equal status on his behalf, such fortunate creatures always made him feel slightly inferior.

"You're very young," he said dismissively, "too young for what I require."

Dando frowned slightly at this frosty reception. Normally people liked him on first acquaintance and he was somewhat nonplussed to realise he had not made a good impression. He was not sure where he had gone wrong.

"I think I could be useful to you," he pleaded. "I could provide supplies for the journey – maybe even a pony to carry them; and I know a thing or two about catering; I could help with the cooking along the way."

Tallis looked at him in surprise. He never cooked when on the road, making do with biscuits, way-cakes, cured meat, nuts and whatever fresh food he came across in the settlements he passed. But the offer of a pack animal and maybe other necessities was tempting.

"I'll put your name on the list – what is it by the way? - but I can't promise anything; I have several more people to see before the day's out."

Dando gave his name absently and then continued in a hesitant manner that seemed to counteract his previous confident air, "I-I'm afraid if you decide in my favour I'll have to tell you where to find me; I won't be here in town from tomorrow onwards (*At least I don't think so* – he added to himself). You'll have to come up to my father's place, that's Castle Dan. G-Go across the bridge here and then take the pike westwards on the other side of the river – it's a few miles – you'll see a road going off to the right through a wrought iron archway – that leads to the Castle."

"I can't promise anything," Tallis repeated somewhat impatiently, feeling it was time to bring the interview to an end, his momentary inclination to employ this young peacock rapidly fading.

"You'd b-better not come to the main entrance," pursued the boy, as if needing to finish what he had begun. "When you get to the gatehouse veer right and follow the wall round to the back. Ask for Applecraft - he's my manservant - he'll let me know you've arrived. H-how soon will you decide?" There was a note of almost desperate entreaty in his voice.

"That's not something I can tell you right now," answered Tallis with finality, "as I said, I can't promise anything." He held out his hand, gave the other's a cursory shake and turned away.

Dando directed his steps back towards the Dan's domicile in a deflated frame of mind. Somehow or other he had made a hash of things, but he was puzzled as to why events had gone so awry. The knight, which was already how he thought of this new acquaintance, had been almost hostile, yet he had a strong feeling, now they had met, that the man was in need of his assistance and that their fates were entwined in some way. As he rounded the corner onto the street where his current abode was situated he saw five horses and three soldiers standing outside the entrance. A more experienced criminal would have turned and fled. Dando, naively, walked straight into the arms of his father's whippers-in. As he reached the house a fourth soldier, a hatchet-faced captain, emerged from the building followed by Potto who was wringing his hands. The fellow looked vaguely familiar to Dando; he must have seen him about the Castle.

"You are Dan Addo of Clan Dan," the officer barked, "presently residing at the Ancient House in High Harrow?"

"Yes," said Dando, "you know I am."

"You are under arrest. Surrender your weapons and come with us."

Dando stared stupidly at the man. "U-under arrest?" he stammered.

"I have a warrant," the captain shouted, apparently expecting resistance. He pulled out a piece of rolled up paper, flattened it and held it within inches of Dando's nose for the boy to read. Dando blinked and tried to focus; he could not make out what was written, but at the bottom he saw the Dan's unmistakable signature.

"Surrender your weapons!" the captain repeated. Dando looked helplessly at Potto who looked back with a stricken expression. He unbuckled his sword belt which also held a dagger and let it fall to the ground.

"Search him!" the captain instructed one of his underlings. The soldier investigated Dando's outer wear and discovered a small penknife which their prisoner had forgotten he was carrying. The captain confiscated it with a triumphant look.

"Now get on board," he ordered, indicating the riderless horse.

"I need my things," said Dando, looking towards the house.

"You'll come as you are. That's our instructions. Get up on the horse. No arguments!"

After a moment's hesitation Dando acquiesced and mounted while the soldiers also vaulted into their saddles, one of them taking the spare horse's leading rein. Immediately they were in motion. The boy looked back at the rapidly receding figure of Potto and the old man raised his hand in farewell, much as if his master were setting out on some pleasant expedition.

"Come after me Potto," Dando called, "bring my things up to the Castle."

Grimly Tallis sat out the rest of the afternoon at the Kings Head, but when five thirty came and went he acknowledged that no more applicants were likely to appear. The day had been a total waste of time. It was bizarre that the only inquirer for the position he was offering had been that upper-class youth whose sincerity he doubted. The youngster had probably been playing some sort of game for his own amusement as boys of his age often do; Tallis was angry that he should have unwittingly been forced to take part in the charade. Gloomily he mounted Carolus and turned his head towards the Justification, feeling thoroughly depressed.

As he led the horse into the stables at the inn he was met by the same servant who had brought him his bath two nights earlier. The man received the animal from him, but did not acknowledge that they had already met; in fact he did not say a word, rudely ignoring Tallis as he led Carolus away. Tallis stared at his departing back, admiring once more his powerful physique and his determined belligerent stride; with such a henchman at your beck and call you would have little to fear from hostile elements along the road. Conceivably he might be able to break through the man's unfriendliness if he tackled him in the right way and suggest they should travel together; what he could offer him would surely be better than the lowly position he occupied in this establishment. But to make such an approach would mean overcoming many years of diffidence and antipathy on his part regarding personal relationships. Well, tomorrow perhaps he might make a move, or maybe the day following.

Eating his evening meal in the buttery he noticed that both the group of soldiers that had been there the night before and the Lord Yan Cottle were absent, but so was the little nibbler girl who had claimed his attention and engaged his sympathies, despite himself, when he first arrived; she was obviously not on waitress duty tonight. He thought again about their encounter on the stairs and got the uncomfortable feeling that he had been involved in something strange and unaccountable for which there could be no rational explanation, but then dismissed the notion. He had simply been taken ill, that was the plain truth, nothing that should concern him now that he had recovered. Out in the courtyard once more and on his way to the stables he slipped quickly past the door to the office, not wanting to encounter Mrs Humpage and have to admit to the complete failure of his day in High Harrow and the fact that her helpful suggestion had come to nothing. Back in his room he omitted his evening prayers, undressed, lay down on the bed and composed himself for sleep.

He was not sure how many hours later he awoke, but his internal clock told him that midnight was long past. What had roused him was the need to urinate, something that had been disturbing his sleep more and more frequently in recent months. He climbed out of bed and reached under it for the chamber pot only to find it absent; the wretched nibbler whose job it was to empty and wash the vessel each day must have forgotten to replace it. He would have to use the public privy which was on the far side of the courtyard. Cursing under his breath he dressed, made his way down the stairs and crossed to the latrine. When, after a delay, he came back into the open, having discovered that he needed to do more than just pass water, he realised he was not the only one awake. For the first time he noticed that the gates under the front archway leading to the road, normally closed overnight, were partially ajar, and the yard, lit by a starry sky and the newest of new moons, was now peopled by several dim figures. Tallis identified Mrs Humpage, prinked out in night attire and curlers, a number of guests and members of staff and, the focus of their attention, the individual know as the Lord Yan Cottle, accompanied by another man. Yantle was just ordering this individual to "Go and fetch her, you know where she is!" while Mrs Humpage was exclaiming that this night-time invasion was, "...a houtrage!" Tallis, unnoticed, surreptitiously made his way round the edge of the shadowy space and then crept up the stairs to retrieve his sword, calling Ralph to heel. As he buckled the weapon on he heard a loud knocking coming through the window from the rear of the inn, followed a few minutes later by a cry. He returned to the downstairs doorway just in time to see Yantle's henchman reappear dragging the nibbler girl, Hilda, by one wrist. She was practically naked. Coming along behind them was an old woman wailing at the top of her voice. Tallis drew his sword and stepped into view, Ralph beside him.

"Loose her!" he cried.

Yantle swung round. "Who are you?" he exclaimed, and then "Stay out of this!"

"Let her go!" commanded Tallis, advancing a pace.

Mrs Humpage intervened. "Be careful, Mr Tallisand," she cried, "'e's got a gun!"

For the first time Tallis noticed what Yantle held in his hand: a device made of metal glinted coldly in the faint moonlight. In recent times he had occasionally encountered a weapon such as this at the waist of some lawman or soldier on duty along the road he was travelling but had not imagined that one could have penetrated as far as this remote valley. He took another step forward and repeated "Let her go!" Yantle raised the firearm and at the same time Ralph gathered himself together for a forward leap, a growl starting deep in his throat. Suddenly death was staring both of them in the face.

"STOP!!" The voice was authoritative. The nibbler girl had stretched out her unimprisoned hand in the classic warding off gesture. There was a flash and a deafening report but it was the man that held the weapon who fell. Yantle crumpled, face forward, to the ground and lay still, blood beginning to ooze out from beneath his body. It was apparent that, on being fired, the gun had exploded, sending fragments of shrapnel deep into its wielder's vital parts. There was a shocked moment of silence and then the serving-man released the girl and ran out of the courtyard through the front archway. They heard the sound of hooves dying away into the night. Somebody, it was the peddler in fact, walked forward and stooped over Yantle's immobile body. "'E's 'ad it!" he said in an appalled voice.

Mrs Humpage pointed wildly at the girl. "It was 'er!" she exclaimed hysterically, "she made it 'appen! - I saw 'er!" A murmur began amongst the onlookers that grew and spread. A lone voice rose above the rest: "Witchcraft!" The old woman, apparently a relative of the accused, gave a shriek of despair.

"They'll burn her!" she cried.

Tallis thought faster than he had ever done in his life before; he strode to the landlady and, seizing her round the waist, put his sword to her throat. The woman screamed.

"Nobody move!" he commanded. "Do what I say and she won't get hurt." He looked around assessing the situation, forming a plan.

"You," he ordered the peddler, "go up to my room and get my things – my pack and the musical instrument – and get a warm cloak for the girl." To the old woman, "Take her and put some clothes on her." The little waitress seemed to be in a daze.

"Orl right, orl right," said the peddler, "keep your 'air on mate!" He hurried away. Tallis was left facing a hostile crowd. Nearly every inhabitant of the inn had woken and was now in the yard, while Mrs Humpage whimpered and trembled in his grasp.

"Get them to saddle my horse," Tallis instructed a boy whom he recognised as coming from the stables, "and load him with the baggage." He waited a moment for the peddler to reappear then dragged the landlady through to the back of the building, the rest of the onlookers following at a safe distance. A few minutes later the old woman emerged from one of the lean-to shacks without the girl. She stood staring stupidly in front of her, reduced now to silence.

"Where is she?" demanded Tallis, "Tell her to come at once."

"I don' be able," the woman replied, almost inaudibly, "she's gone to sleep. I tried to wake she but..."

"Is she dressed?"

"Yes."

"You," said Tallis to a brawny individual standing nearby, "go and fetch her."

The man reappeared carrying the apparently unconscious girl in his arms and, following Tallis' instructions, she was wrapped in the cloak the peddler had provided. Now Carolus was led out of the stables carrying Tallis's equipment and the young Nablan's inert body was hoisted across the saddle bow. Tallis, still with his naked sword in one hand, took the horse's rein in the other and, accompanied by Ralph, chivvied Mrs Humpage through the back gate of the inn and along the path that led to the main highway.

"If anyone follows it'll be the worse for your mistress!" he shouted.

The crowd stood silently and watched him go, no-one having the nerve to make a move. At the first bend he sheathed his weapon and mounted behind the girl.

"I'm very sorry," he said to the terrified landlady who was silently opening and closing her mouth like a beached flounder, "very sorry..." All he could do was to hand over some coins which he took from his purse; words were inadequate to express what he felt. Briefly he stared down at his hostess, trying to think of something he could add that would compensate for what had occurred, but then gave up and urged Carolus forward. It behoved him to put as much distance as possible between himself and the Justification before first light appeared in the sky and then to find somewhere where he and the girl could lie low during the day. Perhaps when the next evening arrived they could steal away without being seen and, all things being equal, be quit, for good, of this misfortunate and ill-starred valley.

The colour of his hair?
That can be changed,
But his heart – never.

Chapter fourteen

Dando stood under guard in the centre of the main bailey of Castle Dan, the inner bastions of the keep towering around him on all sides. The captain had gone off to report and receive further orders. The castle's fortifications were built of monolithic stone blocks reputedly quarried high in the western mountains, and the walls, in their massive proportions, resembled nothing so much as the ramparts of a prison. They frowned down on him now in an accusatory manner, seeming to embody every aspect of his overpowering family and all that it stood for. It was a busy area this quadrangle, and he could not help but feel that he was being displayed in the most public place possible so that everyone would be able to witness his downfall. Lots of people, many of whom he thought he could claim as friends, were crossing and recrossing the open space. He saw how they stared in his direction and then looked quickly away as if by just meeting his eye they might risk contamination. Eventually he spotted the head groom, a long time trusted advisor, emerging from the tunnel that ran under the central part of the house; his demeanour, in contrast, displayed sympathetic concern.

"Hollinger," he called, "how's Attack?"

Glancing nervously at the armed guard, the man came over, an understandable wariness in his manner.

"The vetinary from Low Town be with him now, Lord. He say his racing days be over, but he'll still be able to do his duty by the mares if we can get he to calm down. At the moment we can't even persuade he to eat and drink. The medico say that if his leg improve we could try turning him out to pasture for a few weeks along o' some of his lady friends."

Dando nodded gloomily; he had hoped for better news than this; maybe, given time, he could re-establish his rapport with the horse.

"Let me come over and see him," he said, "I might be able to do something. I mean, tomorrow perhaps," he added, suddenly remembering his present circumstances. They both noticed the captain leaving the rear passageway and making his way purposefully towards them. The groom hovered for a moment in the vicinity and then moved away, a look of awkward pity on his face. The officer approached, stamped his feet and came to attention.

"The Generalissimo will examine the prisoner tomorrow. Squad dismissed!" The three soldiers saluted and marched off. Dando turned towards the main entrance in the west wing and took a step forward.

"Where do you think you're goin'?" barked the mercenary.

"To my rooms." replied Dando mildly.

"You're not goin' nowhere, mate, except where I say. You're under arrest remember."

Dando's shoulders slumped; he turned back submissively realizing that for the moment his life was

not his to command. The soldier marched him through
the archway that led to the warren of buildings at the
back of the Castle. Here were located the stable complex,
barns and storerooms, servants dwellings, workshops and
nibbler shacks. The Dan's private army, about five
hundred strong, were also to be found in this region,
quartered in barracks surrounding an open space
traditionally known as the Punishment Yard. This was
where recalcitrant underlings were taught a sharp lesson
in obedience, and those accused of blasphemy, poaching
or other misdemeanours met their just desserts. What was
rumoured to go on there was apprehensively whispered
about the Castle, though those in the know seemed
extremely reluctant to speak about their experiences. It
was used as a bogey with which to frighten little children:
*If you don't do what your mummy tells you you'll be sent
to the Punishment Yard!* Its fearsome reputation was
universally acknowledged, but whether mythical or
deserved Dando had no way of telling. According to
everyone's understanding it was somewhere to be avoided
at all costs and he had never passed that way. Now he
was about to be introduced to it for the first time.

The captain conducted him through a labyrinth
of passages until they came out into an enclosed square.
On two sides of this area were rows of little doors to what
were obviously cells. On the other sides ran a cloister
under which he could make out various items of
equipment. There was a vaulting horse, dumbbells,
hurdles, fencing masks and epees, but also more sinister
objects. Hanging against the wall he recognised sets of
manacles and gyves, some evil-looking coiled whips and
other instruments whose purpose he could not even begin
to guess at. In the centre of the square were two posts,

one a simple column of wood with a hook about eight feet from the ground; the second supported a cross piece at the top beneath which a platform had been built with steps leading up to it. Dando realised he was looking at a gallows. The officer led him over to the cells and unlocked one of the doors. Dando peered in and saw that the sole items provided for any detainee were a wooden bench and an earthenware bowl.

"In you go," ordered the captain. Dando had to stoop to enter and once inside found he was unable to stand upright. He sat down on the bench as the door was locked behind him. With the door shut there was very little light, the only aperture being a small grill that could be opened or closed at the whim of his guards. There was a strange smell. When eventually the light through the peep-hole had faded away completely and he was convinced that night had fallen he knocked on the door and shouted. He was hungry and he decided his gaolers must have forgotten to bring him his evening meal. At first there was no response, but when he persisted, someone gave an even louder bang on the outside of the door and yelled, "Shut the fuck up!" after which footsteps faded away into the distance and another door slammed leaving nothing behind but a brooding silence. Dando realised he was not going to get anything to eat or drink. He lay down on the bench and stared into the darkness feeling both numb and incredulous. Had his father really ordered this? After a while an idea occurred to him. Here was where Tom had been brought after he was arrested and kept without food or water for several days. He had been imprisoned in this place, maybe in this very cell. Now he was in the same predicament. The thought both comforted and disturbed him in equal measure but it also made him feel less lonely. Eventually he even managed to fall asleep.

It was quite late the next morning before his cell door was opened and he emerged blinking into the daylight looking rather dishevelled after spending the night in his clothes. Two unfamiliar soldiers were on escort duty and had come to conduct him to the Dan's apartments.

"Can I have a drink of water?" he asked.

"No time for that. Can't keep the Chief waiting."

He was brought back into the main body of the house which seemed to be a hive of activity. Crossing the bailey and entering the ground floor he was again the focus of curious sidelong glances from those they passed. The huge ballroom within the west wing which they had to traverse in order to get to the upper floors was full of people climbing ladders, putting up decorations, sweeping, cleaning and polishing. Of course, he had completely forgotten, tonight the Dans' Autumn Masquerade was due to take place, the masked ball that was undoubtedly the valley's greatest social event of the year! This evening people would be coming to Castle Dan from all over Deep Hallow, dressed in their best, wearing decorative disguises, hoping to cut a dash and to set the fashion for the coming season. The kitchens would be in full production, trying to excel themselves; dinner would be on offer to the privileged few alongside all the other diversions; no wonder the Castle was in turmoil. As they made their way up to the Dan's section of the house Dando wondered if his father would put in an appearance tonight. It was incumbent on the head of the clan to preside over such events, yet last year the occasion had been remarkable for his absence. Arriving on the landing outside the Dan's suite he was greeted by two more soldiers, sitting on either side of the door, who leapt up and barred the way.

"Who goes there!" one cried.

"Prisoner Dan Addo, reporting for interrogation," replied Dando's escort. There was a delay while one of the guards disappeared inside the apartment. Eventually they were given permission to enter. Passing through several luxuriously furnished rooms that yet had a subtle air of neglect about them they came to a vestibule where they waited once more. At last a door opened, another man at arms appeared and beckoned Dando forward.

"Go in," he ordered.

Dando walked alone into the space beyond - a big airless chamber - and saw his father standing at the far end. It was almost a year since he had last set eyes on the Dan and he was shocked at the change in his appearance. It was rumoured that the Clan Chief no longer allowed anyone to wait on him apart from his mercenaries, and the state of his clothes and person made it abundantly clear that this was the case. His garments were dirty and stained and he was sporting a straggly beard. He seemed to have lost weight. Dando could even imagine that he smelt.

"Well, boy, what have you got to say for yourself?" his parent demanded in a hoarse husky voice. Dando had been planning for several hours the words with which he might be able to justify his behaviour. He opened his mouth and began his defence in a hesitant manner but was not even allowed to get to the end of the first sentence.

"I – I'm sorry father, I..."

"Sorry! It's too late for that! You should have said sorry yesterday instead of running away from your responsibilities! I've been down to the stables and seen the criminal damage you've caused - do you realise what that horse was worth?! I told you a year ago when I sent you to school that it was your last opportunity to make good but you obviously took not a blind bit of notice! You are a pathetic excuse for a son, a complete freak!"

Dando lifted his hand and nervously twisted an end of hair round his finger bringing to his father's attention the engraved band worn by every heir apparent who was second in succession to the chieftainship. The man pointed at it unsteadily and in an accusatory manner.

"That's the first thing that 's going to happen - repossession of that ring! You'll surrender it as soon as the correct documents have been signed."

"D-documents?" faltered Dando.

"Yes, the documents which will define your new status in this household. You are a total and utter failure in your present position and I've been at my wits end deciding what to do with you. What I can tell you is you are no longer to consider yourself my heir – your titles and privileges are revoked!"

"Fine," muttered Dando, trying to maintain a calm exterior although his heart was beating wildly.

"You are no longer to call me father – is that clear?"

"Right f... I mean sir."

"You will take up the duties of house chaplain. I have arranged for a senior priest to come over this afternoon for your ordination. Later you will have instruction. Do you understand what I'm saying?"

Dando remained silent.

"Do you understand me?"

Dando looked at the loved face, distorted by fury, and quailed.

"Don't make me a priest, father, please. Send me to the stables... or the kitchen," he added with a faint revival of hope.

"The stables! After what you've done?! I'll turn you over to my men if you don't obey me! They won't be gentle with you, I can promise you that!"

To be promoted to the chaplaincy of the Dan mansion might not appear to be a very severe punishment for Dando to undergo but this is to ignore the absolute contempt with which the priesthood was regarded within the fifteen families. The Glepts were fanatical about the observance of their religion. Everyday, services took place, rituals were performed and there was always a good attendance at these ceremonies, but it seemed that at bottom the dominant race sensed, despite their piety, that the whole elaborate charade was pointless, that the god Pyr was not present in Deep Hallow and therefore each family's presiding cleric, whose job it was to intercede with the deity on their behalf was a total sham, an imposter. By tradition the position of priest had to be held by one of their own, a clan member. The padre was supposed to be closer than anyone to the god, but everyone knew in their heart of hearts that this could not be the case. Because of this contradiction such an individual - someone who should have been the most revered member of Glept society - was in fact the most despised. Only those at the very bottom of the pecking order: the semi-retarded, the socially inadequate, the mildly delinquent, were considered suitable candidates for the placement and were banished with relief below stairs where the clergyman's quarters were situated. It was no wonder that Dando pleaded, *Don't make me a priest!*

The Dan was speaking again. Shocked and disorientated Dando tried to focus his attention on what his parent was saying.

"You will take up residence in the chaplain's rooms with immediate effect; the barber will attend you. You won't be needing a personal servant any more; Applecraft will be found other duties. Have you anything to say?"

Dando shook his head.

"Well then, get out of my sight – I'll be there this afternoon – after that I don't want to see or hear from you again except when we have to meet at services!"

The same two mercenaries who had delivered him to the Dan's apartment escorted him through the maze of passages and staircases that led down into the bowels of the mansion where the large and elaborate chapel, more of a crypt really, was to be found. It was in this region, well below ground level, that the priest resided. As they left the daylight behind one of the soldiers took a torch from a bracket on the wall, lit it and led the way. The door before which they eventually arrived was at the furthest limit of a low dead-end corridor. The soldier produced a key and, as the room was opened, a puff of stale foul-smelling air wafted past them.

"Phew, what a stink!" the man exclaimed, going in and finding a small lamp with some oil in it which he lit from the torch. Dando looked around. The *chaplain's rooms* seemed to be merely one tunnel-shaped windowless chamber, sparsely furnished with a few battered items, and a low bed which looked as if its occupant had just got up in a hurry. The room had actually been unoccupied for several months, the previous incumbent, one of nature's innocents, having died suddenly at the age of fifty three. Since then the Dans had been managing by borrowing priests from other families. So this was where it was intended he should exist from now on. He thought of the south-west tower with its spacious living quarters and its tall windows looking out onto airy views. It was hard to realise that that was gone for good.

"OK," said the soldier, "let's 'ave your clothes."

"My clothes?" said Dando puzzled.

"Yes." The man indicated some garments hanging on the wall. "Let's see you get into your parson's rig."

"Oh no!" Dando objected.

"Oh yes – that's our orders."

Dando had no choice but to remove his outer apparel and dress himself in some shabby robes, impregnated with tobacco, that were much too short for him, their previous owner having been a small rotund individual. The soldier scooped up the beautifully made garments he had discarded and fingered the fabric.

"Mm, wouldn't mind a bit of this myself."

A third individual appeared outside the door with an instrument case in his hand. It was the barber. For the first time Dando realised the significance of his father's words, *the barber will attend you*. Of course, Glept priests always went shaven headed; he was going to lose his hair.

"Come in," said the mercenary, and, indicating Dando, "all off."

"But that's the Dan's lad," protested the man, forgetting correct forms of address in his concern.

"It's the Dan's orders – get on with it."

"Is that right Lord?" asked the barber directly of Dando.

"Yes," said Dando after a pause, very white around mouth and nostrils. *Yes* was the only word he felt capable of uttering but his eyes spoke volumes. And so he was shorn, the barber finishing the job gently and expertly with soap and razor. Following this they left him alone, having reminded him of the appointment he was due to keep that afternoon in the chapel with the Head of Clan and his tame cleric.

For a long time Dando sat on the bed, every now and then running his fingers over his bald pate. Eventually he got up and went out into the corridor looking for a tap but drew a blank. Where were you expected to wash he wondered? Judging by the smell of the clothes he was wearing he concluded that perhaps you weren't. He thought of paying a visit to the kitchens in search of sustenance but was ashamed to be seen by the staff in this ignominious condition. He was also afraid of getting into further trouble if he were to desert his post while the evening was still young and people of influence were around to notice. Going back into the room he came across a water jug on a stand but it was as dry as a bone. He also found a chamber pot that disgustingly had not been emptied of its contents since presumably before the previous incumbent's death. He explored further, discovering a thurible and a jar of incense, shelves with prayer books and hymnals but also a few romantic novels. There were some empty wine bottles and a box full of cheap pungent cigars and, in pride of place, a lovingly catalogued postage stamp collection. On the flattened pillow at the head of the bed lay a battered teddy bear. He was facing away from the door and all at once heard an unexpected noise behind him. He jumped and turned apprehensively only to see his first friendly face in several hours.

"Potto!" he cried, overwhelmed at the vision of his dear old companion.

"Oh, Lord m'dear!" exclaimed Potto, taking in Dando's appearance; he did not need to say anything more. Dando smiled painfully and turned away. "It's no good calling me *My Lord*," he lectured, somewhat testily, "I'm not *My Lord* now. You'll have to call me just plain..." and then he stopped as the enormity of having no name struck home, for Dan Addo meant simple *No. 2 son* and he could no longer lay claim to that title. He walked to the door and into the corridor but could see nothing other than the dark mist that had risen in front of his eyes. When the storm of emotion passed he was left feeling light and buoyant. It was as if the table had been cleared of old debris and a new cloth was being spread. He repossessed his nickname – Dando – meaning nothing now – just a sound belonging exclusively to him and then went back to Potto.

"Potto, I haven't eaten since yesterday lunchtime, and I need a drink."

"Di'n't they feed you? Tch, tch, tch, tch. I'll soon fetch you somethin' Lord."

"Mainly something to drink. I don't know whether they've told you this yet but you're not my man anymore. You probably shouldn't be here."

"Oh..." Potto dismissed the idea with a contemptuous wave of his hand, "that's just a burra load of crud. I'll hev you set to rights in no time, you'll see. You jest set here an' I'll be back 'afor you c'n say Jack Robinson."

He was as good as his word. In no time at all he returned with a small acolyte in tow bearing plates of hot food, a carafe of water and in a small flask something much stronger, the sweet syrupy spirit distilled from the Dans' wine. After quenching his not inconsiderable thirst Dando set to work and finished up every last scrap of the meal and was soon feeling much better. He made a remarkable discovery, that the darkness of inhumanity and adversity intensifies your appreciation of the bright light of kindness when it comes your way. *I'll never take him for granted ever again,* he vowed to himself, adding for good measure *or make fun of his way of speaking.*

"An' they've tol' you you've got to live down here?" said Potto with distaste. "It could do with a good clean. I'll see to that. An'..."

"Potto, you'll have to go. My father's supposed to be coming soon and I don't know when he'll arrive. He mustn't find you here."

"Don' 'ee fret Lord m'dear. I'll be back later on – I've got your things. We c'n make this place nice an' homey. It just need an airing. Tell me if you need anything," and he was gone, carrying the offensive chamber pot.

The chapel of the Castle Dan mansion was a vast pillared vault, its walls painted with darkened and discoloured murals, the plinths and alcoves at the sides displaying a fortune in finely wrought silver, some of the figurines and vessels obviously of great age. Dando knelt before the altar, the Clan Chief standing behind him and in front none other than Father Adelbert, the priest from the Kymer Delta. Dando had been overjoyed to see him. Although nothing could be done to change the course of events this late in the day, at least he felt there was going to be someone present at this ceremony who might sympathise with his plight.

"*The form and manner of making, ordaining and consecrating of priests according to the order of the Church of the Heavenly-King,*" read out Adelbert from the prayer book he had been given. "Page 455." Dando and his father found their places. Adelbert addressed Dando.

"*Do you think in your heart that you be truly called, according to the will of our Lord-of-Heaven to the Order and Ministry of Priesthood?*"

He does," cut in the Dan in an attempt to pre-empt any mutiny on the part of his son; he remembered the travesty in the Oath Takers Hall.

"The candidate must answer for himself," replied the foreigner, who, being an outsider, did not stand in awe of the local gentry as a native-born cleric might have done. The two men glared at each other over Dando's head. Dando looked at the floor in front of him and said nothing. Adelbert repeated the question but no reply was forthcoming. He began to have second thoughts about conducting this service despite the juicy fee he had been promised.

"I am not familiar with this liturgy," he demurred, "my sect holds other divinities more deserving of worship than the Sky-Father. I'm not sure that I'm qualified to preside."

"You're a priest aren't you? Just get on with it."

Adelbert looked down at his former pupil.

"The applicant seems rather young; may I ask if he's a willing participant in this ritual?"

"No you may not!" The Dan was becoming red in the face.

"Dando?" said the priest and as the boy looked up he stared searchingly at him. Dando gave a barely perceptible nod. Adelbert sighed and turned back to the prayer book; he was out of his depth in this situation.

"Do you think in your heart..." he began again. This time Dando replied "I do," and, having given the requisite answer, the rite proceeded without further hitches.

"Will you give your faithful diligence always so to administer the doctrine and sacraments of the Church as the Lord hath commanded?"

"I will."

"Will you be ready with all faithful diligence to banish and drive away all erroneous and strange doctrines contrary to God's Word?"

"I will."

Eventually they came to the end of the responses and Dando was anointed with the sign of the Heliosphere as the priest repeated -

"Anoint and cheer our soiled face
With the abundance of thy grace,
Keep far our foes, give peace at home:
Where thou art guide no ill may come."

Finally Adelbert laid his hands on the boy's head with the words *"Whose sins thou doest forgive, they are forgiven; and whose sins thou doest retain, they are retained. And be thou a faithful dispenser of the Word of God, Amen.* Get up, Dando, you are now a priest."

Dando looked round at his father, hoping for a word of approval, having done what had been asked of him, but all the Dan said was "Someone will be sent to instruct you," and swept out.

"I'm not going to ask what this was all about," said Adelbert, "but remember, my offer still stands: I'm quite prepared to write you a letter of recommendation to the owner of one of the restaurants down in the Delta City. If you take it up I don't think you'll regret it."

The boy smiled, rather tight lipped, and nodded.

Two hours had crept by on leaden feet. Sitting in the priest's room with the door open Dando imagined that, very faintly in the distance, he could hear music. If, in the normal course of events, he had attended tonight's ball he would have been the most eligible bachelor there. His elder brother was already married to a similarly spectacled mousy little girl from the Blackler family. Dando had heard they were very happy. As the most desirable catch in the room he would have flirted with, and been teased by, all the most attractive girls present in their frills and flounces as they made the most of their brief reprieve from the gynaceum's sequestration. It was a game he would also have enjoyed playing although it would have been naught but a game to him. As for his own getup, he would have been wearing a very expensive new outfit onto which the tailor had lavished all his skill and ingenuity, hoping for follow-up orders from impressed party goers. In the graceful and stately dances, the steps of which he had known from his earliest days, he would have taken his place among his brothers and cousins and friends, as a first among equals. He could not sing but he loved to dance. All that was gone now and he must get used to being just a despised underling banished to this stuffy dungeon far away from light and life and fresh air. Since leaving the chapel he felt as if his freewill had been curtailed and as if the ordination ceremony had put him under some sort of obligation. What was to become of him? He seemed to be staring down a tunnel into a grim future from which there would be no deliverance apart from the inevitable final escape. He buried his face in his hands.

A peal of laughter came from the doorway and a voice cried "Dando! What *do* you look like!"

He lifted his head to find Damask and Milly standing before him, his sister wearing her festive outfit. Seeing his expression the older girl choked back her mirth and to his great surprise suddenly crouched and flung her arms around him in a rough bear hug. It was so much what he needed at that precise moment that when she stepped away he smiled gratefully at her, his eyes bright with tears that he knew he must on no account shed.

"Death or glory, Do-Do," she encouraged gruffly from behind her mask, using a childhood name known only to the two of them, "don't let the bastards grind you down!"

Dando swallowed. "You've said it kid," he replied.

"Onward the Ds," she continued, "up the twins!"

Milly stepped forward and put her hand on his arm.

"'Ave they 'urt you?" she asked passionately.

"No, no, I'm all right." He grinned.

"But they cut orf your lovely 'air!" she protested almost weeping.

"Well, I can do without that – although it's a bit cold!" Here was an ally who was heart and soul on his side. Whereas a few days earlier he would have felt embarrassed when made aware of her devotion he now considered himself indebted to her. He almost imagined he could warm himself at the fierce little flame of her love.

Dress-wise Damask was prinked out in all her ball finery. "We've only just heard what's happened," she said, "although I guessed you were back at the Castle. Did you go through with it, the priest business I mean?"

"The lesser of two evils," said Dando, "I think he would have had me whipped if I'd refused point blank to co-operate." (But – no - it wasn't exactly like that. As he had acknowledged to himself just now, after the initial shock and the realisation that there was no simple way of extricating himself, it was almost as if he had heard a voice telling him that the whole thing was meant to be and he, as the main protagonist, was required to play his part).

"But you're not going along with it," pursued Damask, "being a priest I mean? The sooner we get out of the valley the better. We can be off down the Gorge in the next few days – you, me, Milly?" She looked at him with raised eyebrows and Dando looked back with an inscrutable expression. Damask stared hard; there was something in her brother's face, something she had never seen before, which she did not like the look of.

"You're not thinking of going along with it?" she repeated.

"Births, marriages and deaths, I'm your man," he volunteered with a kind of desperate levity.

"Don't be an idiot!"

Damask and Milly stayed with him for about half an hour until Damask exclaimed that she must "put in an appearance at this junket," and disappeared upstairs. Milly remained behind, taking the place beside him on the bed and shyly possessing herself of one of his hands which she held within both of hers. It was in this position that Potto found them when he came to the door charged with an urgent message.

"Lord, there be a gent outside who want to speak to you. He say you tol' he to come up to the Castle. Do that be right?"

No reason to stay,
And every reason to go,
Yet is it meant?

Chapter fifteen

"*I bring news from the valley, husband. It looks as if, very soon, the one who could be our nemesis will take to the road! In fact I've seen it along the time-lines! Has he learnt the purpose for which he was born do you suppose? Who could have told him? I'm gravely concerned that our lives may be in danger!*"

"*Don't fly into a panic just yet wife. I doubt he's got the faintest notion of how things stand. Maybe he's going off and away, but once he is out in the big wide world think of the perils that will beset him – perils we can turn to our advantage. We may even get the chance to arrange for his demise, although I'm beginning to wonder if that might not be such a great idea. The girl is with him – the one who has the gift – we can trace him through her – and he will be accompanied by a man whose ancestors vowed to return the Object to me.*"

"*Pray heaven you're right husband.*"

"*Pray wife? I thought prayers were offered to us, not the other way round!*"

At dawn Tallis crossed a low-level bridge over the Wendover, upstream of High Harrow and west of the fair, the fair where everything was in that sad state of disarray which a carnival reaches when there is nothing left for it to do but pack up and go. On gaining the main road he could have turned right if circumstances had been more favourable and mingled with the showmen as they made their way out of the valley, but instead he swung left up river looking for a refuge. Between the road and the bank of the watercourse lay a broad, mainly wooded, strip of land. After about a mile and a half he took to the trees, eventually arriving not far from the water's edge. Here he came upon some lush meadowland surrounding an old ruinous fisherman's hut where Carolus could graze throughout the day and they would be well away from prying eyes, at least he hoped that would be the case. He dismounted and carefully lifted the girl down from the saddle. Laying her on the grass he pulled the cloak away from her face, struck once again by her beauty, only to find that her eyes were still closed and she was breathing deeply and evenly, apparently completely comatose. Ralph, who was looking on, thrust his nose into her face and gave it a rough lick. Tallis uncovered her hands and began massaging them calling "Hilda, Hilda," - he understood that that was her name. She stirred and seemed about to wake, but then mumbled something he could not catch, wetted her lips and returned once more to a state of narcolepsy. He imagined she might have said something about *thirsty* so searched in his pack for a container and brought some water back from the river. Supporting her with one arm he managed to persuade her to take a few sips from the cup but she did so while remaining to all intents and purposes unconscious. He had never seen anyone in such a state before: apparently hale but at the same time impossible to rouse.

He thought back over the events of the night. Something unprecedented had possessed him in that yard at the Justification and had induced him to interfere in an affair that he should have left strictly alone. Now he was implicated in a murder, if murder it had been, and was probably already a fugitive from justice. Whether the girl had had anything to do with Yantle's death or not the people at the inn had been in no doubt. He remembered the old woman's cry: *they'll burn her!* Having saved her from heaven knows what retribution, he could not abandon her now; he must get both of them away from this place as soon as possible. But how? He had no food, no fodder, no suitable clothes for the coming season on the road. Already the air was becoming colder since the wet spell and he was beginning to shiver in his inadequate worn and tattered garments - goodbye summer, so you were mortal after all. He suddenly realised there was another reason beyond just fear of arrest which had led him to turn left on reaching the main thoroughfare instead of taking his chance in the direction he understood was the normal route out of the valley: that young aristocrat whom he had encountered yesterday at the King's Head had directed him this way. At their meeting he had been promised supplies and a pony to carry them. Perhaps taking up the boy's offer was his only hope now of getting away from this place fully provided for and unapprehended, when, to follow the well trodden eastern track, would probably lead to recognition and detention. Anyway, travelling northwards as he had done all his life was his preferred option, but he knew such a bearing might present many challenges, especially as he believed another range of mountains lay in his path, yet it would take him eventually, he hoped, to his ultimate goal.

To cross unoccupied territory in winter, a measure he had
been intending to avoid, he would need to be well
equipped, so it seemed he had no choice but to wait until
dusk after which he would try his luck at this Castle Dan.
He would find out then if the boy had been sincere. He
groaned. What a total mess he had created for himself
and his companions!

Several hours later he prepared to make a move
as the light faded. To pass the time he had taken his cue
from his young charge, wrapped himself in his cloak and
gone to sleep on the grass. Now, thoroughly chilled, he
lifted her still inert body, intending to hoist her back onto
the horse and mount behind her. As he picked her up the
mantle fell away and he was shocked to see that there
were spots of blood on her clothes. He immediately
jumped to the conclusion that she had been wounded by a
piece of flying shrapnel back at the inn and that this was
the reason she was so deeply unconscious; he must get
her to where she could receive treatment. Once astride the
horse he managed, with an arm about her body, to hold
her upright before him; in that way they were less
conspicuous. They must journey a few miles along the
pike the boy had said, and then turn right through a
wrought iron archway, then right again at a gatehouse in
order to follow a wall round the side of the mansion to
the servants' quarters beyond. He obeyed these
instructions to the letter only to find, once he had made
the first turning, that the road was unexpectedly busy. A
string of carriages was waiting before the second
obstruction and his progress was impeded. With some
difficulty he slipped past and then tentatively skirted the
perimeter wall, hoping that he was going in the right
direction. Eventually the main part of the house was left

behind and he came upon an opening in the barrier. Abandoning his dependants in a nearby copse he ventured through and explored the elaborate complex of outbuildings that lay beyond before returning and sitting down under cover in order to wait until most of the exterior activity had vanished inside the castle.

"You must stay here," he told Ralph after some time had elapsed, "don't move from the trees and look after the lady. On guard Ralph, on guard!" He satisfied himself that Carolus was secure, made Hilda as comfortable as possible, then set off to enquire as to the whereabouts of the manservant Applecraft from somebody within the wall.

Having left the inn at midnight and having been away in the woods all day, Foxy was completely ignorant of the events that had occurred in his place of work until he returned late in the afternoon. He found the Justification in a state of chaos, resembling nothing so much as a disturbed ants' nest. Everything was at sixes and sevens because the queen, Mrs Humpage, had abdicated her throne and shut herself away in her office, refusing to answer even the most urgent of calls. He could get no sense from Florence: all the old woman would do was lay on her bed and moan "Her'll have me dismissed! – her'll throw me onto the streets!" The truth, when he managed to piece things together, hit him like a hammer. The manner of Yantle's death took him completely by surprise, yet he knew immediately that he should have seen it coming. Hilda had tried to warn him of impending disaster; he ought to have paid more attention when she told him her powers were becoming difficult to control. Yet now it was done he did not rue the killing one iota; in fact he could not restrain a crow of triumph from escaping his lips, even though he knew the outcome might mean the end of all his hopes and schemes for his virgin priestess. Ultimately he just regretted that his had not been the hand to strike the blow.

He discovered that in the aftermath of the slaying, messengers had been sent to the sheriff's office and to the Yan estate. Later a carriage accompanied by men-at-arms arrived to remove the corpse. False rumours were beginning to spread and some gossips, who knew no better, claimed they had heard that the Outrider regiments were being mustered and that the Dan's army was on the warpath, but at the same time the general opinion was that the perpetrators would be well away by now, *Over-the-Brook* as the saying goes. For the first time in his service at the inn Foxy went absent without leave. After finding out which direction the fugitives were believed to have taken he turned his steps towards High Harrow, his eyes glued to the earth beneath his feet. He was looking for the tracks of a horse bearing the weight of two people and the paw prints of a large rangy dog. In the soft, still moist, margins of the highway he soon found what he sought. As he approached the paved streets of the little town the trail disappeared but he picked it up again on the other side of the Wendover and followed it to where it branched off from the main road and turned left towards the river. Here, down by the water, the runaways had rested for sometime, maybe for several hours, which meant that, at present, they could not be that far ahead of him. He hurried back to the pike and set off again at full speed westward, only to find, after several miles, that there was no longer any sign of his quarry. They must have turned along a side road and the only possible candidate was the drive up to the Dan mansion. He retraced his steps and sure enough that was where the prints finally disappeared from the main thoroughfare. Why on earth were they going to the Castle - into the lion's den so to speak? Although he ventured with great caution along the track for about half a mile, so many other horses and carriages had recently passed that way that the impressions he was following were totally obscured; there was obviously some big event taking place at the Dans' and consequently far too many people around for his liking. Also the light was fading. Greatly disappointed he gave up the pursuit for the night and turned back, intending to pick up the trail at dawn. Then he would make a thorough search of the house's environs hoping to discover fresh evidence of the movements of his quarry. In the meantime he would visit the cave under the southern hills, change his clothes, have something to eat and collect his weapons. Then he would be fit and ready to take up the chase again the next day, however long and however far it took him. As he walked towards his destination he puzzled over the involvement of the stranger from the south. Was he just another potential ravisher seizing his chance to abduct a beautiful girl? Yet he had risked his life to save her they said. At least he had rescued Hild and spirited her away from those who definitely intended her harm, but the sooner she was again under his, Foxy's, protection the better - the morning could not come soon enough.

"Lord, there be a gent outside who want to see you. He say you tol' he to come along to the Castle. Do that be right?" Dando looked up at his former servant noticing that he seemed to be more than usually agitated. "What's he like?" he asked.

"It be that fellow I saw at the Town Hall yesterday," continued Potto nervously, "the one wantin' a companion on the road. You bain't a-thinkin' of gooin' along wi' he, be you Lord?"

"I was," replied Dando with a grimace, "until all this happened," indicating the priest's garments in which he was arrayed. He then turned towards his small comforter. "You'd better be getting back to my sister, Milly, she'll be needing you when the dance comes to an end." He gave the little girl's hand a squeeze and watched as she departed with many a rearward glance.

A question such as Potto had just asked of him would normally have been regarded as insolence when posed by a humble nibbler to the Dan's second son. He realised that their relationship had subtly changed since his fall from grace but he was not unhappy. They were now on a more equal footing, as they should have been right from the start. And he was immediately presented with an even more startling example of the reshaping of their bond. He had already become aware that the worry lines on his friend's face were deeper than usual and his tendency to twist his hands together when concerned was much in evidence. Dando did not believe that this show of anxiety was entirely on his behalf.

"Potto, what's got into you? You're acting like a brood mare with the wind up."

"A funny tale ha' come from the Justification, Lord," confessed Potto, "One of the Incomers be dead they do say – killed by witchery it seem." In fact the castle ballroom, the banqueting hall and the servants' quarters were all of a-buzz with this fascinating piece of intelligence. By this time it was common knowledge that a murder had taken place at one of Deep Hallow's hostelries and the Dan, as the local margrave, would consequently have been preparing to send out patrols after the guilty parties, except that most of his troops had been given the day off to ensure that the castle appeared welcoming to its evening visitors with the inevitable drunken outcome on their behalf. Nobody really had much idea about what had occurred at the inn, but, again, ignorant tongues were wagging, especially concerning the character of the victim. *Yantle was asking for it,* was the general opinion, *it was bound to happen sooner or later.* There was also an undercurrent of unease: *they say that nibblers were involved - the innkeeper's in a bad way - nothing has gone right in this place since... you know what I mean...*

"And..." prompted Dando. He guessed that Potto had more to tell.

"An'..." The Nablan paused, apparently unsure whether to commit himself. Then out it came in a rush: "I be afeared for she, that her'll be blamed. He tol' me her had the gift."

"*Her* – what do you mean by *her*?" said Dando, feeling suddenly extremely odd.

"Why Tom Tosa's girl, Lord. Her was called Ann at the Castle, you ast me about her once, after she'd gone..."

Dando gasped; for a moment he was very glad he was sitting down.

"Do you mean the cobbler's daughter?"

"Yes Lord, you used to play with she when you were childer, and so did the Lady Damask."

Dando leant back against the wall and took several gulps of air. Metaphorically, all the bells of Deep Hallow began to chime at once and the sun came out brilliantly from behind a cloud and bathed the whole valley in a blaze of glory.

"But back then you told me she wasn't at the Justification, Potto, you told me you didn't know where she was," he said in a dazed, dazzled kind of way.

"That was 'acos you were naught but a li'l ol' boy Lord an' you might ha' let slip the truth."

Dando could at last bring into the open a long-festering resentment.

"No it wasn't, Potto," he countered. "You lied to me because I was Dan Addo, the Dan's second son – I suspected that at the time. But how can you be sure I might not spill the beans now, given the opportunity?"

Potto stared at him in alarm.

"Of course I won't," Dando added somewhat bitterly, "anymore than I would have done then." He got up and again walked out into the corridor where he stood with his right arm across his chest while he alternately opened and clenched the fingers of his left hand. So, Ann had been found; she was in this world, no longer just a fantasy but a real live girl. In fact she was only an hour or two's journey away. He needed time to work out exactly how he felt. But now a new idea occurred to him which demanded urgent action and pricked him into postponing his proposed meditation. He returned to Potto.

"That traveller – that Master Tallisand – he was staying at the Justification."

"Be that true Lord? Then he might know what really be a-happenin' along o' there."

"Yes, that's what I thought. Where is he? Let's go and ask him right away."

"He be a-waitin' just inside the back gate - but won't you be in trouble, Lord, if you leave here?"

"Oh, I'm pretty sure no-one will notice my absence while the dance is going on – they're all still living it up in the ballroom and will be until the clock has gone way past midnight, so I believe."

When Tallis saw the two figures coming towards him from the House, the shorter one carrying a lantern, he did not at first recognise the showy exquisite of yesterday in the shaven-headed young cleric in his dowdy vestments who was approaching. It was not until the boy shook his hand with a trace of his old enthusiasm that he knew he was one and the same.

"I need help," he began bluntly, wondering why this job applicant should have changed his appearance so radically. "I have a young female with me who requires medical attention and I'm interested in the equipment you offered. There's no time to lose."

"Mister," cut in Potto, "if you come from the Justification tell us what be happenin' down there. There hev been a killin' they do say."

Tallis was taken aback; apparently news had got here ahead of him; perhaps he should have expected it. Could he have just walked into a trap?

"Yes," he said cautiously, "a gentleman died there last night. The lady and I decided it would be best to leave."

Dando wondered whether he was in a dream from which he would soon awaken.

"What's her name?" he asked, overcome with a sense of unreality and almost sure he could supply the answer.

"Her name? - it's Hilda – Why do you want to know?"

"Is her second name Hannah? Hilda Hannah Arbericord?"

Tallis had a vague memory of the peddler calling the girl something as elaborate as this: *big name for a little tiddler* he had said.

"It may be," he replied, wondering at the boy's intensity.

"I must see her," said Dando.

There was no point in refusing. Tallis led the way through the door in the wall and across to the grove of trees where Ralph, ignoring his master, came forward to greet Dando, his furiously wagging tail almost unbalancing him. Tallis indicated a dark muffled shape on the ground.

"I don't understand what's wrong," he said, "she's completely unresponsive."

Dando took the lantern from Potto and, kneeling, pulled the cloak away from the face of the supine figure. He gazed for a long time.

"I know her," he said.

Potto also bent down to examine the immobile features. "It be Tom Tosa's girl," he confirmed with satisfaction.

"She's been like that for hours," said Tallis. "There was an explosion. I'm afraid she may have been injured. There's blood on her clothes."

Gently and reverently Dando unwrapped Ann from the rest of the cloak and saw the stains on her skirt. He and Potto exchanged glances.

"Her be in need of a woman's care, I be a-thinkin'," said Potto. "We c'n take she to my girl Adelaide, her'll be in her room at this time of night."

"I'll take her," said Dando eagerly.

Despite a natural concern for his charge Tallis felt slightly resentful that all the attention was being lavished elsewhere while his own pressing needs were given a back seat.

"We require supplies and equipment," he said, "and you mentioned something about a horse. We've got to leave before it gets light."

"Yes," answered Dando, showing more animation than he had done for several hours, "I'll be right back."

"Don't let anyone see her," warned Tallis, deciding to be a bit more forthcoming about his situation. "She was unfairly accused, that's why I brought her away."

Feeling as if he had suddenly been given entrée to some kind of eighth or ninth heaven Dando lifted Ann in his arms and bore her like a priceless heirloom through the back alleys behind the castle to Doll's hut. The motherly woman, grey-haired now and matronly, came to the doorway at his call, a half-darned sock in her hand.

"Dando, my love," she said with pleasure and surprise, apparently taking the boy's drastically changed mien in her stride, "who have you got there? Is something wrong?"

"It's someone you know very well," replied Dando, carrying the girl into the room and laying her on the bed. "I think she's all right but she won't wake up and we're not sure why."

"My goodness," cried Doll in astonishment, "it be my little Ann – after all these years!"

Dando showed her the bloodied skirt. "I reckon it's the curse," he whispered.

"Don' 'ee worry lad – I'll soon deal wi' that. But I'll have to borrow stuff - I don' have it here – I've been through the change," (in this case meaning a purely gynaecological transformation). Putting on her hat she went out.

Dando looked down at Ann. He had recognised her at first glance although she was more woman than child now. She was just as he had imagined she would be. No not quite, there was something he had not bargained for and it tore his heart out. Young as she was Ann's features were already marked by suffering. It had not affected her beauty, in fact it enhanced it, but it was there. All at once he realised the girl was returning his gaze. She had opened her eyes and for a moment an unreadable expression appeared on her face – surprise? - unbelief? - shock? - confusion? Then that was wiped away to be replaced by a look of utter relief, as if after a hazardous journey she had finally come home. Her whole body relaxed and for a moment the beginnings of a smile curved the corners of her mouth. She sighed and closed her eyes.

Doll returned. "I c'n see to things now lad. How is she doing?"

"As I said, I think she's ok but when she wakes up she'll need some warm clothes," said Dando, "we're going on a journey. Could you manage that? I've got to get all the other stuff together." He turned to go, his

belief in his vocation as a priest having been completely
blanked by the circumstance of his loved-one's
reappearance.

"I reckon so. Just a minute. Come here dearie."

Dando found himself folded to an ample bosom.

"I hear what happen. It be cruel. But you be one
of us now my love."

Yes I am, he thought dumbfounded, realising that
the weight of presumed superiority had been lifted, once
and for all, from his shoulders.

Returning to Tallis and Potto he found that the
two had become quite friendly in his absence. Tallis had
unbent sufficiently to describe the events at the inn in
detail.

"...the gun exploded and the people there thought
she had done it by witchcraft and so I realised I had to get
her away, otherwise she would have been severely
punished..."

"Yes," said Potto, "he allus say her had the gift."

"Potto," ordered Dando, taking charge, "we need
some warm clothes if we're going to be travelling at this
time of year. Can you find some. - Nothing fancy."

"So be you a-gooin' Lord?" said Potto with
resignation, "You be a-gooin' too?"

"Yes of course. Do you know where that sort of
thing's kept?"

"Maybe I do..." and Potto went off glumly
shaking his head to raid the cavernous wardrobes that
were dotted about the Castle. Tallis saw there had been a
misunderstanding.

"When I said I needed help, I meant I needed
your help in providing for my journey, not your

participation. I can pay handsomely for anything you care to give me."

"You mean you don't want me to come?" cried Dando aghast.

"Correct. Your participation is not required."

"Oh, but I must come because..." he was going to say *because of Ann*, but realised in time that such a reason would be hard to explain and might create the wrong impression. "...I need to get out of this valley," he substituted. "I don't think I can be what they want me to be here."

"Well," said Tallis, "I can't assist you in that regard as I'm afraid it's none of my concern."

If Dando had been of a different mindset he might, at this point, have used blackmail: *no travelling for me, no provisions for you,* he could have said. As it was he just protested "But why? You wanted a companion who would help you along the road – Why won't I do?"

"You're too young (*and too high born,* he might have added). I want a responsible adult. For all I know you could go gallivanting off at the first opportunity. I'm aware of what young people are like."

"I wouldn't!" Dando almost sobbed

"I need someone who I can rely on, someone whom I can trust. Someone who can make a commitment."

"I can do that!" and Dando was suddenly struck by an idea. "You say you want someone who would be faithful – well I know you told me you haven't advertised for a squire, but how about if I bound myself to you as your squire? In the old days people used to do that sort of thing – I've read about it in books. What it means is you'd be my liege lord and could command me in all things. I would have to serve you and do what you told me without question."

Tallis considered this. The men of the Lake Guardians had been knights, so his mother had said, and that made him a knight by prerogative. In song and story knights always had squires, and moreover he could go one better than a knight: his mother had claimed royal descent on his behalf. Why shouldn't he have a squire at his beck and call? The thought of this aristocratic youth as his vassal appealed to his vanity.

"What does it involve?" he asked cautiously.

"Well from the books I've read I just take an oath of fealty, that's all. Then it's my duty to obey you. Will you agree? Will you take me with you?"

Dando knelt before Tallis and put his hands together as if in prayer. What he had not explained, and what he knew from his reading, but Tallis did not, was that promises were also expected from the prospective master, but unfortunately he was too afraid of scaring the traveller off to mention the fact.

"You must put your hands over mine. Now I'll take the oath. This is the sort of thing they used to say - *I do solemnly swear to cleave unto thee, to serve thee with all the best that is in me, and to lay down my life if needs be for thy sake. In so doing I give up all claim to rights, titles and lands in the place where presently I do abide in order to follow thee in clearness of heart with no regretful back-looking And thus I will maintain against all manner of folk until the King shall return – so help me God.*"

Dando stood up blinking and took stock. Did the world seem any different? He had now renounced voluntarily those things that had already been taken from him. He waited for a moment or two straining his senses, or rather that extra sense that perceives what the earthly five do not. A surge of elation swept through him. Yes, there was a subtle shift of perspective which gave birth to a new-born feeling, a greater elevation and conception of liberty that was completely novel. Joy bubbled up and stuck in his throat. Tallis looked at him in dismay. "What's this about a King?" he asked to counter what he perceived to be the other's strangely exalted mood.

"Oh, that's just something my people always put at the end of speeches they make," replied Dando, coming back to practicalities, "I thought everyone did."

"You don't have a king?"

"No."

Unexpectedly, Tallis again had a fleeting intuition that he was on the verge of some momentous discovery, but the insight slipped away; he could not retain it.

"Well," he said, "if we're going to travel together we'd better start preparing for the wild. We must leave before morning."

"The wild?" said Dando, puzzled, "It's not very wild down on the Kymer flood plain."

"I'm not thinking of going eastward. My route leads me north, that's my direction."

Dando was startled. In his experience very few people ever went north. The small track that snaked into the northern hills was overgrown and greatly neglected. The Glepts had a saying:

Who leaves his hearth to northward roam,
Never down that path comes home,
yet Glepts were always buried upright facing north and,
for that reason, the northern road was known as the *Way-of-the-Departed* or the *Way-of-the-Shades,* often
shortened to *The Shady Way.* However, this abbreviation,
if taken literally, was a complete misnomer, as there was
very little shade to be had along the wearisome and
seemingly unending length of the drift.

"It won't be easy," he cautioned.

"I never thought it would."

"OK," said Dando, "I'll go and get stuff
together."

Priest and squire all in the space of a single day
and his long lost love restored to him; Dando felt that he
could barely keep up! As he went to look for a beast of
burden he wondered what on earth was going to happen
next. He was halfway to the stables on a quest for a
suitable workhorse when he remembered Damask's
willing little nag that she often harnessed to the dog cart
on her trips away from the Dan mansion. This pony, that
went by the name of Mollyblobs, had the advantage that
she was to be found in her own separate stable close to
the Castle wall and would be easier to borrow
unobserved. He preferred the word *borrow* to *steal*; it
seemed less like a theft if he took the animal from his
own sister. When he got to the place, he was lucky
enough to find a piece of chalk that had been used to
work out quantities of feed. He scratched the double D
symbol on the door hoping against hope that Damask
would understand his need, found suitable panniers and

saddlebags and led Mollyblobs back to where Tallis was waiting.

"I'll get the provisions if you'll pack and load them," he suggested.

The next place on his agenda was the storeroom adjacent to the rear kitchen, at this time of night almost inevitably deserted. Making his way to one of his favourite haunts he was furiously racking his brains over what would be required on a long journey through inhospitable country. In the end he selected bags of flour, rice, beans, oats, sugar, biscuits and dried fruits. He also took a flask of oil and one of spirits, a cannister of tea, a jar of pickles, a slab of cheese, a block of salt, some salt fish and some lard. With these he included small quantities of fresh fruit and vegetables such as apples, pears, oranges, lemons, potatoes, carrots, green beans and onions. Such perishables would soon be exhausted but would be nice while they lasted. He came across a little gardening fork, good for foraging for edible roots, and added that to the growing pile which, by now, boasted a vegetable and cheese grater plus some banqueting leftovers filched from the main kitchen which he could make use of over the next few hours. Last but not least, in the provisions category, he took out of a cupboard his very own box of dried herbs, spices and flavourings, some of them very rare. Now he needed something to cook in: he ran to earth a large fireproof pot plus a pan, and something to eat and drink from: he found wooden trenchers, bowls and tin mugs. Then of course there were implements for preparation and dining – that meant knives, forks and spoons. He also came across a folding tripod in the storeroom that the gypsies had once given him for use over an open fire and a metal poker that could be used as a spit. All these things he lugged back to Tallis outside the wall after leaving a note explaining what he had taken. Tallis, although gratified at the generosity being displayed, questioned the quantity.

"Do we really need to carry so much?" he asked.

"Well, there are three of us and it may be a long time before we arrive at some-place where we can restock."

Dando went to the outbuildings beside the stables and came back with equipment for grooming the horses and other bits and pieces that might be necessary for their welfare. By this time Potto had returned, various items of clothing draped over his arm. It was with extreme relief that Dando was able to divest himself of the nasty robes that had offended a fastidiousness he had not known he possessed and assume the warm and practical garments his servant had managed to appropriate. Both he and Tallis were provided with flannel shirts, thick broadcloth trousers and cable knit sweaters. Potto had also found two leather top coats. Tallis retained his voluminous mantle despite its damaged condition, but for Dando there was a large handsome cloak, big enough to be used as a blanket at night. Everything was a perfect fit – Potto knew his business.

"Potto could you find me a backpack and put some essentials in it? You know what I'll need. I'll go and see how Ann is getting on."

Performing his various tasks Dando was singing softly under his breath, a strange ear-tormenting eldritch sound that he usually kept strictly to himself for fear of frightening the horses. It was not as though he could not hear the melody within his head, it was just that it got lost somewhere along the way to the outside world, but - what the hell – he was happy. Before he returned to Doll's shack he went to the Key Room and borrowed the key to the armoury. His weapons had been confiscated and he must replace them if he was to be any use to Tallis as a henchman. Fair exchange was no robbery he had always understood and this would be an exchange. When he left the arsenal he was equipped with a well-balanced, businesslike sword far superior to his previous plaything and a lethal double edged blade in place of his toy dagger. On the way to collect Ann he also managed to acquire a bag of high-concentrate supplement for the horses. Doll opened the door with a flourish when he knocked and, with an expansive gesture, like a magician revealing the denouement of a trick, indicated Ann who was standing wide awake in the middle of the room, a shy smile on her lips: "Ta-da!" She was wearing a long woollen felted skirt, a knitted top and over all a fine sheepskin jacket plus the cloak she had arrived in. She had on a stout pair of men's walking boots. Doll showed Dando some gloves and a collection of woolly hats. "I knit them in my spare time," she said. Dando absent-mindedly made a choice for all three prospective travellers and gratefully donned one of the hats. "I put she a spare set of undies in her satchel and all the other things her might want," added Doll. Dando was not really listening. Ever since he had arrived at the hut he and Ann had been unable to take their eyes off each other. They were at the stage of visually devouring their rediscovered sweetheart but as yet had found nothing to do or say. Now it was time to leave.

"Well," Dando began awkwardly (he hated goodbyes), "I think we'd better push off."

Doll, sensing his discomforture, cut things short.

"All right my love – be sure you look after she. And you," to Ann, "see that he behave hisself." Ann smiled and gazed up at Dando in wonderment. Their surrogate mother embraced both her children and then Dando put his arm around Ann and led her through the quiet night-time passageways, at the same time giving her, in a voice shaken by emotion, an account of the recent events in which he had been involved.

Potto and Tallis were arguing about whether Carolus should carry his share of the baggage.

"He's already loaded with my own personal effects," objected Tallis, "and he'll be needed as a mount for the girl."

"I c'n walk," said the newly-arrived Ann.

The two men looked at her in surprise: the fact that she had regained the power of speech seemed to come as a shock to them.

"Have you explained?" asked Tallis uncertainly of Dando.

Potto drew the boy aside. "Here be your pack Lord, and here be something that I doubt you've thought about for many a long year." He held up a beautiful pair of boots made of the finest leather. "Do you remember these?"

"My boots!" cried Dando in astonishment. "Tom's boots!"

"I've kept 'em oiled for you. He reckon you'd be needin' they. I di'n't believe he at the time. *If he take a mind to goo a-wanderin', he tell me, don't 'ee stand in his way.*"

"Thankyou! Thankyou!" cried Dando. He hurried to try them on and was not really surprised to find that they fitted like a glove. This meant more to him than he could say.

A faint light was creeping into the eastern sky. Now nothing remained but to take to the road. Dando turned to Potto and for the first time ever put his arms around the old man.

"I'll never forget what you've done for me Potto," he averred.

His long-time friend searched his face.

"You're a good boy, Lord me dear," he said, his own face wrenched with sorrow.

They left from the back of Castle Dan by a route that took them eastward beneath the northern hills. There was not a soul about, certainly no organised pursuit - Tallis and Ann's whereabouts must still be a mystery to those wishing to detain them and, presumably, no-one had yet noticed Dando's absence. After skirting the iron works and travelling for a few miles they came upon a narrow track branching off to the left, the only road that led northward out of the valley, and as soon as they turned in that direction it began to climb. Within a short distance they were confronted by a large noticeboard beside the path on which was painted the following legend – *YOU ARE ADVISED NOT TO PROCEED BEYOND THIS POINT*. They ignored the warning and left it in their wake. All three travellers were afoot and as they progressed upwards Tallis went ahead with Carolus, Ralph at his heels, while Dando came behind leading the little dappled creature Mollyblobs and, because Tallis' back was turned, holding Ann by the hand.

"Where in the world do you think we're going?" he asked her cheerfully, sotto voce. Ann looked at him solemn eyed; he sensed that she was in the same state of incredulous amazement that he was. He laughed from sheer lightness of heart. "To tell the truth," he continued, "I couldn't care less where we go," but left unsaid the sentence's significant conclusion:- *as long as I'm with you.*

The dance ended between two and three in the morning. The guests donned their coats, called their carriages and dispersed to the four corners of Deep Hallow. Milly put a sleepy Damask to bed and then went to bed herself, but, the next morning, long before anyone else was stirring, she was already up and making her way back to the Castle's undercroft to check on the condition of her adored hero; she had not felt happy when he had told her to leave last night and had been uneasy on his behalf ever since. About five minutes later she was back in the women's quarters shaking Damask awake.

"Come on your majesty! Come on, wake up! 'E's gorn, the Lordship, your brother, 'e's gorn!"

"Milly, what's the matter? What time is it? Is it time to get up?"

"'E's gorn. I went to 'is room an' the door woz open and there weren't nobody there. So then I went to find the ol' man. 'E woz cryin'. 'E said the Lordship 'ad gorn away wiv this 'ere geezer an' a girl. Wot shall we do?"

Damask sat up, alternately shaking her head and massaging her temples, trying to grope her way out of the extremely deep sleep that was still trying to claim her.

"You say Dando's gone? Gone where?"

"Out of the valley – so sez the ol' man – wiv this stranger 'oo comes from the south."

"Old man? Do you mean Potto?"

"Yers, 'e woz cryin'."

"Go and get my clothes and yours, the gypsy ones, and fill the bath. I need a soak this morning if I'm to make any sense of this."

Emerging from the hot water, pink and glowing, Damask dressed herself in the men's garments she used when they were playing hookey from the gynaceum and then got Milly to explain again what Potto had told her.

"...'an there woz this girl as well," the child recounted, screwing up her face, a conflict raging in her breast over news which should be a reason for rejoicing but which instead was causing her a certain amount of pain, "'e said 'er name woz Ann – I fink it woz 'is sweetheart – I fink that's why 'e went."

"This person he's gone with was a traveller, you say, from a long way off?"

"Yers – that's wot the ol' man tol' me."

"Well!" Damask felt her anger rising, "would you credit it? When I suggested yesterday we went away together he wasn't having any. One minute he's setting himself up as a sort of sky pilot, the next he's buggered off with some vagrant or other without so much as a goodbye! You know Milly – I'm not going to stand for it. We'll go after him – then we'll see what he has to say for himself! I should have left long ago, but I was too soft hearted. I hung around because I thought he was going to get himself into trouble and of course he did. But now he's gone, the ungrateful sod, and we can go too. We'll take the dog cart."

Once the decision had been made Milly and Damask flung themselves into frantic preparations for departure before any curious neighbours were awake enough to question what they were doing. They gathered items together that they thought might be needed on a long journey and transported them to the shed where the little cart was housed, but in a much more haphazard manner than Dando had employed earlier. Eventually they could think of nothing else to pack and so decided they were ready to set off. Damask went to the small stall outside the castle to fetch her pony and came back incandescent with rage.

"He's taken Mollyblobs! The cheek of it! How dare he! What are we going to do now?" She stared at Milly and Milly stared back. Damask bit her lip as she tried to think of a solution.

"Well the only answer is Phyllis," she said. Phyllis was a donkey who at one time had often been found between the shafts of the dog cart, but that had been several years previously. For an extended period she had been living out a dignified retirement in a field not far from the Castle wall. Phyllis was a very old donkey indeed but nevertheless, when Damask went to fetch her and bring her back to act as their carriage horse, she seemed pleased to be in harness once more. On the point of departure, Damask and Milly returned to the flat for a last look round in case they had forgotten anything.

"You know Milly," said Damask, "I won't be sorry to be shot of this place."

"No, majesty – you'll get on fine outside the valley – you'll see – an' when we catch up wiv the Lordship you'll 'ave a right ol' time."

"After I've let him know what's what!"

But things were not destined to go quite as the two girls intended. In her interview with Potto Milly had not thought to ask which route the fugitives had taken; as far as she was concerned there was only one way in and

out of Deep Hallow and that was along the Incadine
Gorge. Potto, although he had learnt that Tallis was
planning to travel north and had been forced by the Dan's
mercenaries to admit the fact when they questioned him,
had not thought to pass on the information to the little
girl. Damask and Milly consequently set off eastward
behind their venerable moke, their heads full of thoughts
of the Levels, the River Kymer and the Delta City, not
realising that every mile was taking them farther and
farther away from the route Dando and his companions
were following.

    For the duration of the ball the Dan had
barricaded himself inside his apartment, cutting off
communication even from his hired troopers. With time
on his hands he turned in on himself and chewed over
imagined threats conjured from his rapidly worsening
mental state.

    They were closing in on him, getting closer all
the time. **They** were all round the Castle now like a thick
fog, rubbing themselves against the windows, creeping
outside the walls, whistling down the chimneys. You
could not be too **careful** with all these strangers around;
his **enemies** might well infiltrate the Castle under the
guise of party-goers; he had proof that they could change
their appearance at will. They had **murdered** Fenella all
those years ago and spirited the baby Dickon away, and
ever since then they had been trying to get to **him**, but he
had been too **smart** for them. He had executed their
ringleader and thought he had dealt them a mortal blow,
but the man, although dead, had come back and corrupted
his son. Yes, his son. The Clan Chief brooded in his
solitude. He thought over events earlier in the day and of

the interview with his child. He had been a fine offspring, this boy, a chip off the old block, but you could not trust babies after they got past a certain age, the **rumourmongers** got to them, telling them lies, warping their minds. The **whisperers** had told him that it was his son who was going to be his nemesis, that his enemies had won him to their side, and so it was necessary to exert all his cunning and to act as naturally as possible in order to make people believe he was unaware of what his adversaries were planning. In such a manner those that threatened him would be put off their guard. They came from the Way-of-the-Departed these **ill-wishers** so the **whisperers** said, and that was where they returned. The **whisperers** were all over the Castle now, inside the walls, quietest during the day, loudest at night. They had warned him against his son and so, convinced that, of the many male children he had begotten, this day's wrong-doer was the guilty one, he had put the boy away underground where he would be least likely to achieve his father's demise, and he preferred to put him underground alive than bury him dead. The **whisperers** did not agree, but he was not entirely their poodle yet, not entirely. The **whisperers** wore him down with their constant jabber; the only time he was free of them was when he went hunting away from the Castle.

At first light, as instructed, a guard knocked at the door to the Dan's suite and reported *all's well.* This meant that the hoard of visitors had departed and that the Castle was back to its normal state. A couple of soldiers were admitted to the apartment and informed him that the priest from the Conner Clan had arrived late last night and was waiting to see the Commander. The Dan ordered him to be searched – you could not be too careful - and then granted him an interview.

"Our domestic chaplaincy has been vacant for several months as you know," he told the man, keeping his voice light and non-committal, "and I'm grateful for the way you and your associates have stepped into the breach - but now we have a novitiate for the post. A tutorial twice a week for a couple of months on the duties relevant to a household padre will suffice I think; there will be adequate remuneration for the instructor. Would you be prepared to undertake this task? You will? Good. The sergeant will take you down and introduce you. Goodbye."

The Dan drank from a flask he kept in his hip pocket and then threw on his riding jacket. Meanwhile his chief tracker and trapper arrived and informed him that the men, horses and dogs were in attendance down in the courtyard and were eager for the chase: it was the day of the weekly fox hunt. The Dan armed himself and descended to the bailey where he found a rather smaller party than usual awaiting him. A proportion of his regular companions were sleeping off the effects of the leave he had granted and because he had given the troops permission to indulge themselves he had no legitimate excuse to discipline them. Just as he was getting ready to mount his horse the sergeant whom he had sent below with the priest came hurrying into the square. The man saluted smartly and asked permission to speak.

"The prisoner Dan Addo 'as absconded sir. 'E's not in 'is room and the nibbler Applecraft was there instead, folding some clothes."

"Where is he then?"

"I ast the nibbler Applecraft. 'E d'n't want to tell me, but I found ways of persuadin' 'im." The soldier grinned. "It seems 'e's away wiv a southerner and a woman 'oo were both implicated in the murder at the Justification. They've gorn by the Shady Way."

The Clan Chief stood transfixed, staring ahead at something only he could see. As seconds stretched into minutes the mercenaries around him shifted uncomfortably, exchanging glances one with another. At last the Dan blinked and seemed to recollect himself. "Where is Applecraft?" he asked.

"In a cell in the Punishment Yard."

"Good. I'll deal with him later. Well men, we're going to go after this runaway. We're going to hunt bigger game than fox today."

The troops raised a ragged cheer. They swung up into their saddles in imitation of their leader and clattered out of the Castle entrance followed by the dogs. They turned left around the house and then right along the route beneath the valley wall off which branched the northern path. The Dan led the detail, a feeling of wild exhilaration surging through him.

So his son had been summoned and had gone to **them** by the road with the inauspicious name. Now he had a chance to do something decisive. He would bring him back dead or alive and **thwart** their plans. He would offer them a **battle royal** if that is what they sought and free himself from this continual dread that was eating away at his soul. Perhaps, for once, he could act like a **man**, and in so doing regain something he had lost, something that once had been his but which he could not quite put a name to.

Earlier, before the sun had fully risen, Foxy was back in the vicinity of the Castle, well equipped for a journey, searching the soft ground round the outside wall for a familiar spoor. After a while he found some impressions towards the back of the house but at first glance was not sure what he was seeing. He could make out the tracks of not just one, but two horses, as well as the footprints of three people besides the dog's familiar paw prints. Was this Hilda and the stranger from the Justification? If so they had been joined by a third. Foxy began to get an inkling of why they had called at Castle Dan. He examined the marks more carefully. The hooves of each individual horse are unique and looking closely he confirmed that the larger animal was indeed Master Tallisand's mount. The beasts were carrying heavy loads – that was why all the two legs were walking. But whose were these third footprints in the dirt? He could not forget Hild's soft spot for one of the heirs to this local dynasty and conceived a horrible and irrational fear that the second in line to the chieftainship might be the one who was accompanying them. The idea was extremely far fetched and barely credible yet he got the feeling that the sooner he caught up with the fugitives the better. He followed the trail for a certain distance along the footpath that ran parallel with the hills only to see it turn north onto the little used road that would take the travellers into unfrequented wilderness. He found this so unexpected and hard to accept that he explored slightly further east, thinking he might be mistaken, but the tracks were non-existent past the corner. He went back, began to climb the northerly path, and a short way up the trail found a tuft of the dog's hair caught on a thorn bush. No wonder, then, that they were carrying plenty of provender on such a journey; they would need it if they went far in this direction. The path was familiar territory where he was concerned. How often, as an adolescent, had he crossed it in pursuit of strays, how often, following it down into the valley, had he returned with new insights gained on one of his fact-finding missions. Being on his old stamping ground once more encouraged him to wonder if his foster-father, the goatherd, had taken up residence in his hut, ready for the winter, or if he still lingered among the western mountains. His conscience stabbed him at the thought. He had not been back to see the man for at least two years.

The sound of distant hooves, which he had been registering subliminally for some time, suddenly forced itself on his attention. Gazing down from his vantage point he caught sight of movement on one of the tortuous bends in the path below him. He melted into the rocks at the side of the road and then scrambled like a monkey up the tallest in order to get a good view of the track. A party of mounted militia was coming towards him up the hill, shadowed by several large dogs, and at its head a figure that he recognised. Several times he had seen this tall commanding man out hunting in the woods when he himself had been on a poaching expedition and, although the leader's appearance had changed and he looked more unkempt and slovenly than any clan chief had a right to do, he knew him for the individual he hated with the most wholehearted dedication, the head of the dominant Deep Hallow family, none other than the Dan himself. So he was not the only one in pursuit of the runaways, this nobleman with his well known and fanatical determination to root out witchcraft was also on the track of his little Hild. Well this time there would be no hesitation. Foxy stood up to his full height. Below him, drawing nearer every minute, was a figure that embodied everything that roused him to fury: the violation of his person, the subjugation of his people, the killing of the Culdee, the desecration of the Holy Place. Holding these facts in the forefront of his mind he pulled an arrow from his quiver, fitted it to the string and drew back the bow with a creak of yew wood. A moment of maximum tension followed as he took aim and then, the party coming within range, the quarrel sped to its mark. Foxy did not wait to see if the man were dead; he knew he had to be. Since childhood he had been a crack shot. If he chose to wound he wounded, if he chose to kill he killed, it was as simple as that. He dropped to the ground on the far side of the rock as answering arrows whistled past his head and then fled up the slope. Behind, cries of anger came to his ears and there was the baying of hounds. Having gained height he paused for a second and turned, seeing the soldiers spread out across the hillside below him. He raised one fist into the air. "So perish all tyrants!" he yelled, a slogan he had picked up in Drossi. Then he ran on. He felt invincible and all powerful at this moment as if anything and everything he desired were within his grasp. He would bring Hilda back to Deep Hallow and the great day he had anticipated for years would dawn at last. His people would rise, and revenge would be exacted for every injustice heaped on the Nablar over unnumbered generations. He and all of the long-oppressed would reclaim the valley for its rightful inhabitants and the usurpers would either flee or spend their last moments feeding the fields with their blood.

To be continued...

Printed in Great Britain
by Amazon